HOLY WATER

HOLY WATER

A Novel by Colin Heston

HARROW AND HESTON
PUBLISHERS

Australia, New York & Philadelphia

CONTENTS

1. Confessions

Summer, 2014.

Alphonso scratched his protruding belly. Whenever he was nervous his navel itched. His loose shirt of the finest white silk hung loosely over his baggy Patagonia shorts of twenty pockets. He glanced quickly sideways to make sure his bodyguards were on the ball. They had orders to keep their distance from him. He wanted no eavesdropping, but they had to be ready to jump into action at the slightest threat. Each of them would give their lives for him, he knew. They also knew that failure meant death, or worse, demotion to that of a drug mule. He stopped very briefly at the top of the steps to the cathedral, turned, and surveyed the expanse of the Plaza de la Constitución. A grin of satisfaction struggled to overcome an otherwise grim face, his puffy cheeks pushed up and out by a mouth that quivered at its edges. He stood legs apart, hands on hips, pushing his shoulders back with some difficulty. "We own this city!" he announced to his *banda*. They turned with him, surveying the plaza with their AK 47s. Alphonso quickly noted that all seven of them were there. Seven, his lucky number, after the seventh apostle who guided his life, Matthew the tax collector. That was exactly what he did. He collected money from all of those who believed in him, or more correctly, his enterprise.

The twin bells of the cathedral's massive towers rang out in confirmation. Alphonso took it as his due, turned and entered the great cathedral of Mexico City. He took no notice of the massive carved doors guarding the entrance, walked directly to the small font just inside, dipped his fingers into the water and touched his forehead with the sign of the cross. He marched straight to the Altar of Forgiveness, paused briefly and looked up, imagining the Virgin Mary's assumption unto Heaven, the big event celebrated by the cathedral. It was why he was here today. Virginity was on his mind. He straightened up and marched to the confessional that was nestled away just to the

1

right of the Kings Altar. It was not your usual kind of confessional, most of which are the size and shape of ornate telephone boxes. He had donated a lot of money for its construction, could never understand why one had to be so cramped up in such a small space when there was so much to confess. To his surprise, Cardinal Pollagrande, soon to depart for the Vatican, who would one day be Pope according to Alphonso whose network of influence reached even there, had eagerly taken up the project.

And project it was. Some five times larger than a telephone box, it was beautifully built of Patagonian rosewood, the door inlaid with sweet smelling Palo Santo—thousands of pieces, observed Alphonso with satisfaction. He reached for the door with its brightly polished brass knob, when it suddenly flew open, and out stepped a voluptuous young woman, the kind that Alphonso had bought many times over, long blonde hair, dark at the roots, heavily powdered face, pastel mauve lips, eyes rimmed with heavy eye shadow, and long lashes curled to the ends.

"Oh! Padrino!" she cried, with the broadest of smiles as she stooped down to pull on her high-heeled shoe that had slipped off as she stepped down.

"The pleasure is all mine!" replied Alphonso in his thin voice, certainly not the deep penetrating voice that one would expect of a man of such power and influence. He held out his hand and she took it in hers as she rose, kissed it, a light kiss, one of respect and fear. She looked around at his *banda*. They stood as one trying to hold back grins, pointing their guns in all directions, but not in hers. She walked towards them, and as one, they pointed their guns at the beautiful cathedral ceiling, and stepped aside as she strutted through, clutching her new Italian leather handbag that His Holiness had brought back for her from the Vatican. "Ooh! Love you boys!" she called.

Alphonso gave his *banda* a boss's look, which caused them to quickly resume their roles as guardians of the most powerful drug lord in Mexico, and stepped into the confessional. Cardinal Pollagrande sat back on his black leather recliner, imported from California, arranging his splendid outer garments. "El Padrino," he smiled widely, showing slightly crooked teeth stained yellow from his daily intake of English breakfast tea, his face deeply lined, but skin so white, skin that had rarely seen the light of day, or so it seemed.

The confessional door automatically closed. Alphonso didn't like the mirrors attached to the walls, preferred not to see his aging body, and he had pestered His Holiness to take them down. To his annoyance, the His Holiness had taken a couple down, only to attach them to the ceiling above the recliner.

"Do you have to confess every day? Can't you see I'm busy for my departure back to the Vatican?" complained Pollagrande.

Alphonso stared at this Cardinal, the one he had requested the Vatican, almost twenty years ago, to replace the ambitious Father Benitez. "I have a big confession to make, Holiness. Only someone of your magnificence could possibly absolve me of this one."

"Padrino, who have you murdered this time?" asked Pollagrande with a sigh.

"Holiness! You know I don't kill people, my people do."

"Let's not argue over details, God has no patience for that. What is it?"

"I, I can't tell you here. It's not secure."

"You've got all your guards. How more secure can you get?"

"No one must know, Polly!"

"Of course not. Now tell me, Padrino, what's up?"

Alphonso looked furtively around. He opened the confessional door and ordered his *banda* to move away, then turned and said, "Polly, I, I have a daughter."

Pollagrande looked puzzled. "You mean a new daughter?"

"Yes, Holiness. A new daughter."

"Alphonso. You are such a good Catholic. No condoms for you!"

"No father. You don't understand! It's not a daughter. I mean, he is my daughter."

"You'll have to father a lot more kids to make up for all the ones your cartel has killed," scorned Pollagrande with a frown.

"Holiness! Polly! Listen to me!" cried Alphonso as he kneeled down on one knee before the recliner.

"I am listening, my Padrino. Jesus congratulates you for your children! Why are you so unhappy! Rise and be joyful!"

"Holiness. It's about my son. I can't tell you everything here."

"You mean he objects to having a little sister?"

"No, it's more than that!"

"It's nothing to worry about, Alphonso. It's normal. I'm sure he will grow to love her."

"He *is* his sister, that's the trouble with it!"

Pollagrande slid off the recliner and stood tall, a six foot giant, towering above the kneeling Padrino, his red-rimmed robe brushing against Alphonso's face. Alphonso tried to stand, but fell backwards. He heard the door of the confessional open.

"Everything all right?" It was Pedro, his head bodyguard.

"Get out! Get out!" yelled El Padrino. Pedro quickly retreated as Alphonso managed to stand and turn to Pollagrande. He pulled a wad of money from his pocket, several thousand US dollars, and proffered it to him.

"Come to my office. We can talk there," purred Pollagrande.

They left the confessional, Pollagrande leading the way through the baptistry, each of them dipping their fingers in the water of the baptismal font, and crossing themselves as they left, through the Herrera door to the sacristy, passing by The Virgin of the Apocalypse. Alphonso was having trouble keeping up. Beads of sweat trickled down behind his ears. He could feel his toupee sliding just a little off center. His heart gave a flutter, saliva gushed into his mouth. Pollagrande stopped in front of The Assumption of the Virgin. He was about to retrieve the key to his office hidden behind the Virgin, when Alphonso fell down, his body convulsing, tongue protruding like a lion's, his toupee clenched in his fist.

Cardinal Pollagrande looked down in horror. "Mother of God!" he cried, "your toupee!"

El Padrino's arms and legs shook in spasms. In what seemed an eternity, Pedro at last showed up, waving his gun. The rest of the gang stood crowded against the sacristy door.

Pollagrande stood erect, pointing his long finger at Pedro, then down to the writhing Alphonso. "Well do something!" he scowled at Pedro, "your boss is ruining his toupee!"

"Water! Get him some water!" commanded Pedro at no one in particular. Then with great delight he had an idea. "The baptismal font! Get water from the font!"

"Haven't got anything to put it in," complained one of the *banda*.

"I have," called another as he put down his AK47 and retrieved a small flask full of a clear liquid.

"That will do! Empty it and get the water," directed Pedro.

"But it's Tequila! We can't pour it out in this holy place," complained the gangster.

Pollagrande intervened. "Then drink it!"

Alphonso continued to writhe, white froth now spilling from his mouth. The *banda* passed the flask around until it was emptied. And in no time, Pedro was holding the small flask now filled with water.

"Give it to me," said Pollagrande. "It is God's water, and I am his servant on earth."

Alphonso's eyes were now glazed over. But instead of trying to put the flask of water to his frothing mouth, the Cardinal stood tall, his long fingers gracefully floating through the air, and sprinkled it all over his writhing body,.

Suddenly the sacristy became deathly silent. El Padrino lay still, on his back, his eyes fixed on the Virgin as she floated up to Heaven. He stretched out his arms, his toupee clenched in his right hand, and miraculously sat up straight, without effort at all, as though he too were floating. A calmness came over his round pudgy face, his baldness a gleaming moon above it. The cardinal reached down to help him up, but though he took Alphonso's hand, El Padrino rose of his own accord. It was a small miracle!

Alphonso kissed his toupee then threw it down at the foot of the Virgin. "I no longer need this," he said to the Virgin. "It was only a pretend crewcut anyway."

El Padrino turned to the Cardinal. He tried to stand as tall as he could. He hitched up his baggy shorts with its bulging pockets and rubbed his hands on his sweat-soaked white shirt with its signature black collar. He gestured to one of his gang. "Give His Holiness your gun," he commanded. "Today, I announce a rebirth of our cartel. We will from now on traffic in Holiness and nothing else!"

*

At the risk of indulging in cheap stereotypes, there is no other way to describe El Padrino's compound, other than as a super-rich fortress built around a swimming pool, Greeko-Roman colonnades on both sides, a guard posted at every seventh column, an enormous mansion carved into the slopes of Tláloc, rising above the pool, commanding a fabulous view of the never ending expanse of Mexico City, the cap of the White Lady visible even on smog filled days. The columns, of course, are faced with golden pearl travertine marble, the sprawling single story house of same, decorated around windows, doors and arches, with tropical onyx. The rims around these tastefully (well, in comparison to the inside) bordered with gold leaf.

We need say little of the inside. Suffice it to say that El Padrino was bent on outdoing the fabled gold obsession of the Aztecs, and after seeing a lavishly illustrated book on Saint

Petersburg that contained endless pictures of walls, chairs, beds, fireplaces, altars and whatever else one keeps in a palace, coated with gold leaf, El Padrino had instructed his architects to decorate the interior of his castle as though it were in St. Petersburg. A party of fifteen Italians said to be direct descendants of the Italians who decorated the St. Petersburg chapels and palaces, was imported from Italy and camped off to the side for three years while they labored away. Of course, there was no shortage of gold, since the trade in heroin, crack and whatever else El Padrino could get his hands on, produced enormous amounts of money. In fact, El Padrino had so much money, all of it in US Dollar bills of many different denominations, he employed several couriers and negotiators who travelled the world and bought endless supplies of gold ornaments, some of which were retained on show in his vast living room (the size of an American football field). And the dollar bills that could not be so laundered, he ordered to be put into a machine and compressed to produce his own signature tiles that he used to cover the walls, that is, those walls that were not covered in gold leaf.

At the center of the living room was Alphonso's pride and joy, the fifty foot long dining table—yes, he had broken with stupid tradition and place the dining table in the living room, in fact there was no actual dining room in the mansion. His was an "open plan" along the principles of Australian architecture that he had seen on the HGTV House Hunters International show. But what set this table apart was not so much its length, after all there were such tables in English and European castles reserved for state dinners, but that the table was squared at one end, and at the opposite end tapered in to a sharp curve that seated just one person at its head. There could be no doubt, of course, who sat there. At the other end, fifty feet away sat his wife, son when home, and various other children and relatives, depending on the time of the year, and whether their presence was needed or not, usually if other dignitaries had insisted on bringing their wives or mistresses.

Beside the magnificent swimming pool, always a sparkling clear blue, was a deep sea-green pond, in which El Padrino kept his pet fish, constantly replenished with sea water from the Pacific. Alphonso had been fascinated by a documentary he saw on Netflix, of the ancient Romans who kept man-eating fish in their pools into which they tossed their disobedient slaves. It had taken some time, but he finally managed to import some giant catfish and pirañas from the salty mouth of the Amazon. They had worked out very well when he fed them one of his body-guards who, suffering from a bad case of the flu, so he claimed, had coughed up a wad of green phlegm that had landed on Padrino's bare toes (he always wore leather sandals modeled on those of the ancient Romans). This was taken as a serious case of disrespect, and the guard was punished accordingly.

On August 2014, it was in this palace of El Padrino that the magnificent celebration, or event it should probably be called, occurred. It was also, for Alphonso and his long adoring wife (he had no mistress) the most painful, yet wonderfully joyful, celebration they had ever launched. You may find it hard to believe that Alphonso had no mistress, given the stereotypes of Latino men, macho to the core, always with several mistresses, a count of them a sure indication of their manliness. But Alphonso's apparent celibacy demonstrated his resolve to his hordes of supporters, friends, relatives no matter how distant, and workers no matter at what level, whether they worked in the drug production factory located deep inside the mountain behind his palace, or the salesmen who traveled far and wide distributing product and collecting money. They all feared his iron will, admired his dedication to their welfare and that of their own relatives and friends. They happily mistook his unimpressive exterior, his squat legs, round torso, round moon face and shiny bald head hidden under that ridiculous toupee of a crewcut, not to mention his thin, high-pitched voice, as the awful defects that he had overcome.

And you could not be faulted for wondering how come, if he was so adored by his faithful wife, they sat at the opposite ends of a fifty foot dining table. Surely this represented a gulf between them, one bigger than the Panama canal?

The fact is that Maria, for all her adoration of her wonderful husband, had many, how can one say it without derision, "partners" of both sexes. After all, Maria was a prostitute of sorts; that was how Alphonso met her. But he knew that she was very careful and selective as to her clients, and did not just sleep with any young buck running after her, looking for a quickie. No, her clients, many of them non-paying, came from important stations in Mexican society, professors, doctors, lawyers, judges, business executives and the richest of all from top levels of government, politicians of several powerful parties, in recent

years the Partido Acción Nacional, and the Partido de la
Revolución Democrática.

Maria and Alphonso were married in the Metropolitan Cathedral when they were still in their late teens, a lush affair, paid
for by the generous contributions of Maria's clients. It was the
combination of Maria's money and network of clients, and
Alphonso's own steely resolve, that brought him to the top of a
small drug cartel that smuggled high quality cocaine to a small
market just across the border in San Diego. And so in the hot
summer of 1990 (Saturday, August 24), their wedding was presided
over by a young priest by the name of Vincent Benitez who
some time after was reassigned to Singapore and replaced by
Cardinal Pollagrande. Both these illustrious priests would eventually become top dogs in the Vatican, thanks to Alphonso's
influence (that is, his mafia ways). Pollagrande would become
CFO of the Vatican and Benitez the Pope's foreign secretary.
Together they would make Alphonso's final unbelievable achievement possible.

The possible and the impossible, the lives of Maria and her
husband Alphonso flowed back and forth between the two.
Their world was full to overflowing, of opposites. Being good
Christians, of course, the two big opposites for Maria and
Alphonso were good and evil, often one turning into the other.
Was this not the true basis of Christianity? Pollagrande would
often lecture Alphonso when he had a fit of the doubts. The
robber on the cross next to Jesus was made good. Saul transformed into Paul. He could go on. Peter denied Jesus not once,
but thrice.

But Maria listened to none of this. She was a down to earth
person, had to be, given her chosen profession. Or at least, that
was what she would say when her behavior was questioned, no
less, by Pollagrande. She had her own demon, though, her own
conflict of opposites, buried deep in her belly. And when she
reached menopause, it began to emerge, triggered by a short
visit to America to visit their son Julian, their only child, who
was safely tucked away in St. Robert's College at the highly
recommended Catholic University, Virgin Hall. Cardinal Pollagrande had insisted that it was the right place for Julian, a
coddled boy if ever there was one. He was a gorgeous chubby
little boy when he was a toddler, adored by all, his big mop of
black hair that no girl or woman could resist ruffling, sifting it
through their fingers. Except for the black hair, though, the rest

of him reproduced the squat round body of his father. But then, the impossible happened. He hit adolescence and after a brief period of pimples, his body lost its baby fat, as his aunts and uncles chided him, and developed a, shall we say, shapely body that reflected much of his mother, and along with it her charm. .

2. Julian and Christian

The first problem Julian had to face was his name. His application form to Virgin Hall listed him as Julio, the Latino spelling of Julius, the name that Alphonso had insisted on, but Maria would have none of it. Alphonso unabashedly described himself to his friends and relatives as the Mexican Julius Caesar, after watching the HBO series Rome, especially the last episode of series one, when Caesar was stabbed to death by Brutus and former friends. The scene depicted the nightmare Alphonso had many times experienced when he was deep in slumber, exhausted from overwork, of his closest associates, even best bodyguards, cousins and sometimes even Maria, turning upon him with AK47s. Every morning he prayed to Jesus—he never admitted to his associates that he kneeled at his bedside to pray, concerned that they might see it as a sign of weakness—that he would be sent a sign should such a dastardly deed be in the offing. And it was why, at every opportunity, he asserted his power as dictator, arbitrarily and without the slightest doubt, ordering the deaths and torture when necessary, of his enemies.

Yet in spite of himself and his nightmares, he gave in to Maria. It was a compromise of sorts. She had insisted that they call their son Julian, a much nicer sounding name, especially when pronounced as an English name. Alphonso had complained that it was a girl's name, but Maria countered that it was not, because the girl version of it was Julia. Alphonso said all the English were girls anyway. The compromise was that their son would officially be entered into the registry of births as Julio, but that they would call him Julian. It was a compromise suggested by Father Benitez, a master arbitrator.

Julian's first exchange with the Virgin Hall bureaucracy at check-in at the dorm was to insist on the English form of his name. And by the way, Alphonso, always concerned with principles of spending, had also argued that it was better for Julian to be officially called Julio because it was obviously

10

Latino, and therefore he would qualify for various forms of affirmative action, so widespread in American universities. It wasn't the money, it was the principle, recited Alphonso.

*

And so it was that, in the Fall of 2014, Julian became a student at Virgin hall, his future ordained by the son of God, to become a creature of the church, hopefully, according to both his parents, to become a priest and one day take the place of Cardinal Pollagrande.

Young Julian had shown great promise right from the day he was baptized by Father Benitez (Saturday, August 1990), the naked little thing dipped into the spring of holy water, and lo! a sigh of acclamation came from his adorers, when that little thing fired a thin but powerful shot of pee right in the face of Father Benitez who reflexively raised the little baby, now squawking like a red-winged blackbird, above his head so fast, it almost left his hands to fly up to the curved beams of the whitewashed cathedral ceiling.

Now, don't jump to conclusions. While this may have seemed like a portentous event, a sign from Jesus even, it was nothing of the sort. In fact it directed the attention of the onlookers to the source of the pee, and it had to be admitted, but of course, no one would do so, that the source was very, very tiny. So tiny, in fact, that it was almost not there!

Some might say, along with Napoleon and Freud, that biology is destiny, but none of the onlookers, including Julian's adoring mother and father, at the time had the slightest comprehension of what lay in store for that wondrous, wriggling, now scream-ing thing. Father Benitez handed him off to Maria, who quickly swaddled him and stifled the screams. Deep in her belly, she knew what she held to her breast. The future Pope of the world!

And the event that would ordain Julian's future was about to unfold. Once again, this event could not have been foreseen by his doting parents who had, given their considerable financial and other means, pulled the necessary strings to get Julian into Virgin Hall (all of it unnecessary, since Julian was a very serious young man and a dedicated student, getting the highest scores in the SAT ever obtained by a Latino), but, according to Alphonso, it was the principle of the thing, such principles highly valued in America, the country of high principles.

The fact that Julian now found himself at the entrance to St. Robert's College, the seminary satellite of Virgin Hall University, had been arranged by Alphonso through his considerable contacts via Pollagrande, not to mention a hefty donation to St. Robert's Hall itself, insisted on by Pollagrande, who did not trust the secularized propensities of the main university campus to spend the money wisely, such as on a program on "women's studies," or some such silliness. Furthermore, Alphonso had ignored the fact that, as Pollagrande had warned many times, the seminary was for dedicated men who wanted to become priests and was essentially for those who were doing a graduate degree. To which Alphonso replied with the question, if you've already graduated, why would you be doing a graduate degree? When Pollagrande pointed out that whatever the educational level, the students in that dorm would be in their mid to late twenties and Julian an innocent twenty four, Alphonso asked Pollagrande why were the other students not also innocent?

One should add, though, that Alphonso was not altogether off point here. Julian had been groomed for this occasion. He was already steeped in the intricacies of the Catholic liturgy, philosophy, Papal histories and doctrines. His mentor and tutor Father Vincent Benitez (regrettably promoted to Archbishop of Singapore on Julian's twenty-first birthday, and from there to even greater things) had carefully and systematically groomed him. Besides, he had for most of this time a beautiful soprano voice, which did not break until he was twenty three. In fact, this was why, at twenty four his voice sounded often as though it were hoarse. It was still maturing.

*

The dorm supervisor, a thin acerbic looking young man in his early thirties, closely shaven, constantly sweaty face, a faint sickly yellow, guided Julian down the long hallway, to room 69. The door was already open. "Welcome to St. Robert's College," he said with a smirk. "I am Dr. Scalpel, your dorm supervisor, and this is your roommate, Christian." He softly touched Julian's arm, as if to say, go on, get in there he won't bite you. Julian took an instant dislike to Scalpel whose furtive manner, always seeming to look over one's shoulder, was very off-putting. And his body moved in all directions at once like a pudgy Spiderman.

Julian took two timid steps. And there, silhouetted against the window of a bright fall sky of Hopewell, New Jersey, stood Christian, tall, slender, glistening blonde hair, parted on the left, a long wave carefully groomed to hang over his high forehead.

Neither spoke. Both were momentarily frozen in time. It was one of those moments when there is nothing to say because there is no need to speak. Scalpel sensed it and stepped back towards the door, relishing it in feigned horror. "I'll leave you to it," he said, "Christian you can show Julian the ropes." He departed, gently closing the door behind him, the smirk still all over his pasty face.

Oh yes! It was one of those moments, love at first sight! Christian simply stood there, his slender hand rubbing the back of his neck, a mannerism that Julian would come to know so well. And before Julian knew it, in spite of himself and all that Father Benitez had taught him, he rushed forward, extending his hand to shake, but instead Christian stepped a little to the side, opened his arms and before either of them knew it, they were in the tightest embrace that neither of them had ever felt before.

"Oh Holy Jesus!" exclaimed Julian."

"Mother of God!" cried Christian.

Julian, short by comparison to Christian, found his nose snuggling into Christian's armpit. The odor was intoxicating. So much so that he became weak in the knees and began to sag. Christian responded by hugging him even tighter to his slender body, all its protrusions and joints pushing into Julian's softness. He went to lift Julian up, intending to place him on the bed, when suddenly, Julian cried out, "get thee behind me Satan!"

"Shit! What the fuck!" called Christian, as he quickly let go and Julian managed to find his feet and retreat to the door.

Julian grabbed his big glider bag and pulled it towards him.

"That's your bed there," pointed Christian.

It was a bed that looked exactly like the bed in van Gogh's painting he had hanging on his wall back home. Simple and austere. The way he liked it. "I'd better get unpacked," he said. "What time is Lauds?"

"They have that?" asked Christian.

"Of course, it's a seminary, isn't it?" said Julian, puzzled and a little haughty.

"Oh, I wouldn't know. I'm not a Catholic, you may as well know."

Julian turned to him, aghast. Christian was again standing before the window that opened out on to Hopewell village, his hands back on his hips. "You're, you're not?" gasped Julian.

"Nope, but don't tell anyone or they'll kick me out."

Julian, for reasons he could not fathom, smiled a devilish smile, a smile that reminded him of the expression on Judas's face in a painting of Manuel Reanda's *Last Supper* hanging over the fireplace in their dining room back home.

*

The next morning, Julian was awakened by a soft touch to his cheek, as though a feather had been drawn across it, then to his lips. He went to brush it sway, when he smelled that deep odor of yesterday, Christian's armpit. Semi-conscious, he groaned a little, and smiled ever so slightly. Then he heard the drone of chanting, not quite that, a monotone voice reading from the bible.

"Therefore consider the members of your earthly body as dead to immorality, impurity, passion, evil desire, and greed, which amounts to idolatry," recited Christian, kneeling at Julian's bed, his mouth almost touching Julian's.

"Colossians 3:5" answered Julian, his lips hardly moving, but enough to startle Christian, who dropped his bible and retreated as quickly as his lanky frame would allow, back to his bed.

Julian, like a teenager, rolled over, lay flat on his stomach, a sleeping position strictly forbidden him by Father Benitez, and went back to sleep. It was a dream wasn't it? But it had awakened him. He lay there, pushing his head into his hard, lumpy pillow.

The feather returned. No, this time long slender fingers. They lightly ran through his black cropped hair, short to almost shaven on the sides, pushing up in a crew cut at the top, Indian style, but truly the latest in Mexican fashion. He carefully reached out from under the sheets searching for those long slender fingers. He breathed deeply and bit into the pillow, his body stiffened, the devil was at work so early in the morning. What would Father Benitez do? The drone began softly again, then became a loud, deep incantation.

"Let us behave properly as in the day, not in carousing and drunkenness, not in sexual promiscuity and debauchery, not in strife and jealousy. Instead clothe yourselves with the Lord Jesus Christ: do not make provision..."

"For the flesh to gratify its cravings," enjoined Julian in his thin voice.

The fingers stopped their rhythmic stroking, and Julian rolled over on to his back, the sheet caught up in his arm. He opened his eyes only to see Christian leaping back to his bed, his bible lying on the floor between their beds, opened, its pages crumpled.

*

Dawn had come. Christian sneaked out of bed, so as not to wake Julian, slipped on his robe, and made his way down the narrow passage, still dark, to the communal bathroom. He brought with him his toiletries and his small bible of the New Testament, a Gideon version, and his specially sewn boxers. There were no others in the bathroom, possibly because not all had yet arrived. Though, he knew, according to his evangelist father, that Catholics did not shower as much as Protestants which was why they always had a distinctive smell, rather like animals in the zoo. He had been all for this adventure, concocted by his father, to search out whether Catholics were true to their word. Were we all truly brothers, regardless of who or what we were? Virgin Hall heralded its devotion to diversity. How far would they go? Would they really accept him when he revealed that he was an evangelist Protestant who despised their idolatrous ways? That was what his father had preached to him the day before he drove out of the small drive of their little bungalow in Shepherdstown on Sandpiper Lane, WV.

As he stood enjoying the plentiful hot water of the shower, Julian suddenly appeared. Not in the flesh, that would have been bad enough, but in his mind, no, not his mind either. In his body! He quickly turned on the cold water and yelped when it shocked him. He leaped out and reached for his towel, just as Julian entered, his towel draped over his shoulder, no robe, just his boxers. Christian grabbed for his robe. Julian saw it and beat him to it. "Here you are," he said, his eyes almost closed as he tried not to look at Christian's tall, slender body.

Christian, for his part had no such compunction. He looked straight into Julian's eyes, reached out and gently pushed up his chin with his curved finger so that they could look at each other straight in the eyes. How different Julian was! Talk about diversity! What brother in a seminary would have his hair cut like that? And his dark oily, glistening skin. He quickly retreated and stepped into his special boxers, forgetting to dry himself off.

"We're going to Lauds, right?" asked Julian.

"Would you like to borrow my toiletries? asked Christian, "I see you have none."

"Oh, no thanks. My mom says that all those chemicals are bad for your skin. I just use water."

Christian looked at him, pleased at this affirmation of his father's knowledge. Yet his body behaved differently. It ignored his thoughts, causing his eyes to drop down to where Julian was now removing his boxers, apparently oblivious to his gaze.

"How's the shower? "asked Julian.

"As hot as you want it," replied Christian as he took his bible from the shelf and put it into the special pocket of his boxers, watching the back of Julian's tough and taught little body slip into the shower enclosure. "You'd better hurry, though, Lauds is in twenty minutes."

"Ok. Please wait for me, won't you?"

"Oh sure. I will, I will."

*

"Beatus vir qui non abiit in consilio impiorum et in via peccatorum non stetit et in cathedra pestilentiae non sedit," recited Julian.

The room was suddenly silent.

"Most impressive, Julian, but we do not recite in Latin these days," said Dr. Scalpel, his rubbery lips forced into a kindly smile of fake apology.

Julian's olive face turned red and he bit his bottom lip. Christian sneakily fished for Julian's hand under his novice's robe and gave it a light squeeze, that feather-like touch again. "You're too good for them," he whispered. Julian held back a smile.

Julian said, "Holiness, it's the way Father Benitez taught me. I know it better than in English or Spanish."

A light titter moved through the rest of the small group of seven.

"We thank you, Julian, for teaching us the ways of the Mexican liturgy. If you would like to lead us, in Latin, you are welcome to do so. We will respond in English. Most of us do understand liturgical Latin, I hope," said Scalpel, looking somewhere beyond Julian's shoulder.

"Thank you Holiness, but I am but a humble neophyte, besides I must learn the English," answered Julian with a bright smile, echoing his mother's air of confidence. Christian, standing beside him, tried desperately to see the smile that he knew must be all over Julian's face, but dared not show his inclination.

Dr. Scalpel replied, "Ah, now, brother Julian, although I seek holiness, I am not quite there yet. Please address me as brother Timothy."

All took this as permission to smile and turn their heads to Julian who stood, his head held back, standing straight as one could under the looseness of the novice robe.

"Brother Timothy, a beautiful name, if only mine were Paul," quipped Julian, smiling all the more, a smile that caused Christian's knees almost to buckle.

The titters faded, and the Lauds continued, the soft sonorous droning of incantations and their responses. This was a glorious day to begin a new life of fellowship, thought Julian, feeling the light touch once again of Christian's slender fingers, as they swayed forward and back, in perfect unison, the warmth of their bodies and the smell of Christian's armpits wafting into Julian's quivering nostrils.

*

At the end of Lauds, Julian, his bible clutched in front of him, happily chatted with his new brothers. Christian, shy and a little nervous, held back. A major topic of conversation was comparing bibles. It was the first question Julian was asked because his fellow students were so impressed that he spoke the liturgies in Latin.

"I have the JB," said Julian proudly, "It was given to me by Father Benitez when he left Mexico City to become Bishop of Singapore."

"Oh, the Fathers here will not like that," said one of the brothers confidently. "It's too old fashioned and besides it was translated by Jews."

"What's yours, then?" asked Julian, still smiling, noticing too that Christian was hanging back, hands in his pockets.

"We use the LBCE."

"The what?"

"The Living Bible Catholic Edition. And how about you, Christian, is it?"

"Oh, I have just the New Testament. My pastor said the Old Testament was full of abuse and violence and would not let us read it. And besides it was translated by Jews too."

There was a brief, embarrassed silence. All the room had heard him.

"Of course, when I was a kid I grew up with the Católica Romana Biblia en español," said Julian.

"Brothers, please," called Scalpel, "we must move on to breakfast, or you will be late for orientation. Make sure you bring the forms left for you in your dorm, to register for classes.

Of course, most of them are obligatory, but at Virgin Hall we encourage you also to reach out to the many other classes offered across the university to fulfill your electives."

And so the day began, to be one of many days of learning, meditation and brotherhood. Julian delighted in its rhythm, everything was so new to him. His classmates were so kind even though the skin of their faces was scrubbed so white, and they were so formal and perfectly mannered. They were already acting like priests, even though they were a long way from it. All, that is, except Christian, who seemed not to fit, and only Julian knew the real reason why, though the others suspected it. He was a Protestant, and the worst kind of Protestant, Julian found out later. The son of a far right evangelist Protestant, a little known sect, possibly made up by his father, called The First Episcopalian Church of Judasian Trust, or simply The Judes for short. Julian could not quite understand what the church really stood for, even though Christian had tried to explain to him late into the night, nights that ended in heated argument, followed by regrets on both sides, and the inevitable making amends that followed. But the gist of it seemed to be that his father and founder of the church believed that Judas, the Ischariot one, had been framed as the traitor, and that the real traitor was Peter. What a dreadful blasphemy! In fact—and Christian had sworn Julian to secrecy—his father had revised the New Testament himself to correct this horrible mistake, and published his own version of it on Amazon!

The night Christian told him this incredible story was a night that would be remembered by both of them forever. Events like this can never be taken back, for they cannot be forgotten, not completely anyway. But it was more than simply telling a story. It was what the telling of the story revealed about each of them, or no, maybe it was the other way around. The event itself resulted in the telling of the story.

*

It was the night before parents' day when Julian's mom and dad would visit campus for the first time, and Christian feared that his father would also show up, though he had pleaded with him not to do so. They had returned to their room after Vespers, and found themselves sitting on the edge of Julian's bed, Julian leafing through his bible, chatting about what passage they would read together. His breezy, animated talk had Christian on edge. They sat close together. They had done so every night

when they read their bibles together. Neither quite knew how
this came about, though Christian, deep down, or at least half
way down, knew well enough. Julian laughed and smiled and
chatted away. Christian kept his hands in his lap, his slender arm
and angular shoulder snuggling against Julian's muscly arm that
flinched and stretched as he turned the pages.

"So what does yours say?" asked Julian, chirping away.

"My *what* say?" asked Christian, defensively, looking down.

"Where's your bible?" asked Julian cheerfully.

"It's where I always keep it."

"Where?"

"Here!" cried Christian and he grabbed Julian's hand and
pulled it down to his crotch, where Julian felt a very hard object.

"Shit!" he called out, "that's where you keep your bible?"

"It's in my special boxers pocket. It's where I keep it. It's my
chastity belt," babbled Christian, embarrassed, looking away.

Julian dropped his bible, aghast, perplexed, and totally flustered. But his hand stayed frozen to the spot, Christian trying
only half-heartedly to pull it away. In spite of himself, his hand
and its long fingers pressed hard on Julian's hand, with a
predictable result. Julian slipped off the bed and on to his knees,
how this happened he had no time to wonder, for at that very
moment, Christian's body shook in spasms. They both knew
what had happened. Christian's bible had been violated!

*

The next morning, Julian and Christian woke early, in fact
neither of them had slept. Julian took his bible with him to the
bathroom and took care of his toiletries such as they were.
Christian left his bible in their room, had a long shower, so hot,
it hurt, and Julian was waiting for him when he stepped out.
They glanced at each other, Julian forcing a smile, actually, it
came naturally because he was a smiley person like his mom, as
his relatives always said. But his eyes overtook his smile, taking
in Christian's long, naked body. His smile became broader.

"Stop it!" cried Christian, "stop the lust!"

"Do you not know that your body is a temple of the Holy
Spirit who is in you, whom you have from God, and that you
are not your own?" recited Julian, still smiling.

"1 Corinthians 6:19," responded Christian mechanically.

Each said nothing more as they returned to their room to
dress for Lauds, then breakfast. This morning they would choose
their courses. Julian had made a big decision. He would take all

his electives in criminal justice. And he would try to get out of a number of the obligatory courses, convinced that he already knew most of what was purported to be in them. Father Benitez had done a superb job teaching him. And it was clearly so to some of the professors when they quizzed him.

"Why criminal justice?" asked Christian. "What can a priest do with that?"

"When you meet my father tomorrow, you'll understand why."

"He's a cop or something?"

"Far from it," grinned Julian, "far from it."

The day proceeded with its familiar rhythm, Lauds, classes and tutorials, mass, lunch, classes, holy hour and meditation, vespers, sacrament and penance, dinner, group readings and prayer.

They took to their beds, Julian well satisfied, after another full day. He enjoyed his steady predictable life, it was everything Father Benitez said it would be. So very different from back home, every day unpredictable, strange persons, thugs and policemen showing up at all hours, his dad barking orders to his henchmen, receiving well-dressed rich looking people in his great dining hall. He looked across at his room-mate, slumbering and turning fitfully in his bed, murmuring to himself. He leaned down to pick up his bible, reading bits of it with a flashlight. Last night's incident had disturbed the rhythm of his day. He looked across and wondered. What would it be like? It was clear to him that Christian was driven by a passion, one that he could barely control. Julian was puzzled by this, unable to identify a similar feeling of passion in himself, he never quite had it, especially not as intense as it seemed to be in Christian. Yet the slightest touch by Christian invoked a feeling of tenderness, he wanted so badly to take Christian in his arms and reassure him that it would be all right, that he would take him into his heart, love him. Christian compassion, wasn't that what it was? He rolled over to face the wall and drifted off to sleep. It would be a big day tomorrow when his mom and dad showed up. How embarrassing it would be. His dad would take over everything. Who knew what he had already done with Virgin Hall?

*

There it was again. That light brush of a feather, the touch of Christian's knuckle on his neck below the ear. The smell of his armpits. Oh, such sweetness! Julian turned over, brushing the hand away, but in that hand was also a hard object, and yes, it was Christian's bible. Christian pushed himself away, fumbling for his bible.

"I'm sorry!" he cried, "I've tried, I really have! The bible doesn't help me at all!" Then he opened it up to a well-worn page and read, "Or do you not know that your body is a temple of the Holy Spirit who is in you, whom you have from God, and that you are not your own?"

Julian pushed himself up, squinting in the moonlight that flowed in through their small window, Christian still kneeling beside his bed, his wonderful blonde hair hanging down over his right eye, his face flushed, his lips moistened by a hidden busy tongue. "Christian!" muttered Julian, "it doesn't matter what Corinthians says, it was written so long ago, without any understanding of we young people of today."

"Julian, I'm sorry! I have tried so hard. If my father knew!" He struggled up and stood there, naked as could be, his pure soft whiteness glistening, looking down at Julian, long hands covering himself.

Julian reached out for Christian's hands. He felt a warmth rise up inside, deep down, a horizontal warmth, one he had never felt before. It was the love of Jesus, he was sure of that. "We are not sons of our fathers," he said, "God forbid if that were so. We are sons of Jesus, and I say unto you: come into me, I open my arms to you, feed of my body, be sanctified." He closed his eyes tightly, hoping to see Jesus come down to him. He pulled at Christian's hands and they came to him, his body following, his slender figure dropping with a slow, graceful movement as he slid in beside his waiting love. Now there were no more words, just a whispered silence of warm breath and then sighs.

Was this the end or the beginning? Julian lay back, legs apart, absorbing the warmth of love as it spread by Christian's touch throughout his body. But then, when Christian's hands found their way, Christian suddenly drew back and exclaimed, "Heavenly Jesus!"

Julian, only half conscious, his warmth and enveloping love out of control murmured, "what is it?"

Christian replied, with resolve, "I don't know, but it's too late now!" And he thrust himself into Julian who took an enormous deep breath, and seemed almost to choke, but managed to cry, "Satan! Get thee behind me!" But Satan was already gone.

It was a night of revelation. Christian rolled off the bed and switched on the light. He had to confirm what his fingers had told him. Julian lay still, his eyes closed, flat on the bed, legs apart. Father Benitez appeared to him, "do not be afraid, for you are a special person, you are a temple of two, of Jesus and of Mary." He opened his eyes and looked up at Christian. "What have we done?" he asked.

"There are three of us," answered Christian, "you are two and I am one."

"Father Benitez told me I was different."

"You are twice as holy as the rest of us," said Christian as he pulled on his pajama pants. The fact was, though, that Christian was deeply disappointed and felt guilty about it. When he had grabbed for Julian he found only a tiny little thing, not even the size of his little finger. He bit his tongue hard to punish himself for such ungrateful and sinful thoughts. Besides, it mattered not, for his love for Julian was boundless, uncontrollable, infinite. He knew it and so did Julian as they stared at each other until Christian switched off the light and slid back into Julian's bed.

Tomorrow would be another day, but one to remember. Open day. Julian's mom and dad would be here. And so would Christian's father.

*

The Learjet 70 tilted slightly preparing for its landing at Princeton Municipal Airport.

"The trouble with you," said Maria to Alphonso, as she leaned her head against the window to look down "is that you're so damned impatient!"

"Aren't you glad? That's why we're traveling in this Learjet and not with the rabble."

"Oh shut up you macho goat!"

"Bull," corrected Alphonso.

"I can see Virgin Hall. I hope he's doing OK," said Maria.

"Why wouldn't he be? Everything has been set up for him. All he has to do is work at his studies, and we know he's good at that. Anyway, that's what Benitez and Pollagrande said."

"That's what I worry about. One day he will have to take care of himself."

"No he won't. That's why we're making him into a priest."

Maria sat back from the window. "I can't help feeling that raising my beautiful boy has been too easy."

Alphonso scratched his navel. "The trouble with you is that when everything is great, you look for something to worry about. Be happy, for Christ sake!"

"It's all right for you macho shits. You own the world. And what about we women who have to pick up the pieces you leave behind?"

"And what pieces are they? Dealing with the servants? Giving orders to the gardeners?"

"Putting up with the half dressed women who follow your bodyguards around."

"I've told you, it's my way of controlling them. They are my greatest concern. It's for our safety, yours especially."

"Oh shut up. You're oppressing those girls like all men do. One day we girls will rise up and take over, get rid of the violence that you men do every day with your guns and knives as well as your disgusting looks and glances."

Alphonso leaned across the armrest and grabbed Maria's breast. "You're a stupid feminist bitch," he growled, full of mischief.

"Get out you dirty bastard. Don't touch me!"

"Why not? I own you?" grinned Alphonso. This would really get her going.

"What? What did you say?"

He was saved by the pilot's voice over the intercom. "Seatbelts and seats upright please. We'll be touching down at Princeton in twelve minutes."

"Never mind," sighed Alphonso, "you know that I've set the whole thing up at Virgin Hall. Gave a million to St. Robert's College for them to do what they liked, so long as they took care of Julian. Make a good priest of him. Even though he is a lot younger than the rest of them there."

"Wouldn't it have been better to wait?"

"Pollagrande said the sooner the better. I don't exactly know why. He said it's best for him to mature in the College rather than to be exposed to the rabble around our place, the guards, the women. You know…"

"As I said…"

"It's the surest way that he will never want to be anything else but a priest, and that's what you want, right? So you can have him all to yourself, for the rest of your life?" Alphonso's smirk got the better of him.

Maria looked away. She would not give him the pleasure of an answer. Especially as she knew that he was right.

*

Monsignor Flaccidia, Provost and Dean of St. Robert's College stood at the elbow of His Holiness Bishop Boswell, president of Virgin Hall University. Maria strutted forward, dressed in her favorite professional deep brown dress, nice open collar showing a single pearl necklace against her unwrinkled neck, a white frangipani flower in her lapel, her jet-black hair pulled into a twisted topknot above a tanned smooth forehead, shoulders back, head held high, depicting a depth of inner strength unknown in men.

Alphonso sauntered forward, his bright white shirt, Mexican style, hanging loosely over his long baggy gabardine fawn trousers, wishing they were shorts, but Maria had nagged him relentlessly until he gave in, and wearing his Roman sandals as ever, even though it was a brisk Fall day.

They were quickly whisked away to Bishop Boswell's office where they were treated to refreshing red tea from South Africa, which Alphonso politely (for him) declined.

"The rooibos is grown and harvested at out sister seminary's outreach program of St Francis Xavier in Cape Town," announced the president proudly. "We send many of our trainees to cleanse themselves by toiling in the fields, living and working with real people who are not as fortunate as we."

"This is wonderful tea, thank you," answered Maria. "Will Julian go there also?"

Bishop Boswell looked across to the Dean. "That will be up to the Dean's faculty to decide if or when he goes. It is a very expensive program to maintain, as I am sure you would understand. South Africa is a long way from here."

Dean Flaccidia was about to speak, but was interrupted by Alphonso. "So how much do you need?"

Dean Flaccidia coughed a little and put his cup and saucer down on the edge of the president's desk. "Mr. Garcia, it's not necessary, the large gift you already made will sustain the program for quite some time."

"I don't want my son to go to such a terrible place and live in such poverty and filth!" Maria suddenly blurted.

"Oh. Mrs. Garcia, he has a long way to go yet. Let's not get ahead of ourselves," replied Flaccidia, "and I hear that your son has received an exceptional training from Father Benitez and then from Cardinal Pollagrande himself. His knowledge of liturgy and facility with languages including Latin are quite astonishing."

"He's a wonderful boy, worth far more than any of the money we have given you," replied Maria, clearly bristling at the Dean's patronizing manner. She placed her cup and saucer on the other corner of the president's very large desk. Alphonso had eyed that desk and the rest of the rosewood furniture in president Boswell's grand office. He would like an office like this. And he would build one like it when he got back home, but the furniture would be of Patagonian rosewood.

President Boswell spoke. "Please enjoy your visit, and I look forward to seeing you again before you leave. Your accommodation was taken care of, I hope?" he shot a quick glance at Flaccidia who replied, "Mr. Garcia insisted on arranging his own."

"My people always take care of these things for me," smiled Alphonso, "security, you know." In fact, he had already bought one of the fabulous white Georgian mansions, set back from Princeton road in Lawrenceville, its glistening white structure hardly visible through the four acres of dogwoods that encircled it.

President Boswell stood up from his desk. "Dr. Flaccidia will walk you across to St. Robert's where you can visit your wonderful son."

They walked out of the grand, whitewashed administration building and across the campus in the direction of St. Robert's College.

"Our main campus is all around us," said Flaccidia, waving his arm.

Alphonso looked around. It looked like a bunch of buildings, all of them painted white, richly preserved, but nothing like what he thought a university looks like, except for the green expanses of hockey and football fields. There was no single towering building with endless columns, like he had seen on Netflix when he watched *Inspector Morse* solving his cases at Oxford. All of this was so new to him. And St. Robert's College looked like a church with a sprawling block of two story apartments added on to it.

They were about to enter the arched doorway, when Julian came bounding up the steps behind them. "Mom! Dad!" he called, a big smile on his face, the smile that had caused Christian to melt away. Maria ran straight to him and hugged him tightly. He was, obviously, her life. She kissed him on each of his rosy cheeks. She sensed a slight resistance, a tension of some kind, and she pulled back to look him in the eyes. They were brighter than ever. He was very happy. Something was going on. She was about to ask him how everything was going when there was a sudden boom of a kettle drum.

Alphonso flinched and stepped quickly behind Flaccidia, thinking it might be a sneak attack from one of his many enemies. He cursed himself for agreeing to Maria's demand that he leave his bodyguards behind at the plane. The drum emitted two more loud bangs, followed by an earsplitting screech.

"Ohhhhh! Hear this! Oh Sinners! Thou shalt not worship false idols said the Lord, or you will have your foreskins torn asunder!"

Julian turned around to see a huge man, as wide as he was tall, blonde long hair hanging past his shoulders, a large bushy gingery beard, little rimless glasses sitting on the end of his nose, now beating his drum furiously. And not far behind him he saw Christian running towards him, his face clearly distraught. That lithe body though, caused Julian to gulp. It was a thing of beauty.

The man with the drum kept on. Dean Flaccidia tried to usher Alphonso and Maria up the steps and through the open door. But they were both fixed to the spot.

"And the Lord said, gather thee up two hundred foreskins of the Philistines and make of them a soup, and thou shall eat unto eternity until all the sinners have been consumed!"

"Dad! Dad!" shouted Christian in his big voice, at least equal to his father's.

The preacher turned to see his son racing towards him. He dropped his drum and kneeled, his head looking to the sky and his arms stretched up. "The prodigal son has returned as you promised! Praise the Lord!"

By this time, Christian was upon him. "Come on Dad, it's only me. Let's go to Starbucks for a latte. I haven't had one since I got here." He grabbed his father's outstretched hand and pulled him up. His dad struggled and he went to pick up his drum. "Leave it, dad. We'll get it when we come back."

"Mom, Dad, this is my roommate Christian," called Julian, with the biggest of smiles. In fact, *the* biggest of smiles, and Maria noticed it, because they were usually reserved only for her. "We're the best of friends, aren't we Christian?"

"We sure are!" Christian replied, licking his pink lips nervously, managing a smile as well.

Alphonso nodded and stepped towards Christian, "Ola," he said, "pleased to meet you. Any friend on Julian's is a friend of mine."

"Hello Mr. Garcia. And this is my dad Virgil, but everyone just calls him Jude."

Alphonso looked Jude up and down. "Pleased to meet you, Jude," he said, folding his arms over his protruding belly. There was no way he was going to shake hands with that bag of germs. He needed a good wash.

Julian grabbed his Mom's arm lightly and tried to usher her up the steps. "Come on Mom, let's go in and I'll show you around." He looked at Christian who had stepped back a bit, one eye on his father and one eye on Julian. "See you tonight!" called Julian.

"You can say that again," called Christian with a smile. He tugged at the sleeve of his dad's old Oregon sweatshirt, and they walked off towards Starbucks.

"Well, I will leave you in the care of your young son," said the Dean, "I have many administrative chores to attend to. Enjoy your visit!"

Maria nodded with a smile, but she was more occupied with her own thoughts. Alphonso grunted and brought up the rear.

"First, I'll take you to my dorm and you can see how tidy it is!" said Julian. "And then we can talk. I've made a few decisions."

Maria's heart missed a beat. It sounded ominous.

Julian led the way, and continued to prattle on. "I've signed up to major in criminal justice," he said.

"This is one of your decisions?" asked Maria, full of suspicion and doubt.

"Well, it's nothing special. Father Benitez and his Holiness Pollagrande did such a good job teaching me that I know a lot more than the other students already, and they are much older than I am. So the Dean is letting me major in other subjects, so long as I keep up my required classes, the liturgical lessons and the rest."

Alphonso grunted again. They were now walking down the long hallway of the dormitory.

Julian beamed, "this is my room here. Me and Christian hit it off the first day we met. It's really great."

Maria pushed her way in, eager to see the beds, especially Christian's. "So which is yours?" she asked.

"It's the messy one of course. Christian is very tidy. It's because he's a Protestant, no doubt," Julian grinned. He noticed his Mom staring at Christian's bible.

"What happened to that? Is it the way Protestants treat their bibles?"

"Mom, come on! Our bibles are with us all the time, breakfast lunch and dinner. They get worn, stuff spilled on them, you know?"

"How can you put up with a Protestant? Anyway, what's a Protestant doing in a Catholic seminary?" asked Maria, working herself up, clearly jealous. "And how is it he's so tidy when his father looks like a homeless walking germ factory?"

"Mom, it's not his fault he has a weird father." He was about to say something about his own dad, but managed not to. "And to answer your question, why don't you ask the Dean, you seem so chummy with him. They're proud of the diversity of their student body."

"The student body? What the fuck is that?" asked Alphonso, tired and bored with Maria's constant interrogation.

"It just means the students, you dumb shit," snapped Maria.

"Hey, guys. This is a seminary, no swearing!" said Julian with a mischievous grin.

At that moment, Christian came into the room.

"Hey Christian, thought you were with your dad?" asked Julian, under the watchful eye of his mother,

"I left him doing his thing. He's banging his drum and preaching to the homeless bunch camped outside of Starbucks."

"So Mom," said Julian, taking Christian's hand in his. "Me and Christian, our friendship has developed into something else."

Maria drew herself up and turned to face the door. "I don't think I want to hear this."

Julian reached out and took her hand. "We've become a couple."

Alphonso scratched his belly.

"Do I need to ask what that means?" asked Maria, as edgy as she could be.

"It means…"

Christian interceded, "one day we'll get married!"

"Oh Mother of God! Holy Jesus! Oh blessed Virgin!" cried Maria. "It's an affront to all good women!"

"Mom, it's not like that!"

"Like what? Am I not the only woman in this room?"

.

3. A Wedding and a Funeral

Summer, 2016.

Bishop Benitez, or now, Cardinal Benitez, just promoted to four-star general status by Pope Francis, flew in from Bangkok especially for the magnificent celebration. He was not looking forward to seeing Pollagrande, his former mentor and protector. His status in the Vatican hierarchy was now slightly above that of poor old Pollagrande (a three star general), whom he knew—hoped, but tried not to hope of course, one must not allow pride and ambition to sully one's character— to one day become Pope. Benitez had no such compunctions. His eye was also on that prize, and he stood a much greater chance than Pollagrande because, quite simply, he was twenty years younger than him. He was the youngest Cardinal ever appointed. And that was all thanks to Pollagrande's influence and unsullied reputation. He gazed out the window of the old taxi as they at last entered the plush suburbs of Tláloc and the roads, though winding, became a little smoother. They at last pulled up outside the fortress-like gate of Alphonso's compound.

"You get out here," growled the taxi driver. Had Benitez been wearing his priestly robes the driver's manner would have been different. But he was traveling incognito on this trip for a number of important reasons, the obvious one being that now he was a big shot in the Vatican hierarchy, it was better not to flaunt his relationship with a known, infamous, drug lord, even though rumor had it that he had quit the drug trade. And by the way, Benitez said to himself, if the rumor were true it would be mostly because of his own influence on Alphonso, through the incredible job he had done on Julian, though true enough, he was a boy with exceptional talent.

"Can't you drive up the hill? It's a long way up there and I've got a heavy bag."

Benitez wound down the window and called out to the guards. "I am Cardinal Benitez," he yelled, "open the gates!"

Benitez counted at least six guards within sight, all with their AK47s at the ready. Did that mean that Alphonso was still in the drug trade, or did it mean that quitting it was more dangerous than staying in it?

After a phone call, the guard finally let the taxi through. There was already a long line of limousines sitting behind him, carrying various dignitaries to the celebration. And that was another thing. What kind of celebration was it? The invitation simply said that it was to celebrate the birth of Julian. He fingered the expensively printed invitation, and only then noticed that there was a misprint. They had left off the last letter of Julian's name. Someone will have been dropped in Alphonso's fish pond for that mistake, he frowned to himself.

The taxi pulled up beside the Greco-Roman columns. A guard paid the taxi driver who quickly sped away. Benitez looked up at the dazzling sight, the columns, guards with their guns, Alphonso and Maria standing at the entrance to the great dining hall, the sun reflecting off the pool and on to the columns. Too much white! Blinding light! He jogged up the steps, not even looking for his bag, now assuming that all would be looked after.

At last he arrived at the top of the steps and saw Maria at the head, dressed splendidly in a long, leopard patterned chiffon gown, blowing in the breeze, almost transparent, her hair tied in its usual topknot, an upright confident figure of a woman, broad smile engraved into her face. He hurried straight to her, but then faltered, because he saw out of the corner of his eye a woman standing next to Alphonso, thick ebony hair, hanging well past her bare broad shoulders, slightly stocky, but certainly beautiful in her own right, a strong curvaceous figure. Benitez faltered, but quickly turned to Maria, one hand stretched out to her, the other to Alphonso who stood, sullenly, beside her.

Maria took his hand and curtsied, head bowed. "Oh! Your Holiness," she whispered.

"My dear!" said Benitez, "it is unnecessary. Rise up so I can see your shining face!"

Alphonso reached across and grabbed Benitez's hand. "I'll see you in my office," he said in his thin voice, and withdrew from the welcoming line. And as he did so, the long line of arriving guests, many holding large expensive looking gifts, dissolved.

*

"It's a birth and a death," said Alphonso forlornly looking down at his Patagonian rosewood desk, a perfect rendering of president Boswell's.

"Padrino! please accept this gift, and our best, condolences ...er... wishes. We were not sure what to bring," chimed a guest, bowing and stepping backwards, embarrassed.

The long line of guests had reassembled and now snaked from Alphonso's office down to the pool. A great mound of gifts tied in huge pink and blue ribbons, wrapped in gold rimmed paper, accumulated outside his door. Benitez pushed past them all. He had donned his cardinal's robe. They quickly made way for him.

"Alphonso! I had no idea!" he cried.

"The rest of you, get out!" ordered Alphonso. "What did I do to deserve this?" cried Alphonso.

"Plenty," thought Benitez. "I heard that you had a vision?"

"I don't want to talk about that Holiness. Anyway, it was not a vision. It was a... a..."

Cardinal Benitez came around the big desk. "Come, Alphonso, let us pray together. I am sure Jesus has something wonderful in store for you."

"He already told me. It's why I sent for you."

"But I would have come anyway."

Alphonso did not move from his overstuffed leather chair. "It's Julian, I mean Julia," and then he burst into tears.

His Holiness placed his hand softly on Alphonso's shoulder. "There, there, Jesus has a plan for Julian, er Julia too, I'm sure of that."

"My son. I had a son! We were all so proud of him, and now he's gone!"

"At least he's not dead, Padrino."

"I was going to pass on the cartel to him. Teach him all the ropes. And now he's gone!"

"He's not dead, Alphonso, and besides he wasn't going to fill your shoes, he was training to be a priest, which now..."

"He can't be either. Who ever heard of a woman running a drug cartel? And she can't be a priest now, can she?"

Benitez ignored the question. Instead, he gently pulled on Alphonso to get him out of his chair so they could kneel down together, then said, "anyway, I thought after your episode you had sworn to give up the drug trade, and deal only in holiness.

That's what Pollagrande told me. Though I don't quite know what that means."

Alphonso pulled out an enormous handkerchief and snorted into it, them wiped the tears away. "Did you bring any holy water, Holiness?" he asked, his watery eyes peeping out from his handkerchief.

"Of course, I always carry some in case of emergency. Here, let me anoint you."

By now, they were both kneeling on the plush Aztec woven rug, not side by side, but facing each other. Benitez took out his small vial and opened the lid. He dabbed a little on Padrino's forehead, then gave the bottle to him. Alphonso sprinkled water on his fingers and crossed himself. Immediately, he grabbed his desk and rose up, and became the strong and decisive Padrino once again. He held up the now empty vial, holding it between thumb and forefinger. Looking down at Benitez he said, a big smile on his puffy face, as though he were introducing the heavyweight boxing champion of the world, "here is my answer, here is my epiphany, or whatever you call it!"

Benitez struggled to get up. "The vial? Alphonso, what are you talking about?"

"Your Holiness, it's been there all the time and I never knew it until I fell down, gripped by the high tensile steel hand of Jesus."

"You mean iron fist," corrected Benitez.

"Bullshit, Holiness! Iron is for the dark ages. Steel! We have high tensile steel! Much harder and stronger than iron!"

"I don't follow, Padrino. Are you OK?"

"Never better. Jesus brought us a new world, and he has chosen me to do the same."

"Alphonso, that's blasphemy, stop it! You are not one of the disciples!"

Alphonso grabbed Benitez by his cape. "Of course not! I am El Padrino, and I will spread holiness around the world!"

"El Padrino, please! Don't talk like that!"

"I will tell you, Holiness, and no one else. Jesus spoke to me, his voice was so deep it rattled my very bones. That is what it was, it was not an epileptic fit like the stupid doctors said. It was not a vision. I felt his high tensile hand descend right inside me and heard his voice without there being any sound. I *felt* his voice."

By now, Alphonso was shouting. Pedro the guard rushed in, brandishing his weapon. "Everything all right Padrino?"

"Never better! And send in my secretary. She's probably skinny-dipping in the pool." He turned back to Benitez. "It makes so much sense. Jesus is a genius, no doubt about it."

"Alphonso, maybe we should sit and have a quiet talk over a shot of tequila. You're babbling nonsense." Benitez knew as soon as he spoke that he had insulted El Padrino, who was rubbing his protruding tummy, a sure sign he was pissed off.

"I ought to slap you one," growled Alphonso, raising his hand, still gripping the holy water vial.

Benitez raised his arm, half expecting a blow.

Alphonso scratched his toupee and grinned, "good heavens, Holiness, I'm joking!"

Benitez tried to smile, but he was frightened. He wrapped his red cloak around him as if this would ward off the evil of this over furnished room. "Padrino, forgive me, he said in a soft voice. "Do tell me what you have in mind."

Alphonso was about to speak when the office door flew open (it also laminated with Patagonian rosewood), and in rushed Julian, dragging behind him Christian, looking flustered but as beautiful as ever, though Alphonso did not notice it. Benitez, however, did.

When they saw His Holiness, they quickly dropped to their knees and said, "forgive us, your Holiness."

Holiness put out his hands. "Rise my sons, er, I mean children," rise. It is so wonderful to see you Julian, er Julia, and to meet you too, Christian, I understand?" They both rose, their young faces full of life

"Your Holiness," replied Christian, "Julian has told me so much about you. It is an honor to meet you."

"Likewise my son. And Julian? I hear you were the star at St. Robert's College? The youngest to ever graduate?"

"I have you to thank, Holiness for having prepared me so well. And of course, I had such wonderful moral support from Christian," answered Julian, looking lustfully across to Christian, another detail Holiness noticed, but lost on El Padrino.

"I am so proud of you, Julian," said Cardinal Benitez as he looked up to heaven and added, "I ask your indulgence, Jesus, just this once to feel a little sinful pride."

Alphonso plopped down in his overstuffed chair and coughed loudly to bring the attention of the room back to himself. "So what's the problem, you two, interrupting my business meeting with His Holiness?"

"Me and Christian, we're having a bit of a disagreement."

"Christian and I," corrected His Holiness, ever the teacher.

"It's not the way young people talk, these days, Father, I mean Holiness."

"If it's a lovers' quarrel, go to your mother, not me. I'm in the middle of a big business deal right now," said Alphonso in his cold, business-like voice.

"She said she was coming," said Julian. "She was angry with your secretary because her hair was all messed up and they went off to fix it."

"That was the one that skinny-dipped?" asked Christian, cheeks flushed.

Cardinal Benitez spoke. "Well, perhaps you can tell us a little of your difference and maybe we can work it out. Nothing serious, I hope?"

"It's complicated, rather than serious, though I suppose that anything that's complicated is always serious otherwise it would not be complicated, would it?" said Julian, showing off.

"Out with it, so I can get on with my work," said El Padrino gruffly.

Julian shifted from one foot to the other and looked quickly at Benitez and then to his father. "Christian doesn't want me to have the operation," he said in his thin voice, a replica of his father's.

El Padrino leaned across his desk and asked, "Operation? What operation?"

Christian looked down and fidgeted with his slender fingers. His Holiness gave a small nervous cough and said quietly, though in the heavy silence of the room it sounded like the noon bell of the metropolitan cathedral, "I think he means a sex change operation."

And before anyone could speak, the rosewood door opened slowly and in stepped Maria, her topknot still where it was the day before and every day before that. She stood there, her bikini faintly visible through her leopard patterned chiffon robe. She was, for that very brief moment, the center of attention. Hands on her considerable hips, she spoke to the room in her almost male voice: "Did the Holy Father say what I think he said?"

*

"Do you have a dick or don't you?" demanded El Padrino impatiently.

"Alphonso! How could you be so vile?" cried Maria.

"Now! Now!" called His Holiness.

Julian looked down, embarrassed of course. "I have both."

"Both what?" insisted Alphonso, pitilessly.

"Compassion, please!" pleaded His Holiness.

Julian sniffed and shook with tiny little sobs. Just like he did after a long crying session when he was a baby, thought Maria.

"So what's the problem?" reasoned Alphonso, "you've got the best of both worlds." He struggled to hold back a smirk.

"It's the worst of both worlds," interrupted Christian, looking down, then around the room, avoiding eye contact with anyone.

Everyone stared at Christian. His words had fallen upon ears starved of the truth, and he sensed it. "I love him just the way he is. For someone like me, it doesn't matter what he's got in front." And there, he had said it.

"What the fuck are you talking about?" growled Alphonso.

"He means…" Benitez tried to say, but was cut off by Christian.

"If he has a sex change and becomes a girl, he can't be a priest, can he?"

The room heard him. All eyes turned to His Holiness, who now flourished his robe and raised himself on the front of his feet. "As far as the church is concerned, if you are a man, you can be a priest. Of course, priests can't marry, we all know that. So Christian is right and logical." He looked around the room, perceiving nods of agreement.

"Except, if I'm not a woman," said Julian, "Christian and I can't get married and that's what we want, isn't it Christian?" But before he could answer, Maria chimed in.

"Julian, my love, I always wanted a daughter. But I never wanted another woman in the family, if you see what I mean," said Maria with a soft smile.

"Mom, I don't know. I thought mothers loved their sons more than their daughters."

"We do, but we don't want them to grow up and we don't want any other woman to have them. That's why I was so happy you chose the priesthood."

"That's what she wanted from the day you were born," mumbled Alphonso. "And you're not running the cartel if you're a woman, that's for sure."

Benitez could see that this was going to end badly. "Perhaps we should pray to Jesus for a solution, and meet again tomorrow after we have had time to meditate on this very human problem." The wise man had spoken. Yet against his own inclination, he turned to Julian and said aggressively, "do you mean to say that after all your wonderful achievements and studies to become a priest, you would throw it all away just to marry this young man, and a Protestant to boot?"

Alphonso, ever the decisive executive, leaned down to the bottom right hand drawer of his desk and pulled out a revolver, a magnificent weapon, Hitler's Golden Walther that Maria had bought at auction for his 50th birthday. He waved it in the air and then carefully placed it on the first edition of the Gideon bible that was the only item on his desk. He got up out of his overstuffed chair and leaned forward, a posture he had seen on *Mad Men*. "There will be no marriage and no sex change," he growled in his fiercest voice, an impossibility given its thin high-pitched sound, almost that of a woman.

The room went silent. Maria stepped up to the desk and leaned, her face almost touching Alphonso's, her mature breast almost touching the priceless desk. "Give me the gun!" she growled back, "I'll blow my brains out before I will let my son suffer at your hands."

"Get your own gun! Mine's too good for that!" yelled Alphonso. "Besides, you said you didn't want him to be a woman. And I can't blame you. Who would want to suffer such humility?"

"Fuck you!" she cried, "Fuck all you men!" and ran for the door, but Christian grabbed her in his long arms and pulled her to him. She immediately went limp. She had caught a whiff of his armpits. "Oh my Virgin Mary!" she croaked. "Now I understand!" she looked to Julian, dumbfounded. "My darling Julian," she crooned as she swooned in Christian's arms, "I can see now, I can see why Christian does not want you to change, and why you do."

His Holiness stepped in, waving his red cloak over Christian and Maria. "Then I have the perfect solution," he said, but before he could say anything more Pedro called out from the door where he stood holding his AK47. "Give him a big prick, for Christ sake!"

Christian let go of Maria and she fell to the floor. Alphonso, totally flummoxed by this outlandish intrusion into his family's business by one of his guards, brandished his gun. The tiny

beautiful thing would be no match for an AK47, but then, he
thought, nor would Julian's tiny prick be any match for Christian's.

Pedro stood, frozen to the spot, aghast that he had blurted out
what was surely the obvious solution.

Julian took hold of Christian's hand and held it to his chest.
"Is that what you want?" he asked Christian.

"Please, I'm so embarrassed, I, I..." Christian cried.

Clearly, it was. He had been afraid to say it. Christian was
after all gay, he wanted a man, not half a man.

Julian turned to him and kissed him full on those pink lips.
"Then that's it, I'll do it, and I can then stay a priest."

"But you can't marry him," insisted His Holiness, "even if he
were a woman, you couldn't because you are a priest, unless..."

"What?" asked Julian belligerently.

"You leave the priesthood."

"Oh no! Holiness. Can't you grant an exception?" cried
Maria.

"Not even I can do that. Only God."

Alphonso intervened. "Leave me, all of you! Holiness, you
stay, we have business, don't we?"

"If you say so, Padrino."

Pedro slipped away, avoiding the fish pond, Julian and
Christian left hand in hand, followed by a bedraggled Maria, her
topknot undone, hair hanging over her shoulders, almost to her
waist, looking the worse for her age, tears running down her
cheeks. She had lost her son, gained a daughter, then got her son
back again, only to see him taken over by another man, a Protestant. How could Jesus do this to her? She had been sinful, but
not that sinful to deserve all this! She had tried her hardest to
keep Alphonso from evil, really she had. Especially as now he
was on the brink of giving up the cartel a decision for which she
claimed complete responsibility.

Alphonso closed the door, beckoning to a guard to watch it
and to let absolutely no one in. "Pollagrande talked with you?"
he asked Benitez.

"Indeed, my son. Have to say, it is an unbelievable plan."

"What do you mean?"

Benitez coughed nervously. "That only you could pull off such
a plan."

El Padrino eyed him carefully. "You don't think I can do it?"

"No! No! I mean Yes, Yes! I mean, now that Pollagrande is
also Foreign Secretary, it should work."

"Good. Then this is what I want you to do. First, get me, Maria and Julian, Vatican citizenship. Second, Pollagrande will appoint me special ambassador to the United States. Third, arrange a meeting for me with the engineer who supervises all the cisterns under Rome. I think it would be best if Pollagrande brought him to meet me at my new headquarters in Princeton. Tell him to bring detailed maps. Fourth, *la casa del giardiniere* you know that? It is just a short walk from the *Fontana del l'Aquila*."

"I do. It is my favorite place of meditation in the Vatican," answered His Holiness.

"Good. When you go out, go to Bambola, my secretary, and she will give you one million dollars. Take it to the gardener and tell him that we want to use his house for several months. The million is only a down payment. I will send Pollagrande another ten million."

"Pollagrande?"

"He is also the Vatican CAO and now runs the *Banca di Santo Spirito*."

"But what's the money for?"

"*La casa del giardiniere* will be our HQ. Beneath it, we will construct a modern water purification system and tap into the same source as the Eagle Fountain. We will produce there the holiest of Holy Water."

"But how will you distribute it?" Benitez stared at Alphonso as if he were mad.

"I am head of the largest drug cartel in the world, Holiness. It is what I do. Distributing Holy Water will be much easier than drugs."

"Well, if you say so, my son. Frankly, I think you've gone mad."

Alphonso moved to the front of his desk. Benitez stood quickly. He did not want Alphonso's belly button in his face.

"One more thing," continued Alphonso, "find the engineers who run all of Rome's water supply, the ancient aqueducts that feed the fountains, Trevi, Quattro Fontani and all the rest. Bambola will give you an extra million dollars to pay them off, if needed."

"Padrino. Are you sure you want to go ahead with this? It sounds suicidal. The Pope will never allow it. It will sully the magnificent silence of the Vatican gardens."

"Do you still want to be Pope?" asked Alphonso with a devilish smile.

"What? Me?" Benitez stuttered.

"I will make you Pope, that is if you want it."

"It is a sin to want such a thing, pride and ambition, they are the most dangerous of sins."

"Not if good will result," said Alphonso sagely.

"Besides, I thought that Pollagrande was next in line," muttered Benitez, looking sideways as though someone were there.

Alphonso took off his toupee, opened his arms and embraced His Holiness, who recoiled, or wanted to recoil, in horror. No ordinary commoner ever embraced a cardinal, it was an unholy intrusion. He turned his head away, as though anticipating a kiss, which fortunately did not come. The thought of Alphonso's soft, bare belly, always ahead of him, rubbing against his holy red robe was as much as he could take. He very gently pushed himself away and said, "I will take your leave, my son."

Alphonso waved the hand that held his toupee and called, "do not let me down, now, we are doing God's work." He closed his eyes, placed his toupee back on his head, and was sure he heard God speak to him. Then he opened his eyes and added out of habit more than anything else, "failure is not an option."

His Holiness bowed slightly as he quickly backed towards the door. But his quiet withdrawal was suddenly interrupted by the sound of gunfire, a loud splash and cries of excitement. Benitez recoiled and hid under Alphonso's Patagonian desk. Alphonso recognized the sound. Someone had been thrown into the fishpond. He hurried out to see the spectacle.

Pandemonium. Guards ran to and fro, though most stood by the fishpond pointing and yelling. Then came the distinct sound of a drum. That was what they heard. It was not gun shots. In fact it was nothing like gun shots. Alphonso could plainly see that his men had panicked, and it was distressing. Another good reason for his planned relocation to the USA where he would hire a whole new bunch of guards. He would take only Pedro with him, even he would have to be watched.

As the gang gathered around the fishpond, the drum continued, belting out a marching rhythm, though missing a beat here and there. Then Alphonso saw the slender figure of Christian the blonde, running towards the pond, Julian running after him. Christian hurried down the steps, and arrived just as the gang of onlookers gasped and retreated in disarray. A huge piraña flew out of the pond and dropped flapping madly on the ground. Christian reached the water's edge and there, as he feared, was his father Virgil, a bedraggled, unshaven mass, red-faced, beating at his drum and intermittently using it to beat away the hungry fish.

"Dad! Grab my hand! Throw me the drum!" cried Christian.

His father looked up and cried, "lo! The pilgrim was drawn into the sea of despond!" A piraña flipped out of the water and snapped at his bushy face. He banged it with his drum. "Oh voracious gluttons! Creatures of Satan! I command you! Go back to the fire and brimstone from whence you came! Oh Father! Oh Son of God!"

"I'm here, dad. Give me your hand!" called Christian. He leaned out over the curved, onyx lined pond, Julian hanging on to him.

Virgil cried, "take the drum!"

"Fuck the drum!" blurted Christian, "save your life!"

Christian leaned even further out, eyeing the fish of the devil circling, getting ready for a final, bloody attack. But his dad simply kept proffering the drum, he would not leave until he had finished off the fish or they him.

By this time, Alphonso stood at the edge of the pond. Normally, he would let his men take care of it, but they were half crazed themselves, you'd think they were at a football game. He snatched the AK47 from Pedro. He could not let Virgil die. He had an important part for him to play in his new venture. He sprayed the pond with bullets, the blood oozing from the wounded fish who, smelling blood, feasted upon each other. Christian grabbed the drum and yanked it back, pulling his father out of the pond. It was a miracle! He looked at his dad, hunched up at the shoulders, carrying a full backpack, Lord knows what was in it. How did he keep afloat and fight off those awful fish at the same time?

Alphonso returned the AK47 to Pedro. "See that he has a haircut and all that red beard shaved off. When he's cleaned up bring him to me," he ordered.

Christian looked at Alphonso in disbelief and complained, "you leave my father alone. I don't know why he came here. I didn't know…"

Alphonso stared through him. "I invited him, just as I invited you. Your father and I will be going into business together."

Julian stepped up. "What? You're making him into a drug dealer?"

Alphonso gave them all a look of disdain. "Hasn't Father Benitez told you? I thought everyone knew by now. God spoke to me at the baptistry. I had an epiphany. I am getting out of the drug trade, and will from now on deal only in holiness, spreading it far and wide. Isn't that what Christian's father does? He spreads holiness, except that he does it in a very inefficient way. I have a better way."

Julian and Christian looked at their fathers, one to the other. "You're mad!" they said in perfect unison.

4. Changing of the guard

Maria sat at the top end of their magnificent dining table, the place that, until this historic occasion, was always occupied by Alphonso. Halfway down the table sat Christian and Julian on one side, holding hands under the table, facing Alphonso and Virgil on the other. Waiters bustled in and out. Maria snapped her fingers and the largest person in the room strode forward. She had chosen him from many applicants, all of whom she had interviewed and had her psychologist administer a battery of personality tests. She wanted a gentle giant, as she called him, one who would be gentle with her, but a frightening giant to everyone else.

"Francisco, hold my hand," she said with a soft smile.

He held it gently.

"Francisco, kiss my topknot."

He kissed her topknot.

"Francisco, unravel my hair."

"I will need two hands," whispered Francisco.

Maria smiled and let go of his hand. And now her ebony hair dropped past her shoulders, glistened and sparkled in the light of the chandeliers above. She looked up and said, "You know Gloria's saying. 'A woman without a man is like a fish without a bicycle'?"

"Gloria who?" asked Francisco, perplexed.

"Steinem."

"If you say so, Princess," answered Francisco, addressing her according to her wish.

"Those fish in the pond today. They needed a bicycle." Maria grinned

"Yes Princess, they did."

"And now we eat them," announced Maria as she looked around the table, a smile of superiority addressed to all who were brave enough to look straight at her. She clapped her hands and waiters appeared carrying silver trays aloft, bedecked with grilled fish filets.

"That will be all, Francisco."

She stared down the table at her new family, new, that is, except for Alphonso, but he had transformed into something else. She no longer knew who he was. She snapped her fingers again and pointed to the Champaign. "Francisco, pour us some Champaign, there's a darling." When he leaned over to fill her glass, she whispered, "go down there and stop those two from holding hands under the table. It's disgusting. Women might have no use for men, but what of men for each other? Gloria Steinem said that too."

"No she didn't," whispered Francisco with a straight face.

"Shut up and do what you're told," sniped Maria.

Francisco walked down to fill the boys' glasses. He leaned over to pour, then with his spare hand, reached under and grabbed both their entwined hands. "The Princess says to stop," he whispered.

"Is this the fish from the pond?" asked Julian in a loud voice.

Francisco stood back and looked to Maria for an answer.

"It was at my request," answered Virgil. "It was what God intended, was it not? For the sinner who eats, shall be eaten by his prey, Philippians 3: 19."

"That's not right," said Francisco, "it says your God is your stomach."

"Whatever. You know what I meant," Virgil replied, annoyed, glancing to Maria as if she were responsible for Francisco's brazen interventions. After all, he was just a servant.

Without his bushy red beard, Virgil's eyes appeared too big for the narrow forehead that held them. His gaunt long face appeared almost yellow. He looked across at his two sons to be. He had considered disinheriting Christian, but there was no point to it, since there was nothing to disinherit him from, not even his faith, for Christian's actions reflected his loss of faith. Fancy falling in love with a Catholic! It was the last thing he expected. Sending him to a Catholic seminary that claimed to welcome diversity had been a big mistake. Of course it wasn't so much that he sent him, it was the only program that offered a scholarship. But this! To openly display his sinful lust for that little olive skinned Julian was an outrage. What on earth was God thinking? Unless the God of Catholics was a different one from his Protestant God, the God he had known intimately since the night he copulated with a…(he had told himself never to say that word), that produced his only son, now a snake. His only begotten son who was now giving up his life to a Catholic. "Wait a minute, that sounds familiar, John 3:16, giving himself up so I could have eternal life?" Virgil muttered to himself. He had slipped into a kind of trance and heard only the faint sound of Alphonso who had risen from his chair and had raised his glass to call for a toast.

Alphonso made a nervous little cough, then said, "I know that all of you gathered here this evening are wondering why I am not seated at my usual place at the head of the table. My darling beautiful wife, who has served me religiously ever since I snatched that book "The Thousand Indias" out of her hands in the porno bookstore that she now owns, and she fell down on her knees before me, and worshipped me better than any woman before or since, is now the head of our Cartel."

Maria stood and raised her glass too. "To the cartel!" she called, "And Gloria Steinem rest in peace!"

Virgil looked down perplexed. The only Gloria he had heard of was Gloria In Excelsis. He looked up at Alphonso who dipped his fingers into his glass and flicked Champaign across the table at Julian and Christian, and dipping again flicked some on Virgil and turning to him, looking down, the glass held up close to his eyes, "I see in this glass our future together," he said to Virgil. "You will be my CEO and we will spread holiness together like the world has never seen before!"

Virgil's glass was empty. He was, after all, the kind of Protestant that considered drinking alcohol to be an abominable sin. It was a weakness of Catholics that he abhorred, but relished just the same. Alphonso sat down and called Francisco. "Bring him some water," he ordered, looking to Maria for her permission. She nodded approval. And as Francisco filled Virgil's glass with water, Alphonso said, "this is ordinary water from our local spring. The day will soon come when it will be holy. Drink!"

Christian and Julian raised their coupled hands above them. "We drink to that," they said, giving each other a knowing glance that Alphonso missed but Maria saw, and it troubled her. Perhaps she should have Christian annulled, she thought, as she mused over her new powers as Drug Lady of the Garcia cartel.

*

The next morning, God sent a message. All those who had partaken of that forgettable dinner of grilled piraña, were taken with diarrhea. God had given them all a purgative, Virgil announced knowingly. Alphonso, however, had not eaten any of the fish, for he knew how nasty they were, having been the one who stocked the pond. He was particularly pleased to see that Francisco had been reduced to a groaning bent up figure half his size, a good lesson to Maria never to trust anyone, even one's most trusted servant.

Twenty four hours later, he called Virgil to his office. Virgil had requested that his drum be returned to him, but was informed that the pirañas had eaten it. Perhaps it was the drum that had made them all sick. Virgil entered, looking even more gaunt than usual, bent over double with the weight of his backpack.

"Please be seated, Virgil, if I may call you thus?"

"Everyone calls me Jude," he grunted and pulled up a chair. Alphonso had given up all the trappings of drug lord, except his office, which he would eventually pass on to Maria, once the transfer to Princeton was done. Then she said she would equip her own office. He looked down at his desk, though, and wondered whether he could part with it.

"Pastor Virgil," he began.

"Jude, just Jude."

"Thank you, Jude. As I've told everyone, I am giving up the drug trade and moving into a new field of holiness distribution. I have heard from Christian and Julian that you are the greatest evangelist of all time. I thought that we might put aside any religious difference we might have—you know Catholic and Protestant—I don't care for the details of those silly differences. But I need a really good salesman to head up the entire sales department."

"I don't understand what you mean by holiness. You mean faith? Love of our Jesus Christ?" asked Jude.

"That too. No, I mean that we need a vehicle to spread this holiness, I mean a product that people can see and touch and feel."

"But that's impossible. People have to feel it in their insides, in their hearts. Faith isn't a product," lectured Jude.

"That's the trouble with you evangelists. You deny that what you sell to your followers is a product like everything else that is sold by talking."

"Talking?"

"What else is preaching and singing? Aren't songs products?"

"No, they are vehicles that we evangelists use to convey and share our faith with others."

"You see this?" asked Alphonso, holding up a tiny glass flask the size and shape of his puffy middle finger. He did not wait for an answer. "This is our vehicle, in it is all the faith, good will, and holiness you could want, all of it crammed into a tiny space."

"But there's nothing in it," observed Jude. Looking very serious.

"Ah, but there will be. We will fill this vial and millions and millions more with Holy Water."

Virgil tightened up, pushed himself in to the hard rosewood back of his chair, the protruding lumps in his backpack pressing on his ribs. "You Catholics, you turn everything into products and idols. It's sinful, that's what it is!"

"It's a vehicle for conveying faith, love, holiness. It's something people can hold on to, something that will help them believe, much easier than believing in something shadowy, without form. Don't you see?"

"So you want me to head up a sales force to sell bottles of Holy Water," said Jude with a touch of belligerence. "Sounds fraudulent."

"It's what you do, when you pass around the collection plate in your Church of Judasian Trust, isn't?" countered Alphonso

Virgil went silent. Alphonso had finally driven a nail through his evangelist armor. He could not spread the word without the money to support him and some of his followers to do it. He depended on them to give him money to keep doing what he was doing. Building a physical church had been mostly beyond his means. They had met in peoples' kitchens and living rooms. It made his work seem far too limited. He wanted to change the world. Not just his neighbors. He looked across the desk to Alphonso who scratched his bare belly and blinked at him, a faint smile on his round face.

Alphonso took off his toupee, placed it on the desk before him and said in the deepest voice he could muster, which wasn't much, "place your hand on mine. I swear to you on my toupee, the symbol of my true soul, that we will, together, spread holiness throughout the whole world."

Virgil was deeply moved by Alphonso's sincerity. But he remained skeptical. "There's only one problem. You Catholics, your priests, have the monopoly on holy water."

"They think they do, but in actual fact, their entire business of holy water is a sham and a thorough disgrace. I have spoken with the highest of Catholic sources, none less Cardinal Polla-grande, foreign secretary and chief accounting officer of the Vatican who admits as much. Most priests in their far flung empire of Christ simply fill up their little vials with water out of the nearest tap. They don't care where it comes from, they just pretend they are making holy water by holding it in their hands and saying a blessing. If they said a blessing over my toupee would that make it holy? It's nonsense."

"Then where does real holy water come from? You understand that we Protestants don't believe in it," muttered Virgil.

"Do you believe in Saint Peter and that he is buried beneath the Bernini canopy inside Saint Peter's Basilica?" asked El Padrino.

"Yes, I do, though I think he was the real Judas," Virgil replied.

"Forget the details!" cried Alphonso. "Beneath the basilica, the Vatican, and in fact much of Rome, are natural springs that appeared out of nowhere soon after Peter was crucified. They were not there during the ancient times of the Romans—that's why they had to build aqueducts to bring in water from far and wide to keep the city going. The water of those springs was put there by Jesus, why else would they suddenly appear—and there is an endless supply of it—at just that time? I have no doubt that those springs are the source of holy water."

"You and who else?" asked Jude, losing patience.

"It is enough that Pollagrande concurs. He admits that over the centuries, the Vatican lost control of the holy water, and had no idea of how to distribute it from Rome to its far flung empires. So they just told their priests that all they had to do was bless the water and it was holy, They were, after all, God's messengers on earth."

Virgil sat, dumbfounded. Could this be true? Catholics lied about what they did all the time. They couldn't be trusted. But they didn't lie about Jesus, no Christian ever would, at least not knowingly. And the money coming in would be fantastic, if Alphonso could pull it off. It seemed so far-fetched. Yet he was a very successful drug merchant. He obviously knew how to develop markets and distribute a product.

Alphonso could see that Virgil was on the brink. "I will be setting up a vial factory in Princeton, well, nearby Hopewell actually, where I will establish my Holiness center of operations. I want you to head up the sales force that will distribute the vials of Holy Water far and wide. Of course we will have to do it in stages. And at my end, which will be in the Vatican, I will arrange for the collection and transportation of the water from beneath the Vatican to the USA for its processing and distribution. I have already submitted a patent and trademark for Vatican Holy Water—Aquam Sanctus Pietro, water of Saint Peter—and the vials will be stamped ASP against the Vatican coat of arms, and of course with tamper evident packaging. Pollagrande will get the Pope to issue a Papal edict to all priests at every level and every diocese to purchase only officially approved Holy Water, stamped ASP. And there will be strict quality control on the purity of the Holy Water, so there will be no more holy water infected with typhoid and other diseases as happens frequently. The collection of payments, of course, will be in your province, though if you need help there, you may need to talk with Maria to get some assistance. But I do not anticipate any serious difficulties. After all, the Pope must be obeyed."

"But what if the Pope does not agree?"

"We will worry about that when and if it happens. I have plans to manage that also." Alphonso gave Virgil his most confident and mysterious look. "What about ten percent of wholesale price?"

"How much will you price the vials?" responded Jude, trying not to feel like he was bargaining."

"I am not sure yet. Pollagrande will be doing his accounting magic and come up with a price. The initial cost to set up the water collection, transportation, build the factory, all of that I am paying for. So the Vatican stands to make a lot of money. They will get probably twenty percent on top of that. It's the gift of my epiphany. But the biggest winner is Holiness."

Virgil, not feeling like Jude anymore, shifted on his chair once again and said, "I'm not sure..."

"Don't be a doubting Thomas. Take the leap. It's a much bigger one, and will reap much more fruit than preaching to some bunch of loser homeless drunks."

Virgil winced. But deep down he knew that there was a grain of truth in what Alphonso was saying. He had to admit that he had struggled in a sea of despond with his Church of Judasian Trust. "All right," he said, "I'll do it. There's nothing to lose and everything to gain."

Alphonso stood up from his over-stuffed chair and ran around the desk. He grasped Virgil by the hand, then let go and instead hugged him and was immediately repulsed by the smell of his armpits. "We have a deal then?" he asked, pulling away.

Virgil shook hands. "We have a deal. When do we start?"

"Why, now!" said Alphonso as he retrieved a bulging bag from his desk draw and handed it to Virgil. This will get you to America and keep you going until I get our factory up and running."

The two men, one tall the other short, walked to the door, Alphonso not big enough to put his arm around Virgil's shoulder, but instead patting him lightly on the back. Virgil, Jude no more, reached up to put the sack of money into his backpack and at that moment, the bottom of the backpack burst open and out fell its entire content of stones, yet the money stayed in. The back-pack felt so light, he thought he could fly! Another small miracle! Alphonso and Virgil looked at each other. Indeed! They had an understanding!

Now, everything was now set, everything was in place. Or so Alphonso thought, when Julian, Christian and Maria pushed open the door, knocking Pedro aside, Francisco taking up the rear. Maria was angry. Of that, Alphonso was certain. Her topknot was tied so tight it could have pulled her hair out by its roots. Virgil could see there was trouble and tried to slip past so he could get away from this place and spend some of his money. But Maria barred his way, hands on her shapely lips, prodding Julian and Christian, arm in arm, before her. She screamed the shrill scream of a free-tailed bat, "tell them, you pair of shits! Tell them!"

Virgil stepped back, hands on hips too. He had resolved never to give Christian a cent of his new fortune, or fortune to be. He still had not fully accepted that Christian had pretty much become a Catholic. Or that's what it seemed. Alphonso stood behind his desk, hands on his hips too, an amused smirk on his face. Jesus had warned him, the bolt from Heaven had told him that his son would be taken from him. At the time, he had assumed the worst, that Julian would die some awful death and be transported to heaven. But now he realized that Jesus was

much more crafty than that. He was losing a son but gaining a
daughter.

Julian and Christian turned to each other, their hands clasped
together. They dropped to their knees and embraced, a full-on
sloppy kiss that caused Alphonso to look away in disgust. Maria
stopped screaming and stood speechless. Virgil darted forward
and tried to pull them apart and was easily brushed aside by
Christian. But it was enough to capsize them and the two boys
rolled on the lush silk rug and embraced as one. The Patagonian
desk had seen many a spectacle in this office, but nothing like
this. Pedro peeked in from the doorway, his AK47 in hand.
Francisco peeped in through the office window that looked over
the fish pond.

At last, the office became silent, broken only by the small
sounds of lips sucking and pulling apart. Pedro looked to
Alphonso for an order to do something. None came. Alphonso
had returned to his overstuffed chair. He leaned forward, elbows
on his desk, chin cupped in his hands. "When you two are
done," he said quietly, "you might tell me what's going on."

It was enough. The kissing stopped and the boys—that's all
they were, mused Maria, dropping her hands to her sides—sat
up, their legs folded as though they were once more in
kindergarten. Alphonso had to lean across his desk in order to
see them. Virgil was close enough to kick Christian and had to
quietly mutter under his breath "get thee behind me Satan" over
and over to prevent himself from doing so.

"Well?" asked Alphonso as he let out a deep sigh. "What is
it?" They said nothing, just looked into each other's watery
eyes, so he looked to Maria for an answer.

"Julian's quitting the priesthood! He's going to become a
professor at some shitty New Jersey college! All that education
for nothing!" she cried.

Alphonso leaned further over the desk. "Julian? Is that right?
A pointy-head?"

Julian placed his hand on Christian's shoulder and pushed
himself up. "I've applied for an assistant professor position at
New State College."

"Me too!" grunted Christian as Julian pulled him up.

"But you haven't got the jobs yet?" quizzed Alphonso, his
mind racing, searching, looking for alternatives.

"We both have interviews next week. But we're sure we will get the positions. They're opening a new department and need young assistant professors to teach all the new courses."

"What's an assistant professor?" asked Virgil, at last engaging, thinking beyond his new found wealth.

"What professor will you be assisting?" asked Maria.

"It's not like that," answered Julian, "we won't be assisting any particular professor. We just do what they all do, we teach our courses and mentor the students."

"So if you're doing the same work as the professors, why aren't you professors and not assistant professors?" asked Alphonso, puzzled.

"Because we are just starting, we're the most junior," answered Julian again.

"Sounds like a rip-off if you ask me," said Alphonso casually. He was surprisingly calm. Maria looked at him quizzically.

"Is it a Catholic or Protestant college?" chimed in Virgil.

Christian spoke up. "Neither. It's a state college."

"What's that?" asked Alphonso.

"New Jersey state government run and paid for," said Christian.

"If it's a new department, why aren't you the head of it?" asked Alphonso, his mind still racing.

"Fuck you, Dad!" cried Julian in frustration, "everyone has to start at the bottom, and work their way up, for Christ sake."

Alphonso crossed himself and said, "I'll try to ignore that blasphemy. And what's so new about this new department?"

"It's the LGBTQ department," said Christian, "which makes us both very well qualified."

"What the fuck is that?" asked Alphonso in exasperation.

"I can never remember it, it's too long. But you can look it up on Google," said Julian with a smile. He was beginning to relax. He could see that his father was not at all upset, not like his mom, who now had her say.

"Alphonso! Aren't you going to do anything? Stop them from ruining their lives?" Her hands went to her hips once again.

Alphonso looked up to the beautifully frescoed ceiling, a copy of the Sistine Chapel and said, "it's a big change, I see that. But the Lord works in mysterious ways. He has a plan, and I will work to make it the best plan."

"Dad! You mean we have your blessing?" sang Julian, squeezing Christian's hand even more.

"Well, you do my son, but I can't really give it to Christian because he's not my son."

"But he will be once we're married!" blurted Julian.

Maria's arms dropped to her sides and she swooned with a big sigh and fell to the floor unconscious. Alphonso simply sat back in his overstuffed chair, a quiet, all knowing smile. He had a plan, a wonderful plan.

The office fell silent. Julian and Christian embraced and turned to leave. They stepped over Maria's prostrate body and made for the door, turning as Pedro met them, and called out in unison, "Bye dads!"

Virgil who was now leaning over Maria, prodding her with his long fingers, muttering, waved good bye without looking up.

*

"MICE? Who let them in?" commanded Pedro. He turned to Alphonso. "Padrino, sorry! The stupid bastards at the gate let them in. You want me to turn them away?"

"No. We've nothing to hide any more, do we? We're on our way to a new life in Princeton New Jersey."

The MICE car pulled up by the fish pond. Alphonso walked down to meet them. "What can I do for you, officers?" he asked.

"Good morning. We are from Mexican Immigration and Customs Enforcement. Are you Alphonso Godolphony Garcia?"

"Who wants to know?"

"Born in Barranca del Muerto, Mexico City in 1968?

"So what?"

"Could I see your Mexican passport, please?"

"I don't have it here. Why?"

"You need to come with us."

The officer stood back with his partner at his elbow, each with their hands lightly touching their holstered gun on their hip. Both of them, foolishly, ignored all the training they had received in MICE academy, never to stand with their backs to a pool of water, especially a fish pond. Pedro inched forward. Alphonso gently held him back.

"You better have a good reason for this. Your boss is an old friend of mine," warned El Padrino, speaking with a calm authority meant to scare the hell out of the officers.

"You're being deported," blurted the officer, "you're an illegal alien."

Alphonso's jaw dropped. "But I was born in Mexico, that means I'm a citizen."

"Not in Mexico. That only applies next door in USA. Besides your parents were Californian, right?"

"Right."

"They never registered you as a Mexican citizen, and besides, you couldn't be because they're Californian."

"Were," emphasized El Padrino.

"Oh that's right, they were killed in a gun battle in front of the Cathedral. My grandfather was there. He was a cop. He's probably the one that killed them," the officer grinned, oblivious to the danger of his situation.

"So where are you deporting me to?"

"Your choice. Though I'd recommend California. I hear it's a nice place, though getting too much like Mexico for my liking."

Pedro edged forward. "Padrino, you want me to…"

"No it's OK. I'll take care of this myself." He looked back at the officer. "What about Princeton, New Jersey?"

"Please yourself. I never heard of Princeton, but New Jersey, I hear they'll let anyone in there. All my nephews have gone there. They tell me they work in the market gardens and use their own shit for fertilizer."

"You don't need to deport me, officer. I'll go there myself. Here, see, I have my own American passport."

"Where's your Mexican passport?"

"I've never had one."

"You've been here illegally your entire life! This is very serious. You may have to go to prison instead of deportation. I'll have to check with my boss." He took out his phone and nudged his partner. "Better cuff him," he ordered.

This was too much for Pedro. His Padrino should not be treated with such disrespect. He leaned forward and with two fingers of each hand pushed both of them in the chest. They took a step backwards, but of course there was nowhere to step to and they fell into the pond. Though the pirañas had consumed each other, the tiger sharks were still plentiful and always hungry.

"Shit! Pedro. You better run up and tell Maria. She'll be really pissed. I'm leaving. Make sure all our stuff gets delivered to my Princeton mansion. And don't forget the bricks."

"A hundred million, right?"

"Whatever there's room for on the Learjet. One of his more innovative technicians had gotten sick handling cocaine, and turned his skills to inventing a way to compress ten million dollars down to the size of a brick. The process basically freeze-dried the money then compressed it into a brick. It was then reconstituted simply by dropping the brick in a tub of water and peeling off the bills.

*

Alphonso believed that young people today were coddled too much, and that included his son Julian. He was not sure about Christian because, as far as he could see, he must have had a terrible childhood, forced to sing those horrible hymns with his crazy father, living among the homeless rabble that set up camp outside the town library in Newark. Everyone new about that, how they weren't allowed into the library because they were filthy, peed and shit not only on the steps at the entrance, but inside, if they could get in. So he would not let Christian and Julian come with him in the Learjet, only Virgil, whom he had quietly had one of his henchmen grab and clean him up before he left the compound, dead set on spending his new-found wealth. Instead, he had bought the loving couple business class tickets on a United Airlines flight direct to Newark. They would have to learn what it was like to travel with the rabble.

He paid a quick visit to Jesus, walking down to his private chapel dug into the side of the mountain, underneath the great dining hall. There, he kneeled looked up at his replica of the Pietà of Michelangelo, crossed himself, mumbled his adoration, looked around to make sure no one was watching—he could not afford to be seen kneeling in front of anyone—then arose and, with a determined look, turned towards the marble stairway. But at that very moment, he felt a hand grip his heart, squeezing the breath out of him. He fell down, feeling abandoned and alone, and looked up at Mary. He swore, naturally to no one but himself, that he saw tears of blood trickle down from Mary's sad eyes. And then she spoke to him, or not quite that, because her lips did not move, but he heard her say, "go forth, Alphonso, spread holiness, but do not forsake your son, for he will be denied twice."

Alphonso fell down and crossed himself many times over, scratched his bare navel and said, "oh Mary mother of God, I am your humble servant and will do as you command!" Of course, he had no idea what these denials would be, but nevertheless bounded back up the marble stairs, full of confidence, driven by a mission.

As he sat in the Learjet with Virgil beside him, and relived that vision. Bambola came by with drinks, which he refused, but Virgil greedily lapped up. "We will be landing soon," she said, "the pilot says if you look out the window as he makes his turn towards Princeton airport, you will see the concrete campus of New State University. That is the one where Julian will be teaching, isn't it?"

Alphonso looked up at her well powdered smiling face, plush red lips, eyes happy and bright. What a contrast to Mary! And as he looked down and saw the university, a hollow square with towers at each corner, the dorms he was later to learn, and a round structure in the center of the square, the fountain. He closed his eyes and listened to Mary again, and at once he knew what he must do.

*

Maria summoned the boys, as she had decided to call them, to meet her beside the pool. She imagined them swimming naked together. The image aroused her so much she had to turn away as they pranced down the steps, holding hands, like little children. She made herself look back and tried to convince herself that they were both boys. Christian of course was obviously so. And Julian, perhaps in an effort to please her, had dressed like a boy, not in a bikini as she had expected he might. He was wearing those skimpy Speedos that managed to suggest a male bulge where it was supposed to be. His willingness to play the part she wished for touched her deeply. But she would not show it. "Boys," she said, "have a quick swim then Francisco will show you to my office. I want to have a serious talk with you."

Julian and Christian looked at each other, then, holding hands jumped into the pool, Julian calling out, "OK mom!"

"Make sure they're in my office in five minutes," she ordered Francisco.

Francisco asked querulously, "which office, your serious one?"

"I am the Drug Lady, the one to be feared, am I not?" Maria answered mysteriously. She took one last look at the boys when they surfaced and began jousting with each other, then strutted off to get her office ready.

Francisco ordered them out of the pool and helped dry them off, smacking Julian on the behind when he tried to flick Christian with his towel. "Stop it!" he commanded, "your mother gave strict instructions no mucking around!"

Maria sat at her desk, a desk she had especially made out of an ancient rack, originally used to stretch unfortunate miscreants until they confessed their sins or whatever it might be, usually if they had swiped some of the drug money. In fact it still functioned, but Maria had other devices that were quicker and far more effective.

Francisco appeared at the door, holding each of the boys by the scruff of the neck, shoving them forward. They were still wearing their Speedos.

"Look around you," she said with a superior smile, "I want you to see that the Drug Lady means business." Her voice echoed as though in a torture chamber, which after all, she was, and it was her office.

Christian covered his crutch with his hands. He was frightened. He had heard many stories about Catholics torturing sinners. The inquisition or something, his dad was always going on about it. He looked around the office and saw that it was a torture chamber all right. Many scary looking iron gadgets hanging from the wall, a fire of red hot coals burning in the corner, pokers, pincers, branding irons sitting in it, red hot, ready for use. Francisco stoked up the fire, an evil look of anticipation on his big face, bulbous lips protruding, eyes almost covered by a huge overhanging brow.

"Mrs. Garcia!" Christian cried, "we are innocent boys, priests really, why are you showing us this? So it's true then, what my dad says, Catholics torture people for the fun of it?"

Julian gripped Christian's hand tightly, but said nothing. He was frightened. He knew that drug lords were capable of anything, so he assumed drug ladies were the same.

"Your father is only half right. We Catholics tortured mainly women, called them witches, it's the one inequity that as Drug Lady I am going to correct. I will torture only men. So Christian, you are first. Tie him up to the rings on the wall, Francisco, and we'll give him a taste of the branding iron. M will do, M for male. That will work, and apply it where we can all see it, on his forehead. Gloria Steinem will love me for this. And Francisco, make sure the camera is turned on. We'll put it on Facebook!"

"Mom! Mom! Please don't! Why are you doing this? Have you gone mad?" cried Julian.

"That's it Francisco, a red hot M!"

Francisco brandished the red hot iron and approached poor Christian, arms and legs spread-eagled against the stone wall, shaking with fear, eyes bulging with anticipated pain. Julian ran forward intending to grab his mother by the throat, and certain that he would strangle her if she did not stop this madness. Francisco waved the red hot iron in front of Julian to impede his approach.

Maria sat impassively and said with a horrible smirk, "don't worry Julia, you won't be tortured because you are a woman!"

This stopped Julian in his tracks. He pleaded, "mom! How could you?" And dropped to his knees, hands clenched together, as though in prayer.

Maria nodded to Francisco who stopped his advance. "I will stop on one condition."

Julian looked up and cried, "anything, anything!"

"You must go back to the priesthood."

"But mother, I can't."

Maria nodded to Francisco who inched forward again. "And why not?"

"Because Dr, Scalpel got us kicked out, that's why."

"How? Why?"

"It's a long story. Please! Let Christian down and I'll tell you the whole story."

The Drug Lady nodded to Francisco who returned the branding iron to the fire and released poor Christian who fell down on his knees, rubbing his chafed wrists, sobbing, sobbing, rubbing his eyes with his knuckles, like a small child.

Julian spoke, his face pale with fright. "From the very first day we entered college, we knew there was something about Dr. Scalpel. He was the dorm director and supposedly counselor. And as you know, mom, it just so happened that Christian and me were dorm mates right from the first day. Dr. Scalpel introduced us. But you know, he has that sleazy look about him, and he kind of creeps around everywhere, when you open your closet you half expect him to jump out."

Christian now sat beside Julian, both sitting on chairs without a bottom, rather like a commode, but with a lever that, when trodden on by the torture professional, released two hammers, and if the professional was skillful the ancient contraption would squash whatever it caught between them. Francisco, new to this, trod on the leaver and it made a huge bang as the hammers hit each other. Fortunately both Julian and Christian still had their Speedos on, so they felt only a tickle. Of course, there was nothing of Julian's that would hang down anyway. They both leaped out of their chairs in fright.

"Mom! Tell him to stop!"

"Sorry boys, Francisco is new at this. You can be seated. You won't do it again, will you Francisco?"

Francisco grunted, pursed his bulbous lips over nonexistent teeth looking like he would swallow his own mouth.

"So this Scalpel kicked you out?"

"Sort of. You see, we were madly in love from the very first day, and by the time we were ready to graduate, we just couldn't bear to fake it any more, even though we knew very well that everyone had put one and one together, you know?" Julian looked at Christian and squeezed his hand softly. He then looked at his mom and saw her nostrils pulsing. She was breathing heavily, snorting intermittently. Christian was fearful. He imagined fire and smoke blowing out of her nostrils, just like in the Bosch paintings of Satan and his demons.

Maria snarled. "Go on! Finish it!"

"Well, we went to the Dean and told him we wanted to get married."

"The day of commencement?"

"Yes." Julian waited for the abuse.

"You lunatics! How could you imagine that he would agree?"

"Well, it's a university, your know mom, and in America they pride themselves with being great promoters of diversity. I mean, we took them at their word!"

"And of course he took you at your word and tossed you out. But where does Scalpel fit into this?"

"Well, we kind of expected him to be pissed off, but not to kick us out. Anyway we said if Scalpel would wait to kick us out after we graduated with our degrees, we would not bring charges against him."

"What charges?"

"One night, probably just a few months after we entered college, for some reason Christian got up to look for something, it was, it was…"

"What?"

"You don't need to know," the boys looked at each other and shifted nervously.

Christian took up the story. "I opened the closet and the worst of all nightmares hit me in the face. There was Dr. Scalpel. I won't tell you what he was doing."

"What?" asked Maria belligerently, knowing of course, that she need not know. "Never mind. No doubt Gloria Steinem would know and so do I."

"So that's it," said Julian, "it turned out that Dr. Scalpel had been making videos of various activities in the dorms."

"What activities?" asked Maria, now no longer outraged, enjoying herself instead.

"Come on, mom. Stop it."

"But if he has videos of you two, he could do a lot of damage."

"And to the college too," added Christian.

"Anyway, Dean Flaccidia said they had taken care of it," added Julian. "Scalpel is no longer there. And he said he would help us get jobs in any other university that we applied to."

"They would let you back to the priesthood?" asked Maria.

"No way. Of course they wouldn't let Christian either."

"But he's a Protestant anyway so why would they?"

Julian turned to Christian. "Well he was going to change, weren't you love?"

Maria winced at the term of endearment. Christian just smiled faintly. In a way he had been saved by all this.

Maria then leaned across her rack of a desk and said, with exaggerated secrecy, "you understand, Julian, that your father your Padrino as well, has very powerful contacts in the Vatican. I will have him look into the matter."

Julian leaned over and grabbed both his mom's hands in horror. "Please, Mom, we like things just the way they are, and we have our interviews at New State College tomorrow."

"It's time for you both to go," muttered Maria, looking down at her desk, perplexed, angry, sad, mixed emotions was what they called it. But she kept her outward calm.

Julian was now very worried. She was not upset enough. What was going on?

5. Men of water

Cardinal Pollagrande breathed a deep sigh of relief as he turned the key in the lock of his fifth floor apartment at Palazzo San Carlo. He pushed open the door and patted his kangaroo that sat bolt upright staring into space. "Hello Red, I've missed you!" he said. He surveyed his newly renovated apartment with great satisfaction, all done by his disgraced predecessor whom he had helped to depose. The clank of the elevator sounded and there was a knock on his door. It would be the boy with his luggage.

He opened the door and there was a young, gorgeous boy no more than fifteen, smiling broadly. "Dove dovrei metterlo, la Tua Santità?" Pollagrande made a little bow and smiled, "just by red will be fine." The boy dragged the two large glider bags in and then began to back out. "Would you like a cafè, your Holiness?"

"Not right now, thank you. Maybe later. I have much work to do." He handed the boy several Euro notes, and he departed whistling happily.

"The young have little reason to be happy," he thought to himself, his relief now turning into a morose feeling of loss, "except that they are young. They know not what lies ahead." But he shook himself out of this slump and quickly walked over to the large double doors, pulled open the curtains and threw open the doors. There was no view anywhere in the world that matched that of Rome, an aerial view that had not changed much in several hundred years, especially with the dome of Saint Peters so close, the winding snake of the Tiber. Only the hum of cars disturbed the quiet contours of history. "Don't speak nonsense," he said to himself.

Pollagrande had a lot to be thankful for. Born in Castlemaine, a small Australian country town, of an unmarried lady of unknown origin, but by his own coloring, surely Irish, possibly homeless, he was raised in St. Aidan's orphanage in Bendigo, ruled over by nuns, hard but compassionate, educated in the ways of the Roman Catholic church, constantly reminded by all that he was the progeny of sin and must spend the rest of his life making up for his mother's wayward deeds that created the bastard that he was. He closed his eyes and saw the bright red brick building of the orphanage, the eight narrow arches built into the veranda, connecting at each end to double story oblong buildings, steeply gabled slate roofs, the cross of Jesus at the peak of each. What a contrast when he opened his eyes and gazed at the ancient white of St. Peters, a place he knew so well, better indeed, than the old orphanage.

But enough! There was work to be done, and Cardinal Benitez would be arriving in a week or so with the latest news from Mexico City. What a relief to be far away from that God forsaken (apologies Lord) place, El Padrino, that messenger of Satan, he was sure, even though his latest epiphany heralded otherwise. The deviousness of Satan of course should never be underestimated. He walked over to the refrigerator and found a beer, a bad habit he had inherited from his Australian upbringing. The bells of St. Peters were ringing to announce that midday had arrived, the signal to an Aussie that it was time to have a beer. Sister Elizabeth had stocked the refrigerator with all his favorites, and a Cooper's ale was one of them. Beer in hand he walked down to the first bedroom and called out, "Honey! I'm home!"

He peeped in the bedroom but saw no one. The bed was neatly made up, a small corner of the sheet folded back, a way of Sister Elizabeth saying "Welcome back." But where was his loved one? He scratched his head, took a sip of his beer and walked on down to the second bedroom, the master bedroom. Perhaps it would be there. He patted the still dingo that stood at the door, staring vacantly up at him, its tongue hanging to the side, frozen in time. "Sorry old boy, but it's better that you can't be part of life up here, don't you think?"

"I don't think so," came a soft, but hollow sounding voice from the bedroom. At that moment, his phone buzzed. He took it out and saw a text. "Welcome back! Enjoy it! Benitez." Pollagrande was about to reply when he heard a shuffle and there standing before him stood a resplendent young woman, perfectly made up in every way, glistening reddish blonde hair hanging in wisps down to her shoulders, big round blue eyes, an olive southern Italian complexion, the kind Benitez knew he liked, and a breast the exact size and shape he constantly lusted after, which Benitez also knew.

"Who are you? What are you doing here?" asked Pollagrande, his mouth dry with excitement, licking his cracked lips.

"I am Estelle, at your complete service," she said, blinking mechanically.

Another text appeared on Pollagrande's phone. "I gave your inflatable away to the young boy who brings you coffee each morning."

"No wonder he was so happy this morning," texted Pollagrande. "Where are you?"

"Dubai, on my way. Will be in Rome in the morning."

"OK."

Pollagrande eyed Estelle up and down. She was wearing very expensive underwear, and not much of it either. "You better make me a cup of tea," he said.

"Please let me past." Estelle brushed by him and strutted down the passage. Pollagrande sat on the edge of the bed from whence she came. It smelled of, he was not sure, but not perfume, a very human smell. It set him off. "Forget the tea!" he called, "Come here, darling!"

She came, and so did he!"

*

Pollagrande awoke the next morning alone in his bed. A four poster bed, by the way. There was no sign of Estelle. Maybe it was all a dream. If it was, he hoped he could have them every night. He looked across to the dressing table and spoke to the platypus that lay there, big black eyes staring over its flat bill. "You saw it all," he said, "didn't you? A silent witness, that's the best kind. You see, but you cannot say what you saw." He heard the whistle of the kettle. She was making tea? Where did Benitez find such a creature?" He jumped out of bed and trotted down to the kitchen. And there was Estelle, a nicely ironed apron tied to cover her shapely front, placing the teacup on its saucer, pouring the tea, adding the milk.

"You like it white, right?" she asked with a smile.

"Yes please, and the milk added last, just as you have done. How did you know?"

"Cardinal Benitez told me," she answered.

"My goodness!" Pollagrande was most annoyed, and knew it was ridiculous, annoyed that Benitez might have tried her out before he did. She was soiled! Second hand! Used! "Thank you.

Now go back to the bedroom and make the bed and stay there until I call you, please," he said haughtily.

"Yes Holiness. And there is a warm cornetto too. The boy brought it up. And a big package he left just inside the door."

The doorbell rang. It would be Benitez. He went to open it, but Estelle was already there. "I told you to stay in the bedroom until I called you," said Pollagrande, just as Benitez entered.

"The two of you aren't getting along?" he grinned. "Let her attend to you like she did last night," he said with a wink.

"Benitez! Really!"

"Calm yourself, Holiness. She's just a robot after all. And there's nothing in the bible, whatever version or additional texts, about having sex with a robot, is there?"

"Well, some texts could be re-interpreted…"

"There you go. Stop it! You've earned all this, and by the time we are through with El Padrino, there will be a lot more, and we will be doing great things for our good, deserving, Christian flock.

Pollagrande opened the curtains and looked out over Rome. "I suppose you're right. We both came from very poor beginnings, didn't we?" he turned, his face expressionless, ready for business. "Anyway, let's get on with it."

Benitez lifted his bulging leather briefcase on to the kitchen counter and said, "so, El Padrino wants to make the gardener an offer. You know…"

"He can't refuse," finished Pollagrande with a grin.

"Right. Actually, you can see the gardener's house from here if you look out to the left a little bit, just across from the Vatican train station. And there. Further in the distance is the eagle fountain. Do you know the gardener?" asked Benitez.

Pollagrande replied, "not really, although I see him from a distance almost every day, because I pass that way when I go to meet with the Holy Father and his rapidly dwindling assistants."

"Good. Now, here are two million US dollars." Benitez pulled out bundles of dollar bills from the bulging briefcase. A million is an up-front down payment to the gardener to use his house. Alphonso says he will be sending you an additional $10 million via the Banco di Santo Spirito. The other million here is to pay the engineer and others for access to the cisterni under Rome and the Vatican."

"Why the Vatican?" asked Pollagrande.

Benitez looked Pollagrande in the eye and said, "Alphonso insists that Jesus told him the water closest to St Peter's tomb was naturally holy—it runs right by it on its way to the Eagle Fountain and other fountains in the Vatican. Who are we to second guess Jesus?"

"We are His messengers on earth. Why did not Jesus convey this information to us, rather than through a thug like El Padrino?" asked Pollagrande, annoyed yet again.

"Holiness. There is no answer to that complaint, is there? Jesus has a history of choosing the least worthy, in the eyes of the worthy, does he not?"

There was nothing left to say. Benitez turned to leave and noticed the big package at the door. "Aren't you going to open it?" he asked, "it looks like it's from Australia."

"It's from my taxidermist."

Benitez patted the kangaroo on its lifeless head. What is it this time? A bunyip?"

"Very funny. You'd better leave before I have Satan pull you down to his level, not that it would be very far." Pollagrande called out, "Estelle, would you open this package for me please?"

Estelle glided to the door and proceeded to pull the package apart, though with some difficulty because it had been excessively bound up with sticky tape.

"Here, let me help you," said Benitez with a devilish smile.

Estelle hesitated, then said in her almost monotonic voice, "oh thank you so much, Holiness."

Pollagrande looked on. "The two of you make a good couple," he said, with a snarl laced with sarcasm.

"Holiness, you need to do something about your bad moods. I was hoping that Estelle would be the right antidote for them. But I see that she may have made them worse," lectured Benitez.

The package fell open, revealing a big fat wombat, its dead eyes open wide (rare in a nocturnal animal). Estelle stepped back in awe, since she had never seen anything like that before, and had no memory of it in her databank.

"It's not her, it's you," complained Pollagrande, ignoring the look of wonder in Estelle's dreamy eyes.

"Jealousy, especially unfounded jealousy, is the worst of sins, your Holiness," lectured Cardinal Benitez again.

Pollagrande could contain himself no longer. "You tried her out, didn't you?" he exclaimed.

Benitez replied with a command to Estelle, "Go to your room, Estelle, thank you for your help." He gave Pollagrande his most serious look and said in his preacher's voice, "may Satan strike me dead! I did not!"

Pollagrande seemed lost for words, or maybe it was a senior moment. He struggled to speak, speechless as they say. But the silence trapped Cardinal Benitez into speaking when silence would have been more prudent. "But what if I did? She's only a robot!"

Pollagrande found his voice and heard himself yelling, "you shit! It is like you tried on my underpants!"

"Holiness. Be happy! She is a gift. A wonderful gift! How can you hope to become Pope one day if you contain such selfish, jealous thoughts within you?" Benitez reached out and took Pollagrande's hand in his. He bowed slightly, and pulled his aging hand to his lips, kissing his ring.

A soft voice called from the bedroom. "May I make you a cup of tea?"

*

With some assistance from Estelle, Pollagrande dressed in his working suit. There was a light knock at the door. It would be sister Elizabeth. She had been his assistant for many years, following him wherever he was sent in his Papal duties. She was an accomplished typist and even still took shorthand, though that was these days a lost art. He hurried to the door, then turned back. He realized that he did not know how to make Estelle shut up, or go to sleep. So he went to her and kissed her lightly on her perfect cheek. "It's time for your nap. Draw the shades then go to bed. I will awake you when it's time."

"Yes, your Holiness."

He tip-toed to the door and let Sister Elizabeth in. She was a bright person, always chirpy like a sparrow, darting this way and that, chattering on. "Good morning, your Holiness," she smiled.

"Good morning, Sister. Is it cold out?"

"One of God's beautiful autumn days. Sunny and brisk," she said.

Pollagrande gave her his briefcase and walked out. Sister Elizabeth, curtsying lightly as she let him past, followed closing the door behind her. They stepped out into the bright sunlight of

Rome, the broad splash of well clipped green grass ahead of them as they made their way past the Vatican administrative building, then to the gardener's house.

"I have business with the gardener this morning," said Polla-grande, "are you acquainted at all with him, Sister?"

"No, Holiness, but I have admired him from a distance. He is much closer to God than are we, don't you think? We take God's plants and trees, birds, animals and insects for granted, pass them by without the slightest notice."

"As always, Sister, you are right."

Just as they reached the house and turned to admire the beau-tifully clipped lawn, its bright green so healthy and robust, a very small man appeared before them, dressed impeccably in priest's clothing, tight collar, perfectly shaped and fitted shirt and waistcoat, trousers freshly pressed, closely cropped gray hair with traces of black left over from his youth, and a silvery beard clipped as carefully as was the lawn he stood on.

"Walking on the grass is not permitted," observed Polla-grande, feeling a small tug on his arm from Sister Elizabeth, then realizing that this was, in fact, the gardener.

"I have permission to do so from the gardener himself," said the gardener jokingly. "A beautiful morning to you, Holiness. What can I do for you? Perhaps you have come to give me more money so I can feed my beautiful plants and trees that are always in need?"

"Perhaps. Shall we go inside?"

The gardener showed them to his perfectly arranged office, a small desk, two simple wooden chairs opposite, everything aligned geometrically, right-angles everywhere. This was no ordinary gardener. He too was Australian, but many years ago in the small diocese of Colac, he was caught by a shearer copu-lating with a high class merino behind the wool shed. His defense was of course to deny it, claiming that the shearer, like all shearers, was drunk and didn't know his ass from his elbow. Nevertheless, the archbishop banished him to the Vatican to avoid a scandal, where his supposed shenanigans, if true, would go unnoticed. It was not long before the occasional sheep appeared on the Vatican lawns. The current Pope, however, a city man, found their smell offensive and, at a time when the Vatican budget was heavily in the red, and there was hardly enough money to feed the many hangers-on in the Vatican dining rooms, he ordered them to be sacrificed on the altar of the Sunday dinner table.

"Sister Elizabeth, could you open my briefcase and place it on Brother Gardener's desk please?"

Sister Elizabeth lifted the briefcase with difficulty. She was a tiny person herself, probably over eighty years old, and the weight was a bit beyond her.

"Here, let me help," said the Gardener, coming around from behind the desk. But by the time he reached her, she had dropped the briefcase and it hit the edge of the desk, the lid popping open, and the rolls of money bouncing all over the desk and on the floor.

"Goodness! Why is it that green follows me wherever I go?" joked the gardener.

"I am here representing a very rich benefactor," said Pollagrande officiously, "who is offering you one million dollars for the temporary use of your house."

"Why my house? It's grand for a gardener, but what's so special? If he's got so much money, I could suggest much nicer places. Yours, for example," he grinned, as he rubbed his clipped beard, the sound of which he was sure Pollagrande heard.

"Very funny," said Pollagrande, not amused. "Our benefactor is going to make a much bigger investment, probably another ten million dollars to renovate parts of the building."

"But it's lovely the way it is, has a lot of charm."

"This is part of a much larger project that involves the Eagle Fountain and other fountains of the Vatican and even all of Rome. Besides, the renovations will be confined mostly to excavations underneath the building."

"I wouldn't advise it. Who knows what they will find under there," warned the Gardener.

"In any case, please keep this million, and if you are agreeable, I will help you find temporary accommodation nearby."

"And if I say no? Besides, I don't own this house, do I?" asked the Gardener cheekily.

Pollagrande looked across to sister Elizabeth. She responded by starting to collect the money and return it to the briefcase.

"Will you?" responded Pollagrande with a frown and a look that could deliver an annulment.

The Gardener understood and smiled genially, which was his want anyway. "I am most happy to oblige, and look forward to helping spend the additional ten million."

"Excellent!" said Pollagrande and got up to leave.

"But there's one thing," called the Gardener.

"Yes?"

"Holiness, can you change these dollars to Euros?"

"Of course. Come with me to the Banco di Santo Spirito and we will take care of everything for you."

*

The city of Rome is run by communists, so Pollagrande had been told before he came to Rome, and experienced himself, for many years. It was why many of the city's services did not function, or if they did, functioned slowly. Visitors have long noticed that trash lays around the streets for days uncollected, holes are dug in sidewalks and remain there for weeks or months awaiting some city official or tradesman to come and fix whatever was wrong. He also knew that one did not get a top position in the city government without a seriously powerful, usually Mafia-like connection, communist or not. It was not so much that each and every official of the city's hierarchy had to be a communist, rather it was the culture of communism as expressed and practiced by Italians, especially Roman Italians, that drove the city council and those it employed. Pollagrande had always admired the Italians' zest for life, *la dolce vita* was no stereotype, it was how they lived, and blended comfortably with the communist outlook. And when things went badly they came to their priests to confess, and that was true even for the sworn communists. So the ethos of communism left city workers with a very short working day, maybe amounting to a few days a week, depending on what else was going on in their lives, plenty of time for their long lunches, plenty of wine, an afternoon nap, and shop or hang out in bars for the late afternoon and evening. It was a beautiful life that Pollagrande admired and loved from his high perch in the Vatican, one that, in some respects, he tried to emulate as much as he could, as did his many colleagues. It was why the wheels of the Vatican bureaucracy moved very slowly. So he was not looking forward to this meeting with the city's *curator aquarum*, who was an erratic but brilliant hydraulic engineer having got his doctorate in water management from the University of Rome, never having attended a class, so it was rumored.

Pollagrande's phone sounded a kookaburra laugh and he saw it was a text from Benitez. He had pleaded with him to join this meeting with the *curator aquarum*, as he was anticipating a difficult time convincing the water man to join them, even though his briefcase, containing a million dollars now converted into Euros, would help immensely to turn the cogs of communist action. Besides, could this erratic Mafioso communist be trusted? "Will be there, San Eustachio café, right?" said the text. Pollagrande texted back, "in 20 mins."

It was some years since Pollagrande had been to this café, and when he turned the sharp corner to Piazza San Eustachio, he was shocked to see that its old wooden furniture had been replaced with modern style white plastic chairs and tables, the shopfront itself unrecognizable. But as if this were not enough, there, right in front of the café, sitting at the small round white table poised at the very edge of the sharp corner that sat like an arrowhead at the edge of the piazza, was a large, overweight man, looking every bit like the famous opera singer, Luciano Pavarotti, stroking his beard, lounging back on the chair that buckled under his weight, his legs stretching out into the cobbled street, dressed, Oh Dio! In a cardinal's red cloak! This was the *curator aquarum?*

Pollagrande carefully approached him, concerned that he might trip on the rough cobblestones, many lying loose, trying at the same time to survey the piazza for any onlookers who might be suspicious. He extended his hand, and the water man slid off his rickety chair and landed on his knees, took the hand and kissed it. "Your Holiness! He purred, it is a great honor!"

"You are the *curator aquarum?*" asked Pollagrande, retrieving his hand, but then realizing that he must lean down and help him up. A waiter quickly appeared and assisted them.

"You may call me Sisto," your Holiness, it is my nickname after Rome's great water man under emperor Nerva, Sextus Julius Frontinus."

"Very pleased to meet you, my son, Sisto it shall be."

"I see that you are put off by my dress. I make no secret of it. I always wanted to be a great cardinal such as you, ever since I was an altar boy and sang in the St. Peter's choir."

Sisto beckoned to the waiter. "*Una granita di café,*" he ordered. "*Et tu?*" he asked Pollagrande.

"*Solamente café, grazie,*" answered Pollagrande. "Now let's get down to business."

"So why is the Vatican interested in my water?" asked Sisto, not a little cheekily.

It isn't your water, thought Pollagrande to himself, but managed not to say so, and anyway, maybe to all intents and purposes it was his water. "Cardinal Benitez and I have a major project planned for the Vatican near the Eagle Fountain that requires your expertise."

"My expertise always costs a lot of money," grinned Sisto, raising an eyebrow, leaning across the table, "what is it exactly?" He whispered as though he were an actor whispering to his audience.

"Cardinal Benitez, who will be here any minute, will fill you in on the details. We have an extremely rich and influential benefactor who is going to fund the project."

"Does the Pope know about it?" asked Sisto, now tilting his head, a sly expression, trying to look like Shylock.

"Do you always dress like a cardinal?" asked Pollagrande, trying to change the subject until Benitez arrived.

"Always. I buy all my clothes at the little shop on *Via dei Cestari* near the Pantheon. Not far from here. Do you know it?"

"I just came from there, as a matter of fact."

The waiter arrived with the *granita di café* and placed it before Sisto. "This will help me maintain my shape," he joked.

"I see. But as a busy cardinal, I must stay with just this simple café," said Pollagrande.

"Ah! What an example you set, Holiness," mumbled Sisto as he licked the cream from his whiskered mouth.

At this moment, Benitez appeared from behind the police car that never moved from its place at the corner of the largest of the four narrow streets that emptied into the *piazzale*. He hurried across to the café, dressed in a plain priest's jacket, black vest and nicely pressed pants. "Sisto! How good to see you again," he said. He did not hold out his hand as did Pollagrande, but simply patted Sisto on his wide shoulder. Sisto slurped up his whipped cream and splattered, "likewise!"

Pollagrande looked about him. "It's a rather public place to be doing business," he muttered.

"And what business is that?" asked Sisto.

"Show him the money," said Benitez, nodding towards Pollagrande.

Pollagrande brought up the briefcase from under the table and opened it slightly, making sure it faced away from the direction of the police car. Sisto leaned forward a little. "There's a million dollars in Euros in there," said Pollagrande, "it could be yours."

"Thank you, your Holinesses!" He reached over, took the briefcase and held it under his red cape. "What can I do for you?"

Benitez leaned over and gripped Sisto's hand, causing him to stop slurping at his *granita di café*. "You know the Eagle Fountain in the Vatican?"

"Of course. I know every fountain in Rome, and the Vatican is part of Rome, when it comes to water, is it not?"

"Indeed it is," said Pollagrande. "I pay our water taxes to Rome every month."

Benitez squeezed Sisto's hand a little. "Our benefactor wants to tap into the water that feeds the Eagle fountain. We need you to make that happen."

"For what purpose, may I ask?" Sisto put on his most cunning look, again as though he were addressing his audience from the stage.

"Our benefactor has determined after extensive research, that the water that feeds the Eagle fountain, runs under the tomb of St. Peter, that is…"

"Directly under the Bernini canopy in St. Peter's basilica." Sisto finished the sentence.

"We need you to confirm that this is true, and to then supervise the tap."

"What kind of confirmation and what kind of tap?"

"It would need an official certificate that would be co-signed by you and the Pope, saying that the water is Holy Water, made so by passing through the tomb of St. Peter."

"How exciting! I've always wanted to meet the Pope. You can arrange an audience for me?"

"Any time you like," said Pollagrande, "but you had better not dress like a cardinal."

"Whatever you say. And the connection?"

"Are you familiar with the Vatican gardens?"

"I know it all very well."

"We will be taking over the gardener's house for several months and would like to make the connection to the water from under that house."

"I will need to look at my older plans. But I think there are several waterways under the Vatican that were built by my hero Sextus Frontinus."

"Then you are in agreement?" asked Pollagrande, puzzled that it seemed so easy.

"Of course. How could I refuse the two greatest cardinals of the world?"

"There is more money should it be needed," said Benitez.

"Holinesses. I do not see money as the issue. But I do see one problem."

"Which is?"

"I do not think the Pope will agree."

"That will be up to us to convince him. But tell me, why do you say that?" asked Pollagrande.

Sisto looked around, furtively, his eyes narrowing and hand covering his mouth. "He is a very rigid man, he mistakes rigidity for piety. Should never have been made Pope. He is in the pocket of the rich communists of the North who will stick their noses in."

"You mean the Bologna enclave?" asked Benitez.

"And Milano."

"The Pope a communist? Don't be ridiculous," said Pollagrande. "How is that possible?"

"Ask your brother here," said Sisto, tapping Benitez's hand.

"It is true," said Benitez. "His election was rigged, I should say bought, by the Communists for Capitalism party of Milan. Have you not noticed the sudden plush living style of many of our colleagues? You excepted of course, your Holiness."

Pollagrande shifted uneasily on his hard plastic seat. He looked down at the table and said nothing. A cloud of guilt had descended upon him. He wanted to be Pope, a sinful desire.

6. Holy Mafiosi

The pilot dipped the plane's wing, as he approached the Catania airport via a quick aerial view of the old palazzo inhabited by the Great Godfather, then around Messina, to approach the tarmac from the east. The old man must be in his nineties, thought Alphonso as his hand strayed on to Maria's lap. She had not wanted to come, but he had convinced her that it would help her tighten her grip on the Mexican cartels if they knew she had the Great Godfather's blessing. They would just drop in and receive his blessing, make sure he knew that Maria was now the Mexican boss. But for Alphonso this visit was a must, he knew that the Vatican would be a cauldron of trouble if he went in there without the Great Godfather's blessing. How strange it was that a feeble nearly 100 year old crook still had so much power and influence. But anyone who is worshipped, as was the Great Godfather, naturally has power over his worshippers.

The Great Godfather's consigliere, a tall, dark lean Neapolitan met them at the airport. It was standard practice not to recruit a consigliere who had local ties. There were too many temptations for corruption and double-cross. Besides, the current Pope was a Neapolitan, so was naturally subject to control of the various loosely connected mafia organizations that operated throughout Italy north and south, as well as Sicily. The consigliere whisked them away in his Alpha Romeo Stelvio Quadrifolgio, flanked front and back by four police on classic Laverda 750 SFC motorcycles. Alphonso eyed them covetously. The consigliere noticed and, nodding with satisfaction, said, "yes, they are ours."

Getting a blessing from this old Godfather was like getting a blessing from the Pope, in fact probably more important because the loose network of gangs and gangsters, mobs and even terrorists in some cases, was a source of human capital not available to others. The Pope's blessing was only that, a blessing. The Great Godfather's blessing was a promise, that the services, if deserved, of the network of gangsters were always available pretty much anywhere on earth. They did much more than pray for you. They made problems go away.

Maria sat quietly in the back next to the consigliere, a signal that she was now number one. Alphonso happily sat up front, chatting to the driver who spoke excellent Spanish, real Spanish, not Mexican. Maria turned to the consigliere and said, "I hope the Great Godfather will accept me, as he has all the other capos."

"This is already taken care of. He was a little doubtful at first, but when I told him of Alphonso's bold plan, he became very excited. Without someone who could be trusted—it could only be you—to take over the most important cartel of the Spanish speaking people, he would never have given his blessing. We are all in awe of Alphonso's accomplishments. There is no one else but you who could take over."

Maria nodded sweetly and remained silent. She was still under the influence of the lightly brushed kiss on the back of her hand the consigliere gave her as she alighted from the airplane steps. If only Alphonso was capable of that! But then, this man was obviously the crème de la crème of Neapolitan high society. They passed through the city of Messina, the driver making a brief stop outside the town hall. The consigliere took them to the town hall steps, a light gray of the local limestone, and pointed to a black patch on the stones that started small, then expanded down the steps, like a pitcher of wine had been poured out. The consigliere pointed to the patch and said, like a tour guide, "this is the blood of the dear departed mayor of twenty years ago."

Alphonso and Maria said nothing, not quite taking it all in, looking up at the city hall, expecting some soliloquy about its founding, and architecture. The consigliere continued. "It is where our esteemed Great Godfather put an end to him, right here."

Maria looked down at the black patch. Somehow the violence that it represented did not quite come through. Alphonso casually replied, "Ah, so that's how you own these guys," pointing to the police escort.

The consigliere answered, "the Mayor, bless his soul, told the Great Godfather to change his ways, move into the 21st century, that the city must be the only one to collect taxes, that the police worked for him." He scraped at the black patch with his foot. "The Great Godfather dealt with him in the old fashioned way, no guns. Just a clean sharp knife. One thrust up and under the ribs, a kiss on his left cheek, and a tight hug."

"Ah, a man of principle! That's what I like!" said Alphonso, while Maria shuddered and said with a frown, "with a carving knife, I bet."

"Yes, how did you guess?" asked the consigliere.

"No guess. It's what Steinem has advocated for many years."

"Who?"

"Never mind."

They arrived at the Palazzo, a mansion built on the edge of the ancient Greek stone quarries. It was about the size of Downton Abbey and in its day, the late 19th century, would have been as majestic. Now it was a hovel, its once great spires and delicately carved windows and gables had crumbled away and pieces of stone, mostly *lumachella* gray limestone, from the nearby *Latomia del Paradiso* quarry, lay strewn about the once green lawn of the garden inspired by those of Versailles. The escort left them at the old stone gate, its wrought iron spikes rusted away, vines and oleanders overgrowing them. A cloud of white dust flew up as the Alpha slowly approached the circular drive, negotiating deep potholes, and pulled up at the grand Palazzo entrance, it too covered in vines, surrounded by oleanders, prickly pear growing from every crevice. The Great Godfather awaited them, a shrunken old man, his head seemingly drawn into his shoulders, a chin sporting a Ho chi Min-like beard. His eyes, though, both Maria and Alphonso could not help but notice, were bright and clear. Of course, he spoke no English, Spanish or Italian for that matter—rather his was a species of Sicilian dialect, traced back, so the consigliere mentioned later, to the island of Lampedusa, just as were many of the plants of *Siracusa*.

A contingent of attendants, dressed in old, worn bluish-grey satin costumes of the late 18th century, complete with discolored braided wigs, appeared. The Great Godfather was escorted by his Swiss guard as he called her, a tall, solid, bountiful young woman dressed appropriately in yellow striped pantaloons, her long blonde hair hanging down almost to her considerable girth, and her face one of lips, large and protruding as if she were about to kiss. She pulled the Great Godfather to her side and spoke on his behalf. "Welcome to our beautiful Palazzo, please follow us. Dinner is already waiting." The Great Godfather nodded with a twinkle in his eye, and smiled showing his few yellow teeth that remained. But before he turned to lead the way into the great hall, he handed a small package to Alphonso. "A special gift for you to remember your visit to *Siracusa*," smiled the Swiss Guard on his behalf.

Maria opened her Florentine bag and pulled out a small, satin covered cylindrical package. "And this is for you, excellency," she said, "from me and my husband, your great admirers." Of course it was obvious what the package was, a roll of US dollars. The Great Godfather took it and gave it to his Swiss guard, along with a kiss to her hand.

"He wants you to open your gift," purred the Swiss Guard.

Surely it could not be money, thought Maria. She opened it and there, in her hand, was a small jar containing an ear. She almost dropped it in fright, but managed to keep her composure.

The consigliere spoke. "It is the ear of Dionysus."

"Who?" asked Alphonso, amused.

"The ear of Dionysus is the name of a big crevice in the *Latima de Paradiso* quarry. Great Godfather says that the mayor, whose name was Dino, was a big crevice that had to be closed."

Dinner proceeded in silence. The incredibly costumed attendants brought in all kinds of Sicilian delicacies, some of which Maria had to force herself to eat, fearing that the delicacies might not be animal. The climax (or pre-max to be exact) came when four attendants marched in with a whole roasted goat on a massive silver platter held above their heads, its dead eyes looking out over the edge surrounded by sprigs of local oregano and Italian parsley. They laid it on the table and began to carve. No doubt, with one of the knives that had dispatched the mayor, thought Maria. Again, silence reigned, except for the sucking of lips, and slurping of tongues. Conversation was not possible anyway. The guests were spread far apart along the side of the twenty five meter table, the other side with only the consigliere, and at the head of the table the Great Godfather and his Swiss Guard who, every now and then, fed him a piece of succulent goat which she placed delicately on the end of a knife.

Finally, the dinner was done, the table cleared away, and Sicilian cookies, citrus fruits and grappa passed around. The Swiss guard helped the Great Godfather stand. He raised his tiny glass of grappa and said in a strong voice (in Sicilian of course but with the consigliere translating beside him), "I hold in my hand the beginning of the greatest cartel that the earth has ever seen." He raised the small prototype bottle of *Aquam Sanctus Pietro* Holy Water, which the Swiss Guard filled with a shot of grappa. "You have my blessing Alphonso for your daring venture! And to your beautiful wife Maria, who will shepherd the Mexican cartel with her many talents."

All stood and raised their glasses and gulped down their grappa. They all sat, but the Great Godfather remained standing. The consigliere returned to his seat. Suddenly the Great Godfather said, gesticulating wildly, "*Il papa è uno stronzo!*" then prodded and whispered to his Swiss Guard who stood beside him. "Godfather says that the Pope is an asshole and is not to be trusted. He is a Neapolitan after all! They are all sneaks!" Maria looked across at the consigliere, who laughed and said, "don't worry, he talks like that all the time. But he's right about the Pope. You must be very careful. He is a most artful double-crosser even for a Neapolitan."

*

The needles of the prickly pear glistened in the crisp Sicilian morning, Alphonso and Maria stood on the decaying steps of the Palazzo and said their good-byes to the Great Godfather who stood leaning on his old gnarled walking stick. "*Ricorda*," said the Great Godfather, "*non fidarti mai di un Napoletano.*"

"You understand that?" asked Maria.

"Remember, never trust a Neapolitan, but he need not say it. You know I do not trust anyone and nor should you," said Alphonso, noting, as he looked around, that the several body-guards who inhabited the surrounding landscape carried AK47s. The Great Godfather was not so old fashioned as his Consigliere implied. And as if on cue, the wizened old Godfather pulled out a mobile phone from his pocket, dropped his walking stick and began texting with both his thumbs, their nails chewed down to their quick. Alphonso looked at him dumbfounded. And almost immediately, his own phone signaled that he had a text. "*Fatemi sapere se avete un problema con il Papa.*" The old man looked at Alphonso and to Maria and winked with a toothy grin. Alphonso answered, "thank you Godfather, if I have a problem with the Pope I will certainly let you know."

The police escort arrived and they were whisked away to the airport, and to Rome where Cardinal Benitez gave them a diplomatic welcome and their new passports showing their new titles as Special Ambassadors of the Vatican to the United States.

"Our Papal audience is for midday. He has consented to lunch with us, an excellent sign!" said Benitez excitedly.

"And Pollagrande?" Alphonso scratched his navel. It was going to be a sunny humid Roman day. He was glad he had on, as usual, his shorts, untucked white shirt, and of course his Roman sandals. Maria had argued with him, saying that he should not meet the Pope dressed like that. It was disrespectful. Alphonso argued, "he's a Christian, isn't he? He has to take me for who I am."

Three young acolytes dressed in their dark brown Jesuit cloaks, hovered around. Benitez barked orders and they meekly grabbed the baggage and carried it off to the awaiting black Alpha Giulia. "We will go straight to the gardener's cottage in the Vatican where Pollagrande and the water man will be waiting for us."

"Not the gardener?" asked Maria.

"He has decided to take a sabbatical in New Zealand, where they have a huge variety of plants he can study. The Vatican has an outpost there, a retreat, I believe, on the slopes of mount Cook."

Alphonso nodded with satisfaction. He took this to mean that the gardener had been annulled. He would supply his own gardener for the Vatican. Benitez had his ear to his phone. "Pollagrande says he will be at the gardener's cottage. He's just putting his housekeeper Estelle to bed."

Maria looked puzzled. "He tucks in his housekeeper at nine in the morning?"

"She is not your usual housekeeper," said Benitez, looking away.

"And Pollagrande is not your usual cardinal," joked Maria.

"Perhaps. But I bought Estelle for Pollagrande and he loves her deeply."

Alphonso again looked at Benitez with approval. "You bought him a housekeeper?"

"You mean the Vatican doesn't supply one?" asked Maria.

"It does, but Pollagrande prefers his own, replied Benitez. "That was the only thing that concerned me. When I gave Pollagrande his housekeeper, he had to let his old housekeeper of twenty years, go."

"Why not keep both?" asked Maria, ever the practical one.

"He tried, but it just didn't work out."

"So he fired his old housekeeper and replaced her with a trafficked woman?"

"Not exactly," answered Benitez with a hint of mystery.

"But you said you bought her."

"I did, but you see she's not human, so it's not human trafficking."

"So what is she then?"

"She is an it. A robot."

7. Papal audience

Estelle finished dressing Pollagrande, straightening his collar, making sure his dark well pressed trousers were zipped up. She kissed him lightly on the cheek and crooned, "have a lovely day, darling."

"And after you have done the dusting, and made up the bed with fresh sheets, you go off to bed, now, do you hear?" said Pollagrande, feeling more like a parent than a partner.

"Yes darling. Now off you go. Don't forget your satchel. And be nice to everyone!"

Pollagrande made his way to the gardener's cottage, walking by the Eagle Fountain, stopping briefly to say a prayer of thanks, asking God to give him strength. Dealing with the most powerful drug lord and lady in the world was highly stressful, not to mention dangerous. He made his way to the gardener's cottage—hardly a cottage—a mansion by ordinary standards for a gardener no less. It was almost twelve and the autumn sun radiated down from a clear blue sky. He had heard nothing from Sisto the water man and was worried he would not show. Without him, it would be impossible to give the Pope the assurance that the project was feasible, and more important, would not have any serious impact on the water supply of Rome and the Vatican. He had arranged for a small wrought iron table and chairs to be set up outside the cottage where they could meet. Better there than inside where there could be spies, cameras or who knows what. He was about to sit, when out of the gardener's cottage came Sisto, bedecked in his red cape, a French beret with a stripe of red around its rim, his large round form throwing a shadow over the table. He made a huge curtsey-like bow, sweeping his arm in a wide arc, like a magician does when he is about to produce a rabbit out of nowhere. Pollagrande, of course, remained seated, it was for Sisto to show his subservience, which forced him to bow so low he almost fell forward. Pollagrande took his extended hand and said, "rise my son," fully aware that it was only the Pope who should have such bearing, let alone Jesus himself.

Sisto stood up and sang, "O sole mio!" in his loud, off-key tenor voice, his black Pavarotti beard bristling as his cheeks struggled with his huge open mouth. Yielding to Pollagrande's tight grip, he plopped down on a chair, panting, "I am ready! But is il Papa?"

Pollagrande's phone rang. It was Benitez in a panic. "We are at the main gate. The Swiss guards will not let us enter!"

The guards had strict instructions from the Pope. Visitors inside the Vatican grounds must adhere to the dress code at all times. They had spied Alphonso's shorts. "They will not budge!" cried Benitez.

"Put the guard on. I will speak to him. Guard? This is Cardinal Pollagrande, the Pope's chief of staff. If you know what's good for you, you had better let them through."

"Our orders say absolutely no exceptions."

"They were personally invited by the Pope himself. Would you forbid an ambassador from Tahiti wearing his native dress?"

"I'm sorry your Holiness. One of them is wearing shorts. It's forbidden."

"Let them in and I assure you, he will be dressed properly. Send them directly to the gardener's cottage, where I will see to it that he gets a pair of pants."

"I don't know, holiness…"

Pollagrande looked at his phone and screamed, "Give him yours, then!" He heard muffled yelling, and no sooner had he closed his phone than the Alpha Giulia rolled up. Benitez stepped out, red in the face. He held the door open for Maria, whose hand he took as she emerged, disheveled and clearly angry. Alphonso stayed in the car, refusing to come out. He yelled, "the Pope will pay for this!" The driver stepped out, red in the face with rage, no pants on, yelled back, "then give me back my pants!" Maria got back in the car. "We need you, darling," she purred, "come on. I will help you." She rubbed the inside of his thigh, and gave him a little kiss on his bare knee. "We can't risk our great water project because the Pope is stupid."

Benitez poked his head in and said, "and he is stupid you know, as well as being short of a few inches."

Alphonso stirred, Maria pushed the driver's pants into his lap.

"Pope Shorty's only four feet eight. And do you know what his first edict was? That all Vatican assistants and servants must be shorter than him, and if they were not, they had to kneel or squat so that they never rose above him."

Pollagrande walked to the other side of the Giulia and peered into the window on Alphonso's side. He knocked hard. "My son! Come! Don't risk your holiness for His Holiness!"

Maria stroked his thigh again and pushed the driver's pants into him some more. Alphonso took the pants and began the difficult contortions of pulling on the pants inside a car, something he had not done since he was a teenager. And to save the effort, he pulled them on over his shorts. Maria helped him with the zip and gave him another kiss on his cheek. It was enough to give Alphonso the energy to comply. With Maria's help, he slid out of the car as the driver, his bare white legs crossed the bright green lawn, jumped back in and drove away.

Sisto now struggled up from his chair and announced, "welcome to the Vatican gardens and fountains. I am Sextus Julius Frontinus. but call me Sisto, and I am the water man of Rome and the Vatican, at your service." He waved his red cloak as he offered his hand with a big smile.

"Just shake it," said Benitez, "he's not a cardinal, just dresses like one." Alphonso nodded and said in a very serious tone, "it is upon you that all holiness depends."

Unfortunately, Pollagrande chose this moment to express doubts. "I'm not sure this will work. Everyone knows that the Pope is a woman hater. I don't think Maria should attend."

"If the Pope disrespects me, he will have me to answer for as well as Alphonso," said Maria in her most threatening manner.

"Let's not get ahead of ourselves," said Benitez with relish. Things were turning out just as he had hoped. After all, he could have warned Alphonso that he should wear pants. The Pope's strict dress code was no secret. Pollagrande gave him a harsh, knowing look. And as their eyes met, each knew that they could not trust each other.

Sisto who, once risen, did not want to sit down again, sang heartily in his Pavarotti voice, "come on! I want to get to my first Papal audience!" Pollagrande looked around the gardens, across to the Eagle Fountain. "We're due in the Vatican cafeteria in five minutes," he said.

"You mean it's not a private audience?" complained Sisto.

Pollagrande sighed. "The Pope wants to be seen as one of the boys. There will be a table set apart in the anteroom."

"Then let's go! I hope the food is up to my high standards!"

"Not likely. The cafeteria is run by Wa Wa."

Maria gasped. "What?"

"It's part of the Pope's cost saving initiative."

Pollagrande led the way across the lawn, right by the sign that said, VIETATO CALPESTARE. Sisto grabbed Pollagrande's elbow and said, "let's not walk on the grass. I will show you a better way." He waddled back towards the gardener's cottage, pulled open the door, bowed with a flourish, and called "this way please!" In no time, he turned into an agile denizen of the underground, leading them down a steep flight of damp stone steps, tunnels leading this way and that, the sound of rushing water resonating from every direction. As they went, Sisto pointed in various directions saying, "we are just by the Eagle Fountain, the fountains of Piazza San Pietro behind us, the Trevi is six kilometers that way, the Turtle Fountain four kilometers that way." In five minutes, after several turns this way and that, they came to an iron ladder that led up to a trap door. "I will go first and open the old iron grate." Sisto, with surprising agility climbed the ladder, followed by Alphonso who had difficulty managing his long fitting trousers that kept catching on his sandals. As soon as it opened, the din and echo of talking and dishes clanging broke through the steady noise of the gushing water. They emerged into the cafeteria, an underground cavern polluted by the noise of humans and the smell of cooking. Maria looked around. She was the only woman. All diners were priests of some sort, or acolytes, some of whom were clearing tables.

Pollagrande led the way. "The anteroom is this way. The Holy Father will be here any second."

"Why are there no women in the cafeteria?" asked Maria, knowing full well what the answer would be.

"The Pope will not allow women in the cafeteria, or any other place unless absolutely necessary, such as cardinals with their housekeepers."

"Then why am I here?" asked Maria, offended once more.

"Because I haven't told the Pope you were coming," answered Pollagrande.

Pollagrande led the way into a small room that had one tiny barred window at the top of one wall, the rest bare rock, mostly tufa, probably dating back to Augustus Caesar, covered with a wet, green mold. Under the window was a raised platform about three feet high made of old packing crates. A red plastic table, its smooth lines clearly echoing the renowned Milanese flair for design stood before it, laid with white plastic plates and cutlery. The plates, of course, were stamped with the current Papal crest of an outline of Jesus, his arms crossed over his chest, holding in each hand respectively the hammer and sickle, arranged so that they formed a V below His neck.

Pollagrande bade the party be seated just as the noise of the cafeteria suddenly ceased, broken only by the occasional clanking of saucepans, these also with the Papal crest stamped on to their bottoms, at the behest of the Pope who insisted that the red hot fire of the stove was the devil trying to break into the Vatican from below. The Papal guard entered the cafeteria on his knees and banged his red solid plastic staff on the stone floor, making a dull thud. "All yield to Pope Gramsci the First!"

Now, people had never figured out what "yield" meant. The Italian, "*dare la precedenza*" was just as vague. But it was of no consequence since they were all required, by the Pope's first edict, to lower themselves to a level below his height. So some bowed, some slid off their chairs and kneeled on the hard stone floor (the young priests in training did this, not taking any chances), others (clearly his enemies) stood with their heads slightly bowed. The Swiss guard dropped to their knees and shuffled aside. *Papa Rosso*, the Red Pope as he was called by those who worshipped him (*Papa Corto*, Pope Shorty by those who did not), entered, resplendent in his gold sequined gown, red sequined hammers and sickles sewed into the gold. His tiny little eyes squinted from under his white red fringed pointy Papal hat, the rest of his face covered by a lame attempt to emulate the bushy beard of Karl Marx. He simply did not have enough whiskers. This wily little man from Naples had beaten out all others in the recent conclave that lasted for only two days, a record short conclave. It happened because the Communists for Capitalism of Milan had poured in money and other Italian forms of arm twisting, so that many cardinals who did not want to vote for Gramsci, either went back to their dioceses to attend to urgent matters or changed their votes, and in some cases disappeared altogether.

The trouble was that this little Pope was so short, he could not stand with all the fancy robes and trinkets hanging on his body, or at least that was his excuse for insisting on being carried on a litter, on the shoulders of four big black slaves from darkest Africa, their bare bodies glistening in sweet Sicilian olive oil a lifetime gift from the Great Godfather and his people.

Their bodies were completely shaved from head to foot, bare feet of course, a tiny silver sequined G-string covering their considerable manhood. Their faces were stern and solemn, staring straight ahead. They were forbidden ever to smile in public.

The Swiss guard, with difficulty, crawling on the hard stone of the floor, led the way to the anteroom where they placed Papa Gramsci (in the cafeteria and just about everywhere else now called *Papa Corto*, that is Pope Shorty) and his litter gently on a platform. Pollagrande and Benitez of course, approached at once and kissed the Pope's ring, a red ruby carved into the form of a hammer and sickle. The trouble was that they left Maria sitting on her own and the Pope's beady little eyes settled upon her. Benitez and Pollagrande sat back in their seats, waiting for the inevitable. Pope Shorty stared at Maria. Alphonso's dark black eyes narrowed. He had the Pope in his sights. The slaves backed away, bowed deeply, then went off to bring the food. It was a cafeteria after all, but the slaves did not bother to ask what anyone wanted. They returned with five plates of linguine covered in black octopus sauce. These were placed in front of Pollagrande, Benitez, Sisto, Maria and Alphonso, and one for Pope Shorty who, seated too far above the table on his platform, took it in his hands while one of his slaves lay prostrate over his lap to serve as a table. Yet the weight of the Pope's robe was such that he could hardly lift the fork and certainly could not twirl it. So the largest of the slaves took the fork and began feeding him.

All this time, the Pope did not take his eyes of Maria. She sat, staring at her plate unable to eat this dark oily mass of crap. There was plenty of wine, so she poured herself a glass, not *rosso*, but, making a point, *bianco*.

The Pope suddenly shouted, "this is a woman!" knocked his slave's hand away, grabbed the plate of pasta and with all his might threw it at Maria. She shrieked and pushed back in her chair which, being poorly designed and of light plastic, toppled over backwards and she fell to the floor yelling, "red devil, *diabolo rosso!*"

"Take her out!" yelled Pope Shorty. "Who is responsible for this? Take her out before I commit her to the grand dungeon!"

Pollagrande looked at Benitez and Benitez returned the look. Who was going to take the hit? Until now, Benitez had been the Pope's favorite, no doubt because he had ties to the communists

in south east Asia. Pollagrande he had always eyed with suspicion, which was why he kept him close, appointed him
foreign secretary and CEO of the Vatican, basically his chief of
staff.

It was Pollagrande who stepped up, or more precisely,
kneeled up. "Our deepest apologies, your holiness," he said,
holding his red beret in hand, "but her husband, Alphonso
Garcia, was forbidden entry to the Vatican compound by your
Swiss guard because he was wearing shorts, so we thought we
must have his wife instead, who has taken over his leadership
position of Mexico's movement for the poor."

"Was he not informed of the dress code? Really, Pollagrande.
Are you getting too old for this job?" scorned the Pope. This
was a veiled threat, or taken so by Pollagrande who pursed his
lips to hide his resentment.

Alphonso could take no more. He stood up, but Benitez tried
to pull him back down. "The height edict!" he cried, "stay
down!" Pope Shorty came from long line of Neapolitan fishermen, and everyone knows that the fishermen of Naples are
short, always have been. And the Pope insisted that Peter, the
original fisherman, was also short, and the Naples fishermen
were all descended from him.

All this time, Maria was clinging to the table leg while one of
the slaves tried to pull her away. "Asshole! You'll pay for this !"
she screamed at the Pope, "don't you know who I am?"

Her abuse of the Pope did not help matters. Benitez tried to
draw the French doors to the anteroom closed, but Maria's
kicking made it impossible. And Alphonso looked poised to lash
out at the Pope himself.

At that moment, Sisto saved the day. He stirred in his chair,
having put away in short time the delicious linguini. "Your
Holiness, sir, servant of Jesus, may I say it is a great honor to be
with you today," and he then began in a beautiful tenor voice,
even if off key, to sing *Blazen muz* (Blessed is the man) in
Russian, his Pavarotti voice rising above the muffled sounds of
the cafeteria. Suddenly all was quiet, save for Pavarotti. The
Pope ordered his slave to release Maria and whispered to him to
fetch a nun's habit. Maria could stay, but she must be covered.
And so the French doors were closed, a habit was fitted on to
Maria and a shawl as well, her face contorted as though she had
sucked a lemon.

Pope Shorty dismissed his slaves. "Now," he said, "what is your proposal that it is so important that a woman attend this audience? And why is this water man here? Of course his services to God, Jesus and the Vatican are most valuable. But why is he here?"

Sisto wiped the spit and remains of the black sauce from his whiskery mouth and was about to speak when Benitez cut him off. "Holiness, Alphonso Garcia, Maria's husband and great leader of the movement for holiness in Mexico, has proposed that Holy Water be modernized and made properly authentic."

The Pope frowned and growled, "it is ancient, that's its importance, it does not need to be modernized. Modernize it and you destroy it."

Pollagrande interjected. "If I may, Holiness, Mr. Garcia has pointed out that the majority of priests all over the world participate in something of a scam by claiming the water they use is holy, when in fact it simply comes from anywhere it is available, out of the tap, the nearest river or pond. The priest calls it holy by saying a blessing over it, and that's it."

The Pope replied, "what's wrong with that? Priests are God's messengers, Christ's representatives on earth, they are imbibed with the Holy Spirit."

"Papa Gramsci, your Most Holy One," said Benitez with a smile, "you are among friends and colleagues here. You know that the use of holy water has got out of hand. There are cases reported every day of people being infected with typhus and cholera transmitted from holy water."

"These are exceptions. Most holy water is pure and unadulterated, blessed by God."

"Most is not enough," interjected Pollagrande, "even one case of holy water infected by typhus is enough to indicate that it is tainted by the devil, is it not?"

Sisto wiped his mouth and in a crooning voice said, "if I may say so, your high Holiness, our waters, those of the fountains of Rome and its underground cisterns, especially under the Vatican, are the purest of all water on earth."

"Thank you Mr. Waterman. Your work is certainly the work of God," said Papa Shorty, trying to hold back a smile, for he had ordered all his minions that smiling was to be used sparingly. Life was too serious and God's work too important, to be sullied by smiles. The people of Soviet Russia, as they built that wonderful bastion of communism never smiled, and when they were done and they smiled with pride, so the devil destroyed it with capitalism. It would rise again, with the help of Jesus and of the reformed Roman Catholic Church. He would see to it.

"Holiness," breathed Pollagrande, "a vision came to Alphonso while he was standing before the Virgin Mary. He must do this. He can purify and sanctify the holy water and guarantee the safe international distribution of its holiness…"

Pope Shorty cut him off. "What? Him? Sanctify? I am the Pope! I am the only one who can truly sanctify the water or anything else for that matter! How dare you!"

Pollagrande looked down, he was but a child smitten by his overbearing father. "I miss-spoke," your Holiness. "Of course I did not mean to demean you in any way. What I wanted to say was…"

This time Benitez cut him short. "Holy Father, you are of course aware that the church is severely short of money, if I may anticipate what Pollagrande is trying to say. The sex abuse cases have made a very deep hole in our finances all around the world. Alphonso offers a way to recoup all those losses and to spread holiness far and wide as well."

The Pope leaned over to Alphonso, who was now kneeling before him, his head level with the platform of the Pope's litter. The corners of his mouth twitched, hiding back a cynical smirk, which the Pope did not sense, because at the moment he could see nothing but his own importance.

Alphonso, using the obsequious voice he always used in confession, said softly, "the water will be bottled here in the Vatican, stamped with your Holy Crest, and distributed at a small price to all dioceses in the world. It is rather like distributing drugs, with which I am experienced, if I may say so, Your Holiness."

The Pope patted him on the head. "My son, you may be the lamb of Jesus Christ himself. But I cannot allow the sacred waters of the Vatican to be defiled by capitalism. Holiness is not for sale."

Benitez risked an opinion. "He would not be selling it as a product, Holy Father, but charging a distribution service. If there is a product, it would be the bottles, the containers of the Holy Water, not the water itself."

Sisto intervened. He leaned back in his uncomfortable plastic chair, took a deep breath and began to sing in his almost Pavarotti voice:

"Pale in a liminal moon
And all that you are is a star on the water..."

The Pope raised his arms to God crying, "Rusalka! Rusalka!" and then shook his head in time with the song, lip-sinking it, then held out his hands, palm down, indicating to Sisto to stop singing, and he did so. Benitez and Pollagrande looked at Sisto with considerable appreciation. Maria, still lying on the floor, managed to rise up and take his hand to her lips. Alphonso looked up at the Pope, giving him a look as if to say he had just confessed to the worst possible blasphemy, looking for Papal pity. None came.

The Pope signaled to his African slaves and they came forward doubled over and at the double. They hoisted his litter on to their shoulders and stood, awaiting his next command. And it came, not to them, but to his small audience.

"The waters of Rome and the Vatican shall remain unadulterated by capitalism while I am Pope. Is that clear?" He looked at Pollagrande and then to Benitez. Alphonso was retrieving a thick envelope from his pocket, but Benitez caught his arm just in time. "Not this Pope. Neither money nor sex work with Pope Shorty. We need a different solution."

Alphonso stood up, careful to remain in a bow to keep his head below the Pope's shoulders and pleaded, "your Holiest of Holy Fathers, there is one other very important matter I would like to bring to your divine attention."

"Mr. Padrino, that is what you are called, I understand," answered the Pope, "if you have another matter to raise, do so with my CEO, Cardinal Pollagrande. There are thousands if not millions of people all over the world who want to speak to me of matters of importance."

"I will, Holy Eminence, but just so you know. It is a matter of the church reaching out to Protestants. A famous Protestant evangelist is now working with me, and I promised him that we would bring, through your grace of course, Protestants closer to the church. In fact, I think he would like to bring his very substantial flock into the Roman Catholic church."

The Pope was incredulous. "You mean they would defect *en masse*, into the Roman Catholic faith?"

"Yes, Holy Father. "Several hundred to begin, but it could snowball once the first lot was welcomed by Your Holy Embrace."

The Pope looked at Pollagrande. "Cardinal Pollagrande. See to it that this evangelist—what is his name, Padrino? —"

"Virgil Bunion, your Holiness, though they call him Jude."

"—and as many of his flock he wants to bring, comes to Rome and we will arrange for the defection, I mean an audience."

"Yes, Holy Father, it will be done. I thank you so much, Holy Father, you will not regret this, I am sure. It could be the beginning of a massive expansion of the Roman Catholic Church."

The Pope patted him on the head again. "My dear Padrino, the answer on the water is still no." He made the sign of the cross and the slaves prepared to depart. Alphonso looked up, then down at his navel. Plan B would be necessary. He had expected as much.

8. Our Lady of the Waters

Maria had been forgotten. She lay, sprawled on the floor, picking off the pasta from her ruined dress. As she struggled up, the Pope looked down on her as he was leaving and smiled a kind smile, or at least that is what she convinced herself. This was the Pope. "The infallible Pope," she said to herself. She struggled to stand, but as she did, knocked her head on the Pope's litter as the slaves carried it forward. She fell down and lay there, paralyzed, staring up at the bare bottoms of the marching slaves. Then suddenly in a trancelike state, she spoke, but her lips did not move. She heard the overwhelming sound of rushing, running water. She broke out in a sweat, wet and cold all over. "Holy water, holy water! I am an empty vessel, fill me! Fill me up!" She blinked, but saw only the black mass of the tunnels below. The water gushed over her like a waterfall, now she was thrown this way and that, her body shaking uncontrollably.

"Maria! Sister Maria!" Cardinal Benitez was shaking her. "Speak to us!" he cried.

She felt her tongue move inside her mouth, and her mouth open, lips move. The shaking stopped as she opened her eyes. A deep calm descended. She felt a strange inner feeling of safety, or perhaps contentment. The habit gave her a sense of security, hiding her innermost feelings from all who looked at her. She no longer felt she had to present herself to others, put on a show, so to speak. She could be herself, hidden away inside her nun's habit and shawl. She did not even have to defend herself from the predations of men. Nuns were, she now understood, untouchable. She was a different person.

"Come, Maria, let's get you cleaned up and get this habit off," said Benitez.

"The habit stays. I like it," she said.

Benitez looked at Alphonso, who shrugged and looked to Pollagrande, who returned the shrug.

"I must get back to Mexico right away," she said, grabbing Alphonso's hand. "The cartel needs me."

"I'm sure it's fine. It's in Francisco's good hands, isn't it?"

"Yes, but you don't know what just happened to me," answered Maria with an air of mystery.

"What?" Alphonso scratched his navel nervously and pulled at the long pants that hurt him in the crotch.

"I had a kind of vision, a feeling, the noise of the waters of the Vatican," said Maria in a faraway voice.

"It was probably just a bit of concussion," said Alphonso giving her a light hug.

"No. More than that. The waters spoke to me. I know what I must do. They called me Our Lady of the Waters."

Sisto wriggled in his chair. "I am the water man," he said licking his hairy lips and with a glint in his eye, "so why can't she be the water lady?"

Alphonso sat, pensive, scratching his navel till it was bright red. "Our Lady of the Waters. Hmm. Could be a very good way to reach out to all the women out there who need Holy Water."

Sisto wriggled a little more and in his sonorous voice, said, "sister Maria is most welcome to join me. I am sure that a woman's touch will help us get things done both under and above ground. Besides, what is most beautiful in feminine women…"

"… is something masculine!" Maria cried, smiling until her cheeks hurt against the habit. "Susan Sontag I believe!"

"My favorite American woman," smiled Sisto.

"Not mine. I prefer Gloria Steinem," insisted Maria.

The remaining men looked down, left out of the conversation. Alphonso, not quite understanding what had happened, stopped scratching his navel and said. "Let's get you on to a plane to Mexico, and when we get the OK on our project from the Vatican, you can come back here and get to work with Sisto."

"But the Pope has nixed the project," said Maria.

"That's what he thinks," said Alphonso.

*

It was simply not possible for Maria to lead a life of submission, caring for the sick like the sisters of Mary in Mexico. She was, rather, Mary herself, and all other sisters should follow her. Besides, with a mansion built literally out of cartel money, it was simple logic that she should use it for the good of her followers, her sisters of the faith. So as soon as she arrived back in Mexico City, with Benitez in tow, as insisted on by Alphonso, she set about a complete renovation and reconstruction of the famous sixteenth century Convent of San Bernardino de Siena. Of course, she would not sully the beautiful cloisters that still remained, but she would enclose them in a structure that, if one can imagine it as only she could, was modeled along the lines of the American Vietnam war memorial. She had the surrounding geographical features completely changed so that the cloisters appeared submerged or built into artificial hills and rocky cliffs, planted with a sea of pink coralita vines. Those vines, as prolific as the Roman Catholic church, Maria was fond of saying, would overrun the cloisters themselves if they were not daily trimmed back by her many followers, Sisters of Our Lady of the Waters.

Naturally, there were many obstacles to overcome, which was why Cardinal Benitez had been dispatched to deal with any local resistance from the Mexico City diocese overseen by Archbishop Guevara. But within a few days, with the assistance of Francisco the gentle giant, Maria had effectively taken over the daily operations of the diocese and the Archbishop had gone off on a much deserved vacation in Tahiti. It did require that she take down a wall of money from one of the guest's bedrooms at their mansion, but this was hardly noticed. Besides, Francisco had shown his talent at running the cartel while Maria was absent, so there was really nothing standing in her way to fulfill her new life as Our Lady of the Waters.

Perhaps her greatest achievement, though, was to rid Mexico city of its prostitutes whom she rounded up, with the help of Francisco and his efficient *banda*, and moved into the plush apartments hidden behind the hills of the cloisters. It was there that all the priests whom Archbishop Guevara had identified as having special needs, were reeducated.

When Cardinal Benitez reported back to Rome and informed the Pope of this incredible achievement, the Pope, much pleased, ordered that priests with special needs wherever they may be, should be sent to Our Lady of the Waters for counseling. He did not like the terminology of "reeducation" which obviously reflected the Archbishop's leanings.

Unfortunately, as Cardinal Benitez would have to report to Alphonso, none of this could shake Pope Shorty's refusal to give his blessing for the water project. Plan B therefore, would go forward.

9. To Newark

Virgil was supposed to wait at the airport for El Padrino. The Da Vinci airport at Rome, that is. He waited and waited, but no Alphonso. Why it had to be the Rome airport, he did not know. And after a day of waiting, not wanting to descend into his former life as a bum and spend the night in the airport lounge, he slipped out to see the sights of Rome. Now he could really enjoy his new life of plenty, hanging out with the Gypsies, pestering the tourists who flocked to the Colosseum. Their well-developed techniques of begging and just plain theft from the victims who took pity on them, deeply impressed him. They made his old, unshaven, filthy beggar mates outside Starbucks look like gentlemen. Unfortunately, his visit was cut short when he received a text from Alphonso to meet up in the United Airlines lounge. He arrived quickly in a fast limousine, but because he had bought only a premium economy ticket, they would not let him into the lounge. So Virgil fell back on his old ways, used the counter top as a drum, and began to beat it and sing Onward Christian Soldiers. The flight attendant called security, but Alphonso had already heard the noise and knew that Virgil had arrived. He came out and showed his first class ticket to the age-challenged attendant, her face plastered with a powdery paste in a lame attempt to hide her wrinkles. Underneath the ticket was a nicely flattened $500 bill. He then tightly gripped Virgil by the arm as it was about to bang on the counter, and Virgil immediately came out of his tantrum, smiled at the attendant, and they both entered the lounge. Alphonso pushed him down into a worn lounge chair next to Bambola who did her best to ignore them both.

Virgil looked up, puzzled. "Why am I here?" he asked.

"You were plan B"

"Plan what?"

"If the Pope said "no" I was going to call on you and have you fake a defection from Protestantism to Catholicism in his presence, right there in the Papal audience."

"That would be a severe sin of dishonesty," said Virgil with a frown, "though, come to think of it, the Ten Commandments do not forbid lying."

Alphonso eyed Virgil with amusement. Bambola offered him a bowl of nuts and he took some. She offered the dish to Virgil, who declined, knowing that the fingers that had taken the nuts were the same ones that scratched Alphonso's navel.

"Anyway, as soon as the Pope showed up, it was clear that nothing of the sort would work," said Alphonso, "and I knew there was no point calling on you."

"He withheld his blessing then?" asked Virgil.

"Yes, the bastard. It's true, he's a fucking communist," growled Alphonso. He looked at Virgil with a touch of amusement. The fool, even though Bambola gave him very generous travel allowance, had chosen premium economy, where there were no beds or showers, just Wa Wa meals served with heavily starched table napkins. It was all just as well, for he had plans for the return trip.

After the disastrous meeting with Pope Shorty, Alphonso, in a display of false magnanimity, had dispatched Maria back to Mexico in the Learjet. He could not stand the thought of sitting beside Maria who was now a nun, that tight starched habit turning her face into an expressionless ball with just eyes, nose and tight-lipped mouth peeping out. And now, once aloft Alphonso and Bambola demanded a shower, but were told that it was not available as the pilot and executive flight attendant were using it. Besides, the plane had come into some turbulence and it was necessary for all passengers to remain in their seats with seat belts fastened. After the sparse drawn out lunch had been served and Alphonso's head was a little woozy from the cheap wine, and Bambola had slurped up her third ice cream with hot chocolate fudge, the shower became available and the turbulence returned.

Without further incident, the plane landed at Newark and Alphonso and Bambola, after an annoying wait for Virgil who thought his bags were lost until he remembered that he had not checked any, they headed straight for New State University.

*

"Welcome to New Jersey, America's number one rated corrupt state!" announced the Uber driver, an out-of-work priest whose church had just been sold to Starbucks, "going to New State University, right?"

"Right!" said Bambola, crammed between Virgil and Alphonso, in the back of the Toyota Prius, "and we are in a hurry."

"We'll be there in no time. I used to be a student there, you know, but I left and went to St. Robert's College."

This could have been the beginning of an interesting conversation, but Alphonso chose to stay quiet. He was plotting and planning and Bambola was already asleep with her head on his shoulder.

Uber drove up the circular drive and dropped them off at the university entrance. Everything was gray concrete, an ugly design, Alphonso rightly thought, a typical building of the 1960s, built by a capitalist, obviously designed by a communist. "If you go up these steps then take the door to the right, you will find the president's office. Good luck!"

Alphonso was not sure why he would need any good luck. He never believed in such nonsense. He made his luck, and made it with what Bambola was carrying in her smart Florentine handbag.

"Do you have an appointment?" asked the receptionist, not especially interested in who she was addressing.

"I have an appointment with President…er…what's his name?" replied Alphonso, scratching his navel, and checking to make sure his toupee was there, but then remembering that he had discarded it the day of his epiphany, and also decided then that he must get a new one.

"I don't see you on the list."

Bambola leaned forward over the receptionist's desk. "Tell Dean Fossil that El Padrino is here."

"Who?"

"You heard!"

Bambola reached into her handbag and pulled out a $100 dollar bill.

"What's that for," asked the receptionist, puzzled. She had heard of bribes, after all, she had lived her life in New Jersey, but had never been offered one. She was flattered. So she took the bill and said, "this way, follow me."

They walked down the straight, narrow, dark, ugly corridor to the end, where it opened up into a wide expanse of purple carpeted space, surrounded by thin tall windows, and another door, glass and brass, which, with some effort, the receptionist pushed open. "Dr. Fossil," she said, "Mr. ...what's your name?" she asked, without a smile, "says he has an appointment.

Bambola stepped forward. "Dr. Fossil, please meet my boss, Alphonso Garcia, but you can call him Padrino."

Fossil looked from one to the other. His eyes naturally landed on Alphonso's navel that was now red from scratching, then to his bare knees peeking out from under his baggy shorts. "I'm not aware of any such appointment," said Fossil, clearly annoyed.

Alphonso grabbed one of the two ugly steel chairs, obviously made by inmates of the local correctional institution, and sat, leaning forward. Contrary to the advice of many, he liked to project his superiority from a place that people mistook for weakness: sitting rather than standing, placing himself on a lower level. Provost Fossil leaned forward. "You have five minutes, Mr. what's-your-name?"

"Alphonso, Alphonso Garcia, and I'm here on a matter that concerns my son Julian and his partner Christian."

"These are students?" asked Fossil, nodding to his receptionist to leave the room.

"No. They are, what do you call them, professors?"

"I am not aware of any faculty of the name Garcia, and Christian who?" Fossil reached for his phone and barked, "Dr. Scalpel, would you come in here a minute?"

A door to the side of the office immediately opened, and in creeped Scalpel. Alphonso vaguely remembered meeting him the open day at St. Robert's College. But now, he struck him as the most repulsive person he had ever seen, and he had met many repulsive persons in his line of business. Bambola, never ruffled, put her hand to her mouth as though she was about the throw up. Alphonso blinked and could have sworn for a brief moment Scalpel had turned into a slimy snake that slithered across the cheap carpet.

Scalpel, his pasty white face always looking down, yet eyes also darting this way and that said, as obsequiously as possible, "you called Mr. President?" Scalpel's entire body moved and twitched with every syllable he spoke.

"Scalpel, I've told you, Dean Provost Fossil is enough. This gentleman, Mr. Garcia, is inquiring about two new assistant professors, Julian Garcia and a Christian someone. Do you know anything about them?"

"Yes, Professor Doctor, they are applicants for the new LGBTQ studies department of the School of Social Sciences."

"Are they on the short list?"

"It seems so, Dr. Sir. They are coming in for interviews to-morrow, I think." Scalpel smiled his sneaky smile, looking sideways to Alphonso, then to Bambola. licking his lips as though anticipating a delicious ice cream. Alphonso eyed him warily and Bambola clasped her handbag closely to her chest.

"I would like to make a gift for the new department,'" said Alphonso as he gestured to Bambola who retrieved a couple of rolls of $100 bills and placed them on the corner of Fossil's desk. "This should help you with the hiring," Alphonso said with a smile.

Scalpel slunk forward and reached for the money. Alphonso blocked him with his arm, forcing Scalpel to make jelly-like shivers and retreat, his cheeks now a little red, a forced smile obviously covering for the rage that stirred inside him, his eyes looking out from under his low brow. "There's twenty thousand dollars, and more where that came from, should the hiring process go ahead smoothly." Alphonso had debated with himself and Bambola whether this was too much. He had heard that academics were poorly paid, though they had excellent benefits.

Provost Fossil stood up from his desk and was about to make a pious speech, but then sat down again, staring at Scalpel who, as sleazy as he was, understood immediately that he should withdraw. "If that will be all, then, Dr. Provost Dean?" he said, trying not to sound sarcastic, but for him an impossibility, since every word he spoke was laced with a hidden meaning. Fossil just stared at him some more, Scalpel backed out of the room and through the side door, closing it softly.

"Mr. Garcia, this is a generous gift for the school. I will have my secretary send you a receipt and you will in due course receive a plaque recognizing your generosity and contribution to the University. It comes at an important time as we are exper-iencing severe budget cuts, you may have heard."

"It is my pleasure, Dr. Fossil. But I wish to remain anonymous," answered Alphonso in a most genial manner.

"As is your wish," smiled Fossil.

Alphonso made to go and Fossil quickly came from behind his desk to shake hands, trying not to recoil when Alphonso extended the hand that scratched his belly button. Scalpel sud-denly appeared at Alphonso's elbow, jostling Bambola out of the way. "Mr. Garcia," he said, "let me show you the way out." Alphonso eyed him suspiciously. Here was someone who understood how things get done, he thought to himself. He turned to Bambola and muttered, "I think we are going to need Pedro's services. Have him meet me at the Princeton residence as soon as he can get there."

10. Job talks

Julian and Christian, a pair of innocents when it came to academia or anything else for that matter, had not quite thought through what they were doing. And when Dr. Scalpel, as much as they loathed him, came by their dorm room to offer advice on how to interview for a job, they gratefully invited him in. It was he who advised them to apply for the same position, knowing full well that they had not understood that only one of them could get it. They thought there were two positions. Little did they know that he himself had already been appointed to one of them. Worse, he encouraged them to prepare the same job talk, saying that it was quite common for friends to share the same talk, no matter how many positions were on offer. The two innocents relished the thought of presenting their paper together, and of course loved the idea of writing their paper together. Mind you, this was just a few days before the job interview. Neither of them had given any thought of what to talk about. So they were even more grateful when Dr. Scalpel advised them to give a talk on LGBTQ and Jesus. "Was he any of those?" asked Scalpel gleefully.

So for two days, Julian and Christian sat side by side with their laptops on their knees, their bibles unopened. They Googled and Binged for hours on end looking for the mention of LGBTQ anywhere in the bible and found nothing. There were plenty of self-appointed interpreters of the bible who found pronouncements that could be construed as indicating this or that on homosexuality, and one who even claimed that Jesus was gay because He dressed like a woman. But after two days had passed, they found themselves with no paper at all, though they did have a list of five points that each of them would talk about. The list went like this:

Lesbians were not mentioned in the bible therefore they did not exist.

Gays were not mentioned either, though accidental sex between two men was, especially if they were drunk.

Bisexuals were plentiful in the old testament, but none mentioned in the new testament. Therefore, Jesus eradicated bisexuality. Of course, this did not apply to the Romans who were pagans after all.

Transgenders were unknown, though some cross-dressing might be identified, such as Joseph's coat of many colors. It's all a bit of a stretch. Anyway, none of it was in the New testament. Jesus got rid of that too.

Queer is what Jesus was. It just means that He loved everyone, regardless of who or what they were. It's not sex, the *Pietà* notwithstanding. It's identity.

These LGBTQ points may seem simple, even obvious to believers, but they almost caused a terrible rift between our two lovers, Julian and Christian. They argued loudly, even shouted at times, so much that Scalpel appeared at their door, obviously enjoying it all, asking them to "keep it down," said with the greatest of smirks, of course. And searching the web was no help at all, just made matters worse, because it was possible to find a web site somewhere, that produced a quote from the bible that could be interpreted to support one's particular argument. In the end, they both agreed to put aside their laptops and to consult the bible in their hands, the old fashioned way. It was at this point that their differences came to light. Actually, not so much intellectual differences, but differences that they had to acknowledge were differences in their very bodies and how they had grown in their short lives.

Once they had closed their laptops, suddenly, silence overwhelmed them. They looked at each other and saw clearly in each other's faces their true differences, differences that formed the foundation of their love for each other. For Christian it came from one photograph, a postcard that was pinned to the wall above the bathroom sink in his father's ramshackle house in West Virginia. But the photograph was only part of the story. It was also the small holes dug all over the back yard, randomly spaced, filled in again leaving small mounds of dirt above. And these were tied together by his giant of a father contorted by a raging faith A man of Calvin, more Lutheran than Luther. Plagued by a constipation that threatened to blow him asunder, Virgil sat on the toilet and screamed at Satan, tearing at his belly, reaching for his backside. "Asshole that you are! I will tear you from my body!" At which point he would run out to the back yard, dig a hole, squat over it, bang the shovel on the ground, "get out! Get out! Leave me alone!" Once done, he would kneel forward and fill the hole with his hands. And if nothing came, the rage settled into that loathsome red face and beard, and he would lope forward, looking for Christian, knowing exactly what he would be doing, finding him in the bathroom.

And sure enough, Christian stood gazing at the photograph of the Pietà, Mary's eyes cast down, gazing over the scantily covered body of her Jesus, a look of love-lust laden with sadness, lust that never was nor could ever be, lust lost in a pandemic love spread over her naked son whose ejaculate conception had been denied her. All of this consumed Christian every time he found himself in the bathroom, his disobedient body probing, searching for satisfaction, in a word, throbbing with desire anticipating the wrath, not of God, but of his Lutheran giant of a father, who, having dug his holes and filled them in, came crashing into the kitchen, banging the unwashed pots and pans, screaming at Satan, tramping into the bathroom, its door long torn off its hinges, there to find his son of Satan, naked, his hands covering Satan's protuberances, and with his willow switch, he swung his huge arms down and down again, striking at Christian's hands, the skin torn from his knuckles, the red blood soon oozing out and dripping down on to the rotting floor, now sticking to the willow, splashing blood on Virgil's face as he raised it again and again, licking the splashes of blood that landed on his lips. But always, to Virgil's consternation, the more Christian's hands were whipped, the greater the desire that throbbed beneath. For Christian felt no pain in the ordinary sense, his was one of lustful pain, a pleasure like no other, though accentuated by the look of despair and frustration it engendered in his giant bully of a father, who quickly collapsed in a pile, as happens with all human experiences of ecstasy that appear and depart in a matter of seconds, leaving an abyss behind.

But Christian's youth and his love for Julian shielded him from the terror of his father's violent fits. He knew they were symptoms of his father's crisis of faith, one that could only be cured by love, and that was far away for his dad. But for him, he had Julian, whose voice he now heard calling him from afar.

"Christian! Come on! We have to finish this! Christian, my darling!" came the happy cry, "Christian, for Pete's sake!"

Christian shook his head and blinked his lovely blue eyes. "Oh Sorry! I kind of drifted off." He looked at Julian who was staring intensely at his phone as he two-thumbed it with gusto. "I'm doing a PowerPoint," he said, looking up only briefly while he thumbed away. "I've put in our five bullet points," he added with satisfaction, "Dr. Scalpel says that's all we need."

"You sure we can trust Scalpel?"

"No. But who can you trust these days?" answered Julian with a grin, his broad smile dissolving any doubts or remorse that might lie hidden in Christian's body. Christian, bible in hand, leaned over to Julian and gently removed his phone. They fell back on Julian's bed just as Dr. Scalpel entered their room without knocking. One look was enough. He smirked to himself and left quickly, closing the door behind him.

*

New State University was an enormous campus, ugly in its symmetrical design, aging gray concrete columns and towers, concrete crumbling away at the edges and corners. There was no window wider than one foot, all tall and thin, mimicking the twenty-floor towers at each corner of the campus. Pedro had appeared this morning and announced that he had been appointed Julian's driver for the day. Julian saw this as an ominous sign, but said nothing to Christian. Pedro parked in a spot reserved for the Dean and Provost of Social Sciences. Again, Julian registered this as an ominous sign, and again, did not say anything to Christian.

They went straight to the Dean's office where, now not at all surprising to Julian, Dr Scalpel met them.

Christian expressed great surprise and said, "Dr; Scalpel. We did not expect to see you here!"

"Life is full of surprises, isn't it?" purred Scalpel, seeming to address his question to Julian, who ignored it.

They followed Scalpel as he loped like a monkey down the narrow passage. He did not, however, take them into Provost Dean Fossil's office, but straight into the faculty meeting room, a room surrounded on one side with the tall slim windows that did not open, and the others covered with various presentation paraphernalia, chalkboards, whiteboards, overhead projectors. Enough to scare any novice to academia. There were five faculty sitting in various parts of the room, all young, that is, under sixty. A couple were very young, that is, about twenty five. In the corner, on harder seats set apart from the rest of the room, sat three students, undergraduates, all overweight, sitting behind a high table, holding hands and rubbing legs, their genders indeterminate.

One of the five faculty stood as they entered, and introduced himself. "Welcome, gentlemen. Welcome to the School of Social Sciences. I am distinguished professor Serious Becker, interim chair of the College of Diversity and Discrimination Studies." It was only when he extended his hand to Julian that he realized that this was not a gentleman, but a gentle woman. The trouble was that Julian, unable to decide whether to present himself as male or female had dressed kind of half way. A nicely tailored women's suit, lined and cut to accentuate a female body, a thinly striped pants suit, not unlike those worn by his mother. Very business-like, and quite imposing, as long as one stood tall with head back, eyes intensely focused to look out over one's high cheeks.

Julian spoke, a little choked, but enough to reveal his light high sounding voice. "Thank you Distinguished Professor Becker. I am Julia, or Julian, please yourself. I am honored to meet your extinguished, I mean, distinguished faculty."

"And I am Christian, Christian Bunion. Pleased to meet you," added Christian.

Becker gave a little cough as he always did. "Now I have your CVs here, and I see that you are both graduating from Virgin Hall, St. Robert's Seminary. And such impressive CVs with some two hundred performances each! And if I may remind our faculty, we voted at our last faculty meeting to assess all non-political performances as equal to one tier-two academic publication. Political performances, of course, that is protests, marches and the like, are tier-one performances, especially if they end in arrest.. If you so wish," Becker turned to address the candidates, "you may appeal the classification of your liturgical performances as tier-two, but we will put that aside for the time being. Must say, we are pleased to be interviewing you both, though it is a little unusual for two from the same institution and program to interview on the same day for the same job."

Julian was opening up into full display. His smile, such a disarming smile as Christian well knew, lit up his face, his high cheeks causing his eyebrows to slant in ways that simply took

everyone by surprise, and by speaking ever so quietly, emph-
asizing the softness rather than the high pitch of his voice, the
faculty leaned forward so they could hear him. The students
seemed to take no notice, and continued to feel each other up
under the table.

"We are so excited to be here," crooned Julian, "to be among
the leading world scholars on diversity and discrimination, and
will bring to you our unique background of seminarian studies,
a rare field to shed fresh light on LGBTQ problems of the day."

Becker was about to respond when a gruff voice from one of
the students interjected, "we're not a problem, and I resent your
typically veiled implication that we are."

"Oh dear!" cried Julian, reaching into her handbag for a
tissue. Goodness gracious! Dears! That is the farthest from our
minds!"

"You are the problem, not us," sniveled the student, his or her
friends hugging each other, calling out, "right on! Right on!"

Scalpel stepped forward. "As the Dean's representative, I ask
you to be civil to our guests. If you are going to be rude, then
please leave. This is an important initiative of the school, one
that I would have thought the likes of you would embrace, a
complete department of LGBTQ studies. It is a clear acknowledgment of our seriousness in studying diversity from every
viewpoint."

Becker intervened before the students could respond. "What
Dr. Scalpel means is that the very establishment of the department of LGBTQ studies implies, indeed states, that it is not
looking for other points of view that may be prejudiced in
studying LGBTQ, but in fact is clearly stating that the point of
view driving all the studies that will be offered in the new
department will be those of LGBTQ without being comp-
romised or unnecessarily complicated by other approaches such
as Marxism, post modernism, and other scientific or clinical
methods."

The students looked sullenly at the floor, and held hands
under the table. In fact, nobody had the slightest idea of what
Distinguished Professor Serious Becker had said, nor possibly
did he. But true to his reputation, he had smoothed over an
incipient student riot. He continued, "well, I think that this has
been a very productive introduction of our candidates. We will
take a break and meet again in fifteen minutes when our first
candidate will give his or her presentation."

Scalpel led Julian and Christian down the long passage and into a tutorial room. "You may spend a few minutes preparing your talk. Who will go first?" he asked with great satisfaction.

Julian answered. "Dr, Scalpel. I am not sure I heard Distinguished Professor Becker correctly, but did he say that there was only one position open, not two? If that is the case, then it means that me and Christian are competing against each other, and that's not what we want, do we Christian?"

Scalpel took a step back. "You are very insightful, Julian. I will get clarification from Provost Dean Fossil."

Then Julian did something he had never done before. He grabbed Scalpel's sleeve and pulled him lightly back. "Could you see whether our driver Pedro is still around? I would like to speak with him."

As soon as Scalpel left, Christian, plainly nervous, his hands shaking, lunged at Julian and hugged him so hard it hurt them both.

"Sweetie-pie!" Julian exclaimed, it's OK!"

Christian let go. "I know, I know. But I have to go to the bathroom." He left, quickly calling out over his shoulder that he had seen one down the hall next to the Provost's office. But then he stopped and returned for his phone. Do you have my phone? I don't know where it is. It has our PowerPoint on it."

Julian looked at Christian in dismay. "You're going to pieces, darling, it's not like you. I don't have your phone. Are you sure it's not in one of your many pockets?" He walked over and patted Christian down, just like TSA does at the airport. Christian raised his arms, and then felt a weight in his shirt pocket.

"Oh! I have it!" he said, embarrassed.

"You see? Everything's fine. Now off you go to the bathroom. I will practice our presentation while you are gone."

"Do you want my phone?"

"No, I have my own, don't you know?"

Christian ran off to the bathroom, only then to find himself gaping at the doors. Should he go into the male or female? Male of course, what was the matter with him? There's never been any doubt as far as he was concerned, has there? Boys, men. That's who we are, right? He said to himself. He pushed open the male, then almost doubling up with pain in his belly, rushed over the cubicle. His father was right there in his insides, he felt it. He dropped his pants and plopped down on the seat calling out, his left hand covering his mouth to keep down the noise, "Father Virgil, you pig! Vile pig! Get out of me! Satan get out!" And out it came, in full force, a thunderous evacuation like no other. He sat back with a sigh of relief and looked up at the bathroom ceiling. "Thank you Father, I know you are watching over me." It was not at all clear to which father Christian addressed his remarks. But it was a wonderful feeling of calm that came over him as he attended to the small rituals of toiletry, stood up, pulled up his pants, turned and leaned over to flush the toilet, his eyes closed of course, not wanting to see the work of Satan in the raw.

Only then did he hear the sound of a slight "plop" and was again gripped with panic. He slowly opened his eyes and there he saw his phone lying deep in Satan's murky underworld. He turned away in panic, put his hands to his mouth, which he should not have done until after he washed them, and backed away against the cubicle door. There was nothing for it. He took off his jacket and rolled up his sleeve. No, he could not go through with it. Not like this. He leaned over to flush the toilet again, hoping and praying that the phone would not join Satan's works and go off to wherever that stuff goes. The water in the toilet bowl settled, and there, shimmering in the reflected light of the bathroom sat his phone. He looked away, holding his nose with one hand, and the other he groped in the toilet and clutched the phone. Holding it at arm's length, he backed away from the toilet, but found himself up against the cubicle door, which of course opened inwards. He struggled to retrieve his jacket which had dropped to the floor, to somehow get himself around the door as he opened it inwards, then dashed to the basin to wash his hands, dropping the phone on the bathroom floor as he did so. He shook the loose water from his hands and leaned down to pick up the phone which had slid under another cubicle, its door locked. On his hands and knees, he struggled to reach under the cubicle door, and as he did so, he heard a loud grunt followed by a cough obviously meant to inform him that someone was in there. But the further he reached in, groping this way and that, the more impossible it became. He craned his neck and managed to look under the door, and there he saw the Distinguished Chair of Diversity and Discrimination laying back on the toilet seat, his withered member in his hand. Christian blinked. "Excuse me, professor," he said politely, "have you seen my phone?" Becker grunted again and his foot, clothed in an expensive Clarke's of England shoe, gave a sharp kick and the phone slid forward, hitting Christian in the mouth. This was enough to shake him back to reality. He grabbed the phone and pushed himself back, stood up with difficulty, put on his jacket, placed the phone in his shirt pocket, looked in the mirror to see that all was tucked in and straight, and marched out of the bathroom, where he met Julian just coming out of the women's.

Julian asked, "Everything OK darling?"

"Fine and dandy," said Christian, a sheepish grin overcoming his tight lips.

"That's good. Dr. Scalpel has just come looking for us. We're on now. Do you want me to go first, or you?"

"I'll go first," said Christian, not really thinking what he was doing. He felt the wet patch just above his left breast where his iPhone lay sleeping, and only then did it dawn on him that it was very possible the phone would not work after its small adventure. But he had no time to think because as they entered the presentation room, they met Dean Provost Fossil at the door. "Welcome to our School of Social Sciences," he said, offering his hand. Christian, without thinking, grabbed it and shook it enthusiastically, only then realizing that he forgot to dry off his hands in the bathroom so they were sopping wet. The Dean pulled back slightly. "If you will excuse me one moment, I think I left my phone back in my office. Please start without me," he muttered

They entered the room, the same number of people in attendance, though the students had moved up to the front row of seats, looking a little belligerent, laughing and joking as Christian moved up to the dais, after his introduction by Distinguished Professor Serious Becker, who had only just slid into the room, looking a little red in the face.

Christian began. "LGBTQ is what we want to talk about today, as you can see from our PowerPoint, which I have on my phone." He retrieved his iPhone from his breast pocket and waved it to the audience. It was wet and clammy, made worse by his sweating palms. But the overhead projector did not project the PowerPoint. "Is Bluetooth turned on?" he asked. "My phone was working before." But in fact his phone was not working at all. When he pressed the "on" button nothing happened. The phone was dead. "Oh. Well. I guess I will have to proceed without the PowerPoint." Christian felt his knees sagging. He was about to collapse. He grabbed at the lectern, but it moved with his hand and slid off the table making a loud bang. The room swirled around him, and he would have collapsed right there had it not been for the intervention of the love of his life.

Julian, who had remained standing to Christian's left during this fiasco, raised himself on to his toes, and—there is no other way to describe it—fluttered forward to the dais, gracefully took Christian's hand, and steadily led him across the room and to a vacant chair. He then returned and produced his own phone and waved it in an arc, still dancing on his toes, his engaging and disarming smile filling the room with his love. He placed the phone on the lectern and opened up a YouTube video of a young cellist playing, of all things, Uptown Funk. He pranced across to the blackboard and wrote Julian in big upright letters. And to the beat, he stepped one big step back, then two small struts forward. Then clapping in time with the music managed to remove his jacket and toss it across the room, undid his Virgin Hall tie, dark blue with occasional thin red stripes, and danced between the chairs, dragging the tie over the onlookers' hands, shoulders, or whatever else lay in the way. Then wriggling with contortions to the rhythm he removed his long striped pants and dropped them on the students in the front row. It was plenty to stop their snide remarks and cause their eyes to almost pop out of their heads. Now he sang some of the lyrics, in a seemingly falsetto voice, though his, as we know, was a high pitched voice, naturally. He moved his hands gracefully, fingers extended—he had always envied Christian's fingers, a jealousy he allowed himself—sweeping his hands from his knees all the way up his sides, up to his breasts, pushing up under them to make them pop out over his unbuttoned white Mexican cotton shirt with embroidered collar, ripping off his shirt, revealing a dainty red bras, and with delightful twists of his wrists and hands, pushed his fingers through his jet black hair, raising his arms high. The backs of his hands touching, fingers arrayed in a beautiful feminine manner. As the song reached its strongest beat, he suddenly stamped like a bullfighter across to the blackboard, wrote his name Julian in big letters, then crossed off the "N," and when the song came to an end, she curtsied and, holding up her phone, announced, "I am Julia," and stamped her foot, holding her arms aloft.

A brief silence. Then the students erupted in cheers, the older faculty sat stunned, but found themselves clapping politely none the less. The two younger faculty did not clap and sat sullenly together. They were in fact a married couple and prided themselves on being the first to hold positions of husband and wife in the same school. They could see that their pioneering accomplishment was about to be washed away into oblivion. Distinguished professor Serious Becker did not stand, but twisted around in his seat, still clapping quietly, and then addressed the faculty:

"I think we have seen here a tier-one performance! Almost enough to warrant tenure here and now!"

The faculty sat silent, one shifted a little in his seat, a sign of disagreement. "I thought we agreed that the performance had to be political to get tier-one rating," he said, stroking his lightly bearded chin.

"The choice of song was surely that," chimed in another.

"How could a choice of song be political in itself?" asked another.

"Well," intervened Becker, "we do not need to decide that now. We will refer the issue to our performance and publications committee for further discussion and a report to the faculty at a later date. However, all this is premature, since no offer has been as yet made to Julia or Julian. On this we must await the faculty selection committee's assessment after we have interviewed all candidates."

"Point of information," came a stilted voice from one of the younger faculty "how many candidates are there?"

Becker turned to the Dean. "Are you able to divulge any information on this matter?" he asked.

"We have two positions vacant, but of course it's never guaranteed that we can fill them, and two candidates, Julia, Julian and Christian."

At this point, Julia gathered up her clothes, pulling her pants away from the students who were now laughing and joking as they vied with each other for a sniff of the pants. Julia tugged hard, but they would not let them go, until Christian, still sniffling back a few sobs, leaped across the desk chairs, knocking them over and wrenched the pants away. He buried his face in them and then handed them to Julia with a smile, one that forced his thin lips to part a little. Julia took them, not quite sure whether to put them on or stay with who she was for the moment.

And when they looked around the room it was suddenly empty, except for Scalpel.

"The Dean wants to talk to you both as soon as you're done dressing," said Scalpel with a disgusting grin. "Oh and by the way, I found your driver Pedro. He was hanging around the central fountain, eyeing off the girls. I had to call security. They freaked out when he pulled out a golden gun and waved it around."

"So where is he?" asked Julia, aggressively.

"What do you want him for anyway? It will be hours before you're done with many more interviews with faculty and administrators," lectured Scalpel.

"I don't think that is any of your business," answered Julia, sounding more and more like his mother. "Please bring him to us."

"No problem. He's cuffed to the bathroom sink in the men's room." Scalpel licked his rubbery lips gleefully.

"Where is the gun? It is my father's, a very expensive gun."

"I gave it to the Dean. You can get is back when you meet with him."

Christian, still sniffling, handed Julia her clothes. Of course she could not show up to her meeting with the Dean in her underwear. She had not brought with her a proper dress. So she put on her pants suit, white cotton shirt and striped St. Roberts college tie. Christian made her stand up straight before him as he straightened her tie, and patted down the suit to remove any wrinkles. They walked together down the narrow hall to the men's room, where Julia, now Julian, looked in the mirror and combed his hair. But then he paused and a mischievous smile came over his face, a smile that always made Christian weak at the knees. He rummaged in the side pockets of his pants and produced a small lipstick and powder compact, and daintily applied a little rouge to his cheeks, and a touch of pink lipstick to his lips, the lips that Christian so loved. "How do I look?" he asked Christian who looked over his shoulder into the bathroom mirror.

"You look great," smiled Christian, "though I prefer your lips in the raw."

A cough came from one of the cubicles followed by a gruff voice that growled in a thick Spanish accent, "Get me out of these fucking cuffs! I'll kill those bastards, every fucking one of them!"

"Pedro?" called Julian.

"Get me out, fuck you all!"

Julian was not used to any of his father's men talking to him
like this. He turned and looked at Christian who immediately
strode to the cubicle and wrenched off the door with one huge
pull. There sat Pedro facing backwards, no pants, hands cuffed
to the pipes of the cistern. "Where the fuck are your pants?" he
asked.

"That greasy little fucker tore them off me when he took the
gun. You got to get it back! El Padrino will throw me in the
pond if I don't get it back!"

Julian was about to ask Christian to go get Scalpel when the
door flew open and Scalpel appeared. "Allow me," he said with
satisfaction. He threw the keys to Julian, who threw them to
Christian.

"And I suppose the pants are with the Dean along with the
gun?" asked Julian.

"No. The pants are in the next cubicle," answered Scalpel
looking all around the bathroom. "You better hurry. The Dean's
waiting. He has another meeting in ten minutes."

They followed Scalpel out, Pedro struggling to do up his
pants, his curly hair and black beard ruffled, and a runny nose to
boot. "Anyone got a tissue?" he asked. Julia gave him a look
that could kill, and Pedro reflexively cowered back, having seen
those looks before from El Padrino, knowing full well that they
could really kill. In fact, he himself had made them so. As if on
cue, they burst from the bathroom, and ran into El Padrino
lumbering down the hall, followed closely by Virgil and
Bambola.

"Dad! What are you doing here?" cried Julian in dismay.

Alphonso stopped and scratched his navel. "I am calling on
my old friend Dean Fossil. We are doing business together." He
looked across at Pedro. "Someone give him a tissue, he looks
disgusting," he snarled.

Virgil grabbed Christian by his arm. "Are you OK?" he
asked, observing Christian's red eyes.

"I'm OK dad. We just finished our presentations."

"I heard you are getting jobs here," he said.

Scalpel stopped and turned to face Virgil. "They are only
interviewing today, Mr. Bunion. The faculty meets tomorrow to
decide."

"The tenure decision?" asked Alphonso, a knowing smirk on his face.

"Mr. Garcia, I thought you understood academia. You start at the bottom as an assistant professor and after seven years, if they like you, the faculty votes for your tenure. Rookies don't get tenure straight away." Alphonso looked at him, amused. "And you of course have tenure, Mr. Scalpel?"

"Yes, but I am an administrator not a professor. And it's Doctor, if you don't mind."

"Doctor asshole," said Alphonso in his businesslike voice, "we'll see about that." He took Scalpel by the elbow and steered him away from the others, beckoning to Bambola to join him. "The rest of you go ahead to the Dean's office. We'll catch up with you in a moment." He turned to Bambola. "The small envelope, give it to him," he said. Bambola retrieved a small brown envelope from another of her gorgeous new Florentine handbags. The fat envelope was imprinted with the Papal crest, underneath it inscribed in a flourishing cursive, "The Holy Waters of St. Peter," and handed it to Scalpel. Scalpel's hand automatically closed on the envelope, as though he were a seasoned drug dealer doing a deal. In no time, it was lodged safely inside his jacket. He looked sideways, as was his manner, then almost directly into Alphonso's eyes. Alphonso tried to look into his. "This may help you get the number of votes needed for my boys, er I mean, boy and…"

Scalpel cut him short. "Yes, Julian and Christian. To the extent that I can, I will see to it. But there are no certainties here. Academics are an unpredictable lot."

"Yes," smiled Alphonso, starting towards the Dean's office, "but this envelope will make them more predictable." Alphonso stopped and patted the small bulge showing in his jacket. "You understand me? Oh and by the way. I want my gun back. I hear you have it?"

"The Dean has it. Said he wanted to make an example of it, to teach the students that guns were not allowed on campus."

"He is certainly right about that. Only people who are experienced users like me should have guns," said Alphonso with a superior air.

"I will get it for you," answered Scalpel, leading the way down the hall.

Extra chairs had to be brought into Dean Fossil's office. Alphonso, however, refused to sit, as did Virgil who, unusual for him, was quiet. He had no drum, stood straight as a redwood pine, dressed perfectly in a dark navy pin-striped suit and a bolo tie, sporting a large medallion replica of Michelangelo's Pietà. Julian and Christian sat together wanting to hold hands, but each thinking the better of it. Pedro had moved his chair into the back corner and tried to make himself inconspicuous. Dean Fossil, a tall man himself, was dressed loosely in a grey suit, the jacket hanging on the back of his chair, his sleeves rolled up, Virgin Hall tie loosely tied around his collar. This was a working Dean, a Dean who got things done. That was what he stood for. It was why he was hired. "Now, gentlemen, and er, ladies. I have made my decision." He tried not to look down at the large brown envelope sitting at the front edge of his desk, it too imprinted with the St. Peters Water crest. But he was unable to continue because Christian stood up and cried, "before you do, I want you to know that I had an accident in the bathroom…"

The Dean's jaw dropped. Virgil took his hands from his jacket pockets where he had kept them mimicking the stance of the Duke of Edinburgh, and ran over to his son. "Christian!" he cried, "it's all right!" But Christian continued, "…and my PowerPoint was on my phone and it dropped in the toilet and the phone wouldn't work. I could do it now, it's working again…"

Virgil returned to type. He grasped his bolo tie and pulled it over his head. "Take this son, the Virgin Mary will calm you!" he thrust the medallion into Christian's face, but right then, Julian jumped up and snatched it away. "The Pietà!' he cried. "How did you know?"

Christian turned to Julian and grabbed him with both hands. "What do you mean! The Pietà! What do you know?" he cried, tears coming back to his red rimmed eyes.

"My dad, he has a replica of it in his private chapel. I have worshipped it ever since I was a little kid!"

"You sneaked into my private chapel?" growled Alphonso.

Christian turned to the Provost and cried out, "Oh Dean Fossil! Don't you see? All of this was meant to happen! It's God's plan! Let me do my presentation, in the name of Jesus!"

The Dean stood tall, a very serious look on his face, rather like that of Brett Kavanaugh when he was sworn in as a supreme court justice. With magnificent academic authority he announced: "this is a secular university. We are not guided by religious talk. We think logically and make rational decisions based on that thinking." He looked down at the envelope sitting on his desk, then addressed Julian and Christian. "That is why I am announcing today that our school is proud to offer you each an assistant professor position, in our new school of LGBTQ studies."

A deafening silence descended on the room, broken only by the shuffling of Scalpel in the opposite corner from Pedro. Alphonso stared at Scalpel then said to the Dean, "and the tenure?"

Dean Fossil shifted from one foot to the other and said in as serious a manner as he could, "I do not have the power to do that."

"You have denied me once," said Alphonso in his well-known threatening manner. Pedro immediately stood up and stepped away from his corner.

"You don't understand," said Dean Fossil, deeply apologetic, "the university has three levels of review for granting tenure. It's a faculty wide decision not my decision." And he went on, immediately realizing that it was a big mistake, "an initial appointment as assistant professor with tenure is unheard of. It has never happened in any university I know of."

Alphonso stepped forward and picked up the large envelope, turning it over in his hands, then placed it back down. "Be brave, Mr. Dean Provost Doctor, be brave. There's always a first time, isn't there?" He looked back at Pedro, then looked back at the Dean who sat back in his chair, twiddling his fingers nervously. "And by the way. I want my gun back," demanded Alphonso. "I understand it came into your possession?"

The Dean, relieved that he could do something to please Alphonso, retrieved the gun from the bottom right hand drawer of his desk. "Here it is. But I would appreciate it if you would keep your ruffian assistant away from my campus."

Alphonso took the gun and leaned forward, his bare belly resting on the desk. "It is not your campus, It belongs to the governor of the state of New Jersey, am I not correct?" Alphonso fingered the brown envelope. "I will be meeting with him in a few days about setting up my new manufacturing plant and distribution center in Hopewell or possibly Princeton. Perhaps I could raise it with him. We will be negotiating on many different matters."

The Dean's eyes widened. Was this a threat or was this an opportunity? He leaned over the desk to look closely into Alphonso's face, at least this was preferable to looking at his navel, and said, almost in a whisper, "if you would be interested in developing a business park, maybe, as a training ground and business incubator coordinated with our top rated business school?"

"Business school? What is that?" asked Alphonso.

"It's where you learn to start and run a business," put in Scalpel, now edging up to the desk, sensing something big in the air.

"That's bull shit if ever I heard it," mumbled Alphonso.

"The Governor will love it," smiled the Dean. "Lots of jobs in the area, money, money, money. I'm sure you understand that?" The Dean's mild sarcasm went over Alphonso's head. They looked straight at each other for what seemed a very long time. Scalpel hovered around them, glancing this way and that. He could see that the rest of the room's occupants had no interest in, or any idea of what was now hatching.

Alphonso stood back and brandished his gun. "I will not be denied!" he cried in his thin voice, "I will not be denied!" He leveled the gun at the Dean's chest. Who knows whether he would have fired the gun or not. But it was Pedro who leaped forward and pulled Alphonso's arm away, wrenching the gun out of his hand. "My Padrino," he cried, "it was all my fault. I deserve to die," and he pointed the gun at his head, his eyes wild darting from Alphonso to the Dean, a thick red tongue licking his slime filled beard. Alphonso was aghast. Never before had one of his men touched him, never came close! This was an outrage!

Pedro's finger tightened on the trigger. Julian and Christian held each other closely. Scalpel looked on with an amused smirk. Dean Fossil stood back, his arms folded. But it was Virgil who saved the day. "Wait a minute!" he said quietly, "who's got my bolo tie?" Pedro looked around. "Not me!" he cried, and his trigger finger loosened just a little. "I must have it!" screamed Virgil, "it's got sentimental value! I can't live without it!"

"You silly old codger dad!" cried Christian, you gave it to me, don't you remember?" He threw it to Virgil who quickly stepped forward to grab it, bumping Pedro's elbow. And another miracle occurred. The golden gun fell out of Pedro's hand on to the desk and went off. All present gasped. Who was shot? They looked around at each other and felt themselves all over.

Scalpel looked around and said, "I swear I heard two shots."

"There was only one," mumbled everyone else as though reciting a psalm.

Then Virgil noticed that his bolo tie was not in his hand but on the floor. He bent down to get it and there, to his amazement, he saw the miracle. The golden bullet was lodged in the silver medallion of the Pietà. He dropped to his knees and held it up high. "A miracle, a miracle! Jesus has sent a message to us all! He has saved all our lives, any one of us could have been killed! Oh thank you Lord! Jesus has told us that we are on the right path! Padrino! Thank you for leading us out of the wilderness!"

By now Alphonso and Julian had dropped to their knees, crossing themselves, and Virgil and Christian followed, which did not go unnoticed by Alphonso. Scalpel looked on, arms crossed, mimicking his boss the Dean. No one noticed that Bambola stood whimpering in the corner, a tiny trickle of blood making its way down her shapely leg.

It was that time of the month.

*

Dean Fossil had sent a memo around to all the Diversity and Discrimination faculty canceling the faculty meeting due to administrative issues, but informing faculty that the vice president and academic provost of the university, Dr. Phyllis Phoster, had recommended to president Boswell that Julian and Christian be granted tenure along with their appointments as associate professors in the new department of LGTBQ studies. This was, he informed them, a wonderfully positive start to this new department and indicated the strong support of the university administration for diversity and discrimination. He thanked the faculty for their unwavering support of this brave new initiative and congratulated the new faculty recruits. There would be a welcoming event in a couple of weeks where all the school's faculty would have the chance to make their acquaintance with the new recruits. The new professors would be given only half the regular teaching load while they settled into their new positions.

Unfortunately, Dean Fossil did not quite get away with this trick. It only takes one faculty member to dissent, and everything falls apart. And so it was that assistant professor Azalia Akbari dared to question the unconventional procedures used to hire and appoint these new faculty, especially as they were appointed above her in rank, and presumably also getting higher salaries. And so an emergency faculty meeting was scheduled to which Provost Phoster would also attend and explain why she had taken such unusual steps to hire these two outstanding candidates.

It goes without saying that Azalia was very upset, and her husband, a white Anglo-Saxon atheist from Boston who sat next to her, was embarrassed, so much so that as soon as the meeting started, in his JFK accent, he excused himself to go throw up in the toilet. Azalia, to push home her point had shown up in a full Burka, a slit to show her dark eyes, but then she had cut two large holes in the front that followed the contours of each of her considerable breasts, so they poked out like giant lemons. Trying not to look at the lemons, the Dean called the meeting to order and announced that at the last minute Provost Phoster had been called away to another more important meeting concerning safe spaces on campus, one of which, he was proud to report, would be on the 20th floor, the roof actually, of this building. The university psychiatrist had opposed this choice, arguing that persons who retreated to a safe space might be mentally fragile and choose once they got there to jump off the roof. For this outrageous suggestion, clearly full of hate and prejudice against the mentally challenged, the psychiatrist was paraded across the campus with a sign painted on the back of his best suit coat, I AM A NAZI, and was naturally banished from the campus, denied access to his university email account, and required to return all the books he had borrowed from the university library.

Dean Fossil surveyed the meeting attendees. The four student representatives sat muttering to each other at one end of the table. Azalia sat next to them and her husband's vacant seat, then Distinguished professor Serious Becker, a few other faculty, all men in their sixties, none of them with much hair, and a middle aged African American woman, overweight from eating too many Fritos, a bag on the table right next to her notebook. She was charged with keeping the minutes. And then on his left were Christian and Julian. Alphonso had wanted to come, as did Virgil, but thankfully, Julian and Christian had managed to talk them out of it on the basis that it was hardly a sign of their maturity as professors with tenure if they showed up to the meeting with their daddies. In the end, Julian agreed to have Pedro come and sit inconspicuously in a corner of the room, certainly not at the table. Dean Fossil was nervous about that, given Pedro's violent history, but in the end knew that he had no choice in the matter. And of course, at his right hand was

Scalpel, sitting sprawled low in his seat, almost sliding under the table.

The Dean spoke. "Since this is a special faculty meeting, there is no need to review the minutes of the last meeting. So let us begin. All those in favor of granting Julian and Christian associate professor positions with tenure, raise your hands."

One hand only was raised. One of the old men said, "point of order. Shouldn't there be some discussion before we vote?"

Dean Fossil responded quickly. "Of course, if you need to. I just thought after talking to each of you outside the meeting that no further discussion would be needed." He had not, of course, spoken to anyone.

Azalia now leaned forward across the table, her huge lemons demanding attention and said in a deep voice, rather like that of Christiane Amanpour, in impeccable BBC English, "me and my husband have worked hard to preserve diversity on this faculty. But this is taking it too far. Are these two married or what? We need only one married couple on this faculty. I am against this hire, and so is my husband."

Fossil turned to Julian and Christian. "I gather that you are not married, are you? After all you are both men, is that not so?"

"Point of order, Mr. Chairman!" called a student, "men can be married too. Governor Cuomo said so!"

A student nudged him and laughed, "he's the governor of New York, you dope. This is New Jersey!" The students laughed and sniggered. Then one of them shouted, "anyway, after their performances yesterday, the short one is a woman, isn't he?"

Christian and Julian all this time sat quietly, holding hands under the table, as usual. The Dean, red in the face with anticipated embarrassment, looked at Julian and asked bluntly, "what is your gender, Julian or Julia?"

Julian let go of Christian's hand and said, "I refuse to answer that question which is full of hate, and besides whatever gender I am is none of anyone's business."

The old male faculty squirmed as one, their hands covering their mouths as they tried to hold back sniggers.

Dean Fossil however, pressed on. "I agree that it ought not to be my business, but it is. If you are a woman, it is easier for me to get the line with tenure. In fact, of you were a man, it would be near impossible."

Christian searched for Julian's hand again and they squeezed each other under the table. But then he said, "I can tell you, he is not a woman."

"He has to be a woman, as I've only one line if he is not, and could only hire one of you," answered the Dean.

"Then I'm both!" said Julian priggishly.

"That is disgusting!" cried Azalia, "utterly disgusting! Thank goodness my husband is not here to hear such shit!"

The students huddled together in animated discussion, then one of them, the ringleader, spoke up. "Point of order, Mr. Chairman. We call for gender confirmation."

Dean Fossil stood up. "I thought it would come to this. He turned to the African American, and said, "Dr. Booker, would you go get Dr. Scur, the University Psychiatrist? He is hiding in my office." With difficulty, Dr. Booker grabbed her bag of Fritos and staggered out of the room.

"Wasn't he ejected from the campus?" asked the student rep.

"He was, but it was only temporary. Anyway, the university can't function without him. The campus is overloaded with the mentally challenged and he's the only one who knows who they are."

Julian stirred in his seat and said, "what is gender confirmation, may I ask?"

"You'll have to ask Dr. Scur. He's the expert."

"Couldn't we just get someone in from the biology department?" asked one of the old men, his hand still covering his mouth.

Dean Fossil shook his head, looked down and mumbled, "it's not that simple."

Dr. Booker stood clasping her Fritos in both hands, waiting for Dr. Scur to open the door for her. He had difficulty, as he had never worn a full burka before, so couldn't get his hands free, trying to grip the door knob through the burka. Eventually, he managed with both hands and they entered the room. The students gasped, and Azalia screamed, "Ya Allah! What is this?" In the bathroom, her atheist husband stopped throwing up when he heard her scream. He rushed to his office to get his Japanese world war two sword, as guns were not allowed on campus. He ran in behind Dr. Scur, brandishing it this way and that, just how he had seen Mr. Ip in the cheap Chinese movies. He looked round the room and saw two burkas. "Which of you is my wife?" he yelled, "Azalia, where are you, are you OK?" But then he saw the giant lemons, and said, "Azalia, it's you, right?" The truth was that he had only imagined what those juicy lemons looked like, as he had never seen her naked, only felt the contours of her body, having to imagine what it looked like. He dropped his sword and lunged forward, his hands and fingers extended as open as they could be. He just had to feel them! Could not resist this unexpected gift (from Heaven, but of course he could not say that!).

Dr. Scur stood cringing in the corner, his burka covering both himself and Pedro who was crouched down trying to keep out of the way. He wished he had his boss's golden gun, he'd show them a thing or two. The Dean spread his hands on the table and called, "Order! This meeting must come to order!"

"Mr. Chairman, I demand to see him!" called Azalia.

"See who?"

"This Julian. He must show us! Is he man or woman?"

This was enough to bring gasps from everyone, and they stared in silence at poor Julian. Christian put his hand on Julian's shoulder to stop him from standing, and cried, "leave my love alone! He is innocent!"

"No one in this room is innocent," announced Dr. Scur, "besides, this has nothing to do with guilt or innocence."

Everyone ignored him. Their eyes were fixed on Christian who jumped up on his chair and called out in a pious voice. "I'll show you the truth!" And he began to drop his pants. The students jumped out of their chairs as one, shaking their fists, shouting, "show him up! Show him up!"

Distinguished professor Becker got off his chair and raised it above his head. "Sit down and shut up all of you! There's nothing to see here!" It was a poor choice of words. Christian, now very angry, put his hands down to cover the big bulge in his boxers, and growled, "what do you mean by that, you old fart?!"

Dr. Scur now removed his burka. It was time to assert his authority as a respected psychiatrist whose very specialty was sex, as everyone knew. He stepped forward, the word NAZI painted on both his front and back, the only condition on which the University President would allow him back on campus. He addressed Christian, "You are the person in question? You are Julian?"

Christian said, still holding himself gently, "no. My partner here, is Julian. I'm Christian."

Julian buried his head in his hands, thoroughly demoralized. He had thought that academia here would be like at St. Robert's College. That everyone would be respectful and quiet. That a sensible discussion could be had. He looked up and bit his lip when he saw the NAZI sign. And then he said in a thin, timid voice, "I am her," a trickle of a tear appearing above his left cheek.

"Then I request that the room be cleared while I examine young Julian, after which I will give my professional opinion as to his gender."

A buzz of talk ensued, but it was broken by Julian who looked up and said, "I may be a boy or a girl, that is what I say, and it is my right to say it, and what my body says is my private business and none of yours, including doctors or experts or however they describe themselves."

Christian pulled up his pants and got down from the chair. "I say he is my boyfriend and it is my right to say it if he consents. He is to me a boy and it is my right to say so, and my body's right to feel so."

The room went silent. Scalpel even reached over and pulled at the students to sit back in their seats.

The Dean, unsure what to do next, got up to pronounce the meeting over, unsure what had been achieved. He wished the provost had been present. Then came a timid knock on the door and Scalpel, who had taken up a defensive position right there, opened it carefully. It was Bambola, followed by Virgil then Alphonso arm-in-arm with Vice President Provost Phoster, a buxom woman to his liking, followed closely by the University's Vice President for Research, a well-dressed young Latino, sporting expensive jewelry on his fingers and around his neck. Pedro quickly stood up from his position on the floor in the corner and hurried forward, calling out, "make way, make way." Bambola, carrying an expensive looking leather folder, led the way to the front of the room, Fossil vacating his place and moving to the side.

Vice President Provost Phoster beckoned to Dean Fossil. He obediently came forward. She took the leather folder from Bambola, looked at Alphonso with affection, then opened it and announced, "It gives me great pleasure on behalf of the University and the Office for Research, to give you this certificate that confirms the establishment of the New State College Institute of LGBTQ studies with an endowment of thirty million dollars. The Institute will be located in the new East Hopewell Business Incubator Campus to be constructed thanks to the further generous donation of fifty million dollars from the Alphonso and Maria Garcia Foundation. I am also pleased to introduce the founding director of that East Campus Reverend Doctor Virgil Bunion." Virgil stepped forward, big smile, resplendent in his new pin-striped suit, though no bolo tie, instead a tie sporting the striped colors of New State College, black and blue. The Vice President Provost opened up the folder and displayed the certificate to all present, then handed it to Dean Fossil, who said, "I am overwhelmed."

The meeting was transformed into a joyous occasion, as the promise of a lot of money is wont to do. But after Provost Phoster and her entourage departed, the students, at least, wanted to get back to gender confirmation. And the faculty mumbled and complained that they had not been consulted. Azalia still voiced her concern that the new appointments of Julian and Christian were an insult to her religion and womanhood. But the Dean would have none of it. He surreptitiously pointed to an additional letter from the Provost, enclosed in the leather folder, appointing both Julian and Christian as associate professors with tenure, Julian to be the chair of the department of LGBTQ studies. The faculty would find out about all this later. Right now, he would close the meeting on a happy note, though not before announcing that the Provost had approved a salary increase of 10 percent for all Diversity and Discrimination faculty.

"I declare this meeting closed," announced Dean Fossil leaning over to Dr. Booker, "and please run your draft of the meeting minutes by me before you distribute them."

11. Snake man

Alphonso texted the Great Godfather. "Plan B part one now operational." He had decided to meet with Virgil in the faculty lounge of New State University, now renamed "Virgin Hall University." The change of name had cost him a donation of only $200,000. And it was only a beginning. He looked around the lounge. It was disgusting and would need to be refurnished. All the furniture, he was sure, had been manufactured and designed in one of New Jersey's state prisons. It was a dull gray, the color of all prisons, made of cheap steel, painted roughly by hand. He sipped on his cheap New Jersey chardonnay, something else that he would soon fix. He looked across at Virgil, who beamed in anticipation, neatly dressed in a navy business suit, his signature bola tie glowing under the florescent lights.

"Your Church of Judasian Trust," said Alphonso, "would you like to make it bigger?"

"Like how big?" Virgil timidly asked.

"Say, a few hundred thousand or more?"

Virgil gasped. "But we only number in the hundreds if that."

"I can offer you additional support to attract believers," said Alphonso wisely.

"What kind of believers? Why will they believe in me?"

"Snakes," said Alphonso as though he were simply announcing what day it was.

"Snakes? You mean, like they do down south?"

"Not that far south. West Virginia. I know of a place. In fact I just bought it, snakes and all."

"You, you bought it? A whole church? How do you do that?" Virgil cried out in disbelief.

"You offer just enough money," replied Alphonso sagely, "of course, there is a non-compete clause, but still, you will be able to grow the church without competition."

"But I don't dance with snakes," complained Virgil, ever the doubter.

"There's always a first time."

"They're poisonous aren't they? They'll kill me!" cried Virgil.

"Don't you have faith in God?" berated Alphonso.

"Well, yes, but…" Virgil bit his lip, his eyes watered.

Alphonso frowned and looked Virgil squarely in the face. "You'll find a way. Your faith has got you this far," he chided.

"But, Padrino…"

"No buts. Here's half a million." Go down there and work your magic. I've already paid the church leader and part of our agreement was that he would teach you how to do it all. The money is for acquiring new believers. Make some YouTube videos, get a couple of TV spots. Have a big Pentecostal, or whatever it's called, a meeting. Rent a big stadium."

Without thinking, Virgil took the briefcase bulging with money. Right now, he was full of faith. His life was no longer one of want, lacking of whatever. He lacked nothing, he could draw on what he felt inside was a huge reservoir of faith. It would see him through, even if it meant risking his life with venomous snakes. How venomous could they be? Worse than the humans he had known? Nowhere near it!

"And by the way," added Alphonso, "your name's Virgil, never Jude, got it?"

*

The snake man looked just like Virgil when he hung out with the homeless down at Starbucks. He lived in an abandoned trailer in a park that was also abandoned. He kept his snakes in glass tanks in an old shed that was probably an adapted out-house. Church services were every Sunday afternoon, outside his trailer, or if one of the congregation offered it, at their trailer or living room. He was suspicious of Virgil a first, even after he was offered a couple of thousand dollars. But when Virgil showed him a photo of himself drumming up the homeless at Starbucks, he immediately became friendly, though he warily eyed Pedro who was lurking at the edge of the woods. Alphonso had loaned him to Virgil in case there should be any trouble. Pedro would come no closer, though, because he was very afraid of snakes. He had his AK47 hidden behind his back.

"They're very friendly and great companions, if you treat them right," said the snake man, as he opened the top of a tank and scooped up a large copperhead. "The most important thing is not to feed them too much, just like fish. If you do, it will kill them." What he did not tell Virgil was that if snakes are well

fed, they make more venom and it is much stronger. But Virgil
already knew that. He saw it on a YouTube video. The snake
man scooped out a couple more and with them hanging over his
arm, began what he called the snake jig, bobbing up and down
on his toes. "You have to practice the jig to find the rhythm that
suits them. Each one is different, you know, just like we
unlucky humans."

"What do you feed them?" asked Virgil.

The snake man kept jigging. "A mouse or gerbil, or something like it, every month or so."

"Do they eat vegetables?"

"I dunno, mate. Never tried it. I suppose if they are hungry
enough they'll eat anything. Lord Jesus! Bless these serpents,
keep the devil out of them!" Now he twirled as he jigged.

"Where are you from?" asked Virgil. "Your accent, it's not
southern…"

"It is, as far south as you can get. Queensland Australia, mate,
where there's lots of snakes, human ones too," he joked.

"Why are you here then?"

"This old girlfriend, she saw I was making lots of money with
me snake farm, so she accused me of forcing a snake up her
whats-it, it was all over #metoo, Facebook and everything. I had
to piss off out of there or they would have put me in jail. I didn't
do nuthn."

"And they let you into the US?"

"Nah, I sneaked across the Canadian border. I'll go back there
with all this money you and your boss gave me. Especially as
cannabis is legal. Gunna be great! You got anything to put the
snakes in? You can have the tanks if you want. They're bloody
awful to carry a long distance." Now he held his arm up high
and grabbed one by the back of the neck, just behind the head,
as Virgil had read on the Internet. "You see? They're real docile,
they won't hurt you, unless you rile them up. That's the most
important thing. If you're angry or stressed out over something,
they know it. So you need to keep praying to God as you jig, so
as to keep yourself calm. Here, try one!" Snake man scooped up
another copperhead from the tank and hung it over Virgil's arm,
which Virgil held out well away from him. The snake man
laughed. "You're not a scarecrow, you know, just relax. Come
on! Jig, you gotta jig!"

Virgil began to jig, and the snake man hung another snake, a
rattler this time, over his arm. "You can mix the species?" asked

Virgil trying to sound detached, even nonchalant. He jogged some more, changing his rhythm to match that of the snake man. Now Pedro left the shelter of the woods and advanced toward them, AK47 at the ready. He was under strict orders to protect Virgil, he was valuable merchandise. Trouble was, if the snake was going to bite Virgil, he could not shoot it without also shooting Virgil.

"That bloke's yours, I hope?" asked the snake man, starting to put the snakes back in their tanks.

Virgil called to Pedro. "It's OK. Put the gun away." He then, copying his teacher, went to grab the copperhead by the neck just behind the neck, and in a flash, he felt a piercing pain in his hand, just behind the thumb. In horror he shook the snakes off his arms, and stared at the tell-tale twin tooth marks, a trickle of bright red blood running down his arm.

The snake man looked on, calm as could be. "Hold your arm up, don't want the poison to circulate too quickly. Now's the time to pray to Jesus. We'll know soon enough whether you are his chosen one."

Virgil lifted both his arms up high and prayed like he never had before. His knees felt weak, an awful feeling of dread, as though someone had injected him with ice-water, gradually moved down his arm and spread out over the rest of his body. There was no sweat, just a feeling of goose-bumps all over, followed by a searing pain that throbbed at the very top of his head. He dropped to his knees, and cried, "oh God!" then collapsed on the soggy turf.

Pedro was beside himself. It would be the fish pond for sure if Virgil died of a snake bite. "Call 911!" he shouted at the snake man.

"No use. By the time they got him to the hospital and got the serum it would be too late."

"Then do something! Or El Padrino, he will kill us both!"

"Who?"

"My boss. And yours too."

"Not to worry. You see the color in his face? Those red cheeks? If he was gunna die they'd be white as a ghost."

Pedro put down his AK47 and kneeled over the comatose body. "He's not breathing!" He rolled Virgil over on to his back and started pounding at his chest, like he had seen in the movies.

"You'll break his ribs, mate. He'll be OK, I tell you. Can I make you a cup of tea? And I'll bring old Virgil some sweet tea too. Trouble is, can't get good tea in America." The snake man disappeared into his trailer leaving Pedro alone with his dead or dying boss. He rocked back and forth, sobbing, praying to Jesus. Maybe with the two of us praying, He'll hear the cry for help, he hoped. Pedro gathered up the briefcase that bulged full of money. and for a moment he thought of running off with it. And maybe he would have, had Virgil not groaned and moved his head to the side, saliva dribbling from the corner of his mouth. Pedro quickly slid the briefcase under Virgil's head. Virgil blinked, the pupils of his eyes the size of pin-pricks. "I can't see!" he cried, I can't see!"

"Boss, I thought you were dead! It's a miracle!"

Virgil stretched his arms out, trying to see the hand that throbbed with pain, felt it swollen to twice its size. "I'm not dead, and my hand hurts like shit!"

"The snake man said he was bringing you a cup of tea."

"Tea? What the fuck for? Wine, red wine, the blood of Christ, that's what we need." He blinked some more and gradually the world came into focus. "Help me stand up!" he groaned.

Pedro helped him up and they staggered together back to the snake man's trailer, only to find that he had departed.

News of Virgil's induction into the world of snake dancing spread far and wide via his new Facebook page, Instagram and Twitter. Not to mention the videos Pedro took of him dancing with the snakes. Virgil spent all the money needed to develop his web page, spread his newly reformed Church of Judasian Trust and its wonderful attraction, the exciting communion with Christ through those animals so detested by the whole world, serpents of the devil, showing that even these hated and feared creatures were well within the bounds of Christ's love. And the fact that Virgil had withstood the devil's attempt to kill him, was plenty to convince his rapidly growing congregation of his sanctity.

Money began pouring into his web site, and soon he was ready to do as Alphonso had directed: hold a rally of many thousands, televised far and wide. He even did an interview on Len Pecker's morning show on WUBS, and brought along his favorite snake, an Australian Tiger snake as it turned out, to demonstrate his infallibility and unshakeable faith in Jesus. It was on that show that he announced the forthcoming massive

Pentecostal gathering at CURE stadium in Trenton New Jersey. It would be patterned after the Billy Graham shows, plenty of time after his blockbuster sermon for people to come down to the front, hold a snake and jig if they wanted, drop down under Virgil's divine hand, and be born again.

And then, Christian phoned into the show.

One should not judge Christian too harshly. After all, he had been raised by a bible-bashing, God-fearing father. His recalcitrance was entirely understandable. He refused to live with the homeless scum and took great pride in his own clean cut body. If love was all embracing, as Virgil preached, love absorbed all sins, surely Christian's own love for his body, clean, brushed, nails clipped, closely shaven, all its needs satisfied in every way, served Jesus much better than defiling it among the homeless scum? His question to his father on Len Pecker's morning show was persistent and, some would say, disrespectful: why had he twisted the words of the bible to support an obviously fake infallibility to the venom of snakes? Were not the miracles reported in the bible, especially those of Jesus, enough? By faking his own miracles, was he not committing the worst sin of all, claiming to be Jesus or one of his apostles?

We need not go into the details of their very public argument on Len Pecker's show. Needless to say, Pecker's producers were ecstatic. Their switchboard lit up for hours on end. And the argument ended with Virgil beating the table with his fist, singing "Onward Christian Soldiers" as loud as he could, trying to drown out Christian's challenge: if he were so full of miracles, Christian would come before the audience at the CURE stadium, jig with the most venomous snake and demonstrate to all, the nonsense of it all. And in spite of himself, Virgil was so angry that he yelled into the microphone, "Come on then! You come on down and we'll see just who is fake!"

*

The CURE stadium was full to overflowing. Virgil sang "Jesus loves me, this I know" and the audience enthusiastically sang along. He gave a rousing sermon, all the while jigging around the stage, two snakes dangling from his arm, both of them Australian Tiger snakes. Christian sat in the front row while all those around him stood in their seats, jigging in time with the loud accompaniment of an electronic organ. He leaned forward in his seat, his hands over his ears, the noise too loud. He looked at his father and was repulsed by what he had become. He loved him when he was living with the Starbucks homeless rabble. There was something true and genuine about him then, even though he himself did not follow him there. Besides, he sensed that his father would have been embarrassed if he had. But now, this huge transformation, clearly a result of something that Alphonso did to him, had produced something that was evil. And it had to be stopped.

The singing ended and Virgil now spoke, holding his two snakes aloft. "And now, I bring to you my own personal demonstration of commitment to Jesus, my son Christian, who will join me and I will convey my infallibility to him. We must share our love, and what better way to do it than to spread our faith in Jesus in the face of death—which is what these snakes promise, do they not?"

A buzz of excitement spread throughout the stadium. Murmurs circulated of "surely he won't do it," "the snakes aren't real," "they've got false teeth and can't bite."

Christian stirred from his seat and walked up to the stage. Virgil opened his arms wide, a snake dangling on each. Christian walked into his open arms, the audience cheering and urging him on. The big screen TVs zoomed in on the snakes' heads. "Come to me!" cried Virgil, "come to me, my son, that thou shalt have eternal life!" and he wrapped his arms around him.

Christian responded. "Dad! Dad! You don't have to do this!" He tried to grab one of the snakes by the back of its head, but it wriggled and as well Virgil was still jigging. Virgil cried out again, "take me O Lord! As is thine will!" And then, almost without anyone noticing, all having expected a massive rearing up of the snake's head, ready to strike, one of the snakes simply and quickly bit Christian on the neck. Christian reflexively grabbed at the bite, then saw blood on his fingers. A searing pain shot straight into his head, then slowly sank down to the rest of his body which felt as though it were draped in a heavy, lead cloak. He sagged to his knees, then fell prostrate on the floor, his body every now and then shaking, then still.

Virgil stood transfixed. Someone in the audience yelled out, "blasphemy! He's given up his only son!" Meanwhile the snakes had dropped to the floor and scurried away, off the stage and into the audience. Pandemonium broke out, screams and people pushing to escape. Snake! A fear worse than fire! Virgil looked down. Indeed, he had killed his only son. If only he had listened to Christian this morning on the talk show. Now, his death will be broadcast all around the world, there will be YouTube videos played over and over again. And at what price? The money of Alphonso, the filthy money. His promise to help spread holiness to billions. Had he been misled? Why had Alphonso insisted on the snake dancing? He a Catholic, of all things, surely he did not believe in such nonsense? But it's not nonsense, is it? He himself came back to life after the snake bite. The same would happen to Christian. He kneeled beside Christian, ignoring the bedlam in the stadium. The medics arrived, but Virgil could see it was too late. Christian's face had turned a deathly creamy white and the smell of bad ripe cheese, the smell of death, hung over him.

The medic asked what kind of snake and Virgil shrugged helplessly and said it was an Australian Tiger snake. And was told, naturally, that there was no antidote within 10,000 miles.

"Your son, I believe is seriously ill," announced the Medic. "Has he got insurance?"

"Only that of Jesus," answered Virgil.

The medic looked at him in disbelief. "We're not taking him then. You better call for a hearse. This made Virgil very angry, and he would have punched the medic, had not Alphonso stepped in front of him and grabbed his arm.

"You were here? You saw it all?" asked Virgil, flabbergasted.

"I did. You did a great job. I'm sorry about Christian." He turned to the medic and said, "do whatever is necessary to care for this young man. Here is the down payment. I believe only in self-insurance."

"But we don't take cash," frowned the medic.

"Then change it into a check before you get to the hospital," said Alphonso tersely. The medics carted Christian away, the sheet drawn up over his face, as though he were dead. "And show his face like he's alive," Alphonso ordered.

"But he's dead, it's pretty obvious," answered the medic pompously.

"Not to me, and here's another $500 that says I'm right."

The medics pocketed the money and trundled Christian away. Alphonso turned to Virgil who still knelt where Christian's body had been. "Virgil, this is a time when we must have our faith. We can't let our guards down."

"Why did you want the snakes?" sobbed Virgil, "my only son!"

"You must do this again," said Alphonso ignoring the question.

"Do what again?"

"The snake show."

"But I don't understand…"

"You escaped death from your snakebite, didn't you?"

"Yes, but…"

"I want you to put on a show for the Pope. I promise I'll get him to come here, to CURE stadium. It will be a huge achievement. It will show Catholics all over the world that their Pope is all embracing, that he accepts diversity, even the craziness of an insignificant Protestant sect."

"The Pope? But he's the devil to us, you know."

"Then that's all the better, isn't it? We'll fill this stadium full to overflowing, have it broadcast live on CNN. You will be the star!"

"But I don't want to be a star. I just want my son back."

"You know, Virgil, for a Protestant, I like you a lot. But you Protestants have to learn that every good deed has its price. You will reach millions of souls in your broadcast. Surely the loss of your son, though heart-wrenching, is a reasonable price to pay. And as well, you will contribute to the Christian health of billions once our holy water is in production and you distribute it around the world. The nasty veil between Catholics and Protestants will at last wither away. Even our current Pope has used those words to express what he would like to happen at the inter-faith rallies he has attended."

Alphonso helped Virgil to stand. He even pulled him close to him, so close that he rubbed his belly button against Virgil's belt buckle.

Virgil remained speechless. His thoughts now were of a funeral. But they also drifted to another big consequence. Julian would be without his lover. He looked into Alphonso's dark eyes. Yes, Alphonso was thinking the same. The relationship would be no more. A very big problem that had plagued them both as fathers would be solved.

Though not quite as they anticipated.

12. Identity crisis

Julian sat at his desk looking through the narrow window at the students frolicking around the fountain, opening what he knew would be his official letter of appointment from the New State College president to the position of Associate Professor with tenure and head of the LGBTQ studies department. His mind was brimming with ideas, courses he would teach, activities he would provide for his students, posters he would put up on his wall of famous LGBTQ scientists, authors, poets, and politicians, going as far back as Cleopatra. Then there was Joan of Arc, Lady Ga Ga, Dean Martin, Clark Kent, so many. He would teach a whole course on them and their great achievements. He would be the inspiration of the entire university.

His door was ajar, so when Dr. Scalpel knocked, it pushed open. Julian looked up with his big smile, his cheeks all puffed up with pride. He waved the letter and said, "my appointment letter from the president."

Scalpel stopped at the doorway and asked softly, may I come in?"

"Of course, what can I do for you?"

"I have very bad news." Scalpel slinked around the room, looking this way and that.

"Oh, not too bad for you I hope. Do share it with me. I will always be here for you."

"It's about Christian…"

"Christian? His appointment is not in jeopardy, I hope? It was a joint appointment. I know he messed up his presentation but he's a great scholar, you know."

"He's dead."

"Now don't joke, Dr. Scalpel. Please, that's in very bad taste."

"No. Really. He was bitten last night by an Australian tiger snake."

Scalpel's pleasure in conveying this news was hardly hidden. Julian, aware of his new status as department chair, retained his composure and said in a formal voice, "thank you for informing me."

"Are you sure there's nothing I can do?"

"Not at this moment. Err, how did it happen? How did you learn of it?"

"I met your father on the campus. He said he was on his way to see the president." Scalpel could not hold himself back. "The worst thing was that it happened at his father's Pentecostal gathering, in front of thousands of people."

Julian looked down, glanced out the window at the frolicking students, then, after a long silence, he turned back to Scalpel and said, "I'd like to be alone, if you don't mind."

"Of course." Scalpel feigned a bow and backed out of the office.

Julian went immediately to his computer and did a search for "sex change surgery Newark." The search returned New State University Hospital of Newark, New Jersey. He scrolled down the page until he came to "Transgender health Services and Surgery." He picked up the phone and called the LGBTQ Ombudsman at 973-972-6410. The call was answered immediately.

"LGBTQ emergency care. How may I help you?"

"I want a sex change operation."

"Front or back?"

"What?"

"Reversible or irreversible?"

"I don't understand."

"Never mind. Give me your name and date of birth and you can come down this afternoon and we will go over everything in detail. We offer many different options, tailor our surgeries to suit your individual needs exactly. We cater for every taste."

Julian gave his information. He wanted to act quickly before he could change his mind. He had wanted to be a woman for as long as he could remember, but Christian wanted him to be a little of both, well preferably a lot of man, but Christian liked his little feminine ways. Now he was free to choose. He had loved Christian dearly. He could never feel so close to anyone else. That was why he stayed being a man with him. Now he must act. Do it before his mom or dad found out. The only problem was that the university health insurance would not kick in until after he had been employed for six weeks. But, knowing how careful the administrators were these days, he guessed they would not want any publicity that they denied him coverage as an LGBTQ person. So they would break the rules for him. Of course, his mom and dad had plenty of money, too much, he knew. But he did not want to come out to them directly, could not ask for their help. This was a silly fiction he would cling to for as long as he could. Of course, he was already "out" it happened at their "wedding." But now, he was really changing into a woman. Something his mom would probably like, but his dad would abhor. It did not fit well with his gangster culture. On the other hand he did go through with their wedding. That took some doing, no doubt about it. And he had to admit, if it weren't for his dad, he would be a research assistant in some insignificant place. He took out his phone and was about to call him when Scalpel knocked at his door and entered. "Your dad is here," he said with a serious smile.

Julian rushed to Alphonso and hugged him tightly. Alphonso stood motionless, allowing his body, including his navel, to be crushed against this enigma of a son he had spawned. But he was blood, and that was what mattered. Blood first, his own cartel father had drummed into him from an early age. He lightly patted Julian on the back. Scalpel hung around the door.

Julian cried, "Dad! I don't know what to do!"

"It will take time." He wanted to say, "and it's all to the good," but managed to hold it back.

Then Julian suddenly muttered, "I've already decided what to do."

"But you just said you didn't know what to do," put in Scalpel.

"Get the fuck out!" growled Julian. Scalpel slunk away, pulling the door shut behind him.

"Son," said Alphonso, "I have just made an excellent deal with the university. You are all set for life. Lots of big things are happening. I will support you in whatever you decide. Your mom and me always want what's best for you, and now that you are an associate professor, you are the one who knows what is best for you."

"I have actually made a decision. On the spur of the moment as soon as I heard the news of Christian. I'm becoming a woman."

Alphonso pulled away from the hug. "A woman? I thought you decided not to go that route."

"That was for Christian. Now I am free to be who I want, and I really want to be a woman. Sorry dad. I can't help it. It's the way I was almost made."

"But you could go either way. Your mom and me understand that. So why choose the weaker sex?"

Julian sat back in his chair and clasped his hands together. He looked down, then looked up and stared his father directly in the face, as hard as could be. "There's strength in beauty, and as Jesus taught us, strength in love, which women have far more of than do men."

Alphonso's hand reflexively reached for his navel. Fumbling with words, he said, "you know, son, I should have had you put down. When we saw you didn't have the proper equipment, I wanted to have you got rid of. But your mother could not bring herself to do it. So you have her to blame, and no one else, for your pathetic situation. We could have saved you the choice, right back when you were born, or soon after anyway."

"Fuck you, dad. You're not God. Only he giveth and taketh away."

"Yes. God, not goddess. Only men have the power over life and death."

Julian leaned forward and retorted, "they can kill, but only women can give birth, create. Men are destroyers. We women are builders. Dad, I've made my decision. I'm not going back on it. Christian has done me a great service, in fact God has sacrificed him to give me the life I always wanted."

Alphonso was trying to keep up with the argument. So this is what they do in academia all day, he thought to himself. Take things to pieces bit by bit, just so they can win an argument, make them seem smart. But they are all talk. That's all they are. He stared back at Julian wondering whether he had made a mistake taking a chance on him. He turned to go, but then on second thought turned back and said, "I do have some other very important news to give you, but I think maybe it should wait until after Christian's funeral, and you have had time to reconsider your options."

"I'm having the surgery tomorrow, maybe even today, at the university hospital LGBTQ emergency care center."

"Shouldn't you wait until after Christian's funeral?"

"I'm not going to the funeral. Besides, my operation will be my most reverent act of farewell to him, don't you see?"

Alphonso rubbed his navel and muttered, with a frown, "I think so."

*

Julian had no sooner entered the massive building of the nineteenth century, an icon of Newark overlooking the Jersey turnpike, its carved stone entrance, decked with polished brass, a massive revolving glass door, and inside, various huge brass animals, tigers, eagles, looking down from the ceiling, gray and fawn marble covering everything. He pressed the elevator button that said "LGBTQ emergency care," and he was quickly transported to the top of the skyscraper. He stepped out of the elevator and immediately a robotic voice announced, "Julian Garcia, cubicle five please."

Julian entered, and a robotic voice immediately said, "please disrobe." He looked around for a mirror. Nothing.

"Everything/?" he asked.

"Yes, everything."

"When am I going to speak to a person?" asked Julian, annoyed.

"You are speaking to a person."

"I mean a real person, not a robot."

"If you don't mind," replied the robot in a haughty manner, "we robots are persons too, just like you are. Please do not be disrespectful."

Chastened, Julian disrobed as he was told. The robot continued. "My name is Onesy. We robots use numbers for our names in order to avoid any ascriptions of gender that are always implied by the names people are given."

"I agree with that," smiled Julian.

"Now raise your arms, spread your legs. Excellent! Bend over and touch the floor with your fingers. Very good! Just one moment while your data are analyzed."

"How do I look?" asked Julian, impatient, "what do you recommend?"

"Our deep scan shows that you are an excellent candidate for pretty much any of the LGBTQ options we offer. So it will be up to you to choose the options you want, and whether you want added special treatments for a premium. Do you have insurance, by the way?"

"Yes, I'm a professor at New State, I mean, Virgin Hall University."

"Ah, then. Their health scheme is very generous. You will have lots to choose from."

"Ok. Then what?"

"The possibilities will begin to appear as holographs in front of you in a few minutes. But first a couple of preliminary questions. Do you want memory erasure?"

"I'm not sure I understand."

"Some of our clients prefer not to remember what their gender was before the procedure. It helps to avoid PTSD. But others do not like the idea of forgetting who they were."

"I'll go with erasure. My memories of Christian are too intense. I may regret the change if I can still remember him."

"Fine. Ah, now the list of options is appearing. I will read them for you and you can give your response. Do you want reversible or irreversible?"

"You mean, if I change my mind after you've done me?"

"Not quite. We can make you so you can switch over from one to the other. We call that dynamic reversibility."

"I don't understand. I'll be either one or the other, right? And that will be for good, unless you can undo the surgery?"

"Well, there's that too. We call that standard reversibility. In dynamic reversibility we do the surgery in such a way that you can switch from one to the other pretty much in a few minutes. It's like, if you will forgive me saying this, we do the penis-vagina package. Basically you simply pull a flap and tuck the penis inside and it becomes a vagina from the outside. We do charge a premium for this package."

"Shit! Excuse me, but that's what I have right now only too little of both. I don't want that. I want to be only one, and no other."

"Oh! I'm sorry. I should have caught that from the scan. Of course you do. So you want standard reversible female?"

"I suppose so. But I am sure that once a woman, always a woman it will be for me."

"Believe me, and I am a robot, you can always believe me, one never knows what the future holds. You may change your mind. Though, since you're going with erasure, I doubt it."

"I don't really want to completely forget Christian. Will he be completely gone?"

"I'm afraid so, though you may have a vague sense of having met him before. We are working on partial, but it will be a few years yet until that's available. We do have other premium packages though."

"Like what?"

"We can make your fitting modeled on various famous peoples' vaginas."

"You can do that?"

"Oh yes! Using facial recognition we have algorithms that compute the depth, width, and elasticity of their vaginas. There's a ten percent surcharge for that, sometimes more, depending on the celebrity. Our most expensive is Madonna's."

"You say you do it for penises too?"

"Yes. Though for them, hand recognition works better. Why, are you having second thoughts now?"

"Oh no. I was just wondering." Julian smiled, a little embarrassed.

"Don't be embarrassed," said Onesy, "I'm a robot. I do not pass judgment on others and get no special pleasure from seeing them either suffer or enjoy themselves."

"OK. Now what's next?"

"Well, you have come to the LGBTQ emergency care center. We can move swiftly right away and do the procedure. It's all done by laser, non-obtrusive, though you do have to be naked, wouldn't want a zipper to get caught anywhere, would we? And we do harness you to the operating table."

"Then let's do it!" cried Julian with great enthusiasm, "before I change my mind!"

"Now, before we begin, there is one extra procedure that we offer, for the moment free of charge, since it is experimental. We are proud of our center and of keeping ahead of all things new. If successful, we will be changing our name to the LGBTQO. The 'O' stands for Onan, the masturbator. This procedure will onanly ..." Onesy paused waiting for Julian to see the small joke, but he did not, "...be available for standard reversible clients. We think that if you choose your gender once and for all, you should stay with it, but that means if you cannot find a partner, you have the right to make yourself your partner. It's only fair, don't you think? And from our surveys, we know that there are millions of onanists out there, hiding in their closets."

"So what is the procedure, what does it offer?"

"I'm not allowed to divulge the details, but I can assure you that it will enhance self-pleasure like nothing else."

"Really? I haven't found it very satisfying."

"I know, I know. And there are millions like you. As I said, no extra charge. It's a bonus."

HOLY WATER

"OK. I'll take it. It's going to be very lonely without Christian."

"Yes, and remember, you will be able to fantasize about him. Make him into anything you want."

"But you said I'd forget him."

"Yes, but that makes it easier for you to invent him in your own image doesn't it?" answered Onesy wisely.

Julian could see Onesy's point. He smiled, then firmly said, "Let's do it!"

"Excellent. Just sign there on the screen with your finger then lie back on the examination table, and Doctor Twosy, our laser specialist will be with you shortly."

Julian signed his name, Julian Garcia. Then Onesy said, "Oh, I forgot. There's another option you can also choose."

Julian hesitated. "So many options!"

"You can choose, within reason, where on your body you want your new gender apparatus to be inserted."

"I don't understand."

"Yes, I'm not surprised. We are a radical LGBTQO center, the leader of the free world. Let me put it this way. Were you a thumb sucker when you were a baby?"

"I'm not sure, I think so. I did suck my thumb until I was about three, so my mom always said."

"Then I'd advise against the option that placed it on or near your thumb.. Your life would be one of pleasured exhaustion."

*

Our Lady of the Waters, Sister Maria, retained control of the cartel, but allowed Francisco the gentle giant much leeway in dealing with obstreperous staff and clients. The result was a sudden increase in disappearances in Mexico City of drug dealers and addicts and the number of addicts lounging around the streets of Mexico city dropped markedly. Most importantly, Sister Maria had issued strict orders to Francisco that there were to be no more violent killings, that he should find another way. And at his meetings with Maria every other day when Francisco kneeled before the cross of Jesus in her tiny little chapel for two, he informed her that her wishes had been obeyed. She did not ask how. Francisco had watched a documentary of the death penalty in America and saw that they did it with a lethal injection saying that it was not violent, so he did the same. After all he had plenty of drugs to inject. The trouble was that the offender had to be tied down which required some violence. So Francisco had devised a method of delivering the overdose

mixed in with a triple shot of tequila. He was even exper-
imenting with a drug overdose bullet that could be fired from
any weapon, including the favorite AK47.

On this morning, Francisco appeared a little nervous as they
kneeled together. And when he told her that Julian was her son
no more, but that she now had a daughter, Our Lady of the
Waters wept with joy. She had always wanted a daughter. Now
Julian—no Julia—would be just like her. Strong, decisive, a
solid figure of a woman. She went back to her small apartment
within the cloisters and got out her collection of Gloria Steinem
photographs. She had always liked the blonde hair, shoulder
length—she hoped Julia would do the same—and her big eyes
and big mouth too. Julia was just like her! And as well,
Francisco had reported that Christian, that stiff Protestant who
had taken her Julian away from her, had died of a snake bite at a
Protestant rally. How very fitting! It affirmed her everlasting
faith in God! She packed up her things and immediately called
for the Learjet. She had to see her new daughter right away! She
texted Alphonso that she was coming and would he meet her at
the airport. He replied that she should come directly to the
Virgin Hall Hopewell campus and ask for the Vice Presidential
Academic Provost's office. They were all assembling there and
would proceed to Christian's funeral which would be held in the
university's inter-faith center. But Alphonso did not text the
details. Simply said that he had a surprise for her.

*

Alphonso now occupied Vice Academic Provost Phoster's
office, sitting in the large chair behind the rather small desk.
Virgil stood at his elbow, his face stricken with grief, his new
pin stripe suit looking drab, as though it also knew of the
disaster that had befallen its master. Pedro as usual remained
just outside the door. Scalpel, of course, hovering around the
back corner of the room, every now and again slithering forward
to welcome someone, rub their arm with feigned intimacy.
Maria arrived, her nun's habit tightly bound around her face, her
pale, clear skinned face, bare, no make-up, lips pale. Though
perhaps, there was some eye shadow, at least it added to her
feigned sadness. A low-pitched buzz of conversation ensued for
some minutes until Julia walked in, dressed in a smashing black
chenille dress, tightly bound to her body, down to her knees, a
single necklace of pearls sparkling against her shapely breast,
looking as fresh as the day they were raised from the ocean

bottom, and the highest of stiletto black Italian leather shoes, narrow and pointed. She made such a startling entrance that the buzz of the room suddenly stopped and gave way to gasps of awe. Such was the spectacle that Alphonso even stood up and pulled his shirt to cover his navel. This was his daughter! Brand spanking new!

Julia smiled broadly. "Sorry I'm a little late," she said, "but I see that I have made it here before the Provost."

Alphonso stepped out from behind the desk and said, "Julia, the former provost had a family emergency and had to take an extended leave of absence. She asked me to convey her best wishes to you and that you have been appointed interim Vice Presidential Academic Provost in her place."

"Oh my God!" cried Julia, putting her now seemingly slender fingers to her lips, painted a faint pink. The buzz of the room erupted again, this time much louder. Someone clapped, and others slowly joined in. "But how come it's you, dad? I mean, I don't know what I mean!"

In fact Alphonso was now the president of the new Virgin Hall University which had merged with New State College, a fact not yet officially announced. Bishop Boswell, the former president had been transferred to the University of Malta where he would orchestrate the migration of illegal Christian immigrants who were coming in hordes from West Africa and other places, making sure they ended up in Sweden, or anywhere else in Northern Europe.

Alphonso continued. "I am also authorized to appoint Reverend Doctor Virgil Bunion as Vice President of Virgin Hall University." Virgil looked up briefly, but quickly cast his eyes back down. "I know this is a very difficult time for him, and I hope this wonderful news will help with his grief."

Virgil said nothing, looked up then down again. Mumbles erupted around the room. Puzzled looks on everyone's faces, except that of tightly bound Maria behind whose blank face, or seemingly so as it peeked out from the nun's habit, lurked her sharp discerning intellect. She knew what her husband was up to.

There were a few students and only one faculty, Distinguished professor Serious Becker, who stood well to the side, looking out the narrow window. Alphonso stepped forward and resisted the temptation to put his arm around his daughter and slap her on the back. He announced, gleaming like never before, "as some of you may know, the Maria and Alphonso Garcia foundation has been doing some serious work behind the scenes to bring this wonderful university into the limelight that it deserves. We have now completed the merger of the New State university with Virgin Hall university, thanks to a most adequate donation from the foundation. The next big change will come in a few weeks when we open the new business incubator park that actually fills the ground between the two universities, and will constitute probably the biggest campus in New Jersey. Some of you may wonder whether this means that New State University will cease to be a state university of New Jersey. I am pleased to announce that it represents a new model for public universities, a public-private partnership that retains the best of both models." Alphonso, amazed how easy it was to talk and talk at a university, paused for an applause. None came. He continued, "and now I announce that our very own, Provost Julia Garcia, will coordinate the academies of both universities. Further, as you know, she has just undergone the most amazing trans-formation, one that qualifies for high honors in the performance section of her curriculum vitae, so high that she has been designated by the university's president as Distinguished Professor."

This last announcement stirred Distinguished professor Becker who stood, his arms folded tightly across his chest. He coughed his well-known intellectual cough and said in a haughty voice, "if this is so important why isn't the president here to make this announcement?"

Alphonso had been waiting for this. "Because I am now the President. The Governor of New Jersey made the appointment at 2.00 pm. yesterday when I was caddying for him at the annual LGBTQ golf tournament, where, in acknowledgment of the occasion, he teed off from the ladies' tee."

Julia rushed to her father and hugged him so hard it hurt his navel. He returned the hug, and noted as he did so, talking over her shoulder, "it is also the new policy of the university to require hugging as the official form of greeting and satisfaction among all persons, regardless of gender, age or any other status."

"And if we don't hug?" intercepted Distinguished professor Becker, unable to hide the hostility.

"You will be sent for counseling with our new hugging specialist." Alphonso looked around the room, and just as he did so, the piercing call of a tenor voice echoed through the corridors. The door opened, and in came Sisto, resplendent in his curly beard and red cape. "I present to you our new hugging counsellor, the renowned tenor and water engineer of Rome, Sisto Frontinus!"

At this point, Maria's knees buckled and she dropped to the floor. Something had happened to her! Jesus playing tricks on her again? Sisto reached down and offered his hand. "My dear," he sang, "please rise so I can hug you!"

Scalpel, acting as though he knew all about this new arrangement from the beginning, slithered forward and helped Maria up. Alphonso nodded to Pedro who quietly left and went to meet the funeral director of Christian's funeral. His pocket bulged with rolls of US dollars.

*

Distinguished professor Serious Becker would not let it go. As the group made its way to the University Club for a lavish celebration lunch, he hurried forward to speak with Alphonso. "Would you mind telling me where the President has gone? He and I were doing some important research on discrimination against rats by exterminating companies in Newark. We were about to release our results, which, if taken seriously, will have extensive implications for all people living in downtown Newark."

Alphonso pulled his shirt over his navel and said, "the former president had to leave suddenly. There was an emergency in his family, I believe. Some kind of accident. But don't worry, my assistant Pedro is helping him on his way as we speak."

Having paired off, the group approached the faculty club. Virgil walked arm-in-arm with Julia, Maria with Sisto, and Alphonso with Scalpel at his elbow. They were greeted at the entrance of the club by a young LGBTQ student, dressed in a sharp tuxedo, tapered black trousers with a black satin ribbon down the sides. The club was a large room, obviously two former classrooms turned into one. On the front wall was a large screen on which was projected in real time, the video of the hearse carrying Christian's coffin. The lunch room was décorated in white lilies. Each person as they entered received a glass of Champaign. Large round tables had been set, enough for six at each, but since there were only eight people, two were seated at each table. Bottles of tequila, lemons and salt were ostentatiously displayed on each table, amidst several shot glasses.

"We have ten courses to eat through," announced Scalpel, "so please do not hesitate to get started on your oysters. You may, if you wish, dribble your tequila on the oysters, an old Mexican tradition. If we are not finished in time, we can watch the funeral on the screen. But I think we should make it in time for the eulogy which vice president Virgil Bunion will be delivering. Julia tugged at his sleeve, and Virgil stood briefly then slumped back down.

"Is there any coffee?" asked Virgil, harking back to his days outside Starbucks with his drunken brothers.

Scalpel replied, "President Garcia's assistant Pedro has gone to get some from Starbucks. He should be back here in just a few minutes. The clink of cutlery against china sounded, and on cue, a line of waiters, as many as there were guests, marched in with the soup of the day, Vegan Miso, imported from Kyoto. Now came the deeper clanking of soup spoons. But then, a sound that only those who had known Virgil could recognize, grew louder. The sound of a kettle drum, and intermittent screams of "get away you bastard! Let me go!"

Julia squeezed Virgil's hand, puzzled by her response. She had a strange feeling that she had heard that voice before, and certainly knew the sound of the drum. It was just like the drum of Virgil, sitting next to her, his face long and drawn, his jaw dropping, but mouth tightly closed. It was the face of a man ready to explode. The drum became louder, and there was banging on the door. The tuxedoed student looked askance at Alphonso, then to Scalpel, who nodded to open the door. He did so, and in burst a scruffy, spit covered bearded long haired filthy creature, banging his kettle drum, making guttural noises that were supposed to be the words of the hymn Onward Christian Soldiers. He pushed himself forward, butting the tuxedoed student in the chest, leaving awful gooey slime all down his front. The student recoiled in horror and ran out looking for the bathroom.

"Quiet everyone, please!" cried Virgil looking up at the screen where six students from St. Roberts carried the coffin of Christian to the front of the beautifully flowered chapel of the crematorium. Julia helped him stand and supported him in his moment of grief. It must be terrible for a father to lose his son, she thought. And Christian, she was sure, had been such a good son. Though she had to admit to a strange sense of nothing. She knew Christian, did she not? They roomed together at St.

Roberts for four years, how could she not? But strangely she remembered very little of their lives together. Just the recitation of the psalms at Lauds every day. She pictured him now, as the tall, clean cut young man, the picture of youth. Someone, perhaps in another life, she might be attracted to. But as of yesterday, she thought of herself as the second Gloria Steinem. Indeed, she had her vagina!

The drum became so loud it was deafening. The filthy creature threw his drumstick at the screen and dropped his drum on the hard floor. "Don't let them burn me! I'll not go to hell! I did nothing wrong! Since when was loving another, whoever he might be, wrong? Jesus said we should love each other, Love! Love! Love!" The creature ran forward, knocking Scalpel aside who rolled easily away, and grabbed Virgil by the sagging lapels of his pin-stripe suit. He pulled him roughly forward and their foreheads banged each other. "Do you hear me? I've done nothing wrong!" yelled the creature, spit and dribble flying all over Virgil's distraught face.

Julia made a weak attempt to pull Virgil back, push the creature away. Then she got a handful of the creature's scruffy beard and pulled it as hard as he could. The creature screamed, dropped to his knees, then tried to run out the door, but did not know which way to turn. It was then that he dropped to his knees again and looked up at the screen where the coffin was now slowly passing into the furnace. "I'm coming, Lord, he cried. I'm coming!" He dropped down and rolled around the floor, then became still. Those not standing sat, looking silently at their plates. A line of waiters appeared with trays of the main course, roast hare with apple and cheese garnish.

Virgil calmed down. Julia helped him wipe the muck from his face. He stiffened. Looked down at the poor wretch on the floor. Now it seemed to be sobbing. Christian goodwill enveloped him and he got up slowly then bent down to look more closely at the poor wretch. With Pedro's help, he managed to roll him over, to look more closely at his face. Now he could see it! He saw himself! He looked up to see if Alphonso was watching. He was. He pushed back the beard, pulled the scraggly hair away from its face. And there it was! Another miracle of Alphonso's making! He kneeled, his hands clasped as in prayer and said in a soft voice, "thank you Lord," then standing, raising his arms up to the heavens, he cried loudly and with great authority, "he is risen! My son has come back from the dead!"

It was true what Alphonso had said. Feed snakes cannabis
and it weakens their venom.

*

"I'm not stupid you know," said Distinguished professor Becker
to Dr. Scalpel as they left the lunch room, "that was our former
vice presidential academic provost in the coffin."

Scalpel produced a small roll of one hundred dollar bills. "I
have been authorized to give you this and to strongly recommend that you remain stupid."

Becker quickly took the money and put it away under his
academic gown. "Who are you, Scalpel, anyway? You came out
of nowhere."

"I am here to make sure our country is safe and secure," said
Scalpel with a sneaky smile.

"Oh, I see. You're CIA. No, wait a minute, FBI."

"You had better go back to your office right away or I will
have to have you dispatched," said Scalpel with a grin. Becker
quickly walked away, but Scalpel looked down, worried, walked
a few steps towards his office, then back again; walked towards
the Provost's office, then back again. He could not decide which
way to go. Life had caught up with him. CIA or FBI? Which
was which? The pointy heads over in psychology and even political science were always on about human agency. Whose
agency was he? His own, or some agency of the government, or
even now, a Mexican cartel? It dawned on him that he himself
did not know who he was, or more precisely, who was his
master. He decided to go talk with the one person who would
understand, who must know all about identity crises.

*

There was much work to be done. Julia looked out her narrow
second floor window and surveyed the campus. It was a brisk
sunny fall day. The students were gathering around the fountain,
others hanging about outside the library. Her mom and Sisto had
just left. Maria and Sisto were off to Rome and the Vatican on a
hush-hush mission. Only Alphonso knew the details, at least
that is what she thought. She felt down at her crotch just to
make sure everything was still as it was supposed to be. The
LBGTQO surgery had been such a success. To think, that she
now had Gloria Steinem's vagina! When she told Maria she
almost collapsed with joy, almost ripped off her nun's habit,
wanted to kiss her all over. She was so proud!

A timid knock at the door. Julia sat on her government issued office chair and noted another change that she must make, change all the furniture of the campus, get rid of the prison-made junk. Before she could ask who it was, the door handle turned slowly and Scalpel peeped in. "May I see you for a brief moment? I have a bit of a problem."

Julia, once always the loving one, open to all comers, trusting, suddenly found herself on the defensive. Was this PTSD as Onesie had mentioned? "I am very busy, how did you get by my secretary?" she asked curtly.

"I don't know who I am," blurted Scalpel.

"What? Dr. Scalpel, I have more to do than be your psychologist."

"But I thought that, you know, what you've just been through, I thought…"

"Thought what? Come on! Out with it, man that you are, or should I say, ought to be!"

Scalpel recoiled in horror, his entire body seemed to shrink as though he were the wicked witch of the west melting into the floor. This was not Julian, the fine young man he knew at St. Robert's. It was someone else! Julia stood up from her desk, marched to her window, hands on hips, legs apart, head held high, shoulders back, straight hair hanging shoulder length, a touch of eye shadow around her eyes. Sca;pel edged back towards the door.

"Well what is it? Out with it!" said Julia, firmly, with a smile that mocked.

"I, I, now I know who you are," muttered Scalpel, "you're, you're…"

"Your provost, Dr. Scalpel. And you are one of my administrative assistants, though Lord knows what you do."

"I'm the associate Dean for the School of Diversity and Discrimination studies."

"I know that. But who do you really work for? Not my father, I hope, sent to spy on me perhaps?"

"That's just it. I mean, Dr. Garcia."

"Yes?"

"I work for the CIA, I mean, no, the FBI. Sometimes both. I don't really know whose agency I belong to."

"The human agency, you dimwit," snarled Julia. "Anyway, if you work for the FBI you're a Protestant, for the CIA, a Catholic, for both, you're an atheist. Simple as that!"

Scalpel shrank away even more, horror-stricken by this verbal aggression. And then it popped out, he couldn't help it. "You're Gloria Steinem, aren't you?"

Julia took a step towards him, and looking down at him smiled, "little man, you don't know how close to the truth you are!"

"I. I, don't know whose agency I am any more. There's the CIA, FBI, and then your father, he's so powerful, and now you. I thought that you would know what it's like to be..." Scalpel's voice trailed off into a mumble.

Julia crossed her arms and stood over Scalpel who cowered in a heap at her feet. "Poor little man! You're having an identity crisis. Too bad there's no surgical procedure to fix your conflicted condition." Then she looked away, out the narrow window. The students were walking to and from their classes. She leaned down, offering Scalpel her hand and said with a smile, "I think I know what could help you discover yourself. Who you really are."

Scalpel took her hand and struggled to stand, still cowed over, his shoulders hunched up, chin on chest. He dared to speak, looking out from under his furrowed brow. "You do?"

"I will speak to our new President, my father that is, of course. He has a new project with the Vatican in Rome. He will need someone just like you to keep an eye on the project, if you see what I mean." Julia winked slightly.

"Oh, yes of course." Scalpel had no idea what Julia meant.

"There's a cardinal there, a cardinal Benitez. He needs watching. You're a Catholic, right?"

"Oh, I suppose so, I mean, I can be if necessary." Scalpel looked to the door. He wanted more than anything else to get away from this witch whose fingernails grew longer as he looked.

Julia returned to her desk and sat at her computer. "You may leave now. And please, do not come to me again without an appointment."

*

Virgil ordered a decaf latte with his Starbucks card. He looked outside where the scum were rolling around on the grassy patch, peeing against the brick wall. The new university vice president for sanitary services had issued an order that the scum were not allowed to use the Starbucks conveniences unless they had a university ID. He looked outside for Christian and saw him peeing against the small tree, now wilting, obviously dying from too much urine in its water. How does a father save a son? A son who had, he must admit to himself, become too much like himself, or more precisely, like he used to be until Alphonso saved him. Maybe he could do the same for Christian? Maybe he could try again to get Julia to come to Starbucks to help Christian get over his loss? Julia's transformation, a resurrection itself, had deprived Christian of the other half of who he was. The other half he lost by dying. Why didn't her resurrection affirm his belief in Jesus? Maybe he should join the scum outside once again and try to talk some sense into Christian? But he knew that none of this would work. He had tried, perhaps not hard enough, to get Julia to come with him to Starbucks and she had looked at him as though he were mad. When he told her that she owed it to Christian, she stared at him and snapped, "he's your son. Be a father!" And he responded, "but you loved him" and she snapped back, "I have never loved anyone but myself!"

"Virgil!" called the barista, "nonfat decaf latte!"

He looked at the cup sitting there in its sleeve, the lid pushed tightly on. And then he had an idea. "You know what?" he asked, "could you make me a mocha with lots of cream? And could you hold my latte for a moment? I have to slip out and get my briefcase. I left it in my office. Back in five minutes."

*

Virgil returned, picked up both drinks and went to a quiet corner of the Starbucks, to the table reserved for those with special needs. Christian was still outside rolling around on the grass with the scum. What was needed was a father to take charge. Treat his son like a son, make him do what he was told, and first things first, he must be made clean in body before he can be clean in mind. Cleanliness is next to godliness, wasn't that right? He opened his briefcase and pulled out a razor, a Phillips One Blade razor and set it on the briefcase. Then he turned to the barista and said, "excuse me, do you think I could borrow a Starbucks apron? I have to add a medical supplement to the mocha and don't want to get it on my clothes." The barista complied, though looked puzzled.

Now came the hard part. He donned the apron and marched outside to the tree of pee, where Christian sat feebly beating his drum. Virgil saw, with satisfaction, that Christian's heart was not in it. He kicked the drum away, and Christian looked up, a silly grin on his face, saliva dribbling down through his blonde

beard. Virgil grabbed him by his beard and pulled him up.
Christian did not even yelp. In his sorry state, his body automatically gave into Virgil's physical strength, the strength of a
father about to discipline his son, now very much a child. He
gripped Christian's arm and pulled him along into Starbucks,
straight to the One Blade and to the mocha with extra cream. He
sat Christian down, flipped open the lid of the mocha, dipped
his fingers into the cream and slapped it all over Christian's
beard, making a perfect lather. "Keep your tongue in your mouth
or I'll cut it off!" warned Virgil. Then with firm, long strokes,
pulling the razor up his neck to his chin, he shaved a clean path
through the beard. Christian sat, trying to lick the cream, Virgil
pushing his head this way and that until the entire beard was
gone. The transformation was truly magical. Christian's eyes
came to life, and he looked at his father with wonder. Something
had happened to him, deep inside. Virgil stepped back to admire
his handiwork. "Son," he said, wiping the cream off the razor on
a Starbucks napkin, "welcome home!"

Christian, still licking his lips, gazed at his father, but as he
spoke, his voice was flat. "I love your suit," he said, "could I get
one like it?"

Virgil was so happy, he replied, "I'll get you anything you
want, my dear, dear son. Not only have you come back from the
dead, but you have come back to me."

"There's just one thing," said Christian, "once I'm dressed
up, I want to see Julian."

"You mean Julia, she is now. I can arrange that, I'm sure she
will be pleased to meet with you. But you understand she is a
completely different person. Her surgery changed everything."

"I think I understand. I hadn't realized. She had me erased,
right?"

"I guess you could say that they surgically removed you from
her memory."

"So everything we did together?"

"Gone, I imagine."

Christian sat back and drank the rest of the mocha in one gulp
and said with resolve, "then I know what I have to do."

"Where did she have it done?"

"The University LGBTQ emergency care center, I believe."

"Is it close by?"

"Right around the corner. Why? You're not planning on a sex
change too, are you?" asked Virgil, worried yet again.

Christian was not really himself. He spoke in a flat monotone. "Not exactly." Christian saw clearly what he must do. Get rid of sex altogether. He would be free at last!

*

Christian's meeting with Julia was brief. Virgil had convinced him to ask her advice on the University LGBTQ emergency care center. He had been surprised to find both President Garcia and Scalpel present. And of course, Pedro sat quietly in the corner of the room, then left to stand outside the door as soon as they arrived. Julia walked behind her desk, holding out her hand, which Christian mechanically shook.

Julia, dressed in a resplendent black satin business suit, the shirt open at the neck just enough to invite curiosity, looked Christian in the eyes, blue and strikingly beautiful. They were an object of fascination, but of no interest to her. He was, simply, another faculty member. Christian shook her hand weakly and looked away. This was an impossible meeting, he with his head stuffed with memories of their passionate past, she with none. He was a stranger to her and Christian felt it. It was as though he had died, which of course he had, almost, but for Julia he had not risen. She smiled and said, "you have met our new president, Alphonso Garcia, I believe?"

Alphonso reached over and shook his hand. "I was just leaving. I want you to know how very much relieved we are that you recovered from your unfortunate accident. Your father tells me that you have been through a lot, recovering from that terrible experience. It's a miracle you are here with us. I thank the Lord that you were saved. We look forward to your important contributions to discrimination and diversity."

Julia looked at her father then to Christian. She was amazed to see that her father had changed so much. When he was drug lord, he was a man of few words, just crisp orders barked whenever necessary. Now he was a president of the largest public university in America, and he suddenly talked in paragraphs!

"I'm sorry I put you all to the bother of having to go to my funeral," replied Christian forcing a grin. "I have an appointment at the LGBTQ center for a checkup, just to make sure I am all there," he lied. Virgil nudged him, trying to get him to ask Julia about the LGBTQ center. But Christian stepped away.

In any case, Julia spoke up. "I can tell you that they are very professional down there, a credit to this university. She eyed him closely and wondered what it was he was having done there. But then, it was none of her business, unless, of course, it changed the overall diversity composition of the department of diversity and discrimination studies. "And now if you don't mind, my father, I should say President Garcia, and I have some important business to attend to." The door opened and Pedro stepped in to usher Christian out. Virgil went to follow, but Julia called him back. "The business also includes you, Dr. Bunion. You too, Dr. Scalpel." Scalpel of course, had been there all along, inhabiting his little corner of the room, eyes darting this way and that.

Alphonso turned to Virgil. "You must go to Sicily and meet with the Great Godfather. I have heard that an illness has befallen the Pope. He may or may not die, but we want to be ready with his replacement, who will be Pollagrande. We can't do it without the help of Great Godfather and his network of Neapolitans and Sicilians. Of course, he knows what to do, he just needs to know when, and who must be worked on."

Virgil asked, "and then what do I do?"

"You go to Rome to meet up with Pollagrande and arrange for him to come to New Jersey on a State visit, to your Pentecostal meeting. This will celebrate the joining of the New State University with Virgin Hall."

"And me?" asked Scalpel, feeling left out as usual.

"Why not have him meet up with Maria and Sisto in Rome?" Julia suggested, looking devilishly at Alphonso.

Alphonso said with a straight face. "Yes, they will need all the help they can get. The underground should suit him, don't you think Provost Garcia?"

*

Christian, Pedro at his heels, headed for the LGBTQ center. He pushed Pedro away from him and said, "thanks for your help, but I don't need you."

"I've got my orders," said Pedro, " I have to be with you to make sure you are all right. My boss the President, now your boss too, said I have to. I always follow his orders."

For some reason, Christian felt a sudden revulsion against this small, wizened little Mexican. He imagined him sitting in a desert sleeping under his sombrero, his AK47 lying across his lap.

He was greeted by Onesie, asked the usual questions, signed the usual forms, and finally Twosie came into the room where

Christian was spread-eagled on the Leonardo Da Vinci rack as was the usual practice, naked, incredibly vulnerable.

"I am required by law to ask you again, have you been advised as to the consequences of your medical procedure?" announced Twosie.

Christian stared at Twosie. "I have. I want to be neutered. I want to be free."

"You understand that the procedure you have chosen will be the removal of testicles, but retention of the penis, reduced in size to fifty percent of original, its cap cut off? And that it is irreversible? We do store the parts in our cryo-crypt for ninety days, but frankly, even though we can re-attach the parts, once frozen, they do not function as well as they do when fresh."

Christian squirmed a little to the extent that his body could move while attached to the rack. He looked down at himself. He looked at Twosie. Could you release my right hand? I'd just like to feel myself one last time."

"I'm sorry, but our procedural rules do not allow masturbation before the procedure," answered Twosie in its lilting robotic voice.

"I'm not asking that. I just want to say good-bye to them."

"Them?"

"You know. My equipment down there, between my legs."

"I'll have to call for a second opinion. No one has ever asked this before. Just one moment and I'll have Threesie come in to assist. It has a lot more experience than do I."

Threesie, a small drone robot with a large head, flew into the room and fluttered around Christian's body, It settled on Christian's head and said, "he may touch, but only for twenty seconds. But he must not move them because it will require our setting up the lasers all over again. And if he has an erection, we will have to postpone the surgery."

Christian shook his head, forgetting the drone that cried, "oops" and flew across the room and settled on Twosie's head. Christian looked down again. The memories of Julian swept into his head, his eyes watered with grief. He could not live with such pain. It must be done. "I've changed my mind," he said, "I don't want to touch it. Let's go ahead."

Threesie saw that Christian was suffering and as a good robot it wanted to relieve him. "There is one way that we could reduce your fear of having nothing down there. It is a special option. We can retain the outward form, even skin, and replace their internal flesh and other bodily materials with our patented bio-silicon implants. In this way, you will still be able to feel that your equipment as you call it, is there physically, but there will be no sensation in them at all. Of course, as an extra special option we could also add erection capability, but it is our impression that you want none of that."

"I'm done with sex," Christian sighed. "I'm pretty big down there, as you may have noticed. If I keep anything there that big, even without sensation, I'll start wanting it to work. No. The first option is best. Thanks for the offer anyway."

With that, he slumped down and relaxed on the rack, gave himself up to the surgeon's laser. And when he awakened, he was indeed a new man.

*

Pedro was waiting for him. They stood on the curb outside the emergency room, waiting for the traffic to pass by. A truck, loaded with crates of small glass bottles approached. Christian nudged Pedro just enough for him to step off the curb. Pedro never knew what hit him. The truck screeched to a halt, making things worse, the front wheels skidding over Pedro's squashed body where they came to a halt.

Christian looked at the mess, the blood trickling into the gutter. Medics rushed out from the emergency center. Christian walked calmly away. He was cured. And now he saw clearly what he must do next. The past had to be neutralized too.

13. Erections

"It can't be you," said Cardinal Benitez, "you're too close to him."

"I know. It's up to you, then. But how?" answered Cardinal Pollagrande.

"Can you do without Estelle for a few days?" asked Benitez.

Pollagrande took a big bite of the cornetto that Estelle had baked for him fresh this morning. "That's a lot to ask," he said, his mouth full, spraying crumbs all over the white tablecloth.

"She might appreciate a change of scenery, maybe?" joked Benitez.

"I'm not going to let her get involved in anything nefarious. She's as pure as one could get. Robots are far more trustworthy than humans," said Pollagrande as he slurped his latte. He was serious. After the Pope and the Vatican, Estelle was the most important thing in his life. Perhaps *the* most important.

"Fair enough. I envy you, I do, forgive me Lord," said Benitez, "but I think she is the only way for me to get close to Pope Shorty to do what is necessary."

"If you plan to use her to poison him, forget it. I won't be complicit."

"You must be completely ignorant of how I do it. So I can't tell you what role Estelle would play. Let me just say that she will not be involved in any way directly to annul the Pope." Benitez looked around the room. "This apartment isn't bugged, I hope?"

"No, of course not. I have it checked every week," replied Pollagrande.

"What about Estelle?" asked Benitez, always cautious.

Pollagrande called for Estelle. She appeared at the kitchen door. Benitez was struck, as he always was, by her beauty. Her makers must be close to God too, he thought.

Estelle had apparently heard every word they said and crooned, in her soft Marylin Monroe voice, "no bugs, my love.

Checked yesterday." She trotted quickly over to Pollagrande and gave him a little peck on the cheek. Pollagrande looked up and said, lovingly, "thank you my sweetheart. As always, I depend on you, for everything."

Benitez stirred in his chair. "OK, I get it. Hopefully, I will not need her for more than a day or two. Will she go to another? How much training will it need?"

Pollagrande looked seriously at Benitez. "She can be switched off and attached to another master, I believe. But that's only what her makers told me when I first got her, thanks to you, by the way. I am forever in your debt."

"I am going to loan her to the Holy Father," said Benitez, tugging nervously at his collar.

"What? No way! Anyhow, he will reject such an offer, and will banish you back to Myanmar, or wherever," complained Pollagrande.

"It will be a challenge, I know that. But it's well worth it, isn't it? Given what you want?"

Pollagrande stood up and embraced Estelle, kissed her full on her wonderfully soft lips. Ran his fingers though her hair. "Would you like to attend to the Holy Father, darling?"

"If you say so, holy one," she answered.

Benitez stood to go, put out his hand to touch Estelle. It upset Pollagrande. "I'd like to say goodbye to her, if you don't mind. Come back in an hour, and I'll have her ready. I saw that you are on the Papal roster to see him later this morning."

"That's right. This morning it will begin," said Benitez, backing away.

*

Pollagrande had dressed Estelle according to the instructions he received from Benitez. A white silk blouse, unbuttoned to show a deep cleavage, pulled in at the waist to accentuate her perfectly formed breast. Her lips were painted a bright red, blonde hair pulled back and wound up into a topknot, which she would be instructed to let down as she bowed to the Pope. Her dress, of the purest white cotton from Egypt, blossomed out, in the style of the 1950s, but flared with a touch of gold thread at the edges. And short, reaching only to her knees.

When Benitez and Estelle arrived at the outer sanctum of the *La Clementina*, always busy with people coming and going, the Pope's secretary, a well-scrubbed young man in his twenties tried in vain to ignore the sexuality that oozed from every curve of Estelle's body. "You can't take her in there," he murmured to Benitez, knowing full well that he was out of line speaking to an esteemed cardinal like that.

Benitez smiled, "I understand, but we already have an audience scheduled."

"Of course, your holiness. My apologies." He clasped his hands together and led the way to the door, but in spite of himself, he blurted out to Estelle, "you know, the skull of Saint Peter used to be housed in the Clementine Chapel."

"Oh yes, I know," answered Estelle, "and now it's in the church of St. John in Laterano."

The Swiss guard opened the door and stepped aside. The gold edging of Estelle's frock fluttering as she walked, perfectly at home amidst the gold leaf that decorated the chapel from ceiling to floor. Indeed, it rivaled the Sistine Chapel, in its ornate glory. The room was mostly used for conferences of bishops and cardinals, but this Pope liked to have his private audiences here. It was awe inspiring, gave him a clear edge of authority—as if he did not need any more. He sat at the head of an enormous conference table that would comfortably seat fifty people. Only this short Pope sat *on* the table where comfortable cushions had been arranged for him.

Benitez dismissed the secretary who left and closed the door behind him. He led Estelle up to the Pope where Estelle curtsied deeply. The Pope offered his bare foot, the toes discolored by fungus, and Estelle kissed it profusely. Benitez beamed and announced, "Holy Father, I present to you Estelle, the most beautiful robot in the world. She is at your service."

Pope Shorty stared at her in wonder. "Benitez, you amaze me. Nothing is beyond your grasp. She is truly a robot?"

"Truly, but she's attuned to human needs and desires. The perfect solution to the sex scandals that have ravaged our church throughout the world."

"Solution? How so?" asked Pope Shorty.

"As you know, Holy Father, we are under great pressure to allow our priests to marry. If we provide all priests who want them, a robot like Estelle as their partner, it will eliminate their acknowledged sexual abuse of the young boys of our church."

"But, why would they switch from boys to Estelle? Surely the logic would be to have robot boys?"

"Holy Father, you are way ahead of me. Indeed, we could also offer such robots. But I think first we should begin with women like Estelle to head off the media pressure to allow our priests to marry."

"And what do you say, my good woman?" asked the Pope, uncertain how to address her.

Estelle leaned down and licked his fungus covered big toenail. "I am at your service, Holy Father."

The Pope's usually stern face contorted as he tried not to show a smile of satisfaction. He looked down on her glistening blonde hair that now hung over her shoulders. But he noted that although he acknowledged to himself and God that he wanted her, there was nothing in his body that said so. Benitez suspected as much and smiled solicitously as he said, "I have a blue pill that will help you experience the robot's capabilities."

"Benitez, sometimes I worry that you have been sent to me by the devil."

"My dear Holiness, the exact opposite is true. There is nothing in the bible or Jesus's sayings that can be remotely interpreted to prohibit sex with a robot. It is forbidden with all kinds of beings, but a robot is not a being. It is a creation of man, who was the creation of God. Is it not? Robots are a gift from God!"

"Temptation comes in many forms," muttered the Pope.

"Of course. But you must see that this solution will save the church."

Pope Shorty took a deep breath. "If we gave up our cherished principle of celibacy, our church, our great edifice, would slowly but surely become like the Protestants, divided into endless sects, fighting each other."

"But, holiness, having sex with a robot is not a violation of celibacy. It's true that the bible forbids masturbation. But having sex with a robot is not masturbation, unless you define all sex with another, as masturbation. It's sex, but it's celibate sex. Don't you see?"

"But if we allow it, where will it end up? Once tasted, our priests will want more and more, will they not? That's why sex is prohibited to our priesthood," answered the Pope, sensing that he was losing the argument.

Benitez retorted. "Prohibition does not work, as the Americans of all people know. The scandals that have enveloped our church are clear evidence of that. Sex with robots is a release. Besides, Estelle is only the beginning. I am sure that we will be able to make more and better robots, designed to not only satisfy priests, but also control them. After all, isn't that what happens to married men? Their wives control them. Our robots could do the same!"

Estelle sucked the Pope's toes some more, holding his foot in both her slender soft hands. But she quickly withdrew when she heard a knock on the door. Benitez hurried to the door and took an ornate tray of tea and cookies from a waiter. He returned and set it down on the table next to His Holiness and said, "Holy Father, take this tea and three of these little blue pills whenever you feel the need." He poured the tablets out of a large jar full of them. "I will usher Estelle to your private apartment in the Apostolic palace. It is best that you personally experience what we will be doing for all our priests. Jesus would have it no other way."

Estelle now began to lick the Pope's ankle, slowly creeping up his leg, the varicose veins throbbing. The Pope took the pills and swallowed them with a gulp of black tea. Then leaned down and lightly pushed Estelle's head back, her tongue now licking her gorgeous red lips. It took great effort for Pope Shorty to retain his stern countenance, for which he was well known. But he did, and knew that he must be even stronger. He managed to slide off the end of the table and stand above Estelle, looking down at her. Under his heavy Papal garments he felt a twinge. A twinge that he had not felt since he was himself a choir boy. "Cardinal Benitez," he ordered, "see that this young robot is settled into my apartment, and tell my secretary to cancel all my appointments for the rest of the day." The twinge was now more than a twinge.

Benitez did as he was told. He made sure to leave the jar of blue pills and a glass of water beside the Pope's bed.

*

There was once a Pope who died of the hiccups. He had them for months, maybe even years. And finally they killed him. Something similar had descended on Pope Shorty. But it was not hiccups. It was an erection. His day with Estelle, carefully orchestrated by Benitez, drew him into a vortex of pleasure the likes of which he had never imagined, even as a teenager when he was abused by the choirmaster. It would not be kind to the Catholic church to dwell on such details. The manipulations by Cardinal Benitez were masterful, though even he was surprised at how well plan B turned out. He accompanied Estelle to the Pope's apartment hidden away in the Apostolic palace, and the Pope, having swallowed three of the blue pills, followed on his litter from the Clementine chapel. His erection grew so much and so quickly, he struggled to arrange his heavy robes to cover the bulge.

Pope Shorty's housemaid, a buxom woman from Northern Ireland, one who did not mince words, stood at the door when Benitez arrived with Estelle, and refused to allow entry. She ignored Benitez, looked Estelle up and down with considerable disapproval, then said in her rough voice and thick Irish brogue, "and what business could you have with the Holy Father?"

"This is Estelle, the Holy Father's special guest. She will be staying with him for a day or two. He is coming right behind me," answered Benitez with as much authority as he could muster. He took Estelle's smooth hand and the housemaid's rough hand and pressed them together. Estelle smiled her most beautiful smile which naturally repulsed the housemaid, used only to bitterness and reproach. "I'll not allowed it," she said. And at that moment the noise of the elevator sounded, and the Pope arrived, his four African slaves transporting him on his litter. The housemaid saw immediately the Pope's flushed face, his cheeks as red as hers when she was angry (most of the time), but more important, the arrangement of his robes, all messed up, as though they had simply been dropped on him with no attempt to arrange them. "Holy Father!" she exclaimed, "what have you been doing?"

Pope Shorty's nostrils widened his upper lip curled. "Sister. Be off with you. And do not return until I send for you."

"But Your Holiness, your robes, your blazing eyes! What have they done to you!"

"Woman! Leave us! Or I will have you shipped to Manchester!" commanded the Pope with as much dignity as he could muster, which was not much under the circumstances.

Benitez bowed to the Pope and stretched out his hand to the housemaid. "Come, sister, I will accompany you back to your apartment. His Holiness must be alone with his special guest who brings to him the warmest greetings from Jesus himself. That will be sure to calm him. You know the saying, 'calm follows every storm'."

"No that is not the saying. You have it backwards," barked the sister. She let go of Estelle's hand, stepped aside, and barged past Benitez. "I'll find my own way back," she called over her shoulder. "And I will be speaking to Cardinal Pollagrande about this!"

The slaves let Pope Shorty down at the door. Estelle immediately helped him with his robes and escorted him inside. Benitez followed, only to the end of the foyer. "Make sure you take another two blue pills every few hours, then stop. Estelle will take care of everything."

And so the Pope's descent into the Hell of Heavenly pleasure began. And the erection, while it served many purposes and received many caresses from Estelle, continued to stiffen, throbbed unmercifully, yet the Pope persisted, following Cardinal Benitez's advice, and took the pills, and certainly fell under the spell of Estelle's many seductive techniques.

Cardinal Benitez had the housemaid shipped off to Belfast where she was set up in a little row house of her own, a generous lifetime pension in addition to what she would receive from the government. But she was the least of his problems. The media were clamoring for a sight of the Pope who had been missing for two days. This was unheard of.

*

Cardinal Benitez chose to make the announcement on the steps of *San Giovanni in Laterano*, away from the hustle and bustle of Saint Peter's, where, at this very moment a crowd was gathering seeking a glimpse of the Pope, feeding on rumors that he was on his death bed. A short article had appeared on page two of the *Corriere della Sera*, the headline reading POPE HAS SEXUAL DISFUNCTION? with an anonymous byline. It insinuated that the Vatican was hiding the Pope from the people because he was having a sex change operation, which supposedly was occurring inside the Pope's own apartment. Citing Vatican sources who were familiar with the Pope's daily movements, it referred to Cardinal Benitez as having tried to pass off the unavailability of the Pope as a case of hiccups, referring to Pope Pius XII who suffered from that complaint for a number of years.

Surprisingly, at least to Benitez, not that many reporters showed up at *San Giovanni* where he stood at the top of the steps. He had decided to meet the charges head on, hopefully to dispel any further rumors. There were no TV cameras, though, again surprising. He called the small gaggle to attention. "Ladies and gentlemen of the press. I am here to inform you that the Pope is resting quietly in his apartment. He is not having a sex change operation, but he is suffering from a sexual malfunction that I previously, perhaps unadvisedly, likened to a case of the hiccups. The fact is," Benitez paused for effect, "he has an erection that will not go away, and is in considerable discomfort."

Murmurs and titters spread throughout the small crowd of reporters. Phones suddenly were at their ears and already the sound of police sirens came from a distance as the TV trucks drove at full speed ignoring red lights, to get to the press conference. But of course, all the phones were now recording video. "Could you repeat that please, Cardinal Benitez?" came the shouts. "How long has he had it?" What is the treatment?"

Benitez answered calmly. "We are trying many treatments, including cold showers, ice packs, but so far nothing has worked." Then he added. "I beg you all to stop joking. This is a serious ailment. As you all may know, Pope Shorty has a weak heart, and erections put a lot of pressure on the heart."

"You mean he might die?" gasped a reporter.

"I would not go that far, but I would not rule it out, especially as we know that one Pope in the past died of the hiccups."

"Isn't there an obvious solution?" asked a devilish reporter with a dirty grin.

"What is that?" replied Benitez cautiously.

"Send in a prostitute! There are plenty out on the Via Appia!"

Benitez acted offended, though he was, in fact, defensive. "Really! You know that is beyond question. All we priests, including the Pope, make a vow of celibacy..."

The crowd interrupted with jeers and hisses. Benitez could not face them anymore. He turned and ran into *San Giovanni*, ran down the main aisle, then disappeared into one of the many anterooms, into to the seminary that lay hidden behind. There would be headlines in all the papers of the world in a matter of minutes. What he needed to do was to check on the bottle of blue pills and hope that they had done their job. He borrowed a common brown robe of a student priest, and took the 64 bus to the Vatican. And by the time he arrived, there were already large crowds of worshippers milling about in front of Saint Peter's steps and around the fountains. This would not stop until the Pope's erection went down and he could be seen in public. Of course, he could not be seen in public sporting the massive erection. As he stepped down from the bus, he looked across to the crowd and saw the familiar figure of Sisto and next to him Maria. They held hands, risky, given that Maria still wore her tightly fitting habit. And hovering behind them was that sneak Scalpel, and hovering further behind him was a gaunt figure,

sunken eyes, dressed in ill-fitting jeans and a leather jacket, on
which was drawn in studs, the two symbols of gender facing
away from each other, a red line struck through them, as in a
stop sign. It had to be Christian. But where was Virgil? He
turned away and walked towards the Vatican apartments, stopping briefly to speak with the Swiss guards at the gate. Then on
up to the Papal apartment to retrieve the jar of little blue pills.

*

Sisto slid his arm inside Maria's cape and pressed his fingers
into the soft part of her side, not far from her belly. She turned
to him, her eyes full of expectation. Their time with the Great
Godfather had been too controlled. They were seated at the table
on opposite sides, Virgil had seen to that. And Scalpel had not
left them alone for one minute. But their work had been
completed, the Great Godfather had given his blessing for the
water project once again, and had given assurances that should
anything befall the Pope, his network of spies would immediately begin their work, their pockets bursting with US dollars
thanks to the benevolence of El Padrino, to take care of the
Conclave that would ensue.

Maria listened intently to Sisto's speech about the Bernini
fountain where they stood. "Completed in 1677..." but the noise
of the water drowned out even his high tenor voice. "Come, my
dear, let us go to where we can hear each other breathe," said
Sisto as he tugged at Maria's waist, then led her through a
narrow passageway between the great curved columns, down a
long flight of steps behind the Vatican post office. He unlocked
a heavy metal door and held it open for Maria, followed by
Scalpel and Christian. Immediately he closed the door all became
silent, save the occasional sound of droplets of water falling on
the stone floor. They were now in the tunnels of Rome, through
which the ancient waters of Western civilization had flowed for
millennia. "The most famous fountain in Rome, I'm sure you
know, is the Trevi, thanks to Pope Clement XII," said Sisto as
he put his arm around Maria's waist and pulled her close. Her
body curved into him as he turned into her pressing buttocks,
covering her now shivering body with his red cape. Christian
and Scalpel went on ahead. Sisto yelled, "not that way! Take the
right branch to the Trevi!"

Sisto turned to Maria. "Gloria," he said with a grin, "we will
take the left branch that goes to the Eagle fountain."

Maria was overwhelmed and said, "flattery will get you everywhere." She wrapped her long, solid arm around Sisto's neck, roughly pulling his head down to her bosom. It was basically a headlock. She rubbed his face into her cleavage. Sisto wailed in his tenor voice, but then stuck out his tongue as far as it would go, searching for whatever might be there. "I have a place, quickly, let's go there. The gardener's cottage," he said, breathless. Maria let go his head, took his hand and they pranced along together like young lovers. Or at least that was what Maria imagined. Sisto, after all, was much overweight, struggling to keep up with her, so she pulled on him like a dog on a leash. "That way," he cried, "through that door and up the steps." Maria expected to see the Eagle Fountain, but to her surprise, the door opened into a luxurious bedroom, decorated like any of the plush apostolic apartments, a four-poster bed, satin duvet, huge mirror above the bed.

"This is not the Eagle Fountain," was all Maria could find to say.

"It is not. It is my secret boudoir underneath the gardener's cottage. I planned this the very moment I met you, not far above us in the Vatican garden."

Sisto kicked the door closed behind them and dropped his red cape, revealing a bright white Speedo bikini swim suit, covering barely anything, his fat tummy drooping out and hanging down, shielding all that might be there from Maria's eyes, little spots peeping out from her habit, her mouth wide, rubbing her tongue across her top lip. Sisto stood back, trying to push his buttocks forward, hold his stomach in, but it was plainly impossible. Instead, he took two great strides to the bed and leaped, a superhuman effort, his body charged with anticipation, and bounced on to the bed, rolled on to his back, his stocky little legs spread-eagled. And then he sang in his tenor voice, "take me to your arms, my Charlotte! Take me to your arms!" Maria had no idea what opera he sang, all she could do was put her hand to her gaping mouth, then, driven by a force that went well beyond anything she had ever experienced with Alphonso, she leaped on the bed and sat astride him.

It was another miracle. Sisto's dream had come true. He had always wanted to be done by a nun, preferably a tightly bound nun, and certainly Maria came close enough to that. She went to pull off her habit, but Sisto grabbed her hand and pushed her head, still wrapped in the habit, on to his chest, where his own cleavage lay wide open, then pressed her further and further down, over his hairy and rubbery tummy in search of the small prize of ecstasy that awaited. And when the habit reached its destination, he caressed it, enjoying its stiffness, its starched purity, its tight rigid binding.

*

Later, Sisto would show Maria his plans for harvesting the holy water. His enthusiasm for the project was catching. He spoke so quickly, it was hard to keep up with him. There was an old aqueduct that ran from Naples to Rome, built by none other than his revered ancestor Frontinus Magnus. It began near the top of mount Vesuvius, made its way through the hills and plains of Lazio, thence to Rome. He would reverse its course, not all that difficult with the use of modern day pumps, and feed the Holy water from its source underneath Saint Peter's into the aqueduct, all the way to Naples, then branch off to the bay of Naples thence to large tankers that would transport the precious cargo to the Port of Newark, where it would be offloaded and processed at Alphonso's manufacturing plant at Hopewell New Jersey, in the new industrial park and business incubator established in conjunction with Virgin Hall University.

Now they stood in front of the Eagle Fountain. Sisto scooped up a little water and took a sip. "As pure, as pure as your habit, my love!" he said as he licked his lips, water dripping from his curly beard. Maria looked at him, her true feelings hidden behind her tight habit. "I think I will get one of those habits with the wings on," she said, a little mischievously. Sisto looked at her and gently brushed the back of his hand against her habit where it covered her cheek. "It would give me something to cling to," he said wistfully. Maria lifted his chin with her strong hand and looked into his eyes, covered almost by his black bushy eyebrows. But he appeared to be looking over her shoulder. "What is it you are looking for?" she asked, adopting a kind of motherly tone.

"Nothing beyond you, my dear, except perhaps, I think I see Virgil going into the Vatican apartments."

Suddenly they were business partners. Maria responded accordingly. "Alphonso wanted him to arrange the Papal visit to New Jersey. He's probably going to see Cardinal Pollagrande who does all those arrangements for the Pope."

"But *Papa Corto* is indisposed, haven't you heard?" asked Sisto, showing concern.

"Yes, it's all over the papers. Poor thing. Imagine, Well, actually I can't, but maybe you can," smiled Maria, now worried that she was making fun of the Pope.

Sisto looked into her habit and said, "it would be bliss, my dear, but only if I were constantly in your arms."

*

Christian led the way, Scalpel lumbering along behind, rather like a tired old bull dog. The tunnel followed an underground stream, flowing at a reduced trickle, the recent summer having starved Rome of its water. According to Sisto, they should stay on the main tunnel for some twenty minutes, then take the right fork when it appeared. When they reached the fork, Christian turned to wait for Scalpel to catch up. The tunnel now sloped upward, and shortly met with the gushing *Acqua Vergine Antica* that fed the Trevi.

Scalpel seemed out of breath. Neither had spoken a word the whole way. But Christian had thought of many things he wanted to say, all of them stimulated by the memories that had enveloped his brain, refusing to go away during sleepless nights. The stark pictures of Scalpel peeping out of the closet, transformed his love of Julian into something sinister and evil, objectifying his love. Memories that he should cherish were instead memories that taunted him. And it was all Scalpel's fault, a voyeur of the worst kind, a reptile who slithered under his bed in the dorm, hid in the closet, salivated at Christian's ecstasies. And they were no more, instead they were pallid memories of victimization. That's what it was. He had been brutalized by Scalpel's foul gaze. And now, it was time for Scalpel to pay the penalty, to be held responsible for the distrust and thorough debasement he had caused.

As they proceeded up the slope, the sound of the Trevi gradually became distinct. Christian remembered watching the old movie *Three Coins in a Fountain* at a film festival put on at Virgin Hall. They came to a metal door, that Christian opened, and there before him was an enormous room carved out of the underbelly of Rome, right at its heart, where all the intricate ancient stone and modern mechanisms guided the water through the Trevi's many openings, flowing over and around gods, sea horses, Tritons and whatever else. Massive stone jaws opened out from the room straight to the outside, it was like looking over many waterfalls from behind. A stone wall formed a circular holding pond, probably built by Agrippa way back when, which took up most of the space in the cavernous room. Scalpel, out of breath, sat on the edge of the pool. He cupped his hand and scooped up a little water. Christian turned to him, his hand on his shoulder, his now graying eyes looking down, not a sign of emotion, nothing there, and said, "I think it is about time."

Scalpel looked up, still with that smirk engraved on his face, "What for?"

"To say you're sorry."

"What? What for?" The smirk became a silly grin.

"Your past."

"What?"

Christian grabbed Scalpel by the neck and thrust him backwards into the pool, then pulled him up as he gasped for air. "Think of me as Satan," Christian snarled, "I have a big book full of many pages of everything you've done to innocent people in your life."

"What? But I've never hurt anyone!" whined Scalpel.

Christian thrust him back into the water, this time leaving him under while Scalpel flayed his arms trying to take a breath. Out he came again, this time coughing and spluttering. Christian spoke, a monotone, but with considerable violence in his eyes. "You destroyed the most beautiful thing two people could ever have, their love for each other!"

"I, I, I don't know what you're talking about. I was only doing my job, anyway!"

"Job? That's what it was? And who were you working for?" A quick dunk in the pool and out. "Who?"

"I don't know!" spluttered Scalpel, "ask Julia. I went to her. She might know. Maybe the CIA, FBI, El Padrino, I don't know! Please! I meant no harm!"

"Really? That's what you think? Then you certainly deserve to go to hell."

Now Christian held his neck in both hands, his arms too strong to be thrown off by Scalpel's flailing arms.

"All right! All right! I'm sorry!" cried Scalpel.

Christian loosened his grip and said, "now that's better. Sorry for what?"

"Whatever you want! You can't do this to me! I'll tell Nancy Pelosi! Then you'll pay!"

"Tell who?" Christian's grip tightened and thrust him down deep into the water. This time he did not relent. "Tell Saint Peter you're sorry when you get to the gates of heaven and maybe

he'll believe you. But I think you are good meat for Satan."
Scalpel's body gave one last convulsion, then became still.
Christian let go and Scalpel drifted with the flow of the water,
then out and over the waterfall, into the fountain, caught up on a
Triton's fork.

Christian opened his phone and sent a text to Alphonso,
saying simply, "done." Immediately a text came to him from
Virgil, "Eagle Fountain ASAP."

*

Cardinal Benitez stood beside the Bernini canopy, looking up
at the magnificent dome of Saint Peter's. He looked down and
thought of the rows of dead popes entombed in the crypt under
the cathedral. The thought struck him that perhaps one day he
would join them. Tucked under his arm were the latest editions
of the *National Catholic Reporter* and *L'Osservatore Romano*.
He had fed them the inside story of the Pope's erectile disfunction. It had a simple explanation. He woke up very early
one morning needing to pee, common for all men of his age, but
also with an erection, again a common event for all men. "Did
they not agree?" He had put it directly to the male reporters,
who looked down embarrassed, fingering their phones. The
women reporters present push forward, skeptical, saying things
like, "you're making excuses for him! It's a disgrace, a Pope
having an erection. What was he thinking? In any case, why
didn't he keep it to himself? It's disgusting!"

Benitez replied with the standard answers about the devil
constantly there, even when we are asleep, doing his best to
insert temptations, and what better target than the Pope himself?
"But don't these erections naturally go away after visiting the
bathroom?" asked a reporter bravely. Benitez replied in various
ways. "Usually, as you all know, the erection goes down after
peeing in the morning." "Or after satisfying it," interjected a
grinning young reporter. A ripple of amused murmurs spread
through the gaggle of journalists. This was the call for Benitez to
stand up on his horse. "Really! This is the Pope we are talking
about, show some reverence and respect! This is a very serious
situation. Most of you are too young to remember that Pope
Pius XII died of the hiccups. A common ailment. We are now in
the third day of the Pope's erectile disfunction. Doctors have
tried everything short of putting him into an induced coma,
which would bring with it many very serious consequences not
only for him, but for the everyday operations of the Vatican."

Undaunted, another voice came from the back of the crowd, a reporter from the *New York Daily News*. "So how big is it anyway? He's pretty short, isn't he?" Cardinal Benitez's face went red, as red as his red cape. He threw up his hands and cried, "*cativo!* You are a very bad person! *The Daily News* should be ashamed of itself hiring such people as you!"

Cardinal Benitez walked away in anger, which he had to admit to himself, was a mistake. He looked down and spoke to the entombed popes, "give me strength, holy brothers, please give me strength." He walked out the front door of the church, pushed his way through the crowds waiting their turn to enter, across the piazza and into a tiny bar just around the corner from Santa Scala. He ordered a *café affogato doppio* and gulped it down. Then he headed for the Pope's apartment.

*

A hulking Swiss guard stood at the Pope's door. Benitez wondered whether it was he who had leaked the Pope's erection to the press. In any case he gave him a sour look as the guard stood aside to let him enter. Estelle stood right in the hallway ready to meet him.

"Is there any movement?" asked Benitez.

"Nothing, Holiness," replied Estelle, fluttering her eyelids in a most pleasing manner.

Her nakedness embarrassed him. "Put some clothes on," he ordered scornfully. "What are you doing getting around like that?"

"I'm just a robot, Holiness. In any case, the Pope insisted."

Did Benitez detect a tiny tone of hostility in Estelle's voice? Was Estelle becoming human already? "Really?" he replied, "I would have thought your gorgeous body would be enough to cause anyone's erection, including mine!" He walked towards the bedroom, where the Pope lay naked on his back, his short little legs made smaller by his massive erection. His cheeks were red, his eyes glassy, red rimmed. Benitez dropped to his knees. "Holy Father! My goodness, I feel Satan in this room!"

Papa Corto hardly stirred, groaned faintly. He managed to lift the middle finger of his right hand and pointed to the jar of little blue pills.

"You want more pills?" asked Benitez, "I think you've probably had enough." But Estelle glided forward and retrieved three pills, which she dropped into the Pope's open mouth and lifted his head so he could swallow them with a glass of water. "He's addicted to them," she said with a smile, "and he's addicted to me too."

The effect of the pills was striking. The Pope sat up as if in a trance, like Regan in *The Exorcist*. Benitez expected to see him float up to the ceiling, his head do a 360 swivel. A devilish grin appeared on the Pope's face, his tongue flopped out then licked his lips. "Come! Come!" he cried out, waving his arms at Estelle. "It's lucky I'm a robot," said Estelle, "a real woman would have been worn out by now." She leaped on the bed. "How do you want it this time? Still on your back?"

Benitez wanted to leave. Should have left. No, must stay to see it through. His own erection was emerging. "Get thee behind me Satan" he called, only then realizing what he was asking, a serious mistake, under the circumstances. He backed towards the door, Estelle pushing the Pope back down on the bed, on his back, his erection visibly pulsing, as red as the reddest cardinal cape, but now suddenly, all blood gone from his face, his cheeks a deathly white. He opened his mouth wide, as though gasping for air. In fact, Benitez now saw, he actually *was* gasping for air. Estelle, apparently not noticing, was programed to go forward with this sequence of behaviors, so went down on him, and as she did so, Pope Shorty clutched at his chest, tore at it until his fingernails scratched the skin away, blood oozing out. Estelle was also programmed to cease functioning at the sight or smell of blood, so she froze right there on top of him, squashing him, the weight on his chest too much. And suddenly the Pope's body gave a massive convulsion and an awful croak, the sound of a fart came from his mouth, then all was still. Benitez took out a handkerchief and held it to his nose. His own erection had quickly departed. He tapped the reset button on Estelle. She immediately came to life and rolled off the Pope's still body. He covered the Pope's bloody chest with a sheet. "You better get some clothes on," said Benitez, I have to get you back to Pollagrande."

"But Holiness," cried Estelle, "Papa still has an erection!"

"So I see. Take his pulse, will you?"

Estelle felt the Pope's neck. "There is no pulse, Holiness." She leaned down to listen for a heartbeat. Nothing. Nor was he breathing. "I think he has passed away," said Estelle in a robotic manner. "He was a very good man."

"But how can he be dead if he still has an erection?" asked Benitez, not sure whether he was asking Estelle or himself. He checked again for any signs of life. Nothing. He ordered Estelle to resuscitate him, it was part of her package of options. She went through all the motions, but it was clear to them both that the Pope was dead. "Dress him in his morning clothes, and you better tape down his erection with something. Can't have it sticking up when he lies in state, can we?" said Benitez struggling to hold back a smirk. Then he went to the kitchen, opened his phone and texted to Pollagrande and Alphonso, "Plan B Done." Back to the bedroom, he directed Estelle to grab the bottle of blue pills and put them into a plastic grocery bag. Benitez then called for the Vatican physician.

*

As soon as the Vatican doctor showed up to pronounce Pope Shorty officially dead, Benitez and Estelle clutching her grocery bag, hurried to Pollagrande's apartment. He was, of course, very pleased to have his Estelle back, though he insisted that she be completely and thoroughly cleaned and disinfected before he would allow her to touch him. This annoyed Benitez. "And who would you suggest should clean her up? I'm not your slave," complained Benitez. "Besides, I have to get back to the Pope's apartment and make sure all is taken care of. Then I will have to call a press conference."

"Why not have the Pope's slaves clean her up? They will be out of a job now that the Pope is done for. And I certainly do not want to be carried around by a bunch of slaves. It's disgusting," said Pollagrande beginning to sound already like a Pope laying down the law.

"They are not actually slaves, I thought you knew that," said Benitez.

"What are they then?"

"Haven't you heard them speak? I found them in the wilds of Louisiana, living in a commune, just right for our communist Pope," said Benitez unable to resist bragging.

"What kind of commune?"

"A slave commune. Back when slavery was abolished, the slaves were literally out of a job. A bunch of them got together and decided that slavery wasn't a bad idea after all, so they set up a commune where everyone takes it in turn of being slave and slave owner. You get one year as slave and then there's a big celebration on New Year's Eve, where the slave changes places with the slave owner."

Pollagrande looked at Benitez. Being an Aussie, he was always ready to be played the fool. "You're having me on, right?"

Benitez cocked his eyebrow. "I have to run." He was about to leave when the doorbell rang. Estelle opened the door to find Virgil and Christian looking a little wet, but certainly looking like father and son. Christian, standing taught and upright, his face long and sallow, and Virgil a little over weight, but still in his executive's suit, no longer new, rather damp and ruffled. Virgil's eyes gave him away, the splendor of Estelle moved him in every way. Christian remained unmoved. Estelle ushered them in. "Pardon my appearance," she said, "I have been away on special assignment."

Benitez stepped aside to let them in. "Holiness, this is Virgil and his son Christian. They are Protestants, but a very special kind, as they will explain to you. They represent the core of our initiative to reach out to other Christian faiths. Hopefully..." Benitez looked around the room as though someone were eavesdropping, "the new Pope will embrace this important policy."

Estelle ushered them into the living room. Pollagrande studied the Protestants closely. It was many years since he had spoken with a Protestant, let alone had one in his apartment. Estelle took each of the guests by the hand and guided them into the ornate French carved chairs, patting the cushions as they sat, to make them comfortable.

Pollagrande coughed a little before he spoke. "Thank you, Estelle, you may go to your room now." Estelle smiled her wonderful smile and glided away, still holding her grocery bag. Pollagrande continued, "I hear that Alphonso has done great things in New Jersey, saved New State University from bankruptcy by merging it with Virgin Hal, nowl one of the top universities in America, of which he is now president. He is an amazing person."

Virgil shifted in his soft chair. Christian found it too soft and got up to stand.

"We have just come from a meeting in Sicily with one of your long time admirers," said Virgil.

"Oh yes. Alphonso told me you would be dropping in there. All was well, I hope? My Godfather must be getting quite old by now. Late nineties, I'd say. Seems like yesterday when he coached my football team at St. Aidan's orphanage."

"He sends his fond regards, Holiness," said Virgil.

Christian grimaced, finding this form of address repulsive. The fact was he considered Catholics a shifty bunch, they lied all the time. That was what made Scalpel so despicable.

"Indeed. Now what is it I can do for you?" asked Pollagrande."

"First. Let me tell you of the miracle that brought my son here, back to life, after he had died from a snake bite."

"I read something of it in the *Guardian*. Of an Australian Tiger snake, I understand? For which there is no antidote in the USA."

"Yes, that's right. He collapsed on the spot, in front of thousands of people who were attending my Pentecostal service. He was pronounced dead on the scene, carted off to hospital and pronounced dead again. Then miraculously, he rose from the dead the very next day."

"A miracle, no doubt," observed Pollagrande. "You are both Protestants, I understand?"

"Certainly I am, your Holiness. But it's not altogether clear whether Christian is. You see, I sent him to St. Roberts to gain a thorough understanding of Catholicism. There is much in Catholicism that I admire, not to mention that both our faiths believe in Jesus Christ and in miracles."

"But what has this to do with me?" asked Pollagrande

Virgil looked around. "This room is clean, your Holiness?" asked Virgil.

"I have it checked every day. You may speak openly. Only God and Jesus are listening besides me, and my Estelle is now switched off and regenerating herself."

"Alphonso says that you are the front runner to be the next Pope. He is very interested in promoting an interfaith policy. One day he hopes that Protestants and Catholics will worship openly together. "

"A laudable ideal and one that I support, though you understand that we must take small steps," announced Pollagrande with the authority of a Pope.

"Well, Holiness, Alphonso, you know, is a very impatient man. He gets things done."

"We all have our defects," mused Pollagrande.

Christian shifted on his feet, his face expressionless, his arms folded tightly. Pollagrande looked him up and down. There was something about him that troubled him. "Please make yourself comfortable," he said, gesturing towards the chair.

"I'll stand, thank you," said Christian, hardly moving his lips.

Virgil leaned forward and said in a low voice, "Your Holiness, Christian is still recovering from a major surgical procedure which makes him a little uncomfortable down there." He nodded towards Christian's crotch.

"Oh I see. Not a procedure that would offend me, I hope?"

"I'm not sure. He had himself neutered," blurted Virgil.

"Goodness gracious! A young radical! This happened after the miraculous resurrection?" cried Pollagrande.

"Yes, Holiness. But it has solved many problems. He…"

Christian broke in, "is a sexless creature who lives in the present and commands the future."

Pollagrande was taken aback. The thought struck him, of course, that here was an obvious solution to the sex abuse scandals plaguing the Catholic church. "What clinic did this?"

"The Virgin Hall University LGBTQ Emergency Care clinic."

"I see. Virgin Hall university seems to be expanding in every direction," noted Pollagrande.

Virgil replied with enthusiasm, "oh yes. Alphonso is not a man to leave things lie. And of course, his Holy Water project which I direct, is well under way. All it needs is the Pope's blessing…"

"Yes, indeed. And if I become Pope—of course I do not want the job—but if it happens to me, I will see to it that the project goes forward," announced Pollagrande with an air of authority.

"Thank you Holiness, that is good to hear. And now I would like to convey from Alphonso another offer, which is that, if elected Pope, you will agree to come to New Jersey and attend my Pentecostal service, which would send a huge interfaith message to my enormous audience, now numbering in the millions, since the service is televised."

"I am not sure about that. You will be dancing with snakes? I saw part of your service on YouTube."

"My audience demands it. They love snake dancing. We believe it is a way to show Satan—the biggest, slithering snake of all—that we do not fear him, that we can resist him and overcome him."

"I am not sure of that. Besides, the Vatican guard has an obsessive—you know the Swiss—rigid protocol for overseas travel. I doubt they will allow the snakes," lied Pollagramde.

"Well, if you would agree in principle. I have by the way also discussed this with your Great Godfather who thinks it a marvelous idea. In fact on my visit I gave him a gift of two rattlesnakes which he immediately set free in his garden. When we sat out on a hot night drinking iced tea, we could hear their quiet rattling."

"I certainly would agree to an interfaith meeting, including the Pentecostal. But the snakes, I would have to think about it."

"For the moment, that is all we ask, is that not right Christian?"

Christian shifted on his feet and nodded.

Virgil backed towards the door and beckoned Christian to follow. They were about to exit when here was a knock on the door, and Estelle, obeying not her master but her algorithm, rushed from her bedroom to open it. The loving couple, Sisto and Maria, each of them carrying a large box stood there, big smiles on their faces. "Where do you want these?" asked Sisto, "they're heavy!"

"Not in here!" called Benitez from Estelle's bedroom, "put them just outside the door. He rushed up to Sisto and whispered loudly, "Pollagrande must have nothing to do with this."

Puzzled, Sisto placed the box, almost as big as his rotund stomach, and not an easy task to do without dropping it, on the tiled floor. Maria placed hers on top. Benitez called to Estelle. Could you bring me that grocery bag please?

14. Plan C

Once outside Pollagrande's apartment, the door firmly closed, Benitez took out his phone and texted to the Great Godfather, "Plan C Starts Now," and said to Maria, "text the same to your gentle giant, Francisco, that's his name, right?" Maria nodded. "And you know what to do with this water?" He pointed to the boxes.

"For Pollagrande?" asked Maria.

"No, he must know nothing about it. I take it you have the small bottling plant operating under the Eagle Fountain, as planned?" asked Benitez.

Sisto replied. "All running smoothly. You want to see the product?" He went to open the box, but Benitez stopped him.

"No time now. Take them back to the plant, and what we will need is one hundred bottles of water, they're small sample bottles, right?"

"Right, and stamped with the crossed keys of the Vatican and ASP, for *Aquam Sanctus Pietro*, called "Waters of Saint Peter.""

"I want you to add a very faint coloring to the waters. Fifty a faint pink, barely distinguishable, and fifty blue, colored by dropping four of these little blue pills in each." Benitez handed Sisto the grocery bag. "Make sure the pills completely dissolve."

"But that might affect its pure taste," complained Sisto.

"If it does, then add some fizz to cover it."

Maria, hands on hips, said, "and then what?"

"The Great Godfather's consigliere will be around to pick them up in a few days. They will be distributed to the Cardinals over the next fifteen days as they arrive for the conclave and take up residence in the *Domus Sanctae Marthae*."

"Then what?" asked Virgil, impatiently, feeling cold and wet.

"The guest house, next to St. Peter's basilica."

"And then what? We hang around here for weeks?" complained Virgil.

"You have finished your work. You must return to New Jersey and start preparations for the visit of the new Pope," instructed Benitez impatiently.

*

When Benitez returned to Pope Shorty's apartment, he was confronted by the four slaves jostling with the two Swiss Guards who guarded the door.

"Let them in!" commanded Benitez, "they are *Papa Corto's* most devoted worshippers."

"The doctor said no one was to enter," they announced.

"He's still there? What on earth could he be doing? I am Cardinal Benitez, as you know, the Pope's major confidant and administrator of his affairs. Let me in, and I command you to allow his devoted followers to enter also. I may need their help anyway."

The slaves stepped back. The Swiss guard looked one to the other. Benitez stared them down. They stepped aside and opened the door. Benitez led the way. The slaves followed, whimpering, even crying, and as soon as they came to the Pope's bedroom and saw his flat body, his erection still plastered to his tummy, the slaves began a terrible moaning, then withdrew and began singing in deep baritone voices:

> *"Swing low, sweet chariot,*
> *coming for to carry me home!*
> *Swing low. Sweet chariot,*
> *coming for to carry me home."*

"I can't leave him like that!" cried the doctor, "I've tried everything!" He jumped forward and ripped off the tape, then started slapping at the Pope's erection, trying to get it to go down. But it stubbornly refused. He turned to Benitez. "Rigor mortis, that's what it is. It's set in already!"

And the doctor kept slapping. The slaves saw it as disrespectful. They jumped forward as one, hauled the doctor to the door and threw him out, slamming the door behind him. They then returned and began to assemble the litter. They grabbed the body and dressed it in the finest Papal robes they could find in his wardrobe. Then they forced the body, still pliable, into a sitting position and placed it on the litter. They tied his hands to the side rails, and tried desperately to prop up his body with ornate pillows. Unfortunately, his head kept flopping this way or that and in the end they managed to fix it in a place where it fell forward, his chin on his chest. Then, still singing, each of them took up their place at the four corners of the litter and hoisted it on their shoulders. They got to the doors, double doors as are all the doors in the Papal apartments, and then stopped and stared at Benitez who, without thinking, opened the doors, and they marched forward, still singing.

This would be an event to equal the great battles that mark the turning points of great civilizations. They marched out of the Vatican, through the curved columns of the piazza of Saint Peters, down the middle of *Via della Conciliazone* across the Tiber, straight down the *Corso Vittorio* to *Piazza Venezia*, the traffic completely backed up behind them, throngs of people pouring out of their apartments, hotels and shops, angry drivers getting out of their cars, tourists pouring out of *Piazza Navona*, a complete traffic jam at *Piazza Venezia*, one that stretched many miles and would take three days to untangle. And all the while, the four slaves carried their master weaving in between the cars, down the V*ia Foro Imperiali* and into the great Colosseum. There, they placed their dear master on the ancient stones of the colosseum floor, still singing, now on their knees, heads bowed. Tourists packed the colosseum, it was as though a grand gladiatorial battle was about to begin.

Then the crowd gasped, a collective sound of despondency, or maybe it was terror, when the slaves drew out their gold handled gem encrusted daggers that were assumed to be simply ornate decorations of their costumes, and held them to their throats. They then raised their daggers high above their heads and said in unison. "We give our lives to the Holy Father, our dear leader, that you may be forgiven for all you have done to us!"

The crowded colosseum hushed, and silence descended. The slaves stood like statues, awaiting instructions. Thumbs up or thumbs down? Then a loud voice yelled, just like in a final of the US open tennis match when a player is about to throw up his ball for a crucial serve, "fuck off you heathens!" And all hell broke loose, people ran and stumbled down to the litter, some attacked the slaves others tried to defend them. Pope Shorty rolled off the upturned litter. The sound of a helicopter came from overhead, then it became so loud and the wind generated by its propellers so fierce, that people now ran away, squatted down, and a huge net dropped over the slaves and the litter and anyone else who was there, a net not unlike that used in the gladiatorial combats.

Lives were saved, and the body of the Pope recovered, now stuck in a sitting rigor mortis position. He was the only Pope to be buried in a one meter cube coffin. He could not, obviously, lie in state. Instead, he sat in state. Benitez chose to display him at the top of the Saint Angelo Castle, looking down the Tiber to the Vatican.

*

The work of plan C demanded action of all criminal networks covering every continent. The over two hundred cardinals who would fly into Rome for the conclave to elect the new Pope came from every corner of the earth. The Catholic church, though it was under severe attack for its endemic scandals—nothing new given its long history of abuse and its constant temptations of the flesh—nevertheless commanded an empire that dominated the world. And between the two of them, the Great Godfather and Alphonso rivaled the church in their reach, though each of them had relegated the job of activating their networks to their managers, the Great Godfather's consigliere Giuseppe Di Napolitano, to cover the European continent, and Maria's Francisco the gentle giant, the Americas and Asia. Their mission was simple. They were to contact every cardinal, find out who they were likely to vote for and, if it was not Polla-grande, take steps to delay or prevent their departure for Rome. With the unfortunate demise of Pedro, Maria had dispatched Francisco for the job. Alphonso, however, needed someone by his side constantly in New Jersey as he worked his way through the levels of corruption in order to implement his Great Plan. And Christian would be that man, depending on how he managed things in Italy. So far, he had been the perfect man for Alphonso's many menial tasks.

Maria had insisted that no serious harm should come to any of the cardinals when they were prepared for their visit to Rome. Plenty of money was available for donations to be used for whatever cause the cardinals chose, including themselves. The goal was to whittle the number of cardinals who showed up to the conclave down to one hundred.

Virgil, using his managerial skills as CEO of the ASP corporation, now incorporated in the State of New Jersey, had drawn up a spreadsheet that rated all cardinals: a ten was very sure he would vote for Pollagrande, down to one, not a chance. Of course, this rating depended on the interviewer doing the rating. The cardinals would never divulge their predilections so early, especially to an unknown interviewer. There were, of course, ways to motivate the cardinals to indicate their leanings, which were usually large handfuls of US dollars. Those rated as unlikely (a rating of seven or below) were encouraged not to go to Rome. This encouragement was also usually in the form of US dollars, though in some cases, those who were known molesters were threatened with exposure or offered a robotic companion.

Maria greeted the cardinals as they landed at Rome's Leonardo da Vinci airport. She went out to the little shop around the corner of *Piazza Navona* and bought the most beautiful nun's outfits she could find, resplendent in a habit that had always fascinated her, the one that had the heavily starched white wings shaped like those of a bat. She even practiced her curtsies, and used her feminine charm of which she had much, the power of Gloria Steinem shining through her habit, her strong lips and heavily powdered cheeks forcing her cardinal quarries to look into her dark eyes, and wonder, what power lay beneath that habit what a body to be imagined! Her job was to use her considerable feminine wiles to sort out those cardinals who had dissembled, taken the money, but actually intended not to vote for Pollagrande.

By the time the fifteen days of waiting after the death of the Pope, as prescribed by Vatican law, ninety-eight cardinals had made it to Rome, and were housed in the *Casa Santa Maria*, the hotel located just behind St. Peters Basilica, specially reserved for high ranking visitors to the Vatican. Christian, now endowed with the official title of Monsignor by Cardinal Benitez took over the job of concierge to keep an eye on them all, especially those suspected as dissemblers. According to Virgil's spread-sheet, there were sixty-three unlikely or suspected unlikely to vote for Pollagrande. As each came into the hotel, he bowed and greeted them, took their bags, and showed them to their rooms. Each was given a welcome pack that included various toiletries and essentials, and a small bottle of the Waters of Saint Peter, each with a very faint coloring. Those rated according to Virgil's spreadsheet as dissemblers or no votes, received one tinged with blue, those likely to vote for Pollagrande, a bottle tinged with pink. The former were strongly advised by Christian to keep themselves hydrated, especially after their long travels to get to the Vatican, and also that there would be limited victuals available in the Sistine Chapel. The cardinals were allowed one day of rest, then they were to assemble in the lobby of the hotel and walk together two by two, across the Piazza of Saint Peter, in front of the steps of the Basilica, through the curved columns, and into a door that led through the Vatican library to the Pauline chapel.

The first day of the conclave arrived and Benitez, assisted by Christian, moved quickly to organize the procession. There was a quiet buzz of conversation, but clearly there was something slightly amiss. As the cardinals assembled and began walking across the Piazza, it became clear that quite a few of them were bent over as they walked, their red capes almost dragging on the cobbled stones in front of them. Benitez and Christian looked on them with satisfaction. The blue pills had worked their magic again!

*

Pollagrande imagined himself as Lomeli, the morally upright, self-deprecating character in Robert Harris's fine novel, *Conclave*. Indeed, his assistants and other cardinals as they gathered in the Pauline Chapel addressed him as "eminence." They gathered in the Pauline chapel in small groups, talking in quiet tones, awaiting instructions from Cardinal Benitez who had slipped into the role of administrator and manager of the conclave. Pollagrande noticed, however, that Benitez was assisted by a civilian, most unusual, and probably forbidden, and surely who would not be admitted into the Sistine Chapel where the voting would take place. The civilian had a dark complexion, was tall and gaunt, full of smiles, perhaps too much so given the somber circumstances. He also carried a very large briefcase, the kind that expanded, with a large flap that folded over the top and closed at its base with large gold buckles. Pollagrande beckoned to Benitez.

"Who is your assistant?" he asked.

"You have not met him? I thought you would have by now. He is Giuseppe Di Napolitano, your Godfather's consigliere," answered Benitez.

"I have not visited my Godfather for many years. He is so far away down there, and I have been so busy. I must make myself known to the Consigliere."

Benitez lightly pulled on Pollagrande's arm. "I think it best that you keep your distance. His delicate mission could be jeopardized if there were even the slightest appearance that he was your man."

Pollagrande looked down at Benitez. There was no need for him to say anything. He understood, and felt a slight pang of guilt, largely because it was how Lomeli would have felt. So he just nodded and walked away to join the group from the South Pacific, naturally searching for any Australians or New Zealanders who might have arrived. But he kept an eye on Napolitano who was exchanging pleasantries, his lilting southern Italian voice rising above the somber chatter of the cardinals, speaking English with a delightful Neapolitan accent. Every now and again he would reach into his briefcase and pull out a lavishly printed book with colored photographs of the various Michelangelo masterpieces of the Sistine Chapel and even the lesser masterpieces from the Pauline Chapel in which they stood. The consigliere explained in his lilting voice that the Pope, a Neapolitan, had given him, also a Neapolitan, instructions that, in the event of his death, he was to distribute these small gifts as his thanks to the cardinals' service to him. These booklets bore the photograph on the back cover of Pope Shorty sitting on his litter, waving to a crowd of worshippers, carried by his devoted four African slaves. The booklets were also slightly different. Some had pages edged in blue or in pink. The blue-edged booklets had a tendency, the recipients discovered later, for the pages to stick together making it necessary to lick one's thumb in order to turn the page. These were given to those Cardinals who were bent over as they walked, rather like red hens pecking their way forward, and continued to do so while they stood in the Pauline chapel. Many of these excused themselves while they made for the nearest restroom, located in a cold closet, underground next to the tombs of the popes. Unfortunately, there was a long line of cardinals waiting their turn. Indeed, some even went out and attempted to sneak behind the columns to relieve themselves, only to find, of course, that they had no control over the flight of the pee, nor could this be solved by squatting down. The red cape would have to be completely removed in order to carry out this embarrassing task that God had, in a devilish moment, imposed on the male body.

Each time Napolitano offered a blue-edged book, the exchange was recorded by the camera hidden in the top button of his elegantly tailored jacket. The video was sent wirelessly to Christian who sat in a cheap restaurant in *Trastevere*, sipping rough red wine mixed with Coca Cola, along with a collection of a motley group of Gypsies he brought from the ghetto hidden away in the run down shacks just outside of Ostia. Christian spoke Italian with a heavy Latin accent, and the Gypsies had their own twisted Italian if that is what it was, so there were some communication difficulties.

"The ones who take the blue booklets, they're for us," said Christian as the gang of ruffians gathered around the TV screen. "There, there's our first!" Christian paused the video. He called the bar tender. "Another round for my friends." The grappa bottle was almost empty.

The numbers in the Pauline Chapel, however, had thinned. Many had excused themselves to attend to their "private matters" as they called their erections. Yet when they returned to the chapel they remained stooped over. It seemed, mused Benitez with satisfaction, that they suffered the same infliction as Pope Shorty. Their condition would remain permanent, so long as the blue pills kept coming.

Benitez consulted with the consigliere, who, being Neapolitan, could not hold back a smirk of satisfaction. "I think we should postpone the conclave until tomorrow. What do you think, Giuseppe?"

"I have run out of booklets anyway. All that should have the blue books have received them. It's a matter of waiting to see how long they can stand by their erections," he added with an even bigger smirk. "Of course, if you want to play hardballs, I could round up some choir boys and have then sing in the Santa Maria lobby."

"Consigliere, enough!" cried Benitez.

"Should we let loose with Christian and his Gypsies, then?" asked the consigliere.

"Really, consigliere. I thought you Neapolitans were good at biding your time and striking only when it will have maximum impact. Have you never watched *The Godfather*?"

The consigliere snickered. "I made that movie, didn't you know?"

"*Si, Si. Sens altro.*" Benitez lapsed into Italian.

"Why do you think there were those scenes in Sicily? They were based on the Great Godfather," bragged Napolitano.

At this point, Benitez felt a jolt at his elbow, and suddenly, the entire chapel hushed. Maria, in her beautiful habit, was at his side. Benitez turned to her, aghast. "Women are not allowed here! You must leave!" he cried softly, or so he thought, but his words reverberated throughout the entire chapel.

"Did you not get Alphonso's text?" asked Maria.

"I have been so busy," Benitez replied, frowning.

"He said wait another day. He would rather be sure, and wants the Pope to be elected on the first ballot anyway."

Benitez sighed deeply, then clapped his hands lightly. "Are we all here?" He glanced at the door and waited while a few more stragglers came in, stooped over, holding their capes out like a tent. "Given the discomfort some of you are experiencing, we have decided to delay the conclave until tomorrow." He searched for a look of approval from Pollagrande who stood surrounded in a corner by his staunch Asia Pacific supporters. But Pollagrande carefully looked away. Benitez continued. "However, we think an informal poll might be helpful for us to assess how long we will need to be cooped up in the Sistine. So, if you would please on these slips of paper that Monsignor Napolitano and Sister Garcia will hand out, write down the name of the one person you would most like to be our next Pope, fold it over, and drop it in the box by the door as you leave. Thank you for your cooperation."

A murmur of voices followed, but none questioned the procedure. The stooped were only too pleased to get away and back to their rooms. Benitez placed himself by the door and managed to shepherd the stooped to the right box and the upright to the left box. The boxes were designed so that each ballot dropped one on top of the other, which, when matched to the video taken from the consigliere's lapel camera, would reveal the identity of its owner.

*

Pollagrande was determined to dismiss from his mind any thought of becoming Pope. The mind was an insidious thing, he thought, surely infected by the Devil, perhaps with God's grudging permission. For it demanded strength and resolve, none of which he thought he had in sufficient portions to ward off these relentless attacks on his holiness. The only sure defense against these self-injuring thoughts was to lose one's mind all together. So it was with this in mind that he would get very drunk tonight, go out on the town with his Aussie and Kiwi mates. There was an Irish pub down on *Via del Colosseo* just across from the Roman Forum. He would take them there and they would drink through the night, as long as they could last.

The night began with orders of very large pots of Guinness, poured with perfection, with thick creamy heads. They exchanged bawdy jokes and told stories that would be, if heard by outsiders especially if they were good Catholics, cause for alarm. Soon, they switched to Fosters with whiskey chasers and played drinking games. Pollagrande tried to pay for all the drinks, but his down-under mates protested loudly. It was unmanly, indeed, un-everything to let someone buy you all your booze. They did, however, at various intervals, buy the whole pub rounds of drinks. Had they been dressed as priests, questions would have been asked. How could it be that they had so much money, rolls of it in US dollars?

By two in the morning they staggered out of the pub and into the narrow cobblestone alley that led up the hill then down to the Colosseum. Pollagrande led the way, against the protestations of his mates who insisted that the Vatican was in the opposite direction. Which it was. "We'll fight the fucking Romans, the bastards!" cried Pollagrande. "They'll pay for their murder and torture of our Christian ancestors. May they rot in hell!" He was reminded that there were many worse things that could be done to the pagans in Hell. And probably were continuing right now, and would continue forever. For Hell was an eternity, was it not? As was Heaven. But the former was an eternity of Hell, torture, suffering, pain, every horrible thing that one could think of.

They entered the Colosseum, and Pollagrande led them down to the center of the arena. "I will play Spartacus! You blokes the gladiators! Come on, bastards. Make your move!" And to his horror and consternation, they encircled him, set upon him pushing him back and forth, catching him as he fell. "You're a silly old bastard," laughed the youngest of the priests. "Better get you home to bed!" He took out his phone and called for an Uber black that came seemingly from just around the corner. "Boys! Please don't throw up on my car!" called the Uber driver, as he drove as fast as he could to the Vatican, where they were stopped at the gate by the Swiss guards. They fell out of the car and staggered towards the Swiss Guards who pushed them away. Pollagrande stepped forward, waving his Vatican ID. "I am Cardinal Pollagrande! Make way!" The guards recognized him, but of course, did not know the others. "They are Cardinals here for the Conclave. I demand that you let them enter.!"

The guard quietly informed him that they were at the wrong gate, that the *Casa Santa Maria* was around the other side of the

Basilica. They herded the drunks back into the Uber and gave
the driver directions. Pollagrande was at least sober enough to
push several large dollar bills at the driver, who drove them
around to the *Casa Santa Maria*. He waved good bye to his
mates, and with difficulty made his way up to his apartment in
the apostolic palace. And as he fumbled at the door with his
keys, the door opened, and it was the beautiful Estelle. "Welcome
Holiness. I hope you had a good time," she said, her Monroe
lips dazzling his unfocussed eyes. She took his hand and pulled
him into her arms. The door closed behind them and Estelle
carried Pollagrande in her arms and put him to bed.

Morning came too soon as Pollagrande awoke, Estelle beside
him, caressing him, rubbing the wrinkled skin of his body with
Aveeno. "You must awaken, Holiness," she said. It's your big
day today."

Pollagrande shook his head and sat up. "You must not speak
like that, my dear. It is a day like any other day. Every day
belongs to Jesus, not me."

Estelle was not programed to understand such deep thoughts,
so did not answer. She just kept of trying to rub him down.

*

The cardinals gathered in the lobby of the *Casa Santa Maria*,
to the sweet sounds of six young boys singing hymns. Only
forty out of the original one hundred cardinals showed up.
Christian was dispatched to wake up the down-under cardinals
who had overslept. The rest had mysteriously departed over-
night, though two had checked themselves into the Vatican
hospital for treatment of erectile dysfunction. As they marched
out, two by two, none stooped, though some, the Aussies and
Kiwis staggered a little, holding their sore heads. Orders had
been placed for several shots of espresso that would be awaiting
them when they arrived at the Pauline Chapel. Napolitano and
Virgil stood at the door to welcome them.

Benitez was busy setting up the Sistine Chapel. He had
consulted Wikipedia to check on the required format of the
balloting system, way too complicated to his liking. He decided
that in the pre-scrutiny stage they would not do a written ballot.
Why not a simple show of hands? They were all committed
Christians after all, and Catholics as well, surely they should be
able to trust each other and anyway, keeping one's vote a secret
gave the impression that nasty shenanigans were going on
behind the scenes. The whole thing was a sham anyway since

the new Pope was usually pretty much decided long before the previous Pope died. And why do it all in Latin? Really. This was the 21st century. Why not do it in Chinese?

The cardinals entered. Benitez had enlisted Pope Shorty's four slaves to set up a dais on which Benitez would stand to supervise the proceedings. They then retired to the corner to get the burner ready that would signal that a new Pope had been elected. That was another thing that Benitez disagreed with. The chemicals they used to burn the ballots and make the smoke black or white. He was not going to allow more environmental pollution. And what about the unnecessary carbon released into the atmosphere? He instead had obtained a large electric boiler that emitted lots of white steam when it reached boiling point. The slaves placed it under the chimney that rose out of the chapel. The water was even simmering, at the ready. Furthermore, if black steam were needed, in the unlikely event that the vote did not produce a winner, he had directed the slaves simply to add some black octopus sauce, popular at seafood restaurants around Ostia and Fiumicino.

Benitez stood on the dais and raised his hands, as if to address God himself, and addressed the conclave. "Holy eminences! In the name of the apostle Peter, our founder, I hereby open the election of the 268th Pope of the Holy Roman Catholic Church. I call on you all to repeat after me the oath of allegiance and honesty. Please speak up loudly so I can see that there is no one shirking their duty. I know that many of you are tired from long travels, but also we must understand that given the unusual circumstances in which our Holy Father passed into Heaven fifteen days ago, it is urgent that we get this done as quickly as possible."

A hand went up from someone in the middle of the sea of red cardinals. "Holiness! Are there no chairs for us to sit? Some of us are a little feeble and cannot stand for long periods."

"That will not be necessary, but once we have voted anyone is welcome to sit on the floor, or squat, depending from whatever culture he comes. Are there any other questions? Hearing none, I ask you to repeat after me:

"I call as my witness Christ the Lord..."

Benitez expected cries of dissent, since he had immediately broken with protocol by asking all to recite the oath together, instead of individually. But none came. Instead, they all responded in unison.

"I call as my witness Christ the Lord…"
"who will be my judge…"
"who will be my judge…"
"that my vote is given to the one…"
"that my vote is given to the one…"
"who before God…"
"who before God…"
"I think should be elected."
"I think should be elected."

Now a soft buzz came from the crowd, but still no dissent. Benitez moved on, and announced in a loud, strong voice, "all those in favor of Cardinal Pollagrande to be our next Pope raise your hands and say 'aye'." He beckoned to the four slaves to count the hands and he also counted. "Please keep your hands raised," he called. He noted that one cardinal had both hands raised. "Your eminence, you have two hands raised, each card-inal gets one vote only."

"My apologies, holiness. But Cardinal O'Sullivan from Bris-bane Australia is still in bed with a hangover and he asked me to vote on his behalf."

"So noted."

Benitez huddled together with the four slaves. They had agreed on the number. Then he made the announcement. "Out of forty-four present, we count forty two voting for Pollagrande, plus one absentee vote from Brisbane which makes forty-three."

Someone called out. "Who was the no vote?"

"I think we know who did the no vote," said Benitez with a smile, looking at Pollagrande who sat at the side of the Sistine Chapel, on the small bench that encircles the chapel floor. "Holy Father to be," he said to Pollagrande, "according to Wikipedia, you have to make the oath of acceptance. As Dean of Cardinals, *Acceptasne electionem de te canonice factam in Summum Pont-ificem?*"

Pollagrande stood and bowed his head in silence, praying to Jesus, all assumed. Then he raised his head and stood as tall and straight as he could. "It is with great humility and respect for our great Catholic Church, that I do accept my canonical election as Supreme Pontiff."

The Conclave erupted with cheers and applause. The four slaves brought the huge kettle to the boil, and on Benitez's signal, they opened the lid and the white steam belched up the chimney. The muffled sound of cheers of the faithful who waited patiently in St. Peter's square penetrated the thick walls of the chapel.

"And what name will you take, Holy Father?" asked Benitez.

"Si. Pope Si."

"Si? You mean Yes?" asked Benitez most puzzled.

"I am the Pope of Yes, the first of its kind. Pope Si the first."

Benitez looked at Pope Si, nonplussed. This was not the Pope he had expected. Had Pollagrande fooled them all?

The four slaves approached him. Pollagrande looked them up and down. "Shall we get the litter?" one asked.

Pollagrande frowned. "I think that your services would be much better used back in your own land where you can do the much more important work of Jesus."

"But we have made our lives here, your eminence."

"Go back and preach to your people," insisted Pollagrande.

Benitez interceded. "If your holiness will allow," said Benitez, "there may be a place for them back in New Jersey. Perhaps they could attend college at Virgin Hall. I am sure there is a bene-factor there who would provide the necessary financial aid."

Pollagrande looked at Benitez, slightly annoyed at having been upstaged in goodness. "Certainly, Cardinal Benitez. That is an excellent idea."

*

Pollagrande insisted on keeping his old apartment. Besides, the smell of death still hung in the air of Pope Shorty's apartment. The always reliable Cardinal Benitez managed to shoo his many fawning attendants away and spirit the Holy Father across the Vatican gardens to his apartment. The tedious rigmarole of Papal dressing, loading him down with the unbelievable weight of many layers of garments, topped off with that high hat shaped like an avocado fastened tightly to his head, caused Pollagrande for just a few moments, to regret what he had allowed himself to become. Worse, he felt pangs of pride when his mind, always poised to challenge him, reminded him of his impoverished beginnings, born a bastard no less. They reached his apartment, Benitez having kept admirers away, loud cheers and bells ringing, telling Pollagrande that his life was on the brink, it would no longer be his own. But he hoped for just this few minutes, to drop by and say hello to Estelle, perhaps it might even be good-bye. A most unsettling thought.

They reached his apartment to find Christian standing at the door. There were no Swiss guards in sight. Christian stepped aside, looking down. The Holy Father put out his hand but Christian did not take it. So Pollagrande reached out and took Christian's limp hand and kissed it. "Bless you, my son," he said. He then opened the door, Christian following him in. It was probably the last time Pollagrande would open a door for himself, and inside El Padrino, Maria, and Sisto awaited him. They came forward, smiling profusely, overwhelmed to see him dressed like the Pope, and even more that he really was the Pope! Pollagrande offered his hand and each took the opportunity to kiss the ring not yet on his ring finger, that would come with the inauguration tomorrow. Pollagrande's mind was not on his guests, though; he looked around instead for Estelle and could not resist calling for her. "Estelle? Come meet our guests!" Out she came, that big Marilyn smile, the red lips, even Alphonso's eyes widened. It was the first time he had seen her. "Estelle, please meet our guests, El Padrino, Sister Maria, and, Sisto, I believe?" Each smiled broadly and muttered hello. "Could you make us all a cup of tea, please?"

"Yes, Holy Father, I would be delighted," replied Estelle.

"And tell me," Pollagrande turned to Maria, "how is the convent coming along and the seminary for the poor and homeless?"

"It is doing very well, Holy Father, thanks to the generosity of the Alphonso and Maria foundation. We are saving many souls, day after day."

"That is so wonderful. Please keep up the good work. And Alphonso, to what do I owe this visit? We must hurry, now that I have a life that is owned by others. I am spread far and wide, too little time for too many people."

"Unfortunately, Holy Father, I am here for the worldly matters of money and product. Sisto here, has joined us in case you have any questions about the Holy Water that will be taken from the cisterns of Rome and the Vatican, the connection to be made just near the Eagle Fountain. Perhaps you have not met him? He is the genius who engineers and commands all the waters of Rome and the Vatican."

"We had coffee together, I believe," answered Pollagrande.

"And the best espresso I ever had, your Holiness." Sisto stepped back a little and bowed graciously, his rotund body looking like humpty-dumpty about to roll down the hill. "God has blessed me with these talents," he said in his lilting voice, "and I am so privileged to apply them to your new holy enterprise."

"Yes, now quickly, tell me what is the plan," asked Polla-grande officiously, his voice now that of Pope Si.

Sisto replied, "we will take the water from beneath and near the Eagle Fountain, these waters that run directly below what we all know is St. Peter's tomb. They are, we think, the waters of St. Peter. And they are truly the Aqua Santa of God. We have all the equipment ready and in place. All we need is your permission to begin the project."

"And the distribution, El Padrino?" asked Pope Si.

"I and my network will take care of that, probably also with a little help from the Great Godfather's network, that will be handled by Christian. It will be facilitated by our production plant in New Jersey that will bottle the water into small vials, stamped with the Vatican logo, marked with ASP, *Aqua Santa Pietro*—Holy Water of Saint Peter —and the Papal keys on the back."

"I see," said the Holy Father, rather too slowly for Alphonso's liking.

"Of course, all with your blessing, Holy Father. We estimate that we will be able to pay you, the Vatican that is, point one of one percent for every vial we sell. They are tiny 3 ounce vials, so we expect to sell many, many millions," added Alphonso.

Benitez hovered in the background. Pope Si looked to the kitchen where Estelle was pouring the tea. "Shall I bring the tea?" she asked, sensing the difficult moment.

"Thank you Estelle. Cardinal Benitez will help you," answered Pope Si.

"Oh no! Let me help," said Maria. "It is a woman's role to serve, don't you think, Holy Father?"

Alphonso and Sisto looked at each other. Benitez frowned. Did he detect sarcasm? It was hard to tell. Best to ignore it. As did the Holy Father. The teas were delivered while they all sat around a small table, the Pope having difficulty because of the many robes getting in his way. "Bring me a pen," he said to Estelle.

Alphonso gave a little cough. "Holy Father, I do not think that we need sign a formal contract. Your Holy Word is good enough for me."

"But what of the Vatican?" asked the Holy Father.

Benitez intervened. "Perhaps it is better to avoid leaving any paper trail. Now that you are Pope, one never knows who one's enemies are."

Pope Si rose, helped by Estelle, and said, "then let us consider it a deal."

Alphonso scratched his navel and smiled. "Thank you Holy Father. You are making my miracle come true yet again."

Pope Si made to leave, but Benitez looked to Alphonso, and said, "There is one other important matter to discuss, Holy Father."

"Quickly, I have many audiences to attend," said His Holiness.

"As a clear signal of your policy to expand the interfaith initiative of the Roman Catholic Church, Alphonso is prepared to arrange a Papal visit to New Jersey, the highlight of which will be the consecration of the amalgamation of the New State University and Virgin Hall as one University, and as part of the celebration, you would attend a Pentecostal meeting at CURE stadium, organized by Virgil, who I think you have met. He is the CEO of the manufacturing plant that will produce the vials of *Aqua Santa*. Of course you know that Alphonso is now president of the Virgin Hall University, and is also a close confidant of the Governor of New Jersey."

Pope Si frowned. "This is a very big thing you ask, Cardinal Benitez."

There was a knock at the door and Estelle darted forward, closely followed by Christian. The Swiss guards had now taken up their posts on each side of the door. She opened it and there stood Giuseppe Di Napolitano, his swarthy features cutting quite a contrast against those of the beautiful pale Estelle. Though it was not intended, his appearance could not have been better timed. His sight was enough to remind Pope Si where the powers lay, that he as Pope had most likely much less power than he had when he was the Pope's manager.

The Holy Father spoke. "All right. We will do it. I leave it in your hands." He turned to Di Napolitano and said, with a slight edge, "thank you consigliere for all you have done," and left with Benitez trailing behind.

.

15. Affirmative action

As Virgin Hall's Provost and Academic Vice President, Julia was expected to abide by certain rules of decorum and promote particular policies. These were that she should on many occasions meet with her esteemed faculty to explain to them the policies of the university, announce that the university adhered to the highest standards of education, and above all else, observe that its faculty were there to devote themselves to foster a love of knowledge among the students, that they be free to pursue knowledge in whatever way they chose, that they learn, perhaps most importantly, to worship and adore their esteemed faculty.

Julia was careful in every meeting she attended, to state that she was dedicated to promoting excellence in higher education. To this end, she insisted that all faculty be excellent in every way, especially the male faculty who, in her opinion, were a slovenly lot. So one of her first rules of decorum was that the male faculty must come to campus properly dressed, at a minimum a collar and tie, and jacket. She preferred dark suits, but would accept a neat sports jacket, but definitely no jackets with leather sewn into the elbows, and no corduroy. As for the administrative staff, she insisted that, if they were male, they not wear formal suits or ties, but in the summer shorts and t-shirt, and in the winter, old baggy jeans and definitely no worn out green knitted sweaters. She directed some of her assistants on a number of occasions to go to the local Goodwill store to purchase appropriate clothing for particular faculty.

As for the female faculty, in summer, short skirts above the knees were recommended, and whatever revealing tops they chose. They were to wear the most provocative clothing they could muster from their wardrobe and were not to walk around in academic gowns, unless they were left open at the front to reveal their enticing bodies. The female administrative staff were required to dress like male bureaucrats used to dress, in second hand gray suits, unbuttoned collar and wrinkled tie. The fact was, Julia often complained that, while there were many more female students on campus, there were too few female faculty. She therefore announced that during her tenure as Provost, only women or LGBTQ individuals would be hired. She made it quite clear that men were welcome to apply, but that they would not qualify for any position unless they were women. The university, after all, provided excellent emergency LGBTQ care at its special clinic in Hopewell. She also warned that men should not try to pass as women simply by dressing like them. Because of her unique experience, she could tell by looking at them whether they were genuine women or not.

As for herself, Julia flaunted her feminine charms in ways that perhaps were misunderstood around campus. Her rather stocky build had remained so, even after her radical gender change. But she countered this by first, growing her hair long and dying it blonde, then pulling it up to a top knot just like her mom's. This helped make her appear taller than she was, made her face seem longer and thinner, and with a little carefully placed make-up, rouge at the tips of her cheeks, she manage to convey an almost gaunt look, a thin face, cheeks concave, but not sunken, a longer chin, perhaps jutting out a little more than it should. But attention could be drawn away from that small defect by the artistic application of deep red lipstick, helping shape her lips to appear narrower than they might, reinforcing her now dominant face and high forehead. So when she stood up straight, a posture she practiced every morning when she arose from her slumbers, she pushed her head back, stretched her neck up and raised her chin. Here was the posture of a very confident woman, certainly one not to be messed with. She dressed conservatively, for a Provost a necessary characteristic. In fact, she dressed in the same style as her mom. Black slacks, of stretchy cotton spandex, pulled tight around her flat belly (more on that in a moment), and a black silk blouse open at the top, buttoned so that her cleavage showed enough to attract attention. And as she spoke to her faculty, she often fingered the button of her blouse closest to the cleavage. Indeed, it became a habit that her young straight male assistant sniggered about. And the sniggering was much more evident at the university gym.

*

The university gym was located at one corner of the low rise concrete building that made up the square podium surrounding the central fountain with its dull, plain tower. That tower would be one of the first small changes that Alphonso would make, replacing it with a copy of one of the handsome towers from the small town of towers, *San Gimignano* in Northern Italy. Actually, he wanted to move the whole tower from there to Hopewell, but the local residents of San Gimignano made such an outcry, that he dropped the project. It was just as easy to build a new one, and besides cheaper and easier to install in it church bells, electronic ones of course, that could play some twenty hymns and even broadcast chants and singing by the local boys' choir.

Julia made it a point to attend the gym every morning, usually at eight, a time that was too early for most students, though, as word got around that the Provost went to the gym early in the morning, students started to show up, and even some overweight faculty. The fact was that, now she was a woman, she wanted to make of her body what she could. The trouble was that she had inherited her father's stocky build, but her mother's long neck and face, and her quite fulsome bosom. The three did not go all that well together. Some of it could be overcome by careful choice of workout pants. These were very tight spandex down to her knees, her bottom thankfully still tight and curvaceous, then a bikini-like top that tightly held her breasts in place as she jogged and walked on the treadmill. She had tried the cross-trainer but had concluded that it demanded bodily contortions that were not lady-like. The trouble was that her stocky build stood out in the gym, her arms and legs curvaceously muscular, making her look as though she was a woman with, in part, a man's body, though very much a woman, maybe one who worked out with weights, which she did not.

It was on the treadmill that Julia made many of her tactical and policy decisions. And she did not hide her annoyance if anyone tried to speak with her while she was working out. That included, on this brisk November morning, Virgil who appeared on the treadmill next to her, walking at a medium pace, now sporting a ginger beard nicely groomed in the latest fashion. In response, Julia ramped up the pace and began a fast jog. It was not, all things considered, a sensible choice, since the jogging caused her fulsome breasts to rhythmically call out to Virgil whose head bobbed up and down in unison with her calling tits. He had come to see the Provost for her help. He needed willing workers to get the production of Holy Water vials up and running. The Holy Water would soon arrive by tanker direct

from Naples where it was loaded from the pipeline that Sisto
had, incredibly, hijacked from the old Roman aqueduct that led
directly to the Bay of Naples. Students, though unreliable, were
the cheapest labor, in his opinion, and as well, he only needed
them at this point to get things up and running. Once the
modern machinery was in place, it would not require many
hands on.

Julia eyed him suspiciously and nodded slightly to acknowledge his presence, then stared straight ahead. Virgil, for his
part, looked down at his patent leather shoes as the heels banged
on the rubber roller, now feeling rather stupid getting on a treadmill in a gym, better dressed than he would be at his Sunday
Pentecostal meetings. He slowed the speed down to a walk And
looked sideways to see if she showed any inclination to slow
down. She did not. He wondered what they did to her at the
LBGTQ center, whether she had changed in more ways than
just who she was. He could not believe that just a short time ago
he wanted to throttle her for having enticed his only son into
bed with her, or him as she was then. He had promised his wife,
now long gone to who knows where, that he would protect and
save Christian who was just turning seventeen at the time,
raging hormones, vandalizing school property, grabbing girls
where and when he should not, it seemed he was in the prin-
cipal's office every day. And then that gang of boys he got in
with at Boy Scouts, that seemed to solve things for a while.
They went away on camps together, sometimes for days on end,
and Christian would come back filthy, but in very high spirits.
Too happy, in Virgil's opinion. He suspected then that something was going on. And it seemed that all his time at home was
spent with arguing, Virgil complaining that Christian was not
working hard enough at school to get into a good college. And
worse, he would not go to church. Finally, he decided in des-
peration to send him to a Catholic seminary to straighten him
out. The logic of that decision eluded him now. There was no
logic, just frustration and despair. Virgil had taken to the drink
more than ever, had trouble himself getting off to church to
preach the gospel, and in the end lost all his money, not that he
had much of it. His wife had seen it coming and left him,
threatening that, if he did not straighten out Christian, she would
come back and take him away with her. So he ended up cam-
ping out, literally, at the Newark public library, researching
seminaries for Christian, and chose St. Roberts college as a

place that might take him for free. It was around this time that he lost his house because he could not keep up payments, and became homeless. Christian seemed not to mind, though to his amazement started carrying around a bible with him and apparently was staying with one of Virgil's more serious church brethren. In those last few months before Christian went off to the seminary, he often came by and dropped a dollar or two on Virgil where he had made his home sleeping on the library steps, begging for a few crumbs.

Virgil's treadmill had slowed to a stop. He stood there, looking blankly at the wall, ignoring the looks he was getting from the students who trotted by, slimmed down, their muscles flexing, their sexuality oozing through the pores of their smooth skin. He stepped off the treadmill and turned, his hands on his hips, to Julia waiting for her to stop. She ignored him. He found himself staring at her, unable to think of her as his son's Julian. She was now a woman, someone who would not be at all of interest to Christian, which, he supposed was a good thing. But there was something about her, her obvious aggressiveness, a male attribute surely, unless one considered all those Lesbians as female, which they weren't, but her features, her beautiful face, high cheeks, a nose sweetly small with a slight downturn like that of a Maya Indian, a mouth that to him was full of sexuality. He wanted dearly to see her smile. He reckoned that those small lips that brought her mouth into one that was ready to kiss, would expand into a voluptuous welcome to any admirer. He turned back to the treadmill. Something inside of him stirred, something he had not felt for a long, long time. He looked down at his shiny shoes and saw his nicely groomed face contorted in the reflection. He looked across once more at Julia who had given him a very slight sideways glance. He started his treadmill again, but now cranked it up to a running pace, and soon he was sweating profusely, a long time since he had done so, he ripped off his tie, shook off his jacket, unbuttoned his shirt and ripped that off too and the treadmill drummed louder, he ran and ran much too fast, could not keep up with it, looked across at Julia who now was slowing down, reaching her cooling off stage. But he lost control of the treadmill, slipped on the sweat that had dripped onto the roller, and fell down, the machine automatically coming to a stop, his pants caught up in the machine and stripped right off him, as his almost bare body was wrapped around the front of the treadmill.

Julia was immersed in her daily planning, which was what she did every morning in the gym. So she became at first angry when she noticed that Virgil was—how did they say it years ago—perving at her while she ran. A typical male gesture, she was sure that he had already raped her in his mind. And this, a Protestant preacher! How dare he have such thoughts! And so outrageous that she should condemn him for thoughts that she had no way of knowing were there or not! But Gloria Steinem spoke to her. "Never doubt a man's penis. If he has one, he can only think about where to put it next."

She stepped off her treadmill, grabbed a towel and wiped off the small drop of sweat from her brow. She stood up straight, looking down at Virgil, who now lay naked, having ripped off his underpants as he writhed in pain, a corny attempt to gain pity, and who knows, a rare chance to expose himself to a powerful woman. One couldn't blame him for that! She stood up straight in her typical manner, head back, breasts pushed forward, buttocks pulled in. If ever there was an invitation, this was it, thought Virgil as he lay there, looking up at the manly arms and legs and a beautiful woman's figure. Julia then did something that shocked him. She did the sign of the cross, touching herself so daintily, up, down, left nipple, right nipple. He rose up, like Lazarus, seemed to float up, against gravity. Of course, that was not what happened. Julia leaned over and took his hand to help him up.

"I, I…" stuttered Virgil.

She placed her exquisite fingers lightly over his mouth. "This way," she said, and pulled him after her into the sauna and locked the door behind them. Need one say any more? Gloria Steinem had put yet another man in his place.

It was left to Julia to saunter out to retrieve his clothes from the treadmill. When she did so, there was a rousing applause from cheering students. All of whom were looking at each other wondering why they should not emulate her. But there was a strict rule in the university against sex in public places. That was why Julia had led Virgil into the sauna room. Besides, all students had to obtain written permission from their parents in order to consummate themselves. In fact there were many such rules of behavior on campus that had been introduced by the new Provost.

Virgil staggered out of the sauna, fully dressed, shoes and all. The sweat made his collar sticky and rubbed his neck. "So I can depend on the university to provide student assistance in our manufacturing plant?" he asked Julia, as though nothing had happened between them.

"My budget will allow for twenty work-study students per semester. Will that be sufficient?"

"Provost Garcia, that would be ample, I think."

"Of course, there must be an educational component to the work experience. I take it that you will provide that?"

"Oh yes. Each student will write an evaluation of their experience."

"Excellent! Now if you will excuse me, I have an important meeting of the campus code of conduct committee."

"With pleasure, Provost. My deepest thanks." And with that Virgil reflexively did the sign of the cross on his own chest. Julia stopped in her tracks. Virgil's face blushed bright red. She smiled her biggest smile, her wonderful lips lighting up her gorgeous face and said, "my dear Virgil, I am overwhelmed!"

Virgil's mouth tightened as though he had just sucked a lemon. What had happened to him? Was it the insidious power of Catholicism or a sign that his Protestant ethic had withered away?

*

The Campus Code of Conduct committee was patiently awaiting Julia's appearance. Distinguished professor Serious Becker munched away on his morning croissant and Starbucks coffee. Crumbs dropped on his academic gown, and there were faint smudges where the butter from past croissants had found its way, other spots where the coffee had dribbled down his chin and on to the gown. The usual group sat chatting, student representatives in a corner gathered around an iPad looking at Instagram, pointing and laughing. Someone had posted a video of Virgil when he came out of the sauna, all sweating and red in his face.

Provost Julia entered full of composure, managing to look around the room, staring at each member just enough to scare them. She did, after all, have a lot of power. Universities were not democracies, as she had quickly found out. And thank goodness for that. Though she did think that the students had way too much power. They were, after all, just students. That was Distinguished professor Becker's constant complaint. It all started back in the anti-Vietnam war movement in the sixties, the student riots, demands, one of which was always that they should be represented on all university governance committees.

Julia began with her usual banter, always careful to use the word "excellence" at least once every five minutes. The university was, of course, dedicated to promoting diversity in all its colors, providing an environment where all students felt free to express themselves in whatever way they wanted. And yes, the university environment must above all else, provide a safe and secure environment where students could feel free to pursue their dreams. But above all it strove for excellence in everything that it did. She then made her most impressive announcement:

"I am pleased to report that our university has been rated in the *US. News and World Report* the top school in the USA in enforcement of diversity and inclusion. Our policies and procedures are the envy of every institution of higher education. We have the highest number of successful prosecutions for sexual harassment, insult and inuendo, and our unique ways of handling sexual abuse are the envy of the world, especially our introduction of public whipping of men suspected of abuse. Of course, we only smack them on their buttocks, but that seems to be enough."

A male student raised his hand. "But we don't smack the women for their abuse, do we? Isn't that unfair?"

"We would if there were any female or other gender types who indulged in sexual innuendo and insult, but we know of course, that women do not do that. They are the ones discriminated against so it is impossible for them to be abusers. I thought that issue had been debated thoroughly and settled on this campus."

Distinguished professor Serious Becker stirred in his seat. The Provost turned to him. "Distinguished professor Becker, you wish to say something?" Becker licked the crumbs off his lips and said, "we had one case, Madam Provost, of a male student complaining that he had been abused, but on investigation it was found that he in fact wanted to be abused."

"And how was the case resolved?"

"The punishment committee sentence him to public shaming. He was required to stand at the entrance to the university library, his pants dropped to his ankles, and a sign hung around his neck saying PLEASE ABUSE ME."

"And what was the result?"

"He was eventually abused by a group of female students, I think they were students who had taken your seminar on Gloria Steinem."

"And?"

"They led him away to their dorm, his hands tied behind his back, so I understand. After some days he reappeared at the entrance of the library, a sign around his neck again, this time saying, I WAS ABUSED AND I DESERVED IT."

One of the students raised his hand. "I'm the student, Professor provost. I learned my lesson, learned it thoroughly and I am pleased to report that the good women who abused me have taken me into their fold and we are now very intimate friends."

"That is a touching story. There should be more of it in this country. The transformation of abuse into inclusiveness. Wonderful and uplifting! Restorative justice at its best! Now I must take my leave and go to my next meeting, which is, I think, the affirmative action committee."

Julia looked around for her assistant, who should have been Scalpel, but he had gone missing for some time now and she had no one to depend on to get her from place to place. Distinguished professor Serious Becker stood and opened the door for her, which she thought was certainly very gentlemanly of him, so was an act of discrimination. "Distinguished professor Becker, if you don't mind, I will go first," she said with a cutting edge, "but you may lead the way to the next meeting. I believe you are a member of the Affirmative Action committee?"

"I am its chair, Professor Provost." In fact, Distinguished professor Serious Becker was the chair of almost every committee of the university. He taught rarely. His job essentially was to attend committee meetings and schedule them.

Becker led the way down the hall, across the campus passing by the fountain, then into another larger room, a small lecture theater. He went to the front and stood at the dais. Julia sat at the end of the front row and was surprised to find herself sitting next to none other than Christian.

"Christian! Where have you been? I haven't seen you for quite some time."

"I have been busy elsewhere, helping out your father," answered Christian in a monotonal voice.

"Is it true that you paid a visit to the LGBTQ decency care center? I heard a rumor," asked Julia.

"It's true. I had myself straightened out, you might say."

"Oh? I don't remember seeing that on their list of procedures."

"Never mind," said Christian coldly. "It was nothing really." An understatement if ever there was one.

"But everything turned out fine?" asked Julia, trying to be genuinely concerned

"Perfect, I would say. I am a different person." Christian looked away.

"Excellent." It was time for Julia to respond to Distinguished professor Serious Becker's glowing introductory remarks. She touched Christian lightly on his hand as she rose, an accidental touch. Christian looked at her coldly. "Perhaps you would be interested in taking up the position that Dr. Scalpel held—my assistant and basically chaperone. He seems to have gone missing."

Christian responded flatly, without hesitation. "I would be delighted."

"Good. See me after this meeting."

Julia took up her place next to Distinguished professor Becker at the dais. "Faculty and students, you have all read the report of the committee on affirmative action. And we will put the findings to work right here in our committee. Please let me see a show of hands of those who are different, or should I use that horrible term, are discriminated against in any way because of their personal characteristics."

There were around forty people in the lecture center, and all raised their hands.

The Provost continued. "We can't hope to eliminate all discrimination, but we can certainly try. Here are in summary form the main points of action arising from the committee's deliberations, all of which I will put into practice as of today. Distinguished professor Becker has kindly printed out the list." She gestured to Distinguished professor Becker who passed the handouts around. They were received with considerable buzz of excitement. "I will leave you for ten minutes while you read them." Julia left the room, followed quickly by Christian.

"So, what can I do to get started?" asked Christian.

"You can carry my bag, for one thing."

"Of course."

"And here is my schedule of meetings and events. You can make sure I get to them on time."

"That's it?" asked Christian.

"Well, from time to time, it will be necessary for you to deal with difficult people. I will leave it to you to decide how you deal with them. I have enough to do without being bothered by pedantic or plain silly academics. Understand?"

"Understood. And must I continue to teach my classes?"

"No, not if you can find someone else to sub for you."

"OK. Anything more?"

"You had better look over these points of action I handed out. Make sure you understand them so that you can help me enforce them as necessary.

The Affirmative Points of Action were as follows.

1. Hate speech. Speech that refers to individual characteristics is forbidden. Examples include, but are not limited to: fat, skinny, tall, short, allergic, blind, deaf, crippled, deformed, musclebound, male, female, gay, lesbian, bisexual, transgendered, black, white, yellow, brown, pink, red, ginger, beautiful, ugly, worker, malingerer, mother, father, married, single, daughter, son, grandfather, grandmother, sister, brother, bald, hairy. Big or little applied to: nose, breast, penis, vagina, hands, feet, torso, buttocks, ears. Speech with sexual undertones such as, "you look beautiful this morning," "I love your dress," "After you!"

2. Hate looks. Staring at rings, tattoos or other adornments of the body, staring at any naked part of a body, lustful looks, licking one's lips as one stares.

3. Hate thoughts. Some examples: "Want to get a coffee at Starbucks?" "Can I walk you home?" "Let's have dinner together."

4. Hate touching. No person may under any circumstance touch another in any way, unless prior consent is obtained. Shaking hands, hugging etc. are forbidden unless preceded by speech that indicates mutual consent. There is no such thing as an accidental touch. Public touching is permissible as long as the parties agree and the onlookers are either invited to watch or to look away.

The above offenses are mitigated or aggravated according to the affirmative ratings that will be published and revised on a monthly basis. These affirmative algorithms are driven by the demographic class to which the offender or victim belongs as defined by the population of the University Campus. These affirmative or negative classes are computed according to the ratio of the personal characteristics listed in point 1 above: that is applied to each class. For example, if the population of the university is 80 percent white and 20 percent black, then the severity of offense of a white person will be 4 times greater than that of a black offender and the punishment computed accordingly. The algorithm will be computed according to all personal characteristics involved in both the offender and the victim.

Provost Julia crossed herself then moved towards the door as she announced, "the penalties for all the infractions listed in this notice will be decided and delivered by the Interfaith Center, the head of which I will be announcing later today."

Distinguished professor Becker, in an unusual manner, rose from his seat, pulled his academic gown around him as though he was keeping out the cold, and placed himself at the door, blocking Julia's exit. "I really must protest, Madam Provost. The list of affirmative rights does not mention religion. Surely this is a class worthy of its own affirmative action points?"

Julia stopped and crossed herself again. "I know that this is an important issue, but I assure you that we are dealing with this matter in a different, and certainly better way. I will be announcing the exciting solution to this issue at the next meeting of the Interfaith Council, which I am due to attend right now. If you want to register your complaint, please do so with Professor Christian Bunion who will be its chair." She pointed to Christian who stood and nodded in Becker's direction. "Will you deal with Distinguished professor Becker please Dr. Christian?"

"Only too pleased to do so," replied Christian, a straight face, and in his now typical monotonic voice.

Julia turned to Becker and continued. "You will find Dr. Bunion an impartial judge in all matters. His qualification for the job is impeccable, having undergone neuteronomy. Isn't that so, Dr. Bunion?"

"If you say so Madam Provost."

Becker stepped aside and went towards Christian who scowled and walked past him, giving him a slight nudge as he passed and muttered "please make an appointment with my secretary. I must accompany Madam Provost to the Interfaith Council meeting."

"Then we can speak on the way, as I am also on that committee," answered Becker.

"Of course you are," noted Christian in his monotone.

"I have been a full time, tenured committee member for some thirty years," boasted Distinguished professor Serious Becker.

The Interfaith Council was the hallmark of Julia's administration. In her opinion, all religions existed for one single purpose: to bring down punishment on those who did or thought bad things. And since all people, no matter where they came from or what characteristics they were born with, thought and did bad things, it made no sense that only one religion was the right one. In fact, she often argued, if you scratch the surface of any religion you will find buried beneath it, the punishment that wrong doing brings upon itself. She therefore viewed the Interfaith Council as the most important council on campus because it all came down to everyone agreeing on how discipline—and that's what keeping bad thoughts in check was all about—what pain should be administered and who should administer it. The Interfaith Council, because it represented all religions was the perfect mechanism, and could draw on any religion it liked to decide on punishments.

Those who broke the anti-discrimination and diversity rules were assessed according to the affirmative action algorithm that applied to them, and a sliding scale of punishment, usually the Islamic punishment of whipping. Some of the Christians on campus had complained that this was unfair because whipping was not owned by Islam, but that Christians had long looked to it for salvation. The more extreme Christians even campaigned for a while to have crosses erected around campus where they could, should it become necessary, crucify a severe hate speech wrong doer. Of course, Julia vetoed that preposterous idea, and pointed out that crucifixion was actually a pagan punishment invented by the ancient Romans. And yes, as one would expect, a number of students protested that there were no pagans represented on the Interfaith Council. That issue continued to be unresolved, and there were constant parades in front of the library, of students carrying placards "MORE GODS! MORE GODS!" Julia placated them by agreeing to admit more Japanese students into Virgin Hall.

Distinguished professor Becker called the council to order. The minutes of the last meeting were read out by Christian's secretary who had the job of keeping the minutes. They basically were a list of individuals who had been found guilty of various hateful infractions, and the recommended punishments. Now here was the most interesting part. Every member of the Interfaith Council—there were fifty active members of whom usually only half showed up to the regular meetings—had voted against appointing one of their members as the administrator of the punishments. Christian had volunteered to do it, but since he was not a student, this was not allowed, because it would have been an act of authoritarianism for a faculty member to punish a student. He pointed out that, as a former Christian (he had lost his faith as a side effect of his neuteronomy surgery) he was sure that self-flagellation was a much more just and fair form of punishment. This proposal was unanimously adopted.

However, Distinguished professor Serious Becker, who was an atheist but insisted that it too was a religion so that he could be a member of the Interfaith Council, pointed out that it was also an important principle of the Christian faith, and maybe other religions as well, that one should be forgiven for one's infractions. There was a long debate on whether doing bad things should be called sins, offenses or crimes even, and, since he was an atheist, he argued that there was no such thing as a bad thought or act. For this he was howled down and came close to being charged with heresy. In the end he withdrew his argument and apologized constantly for the rest of the meeting. The final resolution was that, certainly people should be forgiven for their bad thoughts or actions, but that could only be done after the person was punished.

Julia was about to announce the close of the meeting, when a student called for a point of order, having no idea what that meant, and asked was it intended that all punishment should be done in public, and if so, why not use shaming instead of self-flagellation? Distinguished professor Becker should have spoken up here, but he was so ashamed of his own hateful speech, he remained quiet. This was the question Julia had been waiting for.

"Thank you for that insightful question. If I may suggest, we should table this question, or perhaps even better, refer it to the Committee on Safe Spaces, which meets first thing in the morning. That committee will also be considering whether the names of individuals and their bad deeds and their prescribed punishments should be publicly posted."

*

The Committee on Safe Spaces met off campus in the nearby Starbucks. The chair of that committee, Distinguished professor Serious Becker insisted that, since safe spaces were about keeping people safe in public places, their meeting should be conducted in a public place. That there were too many members of the committee to fit into the relatively small space of the local Starbucks, did not occur to him, not to mention interfering with the regular customers and there being a constant line asking for the key to the bathroom. The manager of the Starbucks sought to ban them from entry, complaining that the permanently resident homeless outside would sneak in and use the bathroom too. After all had their lattes, double shots, mochas and the rest, Julia asked Distinguished professor Becker to open the meeting, and also introduced Dr. Virgil Bunion to make an important announcement. He had just returned from Rome where he met with none other than the new Pope Si. Virgil, dressed in his impeccable businessman's suit from Mens Warehouse, eyed the homeless rabble with concern, hoping that they would not recognize him. He was also a little embarrassed that it had fallen to his son Christian to herd the rabble out of Starbucks back to their makeshift tents.

Julia spoke. "I am honored and very pleased to introduce to you Dr. Virgil Bunion, eminent Protestant preacher of the church of Judasian Trust. He has a very important announcement to make."

"Thank you, Professor Provost. I am the reverend doctor Virgil Bunion and I am the director of the Virgin Hall University business incubator park. Many of you here I know will be interning in our various business operations, the most important one being the initiative to modernize the production and distribution of Holy Water. I met with the new Pope at the Vatican last week. He has given us the green light to proceed, and as well additional financing for campus improvements."

A couple of students were chatting to each other and laughing, clearly those who had been in the gym and witnessed the tryst in the sauna room. Christian grabbed them by an ear in each hand and escorted them out of the Starbucks, just like they were little children.

Virgil continued. "We have received a generous gift from the Vatican to establish safe spaces on campus that will be available for individual student use. These spaces will fulfill a number of important purposes: First, they will provide a place of complete privacy where one (and only one at a time) may do whatever one pleases, including dealing with various bathroom issues as may be necessary. Second, they will be equipped with a window that may be made one way in any direction. If you want to see out, but no one see in, you can do that too. Or if you so want, you can make it so that people can see in and you not see out. Or, the default which is like any ordinary window. Third, these spaces will be created all over campus. They will be the size of a small pod, to be called popods, basically like portable potties with windows."

A student raised his or her hand. "So they're just toilets?"

Virgil sternly answered. "No, not just toilets. You can use them for that if you want, but there will be various odor options that you can create with the push of a button, generally intense of various kinds, including, I understand on the last communication I received from the Vatican, the smell of marijuana."

"So you can smoke pot in them?"

"You can do whatever you like in them. They are your safe spaces. There for regular or emergency use," Virgil answered with a smile of satisfaction.

Distinguished professor Serious Becker spoke up. "Will they be equipped for punishment?"

Julia interjected. "They will contain basic instruments for self-flagellation, or other means of administering pain to one's self. These will contain computer chips that will record the number of painful administrations applied, so that the Interfaith Council can be assured that the correct amount of punishment was carried out."

Another student complained. "But if you're going to whip yourself, you need a lot more room to swing your arm than there is in a portable potty."

"Quite right, thank you for your astute observation. We do plan to make them big enough for that," replied Virgil.

"Keep in mind," said Julia, "that for those who want to punish themselves publicly or have someone else punish them, there will be whipping posts erected at various public places around the campus. Now, are there any other questions?"

Distinguished professor Serious Becker gave his deep cough. "Hearing none, I declare this meeting closed."

Christian followed Becker out and to his office.

"Professor Serious Becker, we have not been formally introduced. I am Christian Bunion, assistant to the Provost. That was my father Virgil Bunion, who is heading up the new university business park."

"Yes, I am aware of that. You seem to have forgotten that I was present at your faculty presentation," answered Becker in his haughty manner. He made for his desk, picking his way between piles of books and papers that sat on the floor, some of the piles waist high. Christian followed him and stretched out his hand. Becker ignored it.

Christian persisted. "Professor Provost asked me to check with you to see if there is anything more that you are concerned about."

Becker sat down at his desk and began to leaf through some papers. "If I have anything to say I will say it in the meeting as I always do," he said curtly.

"It's just that she does not want to be embarrassed should you take a position that is unexpected." Christian leaned against Becker's desk, knocking one of the piles of papers over the side.

"And what might that be?" asked Becker as he leaned down to pick up his papers.

"Well I wouldn't know, would I? That's why I'm talking to you now." Christian's icy cold manner should have been enough to warn Becker, but he seemed not to notice. "She is concerned about the next meeting which is tomorrow, I believe, of the Tenure and Promotions Committee. You have read the draft rules that our esteemed Provost has proposed?"

"I do have some disagreements. But that is my right, isn't it? This is a university, not a corporate headquarters," snarled Becker. Sarcasm filled the cluttered room.

Christian appeared not to hear what he said. Instead he changed the subject. "By the way, a prototype of the new safe space popods has been installed in front of the library. Would you like to look it over? The Provost would greatly appreciate your input. We can still make adjustments to them, should they be necessary. It's been a challenge to make them aesthetically appealing, to blend in with the academic environment and the Frank Lloyd Wright design of the campus."

Becker grunted and looked up from his papers, peered at Christian over his spectacles. "The new tenure rules go too far. Must I repeat. This is a university, not a corporate headquarters."

"Oh, indeed. But I don't think you quite understand. This is now a faith based university, not an arm of the New Jersey State government, and certainly not as you say, a corporate entity, which the Provost abhors as she should. The obsession with money is the faith of corporations, if you will excuse my abuse of words."

Becker stood up from his desk with a sigh. "All right, then, lead the way to the popod."

*

Provost Julia sat at the head of a large polished oak table that seated some twenty or more faculty, each with adjustable office chairs, black leather and chrome. Another twenty or so junior faculty and students sat behind them. Christian remained standing, his passive face staring straight ahead at no one in particular. It was a gloomy day outside, the leaves falling off the trees, a brisk wind, intermittent hail and rain. He did not want to be here, as the meeting had interrupted his routine of caring for Virgil's snakes, a job that he had taken much more seriously than anyone expected. He fed them carefully, one by one, spoke to them as though they were pets, even occasionally risked patting or stroking them as though they were cats. A couple of times one had snapped at him, but he was quick enough to draw his hand away. He named that snake, Tiger, of course, since it was a tiger snake, its beautiful yellow stripes and shiny healthy skin glistening in the pale light of the basement. He had argued with Virgil who wanted to add a dozen more rattlesnakes to the collection, that there was no need for more than the current four tiger snakes and one rattlesnake. If there were any more during the Pentecostal service, with all those people running down to partake, there would be pandemonium if someone were bitten. Better to keep it small, and choose only carefully vetted persons from the audience to come forward and do the snake dance. But now, his attention was drawn to Julia who had decided to stand at the end of the table to make her presentation.

Julia had waited for Distinguished professor Serious Becker to arrive, but he did not. She gave Christian a look, but he remained passive and did not respond, unless one takes an empty stare as a response. Provost Julia, as she now called herself, an expression of informality, a good way to have the faculty feel close to her, switched on her PowerPoint. She stood as tall as she could, her office slacks tightly bound around her waist with a bright yellow and purple sash, the university's new colors, and her now characteristic black blouse, the top buttons undone to just the right level of cleavage. Her hair was tied up as tight as ever into a top knot, her face made up with rouge, perhaps a little too much to impress with Asiatic cheeks, and a soft powder to her neck, hiding the wrinkles that had appeared very soon after her corrective surgery. She began, the room silent.

"Of course we all know that the three pillars of faculty assessment are publications, teaching and service, in equal

weight, though it has generally come to be informally acknowledged that really, it is publications that are the most important,
and it is on this that the national ratings of universities and
colleges are made. After consultation with selected and represented faculty, I have decided to radically change this formula to
bring it into line with the twenty-first century."

Faculty pushed back on their chairs, the students sat passive
having no idea what all this meant.

"What I am most concerned to emphasize in our evaluation of
faculty is their *performance* in the life of our university and
community both local and national. As we all know, there is a
great concern about fake and fact, so much so that it has become
almost impossible to separate fact from fiction. Therefore, to
use publications as the key factor in determining faculty
performance, is simply not possible any more. I know that many
faculty along with their students frequently attend rallies and
protests where the push and pull of fact and fiction are played
out. Such experiences are to be encouraged and certainly also
come within the realm of teaching, since those experiences are
very instructive, and more important are directly a part of real
life, not abstract ideas that are the traditional fodder of the ivory
tower."

Christian shifted from foot to foot and Julia got the message.
He was telling her to "get on with it."

Julia switched to her PowerPoint. "Here are the criteria for
evaluation and they will take effect immediately. They are self-
explanatory, so I need not read them out. They will also be
distributed to all members of the university by email."

CRITERIA FOR ACADEMIC ASSESSMENT OF
FACULTY

Academic Performance:

The number of protests attended, weighted by the number of
people in attendance.

The number of views published on the web of protest part-
icipation and rants that uncover fake performances of others,
including faculty, students and politicians or other officials.

Number of blogs that deconstruct fake academic claims, especially fake science.

Number of Twitter, Facebook and Instagram followers.

Service:

Number of committee meetings attended, weighted by the
length of the meetings, the longer the more heavily weighted.

Number of arrests for protesting.

Number of convictions for protesting.

Amount of damage caused by the protest, the more, of course, the greater the weight.

Teaching:

Number of student parties attended by faculty.

The faculty mentoring of students—hot tub counseling, basement raves, sharing joints and other drugs.

Supervision of Holy Water Internships.

ALL THE ABOVE TO BE WEIGHTED BY AFFIRMATIVE ALGORITHMS

Julia sat down and asked, "are there any questions?"

A student raised his or her hand. "What are Holy Water internships?"

Julia looked around the room. "That question is best answered by the CEO of the Holy Water initiative, Dr. Reverend Virgil Bunion. Virgil, where are you?"

"I'm right here, Provost Julia," came a muffled cry from under the long table. Virgil had attempted to sit forward on his office chair, but not used to such chairs, it rolled backwards and he slipped off and under the table. The students giggled some faculty sniggered.

Julia stood up again, indignant. "My goodness! I am appalled that any of you would react in this way to a simple slip under the table. We must learn civility, it is the most important thing in a university, indeed, in this modern age, in our civilization. That is, after all, where this word civilization came from. We must be civil to each other!"

Virgil clawed at the table and managed to struggle on to his chair. "I have fifty internships available. These are paid at equal to the national basic wage which is twice what the university research foundation pays. Or, we offer instead, all or in part, stock options in the Holy Water Foundation."

Another student raised his or her hand. "What is the Holy Water Foundation, exactly? I mean, I thought you only got holy water in a church or something."

"An excellent question," Virgil replied. "Would you like to answer that, Christian?"

"No." Christian was annoyed and disliked the stares it invited.

Provost Julia offered a fake smile and intervened. "The Holy Water Foundation has been established as a result of a wonderful partnership between this university, led by Doctor

Alphonso Garcia, our university president, who has contributed a fortune to underwrite it, with the Vatican where all Holy Water originates." Buzz and mumble rippled around the room. "Perhaps I could confide in you all, but you must promise that this information will not leave this room any time soon, because it is not official as of yet." Julia paused for effect, looking first at Virgil and then to Christian. "We are in early talks with the Vatican for the new Pope, named Pope Si, to visit the University very soon, possibly as early as next month."

"That's tomorrow!" chirped a student.

"Oh so it is! Then let's say possibly within a week or two. In any case, you can see that our Virgin Hall University is getting off to an amazing start."

Students and faculty alike began to stand, ready to leave. Provost Julia immediately sat down." If you don't mind, civility please! I have not yet declared this meeting closed. But when I do, I expect that all those who define themselves as ladies should leave first of course, to retain decorum, followed by LGBTQ, followed by SM."

Christian was puzzled and asked even though he didn't want to, "What's SM?"

One of the students turned to him and whispered loudly, "straight men."

Provost Julia stood again and announced in a loud voice: "In the absence of Distinguished professor Serious Becker, I forgot to announce that there is a meeting in this room starting in five minutes of the Campus Civility Committee. I have another meeting to attend so I am asking Doctors Bunion to co-chair the meeting. Here are the notes I have made for our new policy on this very important matter."

Virgil raised his hand. "Provost Julia, I believe I am technically not qualified for any committee chair-ship because I am not teaching faculty, but a full time university research director."

"Yes, that is true. But given your extensive experience in dealing with uncivil matters, especially in respect to those savages who gather outside Starbucks, I think you are specially qualified."

*

"I am honored to present to you Professor Ito Reo from the Japanese Institute of Powerful Manners." Virgil turned to Professor Ito and bowed his stiff bow following the directions he looked up on Wikipedia. He looked at the floor as directed, and kept his bow until Professor Ito stopped his, which seemed like forever.

"I am most warmly pleased and wisely happy to be in your sacred presence," answered Professor Ito, turning to the audience and bowing once again. Christian, who never liked Japanese because of what he heard they did in World War II, put out his hand and offered a handshake and at the same time indicated to the audience that they should rise and bow.

Professor Ito lectured the members on how and when to bow. It was most important, he said again and again, that one hold one's bow much longer when bowing to superiors and only let up when the superior ended his/her or its bow. And of course, as everyone knows, one must never look the bow in the eye, but always look down. Unfortunately, there were no faculty attending the meeting, only students, so there was an air of irreverence and just plain recalcitrance. The students bowed in all directions, leading sideways, falling over frontwards from bowing too deeply, bowing on one leg, and other nonsense. It was left to Christian to return them to order, which he did by walking around the room and giving any particularly rowdy students a smack behind the ear, which brought howls of defiance, but nevertheless got them to sit down at the conference table. After several more bowing sessions, Virgil ushered the Professor, most embarrassed and thoroughly confused, out of the conference room.

Christian spoke in his quiet monotone, and all listened. They did not want a smack over the ear. "As of today, Provost Julia has signed an order that all students must bow to their professors using the Japanese way. Any who do not will be subject to the appropriate disciplinary action, which will, initially be time out in a popod. There, you will be able to have time in your own safe space, silence to meditate upon your incivilities, self-flagellate should you feel it necessary. Provost Julia has also issued additional guidelines as follows:

"Individuals must keep a distance from each other of roughly two feet, and should never breathe on each other without the other's consent. If touching is desired, the university will be issuing official touching coupons which individuals may exchange to gain permission. Purple coupon means permitted to touch, yellow coupons mean not OK to touch."

An insolent student raised his or her hand. "Can you touch anywhere once you have permission?"

Christian answered quietly, "the guidelines are silent on that issue." He continued, "prayer dropping will also be required of each student at least once a day. Virgin Hall University is a faith based university, so it is necessary for all students, including also faculty, to show their faith by dropping to their knees at least once a day, and in public, to affirm their faith. Of course, because we are an inter-faith university, whoever you pray to or for is your personal business. But you must drop to your knees and pray at least once a day. You may also download the University App which will keep count of your prayer drops, so you can monitor your faithful progress. An award will be given out at commencement to the most faithful student on campus."

"How much is the award?" asked the obstreperous student.

"I'm glad you asked. Doctor Virgil here will answer that."

"The inaugural faith award will be the opportunity of a special personal audience with Pope Si I, who, it is now confirmed, will be visiting New Jersey, specifically our very own faith based campus, to deliver his blessings to all, to dedicate our new Holy Water business park, and he will receive the winning faithful student in a private audience. You will be photographed and this will be included on the award certificate signed and sealed by Pope Si himself."

"Will I have to do a sign of the cross like Catholics do?" called out one student from the back, "I'm not a Catholic, I'm a Vegan."

"As a matter of fact, Professor Julia and members of the inter-faith council will be working on this very issue, since as you know, Virgin Hall University is a Catholic university primarily, although we welcome all faiths," answered Virgil. "For the moment doing the cross will not be required. The prayer drop is probably enough, though those who want to practice being Catholics are welcome to cross themselves any time they have a bad or good thought. As for me and my son here, Christian, we are Protestants so we do not do the cross. Instead, we bite our knuckles or bottom lip until it hurts."

"Are there any more questions?" Christian asked.

Silence.

"Then please go to the student center to collect your touch coupons. There you will also be issued a free pass to the Pentecostal meeting in honor of Pope Si I that will be held at the CURE stadium on Sunday. Be sure to have plenty of touch coupons for that event because the seats are close together and it

will be difficult to sit or move around without touching someone."

16. Pentecostal

On the stage there would be all the top academics of Virgin Hall University, Maria, Sisto, Francisco, Pedro, Christian, Julia, and of course, El Padrino Alphonso, dressed in a gold leaf academic robe with platinum braid. The Great Godfather had also been invited, but news came that he had gout and had taken to his bed with his robot partner Angelina (a gift from Cardinal Benitez). Di Napolitano would come in his place, accompanied by Cardinal Benitez who these days seemed to be everywhere. And of course, the main attraction, Pollagrande, now Pope Si, the people's Pope, would be there in all his spiritual splendor.

There was some debate whether Pope Si should retain his predecessor's slaves, and in the end they decided to make an exception at least for this Papal visit, and use them along with the litter. The slaves were, understandably, jubilant. While New Jersey wasn't Louisiana, it was closer than was Rome. And the Pope had offered as well to pay for any of their relatives from New Orleans to come to New Jersey to attend the Great Pentecostal.

Pollagrande, for his part, had difficulty settling into being Pope Si, the name insisted on by the Milanese caucus of communists for capitalism who claimed to have got him elected, yet they claimed not to believe in singling out any individual as number one. He had little time to himself, which meant that he had almost no time with the love of his life, Estelle. In his regular early morning consultations with Benitez, he even sometimes whimpered that he couldn't go on without her and that maybe he should quit. Benitez comforted him by pointing out that if they scheduled his time carefully, and Benitez programed Estelle into going through her duties more quickly, perhaps that would help. But Pollagrande, as Benitez well knew, could not manage quickies. "Maybe you should take one of my blue pills," joked Benitez, but this made Pollagrande even more despondent. And in his maudlin moments, Pollagrande grasped

Benitez by his shoulders and demanded, "promise me one thing. That I will be buried alongside my dear Estelle in an unmarked grave in the grounds of Saint Aidan's orphanage in Bendigo."

"Polly, really! That's enough of this talk!" complained Benitez.

"Promise me!"

"Of course, I promise. But who knows, I might be the one to go first. In which case, may I have her beside me when I go?"

"Oh! Shut up!" said Pollagrande, at last with a grin.

"As you wish, Holy Father," said Benitez as he bowed deeply.

*

Benitez called the Pope's plane Eagle One. He rented it from Al Italia, charged all the press corps super first class prices to pay for it, and herded them into the back of the plane. Pope Si I took up the entire first class section, all but two beds removed and the section completely separated from the press and Papal staff by a thick bulkhead. The Papal bed had been especially widened to make room for Estelle, a big surprise for Pollagrande. Benitez had gone to a lot of trouble to have Estelle dismantled and packed into a large crate which was loaded into the first class section where they rebuilt her just before take-off. And once they got to Newark, she would quietly alight from the plane dressed in a simple nun's habit, posing as a reporter for the Virgin Hall Daily Express. This required a lot of new programing and there had been no time for testing for any bugs.

The landing at Newark was sensational. From the air, Benitez pointed out the massive array of buildings that made up the new Virgin Hall business park that was now the headquarters of the Holy Water project. A huge tanker had already arrived at the port of Newark, and a cohort of trucks, marked with the Papal keys was clearly visible moving along the highway to Hopewell where it would be unloaded into the enclosed holding pool, then bottled in the vials made of recycled glass, tamper proofed and marked with the Papal keys. As the plane came in lower to its last approach, huge throngs of people could be seen waving at the road side, others in rowboats with oars or outboard motors, waving from the cesspools of Newark's polluted outer suburbs that were, naturally, all on the New York side.

Someone, most likely an illegal immigrant who was used to climbing fences, had cut through the fence that surrounded the Newark Airport and throngs of people had pushed their way through and ran onto the tarmac, waving frantically, many dropping to their knees, crossing themselves. Pope Si was overcome. Water came to his eyes. "The faith of the living!" he thought to himself. "Sinner that I am, I do not deserve this adulation! Oh! But it is not for me! Jesus, my deepest apologies! They are here for you! I am just your pawn."

Benitez smiled to himself. It was amazing what an orchestrated campaign on social media could achieve. The plane landed to a huge applause, a tradition of passengers who flew Al Italia. Not so much tradition, as an expression of relief. There was a loud knock on the door and Benitez opened it. The four slaves were bursting to go! He had never seen them so happy. Papal assistants ran in and began to dress Pope Si. Estelle had been quickly moved into the cockpit out of sight. The pilots, all women, were displeased and wanted her out. They found her habit disconcerting. Besides, civilians were not allowed in the cockpit. One of the pilots pinched her to get her out of the way. But Estelle felt nothing. Benitez had put her into hibernation mode.

The next several hours went like a fast forwarded movie. Pope Si stood at the top of the steps of the plane and did the sign of the cross to the crowd, turned first to the right then the left. The slaves lifted him on to his litter and they lifted him high. "I bless you all, God bless America!" he cried, his head held high. How could one not feel the power of a swooning crowd, how could one not avoid thinking that it was him who they worshipped, not He whom he represented?

Alphonso, garbed in his gold sequined academic robe, stepped forward from the crowd, Christian hung behind to beat back the crowd with his riot gear shield he had borrowed from the Newark Police Department. Alphonso dropped to his knees and crossed himself. Pope Si placed his hands on Alphonso's head and said, "I bless you my son and father, you are a person of great magnificence. Rise! You are twice blessed!"

Alphonso tried to stand tall as he announced, "on behalf of the governor of New Jersey, who stands beside me, as proud president of Virgin Hall University, and father of Provost Julia, I welcome you, Pope Si the first, to the Great State of New Jersey!" The crowd swayed and rippled like an ocean, as people shouted and screamed.

The slaves placed their Pope and his litter on the back of a specially painted black pick-up truck and it inched its way through the unruly crowd. The motorcade slowly emerged from the airport, but no matter which way it went, thousands of cars seemed to follow and clogged up the many freeways that entered and left the airport. There would be a huge traffic jam reaching as far back as the Holland tunnel, taking two days to untangle.

The crowd that awaited them at the CURE. Stadium was even larger, and more unruly because the stadium was full to overflowing. Virgil set up oversize screens outside for the crowd, but of course, that was not like being able to see the real thing.

*

Virgil took great care with his grooming. He decided to forego the jacket and tie and instead emulate the simple dress of the digital giant executives, like Steve Jobs, and prune his ginger beard to a light stubble, carefully trimmed, and shaped above his upper lip, his thinning hair also cut short to maybe half an inch. And his eyebrows he had cropped so that in the bright light of the cameras, they gave a faint reddish glow. It was youth that he wanted to portray, youth and energy, an exciting future ahead of all. He sported an untucked shirt and tapered casual pants. And underneath he wore a new compression t-shirt that pulled in his aging belly. All in all, he looked very much the part of a vibrant young executive.

It was his show, so he led his entourage of Incredibles on to the stage. He and Christian jogged out together, Virgil so proud of his son, Christian, slightly embarrassed, but overwhelmed by the feeling of exhilaration when the crowd erupted into enormous cheers of adulation. How could one not feel so great? And Christian carried snakes draped over both arms, two tigers on his right arm, a rattler on his left. Virgil sent him forward to get closer to the crowd, and Christian jigged lightly, the snakes winding and every now and then lofting their heads as if to survey the crowd.

Then huge applause erupted when Pope Si I appeared on his litter, carried high by his four slaves who were also jubilant. They even began to jog in unison with Christian. The University band struck up the Papal Anthem, as the procession of Incredibles marched on to the stage, Alphonso in his gold sequined academic robe, Sister Maria in her simple black robe and white winged habit, and Sisto, crooning "O Felix Roma!" in his off-key tenor voice that penetrated the cheers of the crowd with ease, his round body seeming to float on his fluttering red cape. Francisco took up the rear, dressed as a soldier of the Holy Roman Empire.

Virgil took up the microphone and walked across the stage. He had watched Steve Jobs many times. It was confidence he must portray, supreme confidence. Then he began. He would not speak in matter of fact tones like Jobs. He would speak in rousing tones, shouting at times, shouting out the love of God and Jesus Christ. Most important was to engage the audience, have them chant and respond.

"Our Father who is in Heaven!" he cried, starting at a high pitch. "Speak to me!" he bade the audience.

The crowd answered. "Hallowed be Your name!"

Virgil: "Thy kingdom come! Thine will be done on earth as it is in Heaven!"

The worshippers: "Give us this day our daily bread!"

Virgil: "And forgive us our me-toos!"

Worshippers: "As we forgive those who me-too us!"

Virgil: "Lead us not into temptation!"

Worshippers: But deliver us from evil!"

Virgil: "For Yours is the Kingdom of power and glory!"

Worshippers: "Forever and ever!"

And all together: "Amen!"

The band struck up "Come Down O Love Divine" and Virgil beckoned Sisto to join him. They sang and Virgil called to the audience, conducting, and the audience quickly joined him. The crowd was ready, almost swooning. Christian was even swaying with the beautiful melody, waving his arms, jigging a little so that the snakes also swayed, but then Christian raised his right arm a little too suddenly and one of the tiger snakes flipped off and slithered across the stage. The slaves had placed the Pope's litter down and were happily singing along as well. The Pope struggled to stand, weighed down by his heavy robe, a bright white with gilded braid, but he managed to make the sign of the cross to the audience turning to the right, center then left, "in the name of the Father, the Son and the Holy Ghost, I bless you all!" he called out in a weak voice.

In the excitement and noise no one but Christian had noticed the snake slip off his arm. Christian stood rooted to the spot fearful that should he chase the snake, the others would drop off his arm and there would be pandemonium. He had fed them and looked after them as Virgil had instructed. The problem was clearly that they were too healthy and looking for action. But he was too late. He saw the tiger quickly slither under the Pope's robe just as he sat down after delivering the blessing. The stadium now became quiet in anticipation of the Pope's prayer that would bless them all and Virgin Hall University. He went to stand again, but just as he started to rise his whole body shook and he fell back on to the sedan chair of the litter. He convulsed once again, as though he were about to vomit, but instead, through the robe from his crotch, the snake leapt out, lifting its head in the manner of a cobra for just a second, then slithered away across the stage and into the crowd.

"The Devil! It's the devil!" someone cried, and all hell broke loose, and worse, Christian had run forward to grab the snake, but of course, the others fell off his arms and scurried away into the crowd. Francisco, good Papal soldier, moved forward to protect the Pope, but then stopped. For before their eyes, his robes had split open, and a massive bulbous thing of swollen testicles burst out of his pants, two bite marks clearly apparent, a trickle of blood running down a closely shaven crotch.

The first to arrive were the pest control people who had never chased tiger snakes before. Their technique, proven they said on American snakes, was to release a bucket full of mice that had been fed on marihuana and wait for the snakes to go for them. It turned out that the crowd was just as freaked out by the mice as they were the snakes. The problem was solved, however by the good soldier Francisco who rid himself of his 17th century armor and used his Beretta 9mm pistol to shoot them.

Unfortunately, the problem of the Pope was not solved so easily. The ambulance arrived and he was rushed to the LGBTQ emergency care center where a neuteronomy was performed. But it was too late. The poison had quickly overtaken his whole body and he died on the operating table. The genitalia were, however, frozen and kept in storage should the Vatican request that they be used to spawn a new Pope, maybe. The rest of the body was parceled up, frozen, and prepared for transport back to the Vatican. The world was aghast at this terrible event. Pope Si I was revered and loved by all good and bad Catholics, certainly far more than JFK.

17. Pope No

The story might well have ended with the death of Pope Si, but it was only the beginning for Alphonso, whose first epiphany had spawned all of these events. In truth, Alphonso, who, by the way, no longer scratched his navel in pubic, had underestimated just how enormously rich he would become, indeed, there appeared to be no limits. The constant flow of money that came in from the monopoly he had on Holy Water vials and the spin-off products, was far greater than he could have imagined. And best of all, the money was legal, so it gave him an easy way to launder Maria's drug money. Their houses in Mexico, built literally of drug money, were gradually being laundered away. His net worth was easily equal to that of the digital giants, and he had the advantage of his business being relatively hidden in the shadows of the Catholic Church. There was no end in sight for his riches. Yet it was this lack of an horizon that caused him some restlessness.

He woke up each morning and wondered what the day would bring, yet knowing full well that the day was perfectly predictable. He had even grown bored with his sprawling white villa, set among the native dogwoods of the forests that surrounded Princeton, eight bedrooms, a room for every day of the week, and one for a guest. He had only the undocumented housemaid to order around, and ordering Christian around was like ordering one's dog. There was no satisfaction in total obedience. His navel was no longer the source of irritation. It was his head that itched to be scratched, or at least what was inside it. He had reached the pinnacle of success. Yet his brain kept asking each morning he awoke, what next?

A man of success, Pollagrande used to say, bless his soul, always looks to the future, forgets the past. This has its advantages, but also one serious disadvantage. Men of success cannot be so without having made enemies. And to forget who one's enemies were or might be, is a fatal mistake, especially for a man whose business was one of violence. And who were his enemies? He could think of none. After all, as he had said to both Pollagrande and Benitez during confession prior to his epiphany, he never killed anyone. And as his acumen grew as El Padrino, he didn't even have to ask his minions to do violence, because they anticipated his every wish.

This was his state of mind when there was a light knock on the door and the maid ushered Benitez into his Friday bedroom. He lay flat on his back looking up at the ceiling, hands behind his head. The ceiling was of course, decorated with a copy of the Michelangelo depiction of God and man, the fingers reaching out, set against all that blue sky.

"Padrino! I have caught you napping," laughed Benitez.

"What is it? I thought you went back to Rome to replace Pollagrande, poor fellow." Alphonso crossed himself.

"You know that it is not all that straight forward. But it is why I am here."

"Oh?" Alphonso sat up, suddenly invigorated. There might be an excitement to make his day.

"The Great Godfather has refused to support me," muttered Benitez, trying to control his anger.

"But I thought we paid him off most handsomely. Was it not enough?"

"It's not money. It's because I am not Italian, or actually, not a Neapolitan."

"But neither was Pollagrande," said Alphonso, "nowhere near it."

"Yes, but the Great Godfather says the Anglos have had their turn and messed it up, so now it was time to get a solid Neapolitan in there."

"Messed what up? It was an accident. The poor bugger got bitten by a snake. Who could have predicted that?"

Benitez shrugged. "He blames you. Says you fixed it all. And Pollagrande was a favorite of his. Claims he was his genuine Godfather. Nobody believes that, of course. Pollagrande was an Aussie orphan."

"You want me to send Christian to take care of it?" asked Alphonso. warming to the prospect.

"It will take more than Christian. You've been there. The place is like a fortress. Besides, I think things have gone too far already. I think he's out to get you."

Alphonso sat up and burst out laughing. "The old shit! Who does he think he is? I'll go over there and take care of it myself."

"You're joking, right?" asked Benitez.

"Me, joking? Since when did I ever joke?"

"But you've never killed anyone in your life. You told me that in your confessions."

"True. But there's always a first time."

Benitez shrugged again. "Anyway, you would have to deal with the consigliere. He's already campaigning among the bishops and cardinals who will be descending on Rome in the next few days to elect the new Pope."

"Who does he want?"

"Don't laugh at this," replied Benitez, "he says the Great God-father wants to be Pope. Says he's earned it, and of all Italians in the world, he is the one who knows how to order people around and make them obedient. That's what popes do, isn't it?"

"He's right about that. Maybe I should consider throwing my hat in the ring," mused Alphonso.

Benitez looked at him in consternation. Then Alphonso scratched his head and grinned. "Just joking!" Though neither totally believed him.

Benitez was suddenly afraid. "If you like, I will take care of it. But I will need a lot of money to pay out, and Christian's muscle, if he will do it. I doubt that Di Napolitano can be bought off. "

"Why not borrow one of Virgil's snakes?" grinned Alphonso.

"Too obvious. I can do much better. I have contacts from my time in Singapore. Islamic contacts."

"What? You'd deal with that filth?" scowled Alphonso.

*

Provost Julia loved her job. And what a difference she had made to the university. She had Christian elected to the faculty senate and he became chair of that august and gutless body. Her latest achievement was the introduction of a revolutionary curriculum that she called the double core curriculum. She had been impressed on a recent visit to Columbia University as part of the external review panel required by New York State. The core curriculum was its major and shining achievement, even after many attempts to abolish it for many different reasons, but mainly because the new guard claimed that it was old fashioned and irrelevant to the demands of modern life that faced its new graduates. She returned to Virgin Hall and immediately proposed to the faculty senate what she called a double core curriculum, a traditional curriculum that had Latin and Greek at its core, and of equal value, a core of LGBTQ studies. Courses from these two cores would be required for all students entering as of the current year. She charged Christian with the mission to get it through the senate, and it was achieved within a week of its proposal. Though, Christian had to report, it was too bad that half the members of the senate were unable to attend the meeting when the final vote was taken. In any event, the vote was unanimous in favor.

Provost Julia looked over her big desk at Christian who sat with his arms hanging down, his placid face, now a sickly gray, perhaps because his hair was turning gray or so she thought. Even his eyes seemed to be dull, also gray. For some reason, she thought that they used to be blue, and almost asked him, but didn't. He was a great puzzle to her. She knew that her LGBTQ procedure had erased many of her most intense memories and guessed that Christian must have been part of that loss. But this was unknowable, unless she asked him. And he showed no indication that he was interested in her or had been interested. In fact he appeared to have no emotion, no life in him, so she wondered what it must have been that she apparently saw in him. She decided to risk it and said, "Christian, I'm trying to remember where we met some time in the past. We have a history, don't we?"

Christian looked blankly at her. In fact, he remembered everything, except that it wasn't everything. The intensity of them together in each other's arms, the sex, was absent. He knew they had been close, but there was nothing to remember. He was about to reply that he had no idea what she was talking about when Bambola knocked at the door and entered.

"Cardinal Benitez to see you, Provost Julia."

Benitez, getting more cocky by the day, stood beside Christian and said, "don't get up Provost Julia," even though she had made no move to do so. "I am here to announce a wonderful piece of news."

"Don't tell me, you've been elected Pope,' said Julia banging her open hand on her desk, a big grin on her face.

"Not quite, but I will be," boasted Benitez. "I am here to offer Christian a Fulbright scholarship to Jerusalem and then to Rome, to work with the Palestinian Christians of Jerusalem and bring them under Vatican protection." He looked down at

Christian who remained passive. "I understand that you are good at languages?"

Julia leaned across her desk. "Latin and Greek, they are his forte, and he is essential for our double core curriculum. I can't spare him right now."

Ignoring her, Benitez addressed Christian. "Part of your Fulbright studies would be to learn Arabic. Palestinian Christians speak Arabic, of course."

Christian still remained quiet. Julia looked at him, more puzzled than ever. There was something missing in this man. "Christian, you must remain here. It's for the good of the university."

At last, Christian stirred just a little, sat back in his chair and crossed his legs. "My father could sub for me. He knows Greek and Latin. Not as good as me, but still better than nothing."

"Too bad we lost Dr. Scalpel. He was proficient in both," put in Julia.

"Yes, too bad," answered Christian blandly.

Benitez squeezed Christian's shoulder. "Then you will do it?"

"Why not? I'm a great supporter of Christianity. Aren't we all?"

There was no need for anyone to answer. Provost Julia also knew that a proposal from Benitez would not come without it having been cleared by her father Alphonso.

Benitez clapped his hands. "Excellent! Then I won't take up any more of your time. I leave on the Papal jet along with poor old Pollagrande's swollen body the day after tomorrow. You can join me if it's not too soon?"

"No. I always travel lightly. When I was a student at St. Robert's college, I made a vow never to accumulate physical possessions or get attached to inanimate objects," answered Christian, his face straight and expressionless.

Julia looked startled. She had no memory of that, though she could recall that they were at the seminary together.

"Then come, Christian. There's much to tell you about Jerusalem. I have many contacts there, some of whom I met in Singapore when I was the bishop."

Neither Julia nor Christian asked the obvious question, "what were Palestinians doing in Singapore?"

*

The narrow winding streets of old Jerusalem are teaming with life, much of it beyond the vision of the tourists who descend on it each day, buying relics, trinkets, souvenirs and what have you, visiting the stations of the cross. Divided into quarters, according to religious devotions, the old city exudes an atmosphere of mystery. The tourist moves from one section to another largely oblivious of whether it is Muslim or Christian, or Greek orthodox. And while certain personalities who wield power sit quietly hidden behind the narrow doorways that lead into enclosed courtyards, much of the serious action takes place outside the city walls, in the suburbs.

Christian, following the directions of Benitez, found his way to the end to the first station of the cross, in the Muslim quarter. Lines of pilgrims and tourist groups jostled each other. A gruff old man wearing the checkered scarf of Hamas pushed through with his motorino and with a nod of his head, told Christian to mount the bike and immediately the old man drove off, Christian clinging to him for dear life, through the Lion Gate, and off to the surrounding hills and suburbs.

They rode into an old windowless garage, the door closed behind them, and bright florescent lights fluttered on. Christian looked around for other operatives. He had expected a hive of activity. The old man set his motorino against the garage wall and spoke in broken English.

"If you are looking for my colleagues, I don't have any. I'm a one man show. It's safer that way. No spies, if you see what I mean." He licked his very large moustache, the size of Stalin's. Christian nodded passively, and the old man continued, "I hear you're a man of few words." Christian nodded again. "So just call me Bomber, and I'm pleased to meet you."

Christian extended his limp hand. "Likewise."

"I'm told we don't have to go through all the nonsense about you're doing this for God, or Palestine, of freedom or whatever, and there's to be no video, right?" asked Bomber.

"Of that I am sure," said Christian, "I just need a first rate explosive and a failsafe means of detonating it."

"I have a number of standard vest sizes and their explosive capacity can be adjusted according to the circumstances in which you plan to use it," said Bomber with the authority of an expert.

"I want one that will take care of anyone within ten meters," said Christian casually.

"May I ask whether you have a specific target?" asked Bomber, cautiously.

"What do you mean?" Christian stared at the bomber enough to scare him.

"Well, are you after a particular individual or do you just want to create a big explosion in a crowded café or bus or something? Here in Israel, crowded busses are a favorite target."

"As I said, I want to be sure that it kills anyone within a ten meter radius."

"You want a vest, right? Not a car bomb?" Bomber asked, raising his voice.

Christian rubbed the back of his neck. "Actually, I want a motorino bomb," he said.

"But I was told you wanted a vest. They are my specialty," complained Bomber.

"I had thought of a vest, but now after riding with you on your motorino I think that it will be a far more effective delivery vehicle. You see the main problem is to get close to the target," explained Christian.

"I see. Perhaps an explosive is not what you want then? Maybe you should consider a sniper?"

"No. Explosive. Packed into a motorino," insisted Christian.

"Where exactly is this motorino that I will work on?"

"Yours will do," said Christian almost with a grin.

The old bomber wrinkled up his nose and licked his moustache again. "You mean the target is here in Jerusalem?"

"No. In Italy."

"And how will you get the bike across the Mediterranean?" asked Bomber.

"My old bishop friend from Singapore did not tell me that I would be dealing with a fool," replied Christian, losing patience. "Don't tell me you guys don't transport explosive to Europe. Those bombers in France. They were yours, right?" demanded Christian, edging closer to the bomber, close enough to smell the Turkish tobacco that oozed from his jacket.

"Questions like that could get you killed," snarled Bomber.

"Here's the deal. You fill the handlebars with enough explosive to annihilate everything within 10 meters. I will drive it to Tripoli and pay for a refugee boat to Lampedusa, then on to my target."

"I can, but you're crazy. I will have to show you how to attach the detonator, assuming you need one? Unless you're planning on slamming it straight into your target?"

"I need a detonator," said Christian, stepping back.

"If you say so. Then I will need to fill every hollow space in the motorino with Semtex in order to get the maximum impact you want."

"How long?"

"A day. You can stay here if you like."

"No thanks. I want to do the stations of the cross. If you can take me back to the old city. I'll stay there until you are done."

The old man looked at Christian, a slight smirk on his face. "As you wish. The money up front. More of course if you want the motorino."

"Twenty thousand should do it, no?"

"That's US dollars?"

"Yes, of course."

*

Cardinal Benitez arrived in Messina with a considerable entourage of assistants. He was acting as though he were the Pope, and many people came out to see him alight from the Papal Alitalia rent-a-jet. He gave them all the sign of the cross, and many cheered. Consigliere Di Napolitano stepped forward and whisked him away in the big black limo, flanked by two carabinieri on their motorbikes. "The Great Godfather is not well and stays in his bed, I'm afraid. It's nice of you to come. It may be the last time you will see him alive."

" I hope so," said Benitez to himself. "I was to meet Christian here. Has he shown up yet?"

"He arrived yesterday on a motorino, of all things. Looked pretty beaten up."

"Him or the motorino?" asked Benitez with a grin.

"The motorino. He tried to get Great Godfather to go for a ride with him. But he wouldn't get out of bed."

"How long has he been in bed now?" Benitez asked.

"About three months. I don't think it's gout. He's depressed," replied Di Napolitano

"A crisis of faith. I can fix that," said Benitez adjusting his red cap.

"It doesn't really matter. Everything's running well. Don't really need him," muttered the consigliere.

"No wonder he is depressed." Benitez looked across at Di Napolitano who met his stare directly, expressionless.. He wondered if the consigliere was telling him something. It would be risky, but maybe he should try him out. "I'm surprised you haven't dealt with it yourself."

The consigliere blinked. "I was waiting for you."

"Your mean to give him his last rites?" asked Benitez.

"Something like that."

The car turned into the dusty drive to the Great Godfather's villa. There were peasants working in the fields. One of them looked familiar. It was Christian. And the motorino was leaning against the stone wall of the field.

Benitez called to the driver. "*Ferma*! Stop the car!"

He stepped out into the long dried grass.

The consigliere cried out, "watch out for the snakes!"

Christian looked up from the vines he was pruning. "Cardinal Benitez! At last you are here." Many of the peasants dropped to their knees and Benitez blessed them.

"You have not carried out your task," growled Benitez as he shook Christian's hand.

"Haven't been able to. He won't get out of bed. Anyway, I don't see why it's necessary. Everything down here runs without him."

Benitez looked back at the car. Di Napolitano sat reading his *Il Messagero*. "And the consigliere?"

Christian shrugged. "He's the boss, he's really the godfather."

"Your instructions were to deal with them both."

"I know. But Di Napolitano is a slippery one. Can't pin him down. Anyway, I think he might be one of us."

"What do you mean?" Benitez asked.

"He wants the Great Godfather out of the way."

"He told you that?"

"Not exactly," replied Christian. "He told me he wanted to be Pope."

"Di Napolitano?" Benitez looked out across the field of vines and olives. "Then I think you need to take him for a ride on your motorino. You rode it all the way from Jerusalem, I take it?"

"Pretty much. But if I take him for a ride, it won't solve things. All the power resides in the Great Godfather. He may be just lying in bed. But everyone around here worships him."

"So you're saying you don't want to do what I instructed you to do?" Benitez looked back at the car.

Christian then said in a most matter of fact way, "I slept with the Great Godfather."

Benitez put his hand to his mouth to hold back a gasp. "You what?"

"He was crying and asked me to lie down beside him. He thinks I'm the son he never had, or something."

"Does the consigliere know?"

"Yeh. He came into the room and saw us. I mean, it was just a friendly thing, you know. What else could it be me being neuter-onomized and all."

"It was just once?" probed Benitez.

"We sleep together every night now. Godfather says he can't live without me."

Benitez nodded knowingly. He had a solution. He returned to the car and it moved off towards the old villa, Christian follow-ing them on his motorino. It was dusk, and dinner would be waiting for them. The young attendants dressed in their old spoiled satin costumes and powdered wigs greeted them. They ate and drank well, and Christian went off to sleep with the Great Godfather who had drunk a copious amount of wine and lay on his back snoring. Christian lay on his side whispering in his ear, his hand stroking the shriveled skin of the old man's neck. Slowly the strokes became stronger until his hand grasped the Godfather's neck, gripping his Adam's apple, the fingers pushing into the aged, loose skin, closing around his wind pipe until the Great Godfather could snore no more.

What a scandal it would be for all his Sicilian servants and followers, all those who owed him a debt for all his good deeds and favors he had done them, to be told that their Great Godfather died asleep in his bed. Great Godfathers did not die like that. They always died a violent death. So it was that Christian, when the light of day arrived, lifted up the lifeless body of the Great Godfather, a legend throughout all of Sicily and the entire world of drug cartels, placed him on the motorino, pointed it towards the ancient quarry, folded the dead hands around the handlebars and revved it up, then drove to the edge of the quarry, slipping off the back as it took off into the pink light of dawn, carrying the Great Godfather into the land of myths and legends.

The headlines in *La Sicilia* would read, LA BOMBA DELLA BICI UCCIDE IL GRANDE PADRINO.

Di Napolitano did not like Christian's cold, icy manner. He resented Christian sleeping with his Great Godfather. He had always been careful not to get too close to the Great Godfather himself because he was after all the consigliere and it was a necessary part of his job to remain aloof so that he could give wise counsel unaffected by any emotional attachment he might have. Now that Christian had dispatched his Godfather, he felt an emptiness he had not anticipated. And he had to admit that he was jealous of Christian. If anyone was to dispatch the Great Godfather it should have been himself. He was angry and his Neapolitan gut told him that vengeance was demanded for Christian's merciless act. Paralyzed by rage, perhaps against his better judgment, he went to Cardinal Benitez to ask his advice and counsel.

Cardinal Benitez, for his part, looked on the consigliere as his competitor, certainly one who could not be trusted. Yet he needed him now more than ever, to carry out the project of making himself Pope, just as he had done very effectively for Pollagrande. He looked out over the vineyards and olive trees as they glistened in the morning dew and the hot Sicilian sun rose above them. Working away in the fields was Christian, whose slender form seemed to bend with the rays of the sun as they shone through the vines. The consigliere was a competitor and a threat. He had better keep Christian close to him, though when he looked out to Christian, happily working in the fields, laughing and joking with the peasants, he could see that this may be the place for Christian to call home.

In the end, Di Napolitano did not consult with Benitez, except in a perfunctory way. He simply asked him for his blessing, and then proceeded as though he was Benitez's advocate for Pope, and saying he would do everything and more for Benitez just as he did for Pollagrande. However, Benitez pointed out that now, if he himself were to campaign for Pope, he would not be able to organize everything like he did for Pollagrande. He decided, therefore, to enlist Christian to take on the organizational chores, though Di Napolitano would have to guide him through, since Christian of course had no experience with Vatican ways.

Never before had Di Napolitano's self-discipline been so challenged. But he told himself that it was the way his Great Godfather had taught him, always to wait. That vengeance was a dish best served cold. So for now, he would make Benitez Pope, and he would mentor Christian until the right time came.

At first Christian resisted, happy as he was with the peasants and the vines. Indeed, he had no recollection of any other happiness in his life. It was only when Benitez promised to have his father Virgil join them that Christian agreed. His dad, after all, was the organizer and campaigner of the family. At first, Di Napolitano saw this as Benitez trying to squeeze him out. But then told himself to be patient. The time would come. If necessary he would annul them both. They weren't even Italian anyway. Just sallow, insipid Anglo-Saxons of the worst kind, Americans.

La Sicilia called Cardinal Benitez the Courageous Cardinal for presiding over the funeral of the Great Godfather that nobody attended. None of the Great Godfather's worshippers, hangers on, underlings, clients, customers, acquaintances or enemies deigned it wise to attend. They sent flowers instead. Inter-flora and local florists must have made a fortune. Not even the carabinieri showed up, though they did send someone to scrutinize the cards attached to the flowers. Cardinal Benitez, dressed like a Pope, stood in the small stone church, as many priests before him had done, waved his arms with the per-functory blessing of the cross, standing over the casket of the Great Godfather. Unfortunately, it was a very small casket, roughly the size of a pill box. The explosion had turned the Great Godfather into dust. Only one of his rotten teeth was found in the rubble of the quarry where the tiny bits of motorino and Great Godfather fluttered down from the massive explosion.

*

Poor Maria. Sisto had insisted on joining her at the seminary. But it was not the place for him. Nor was it for her. She had toiled day and night to build her beautiful seminary into what it was today, a shining beacon, a thousand points of light, literally. She had placed Christmas lights along the contours of every building and window. At night is was so beautiful. And she and Sisto could retire to her luxurious quarters in the newly reno-vated spire of the church, make love, looking out over the thousand points of light.

Except that, well it's embarrassing to admit it, but after just one night together, Sisto found to his consternation that he was no longer himself. He even tried a couple of Pollagrande's blue pills that he had swiped the day he was elected Pope, but they didn't work. Nor did it help that after the first night, Maria insisted on wearing her tight habit, a new design that left only enough room for her lips and eyes to poke out, the rest covered. "Might as well wear a habib," muttered Sisto to himself.

"Did you say something, my love?" purred Maria as she snuggled into him, the points of her flying habit sticking into his protruding belly. Sisto responded in the only way he knew. He rolled off the bed and rose up, his belly covering everything, not that there was anything to cover, in fact there could be no cover-

up here. He stood as tall as he could, his arms out wide as
though to hug the world, his head thrust back so his curly beard
poked out, his sweating neck exposed, and he sang in his
loudest possible off-key tenor voice:

> *"One happy day*
> *You flashed lightly into my life;*
> *And since then I've lived*
> *In tremulous possession*
> *Of that unspoken love,*
> *The pulse of the whole world,*
> *Mysterious, unattainable,*
> *The torment and delight of my heart."*

It may have been off-key, but Maria was stricken. She ripped
off her habit and lay back flat on the bed. She was not a fallen
woman! What she did was out of love, no more, no less! It was
love for Sisto, pure and simple. His off-key voice had swept her
off her feet in Rome, and now here, in Mexico City. Sisto leaped
on the bed and it collapsed under his weight. He grabbed the
habit as they both fell on to the floor. And he wrought that habit
into a thousand pieces. He kneeled, crossed himself, and cried,
"Unbind yourself woman! In the name of Gloria Steinem! Free
yourself and with it my love!" By now Sisto was babbling with
no idea what he was saying.

Maria sat up. She crossed her arms over her fulsome breast,
pulled her legs up under her chin. "You can't bear to be here, can
you?" she cried. Bursting into tears, she ran into the bathroom,
turned the shower full on and jumped in. The sound of rushing
water awakened Sisto as never before. His eyes lit up as did the
nether parts of his body. The waters of Rome! Those sounds he
could not live without! And soon they were far away from the
thousand points of light, in their own water world.

*

Alphonso mourned the Great Godfather. He called up inter-
flora and sent a truck load of lilies and whatever other flowers
that were white. It was a shame that it had to be done. But it was
a necessary evil, so many of such evils in his business. Alphonso promised himself that it would be the last such evil he
would countenance, now that he was out of the drug trade. He
stepped out of the limousine, accompanied by Julia and the
newly elected governor of New York, Governor Pillsbury, who
had graciously agreed to come and preside over the dedication

of the new Holy Water factory on the business campus of Virgin Hall.

Virgil stood at the entrance on the marble steps—Alphonso insisted on Mexican marble wherever possible—to welcome them. They all stood on the top step on which was inscribed:

DEDICATION
NOVEMBER 23, 2018.
GOVERNOR PATRICK PILLSBURY,
PROTESTANT, CATHOLIC, CAUCASIAN, LATINO,
AFRICAN, NATIVE AMERICAN,
AND LGBTQ FRIENDLY.

He beamed with pride. He had bought a Coca Cola bottling plant lock, stock and barrel, and moved it from California to this place in Hopewell, New Jersey. The plant had gone broke in San Francisco after the local homeless rabble, paid by special interests, paraded in front of it night and day with placards, reciting, "Carbon Coke! Carbon Coke!" Riots had followed, someone set fire to the factory, the owner had no insurance, he sold out to Virgil and was glad to do so.

For this special occasion, Virgil put on his new priest's uniform, carefully tailored dark gray tapered slacks and matching jacket, priest's starched white collar, (actually no longer starched, but made of a super fiber that was easier on his sensitive skin), and black shirt or vest, he wasn't sure what it was called, all imported from Rome for this special occasion.

Appropriate speeches were made, the governor departed, and Alphonso remained to speak with Virgil about his coming trip to Rome to supervise the Benitez campaign for Pope. Julia stood at his side, displeased. In fact, she turned her back on them, sulking. What would happen to her double core curriculum now without not only Christian but Virgil? Who would teach Greek and Latin?

Alphonso, more and more a sensitive fellow, scratched his head and as soon as he had shaken Virgil's hand and congratulated him on such a great job of getting the first Holy Water bottling factory up and running, he turned to Julia. She looked back at him defiantly.

"You're ruining my double core curriculum!" she blurted.

He went to put his arm around her, but thought twice about it, given the new university rules about touching. "My darling daughter," he said, trying to show that he really meant it, and really he did, "why don't you hold the fort while they are away, and teach the courses? After all, your mother and me paid for your expensive education at St. Roberts, and you were the best in class there, weren't you?"

Julia felt herself shrink. She knew this was what he would say. "I could, but I'm overloaded already with my administrative duties. I have the whole faculty of Virgin Hall to manage."

Virgil intervened. "May I make a suggestion?"

Julia knew what he would say too. "What?"

"There are many priests and lay priests at St. Roberts," answered Virgil. "Why don't you reach out to them? Have you forgotten that they are part of your faculty too?"

"Seems logical to me," said Alphonso scratching his head.

Julia was cornered. She had purposely not gone to St. Roberts faculty because she wanted Christian to be her main guy for her core curriculum. She did not quite understand why she had this obsession with him. But she knew that she just always felt better, somehow calmed, by Christian's presence. She gulped and looked at them both.

"You're ganging up on me," she said, forcing a smile. "It's just that Christian is easily superior to any of them. As his dad, Virgil, you would surely agree with that?"

"Indeed. But he has a much more important task ahead of him, and I will also be there to guide him. Not to mention that we will both be mentored by Di Napolitano, the master of all ceremonies."

Julia was silent. Alphonso scratched his head and said in a soft voice, "it's not like it's forever." Then he took a big risk, but deemed it worth it. He put his arm around her and gave her a big hug. It seemed to Julia like all the blood had run from her head. She became dizzy, overcome by her father's caring. She had never seen him like this. So sweet! How could she refuse? Some things were more important than core curricula. "OK," she said, and hugged him back.

Virgil looked on in wonder, and decided that his becoming a Catholic was a good idea. Not that he had done all the silly catechism and the rest. All he needed was the uniform, and he had that already.

*

Cardinal Benitez kept a tiny apartment hidden away on the *Corso dei Rinascimento*, just beside *Piazza Navona*. It was nestled under an ancient stone stairway, basically a small passage no more than a couple of meters wide and maybe ten meters long. There was hardly room for a cot, no toilet, just a wash basin. The entrance was a narrow steel doorway, painted a faint beige, large sections showing rust. The only sign of its use was a shiny brass lock. One of his appreciative Singaporean flock had given it to him, or more precisely, loaned it to him for life. He kept Estelle, currently in hibernation mode, laid out on the cot. He had been tempted to take over Pollagrande's apartment, but decided that it was too much and too public, if he were going to keep Estelle. Though he was not sure why he wanted to keep her, given that he had not felt the slightest inclination to sleep with her. It somehow seemed to him inhuman to do so. Though he did sleep on the cot next to her when he was exhausted and wanted to get away from the hustle and bustle and mutual surveillance of the Vatican. But a great advantage of the apartment was that he could reach it from the Vatican entirely underground, following the tunnels of the water distribution that, naturally, fed the fountains of *Piazza Navona.* He had once run into Sisto under the Bernini fountain, the one with the huge obelisk stuck in the middle of it. This time he had arranged to meet Di Napolitano, Virgil and Christian under the Eagle Fountain. He was not sure whether it had been a smart idea to bring these three together, each of them with their own agenda, though perhaps as far as Christian was concerned, he did not appear to have an agenda. He was, maybe, rather like Estelle—inhuman.

Di Napolitano for his part, was annoyed at this demand for a meeting. He had worked hard to line up all his cardinals, first the Sicilians, then the Neapolitans, and regrettably the North-erners, the arrogant Tuscans. And now he had to work with the rank amateurs Virgil and Christian neither of whom had the faintest idea of Vatican protocols and procedures. Not that he kept to them. Of course, with the assistance of Benitez, he had broken with Vatican tradition, even law, to get Pollagrande quickly elected. He would do the same now, except that he had to do without Benitez. He sat waiting in the campaign head-quarters set up beneath the gardener's cottage, as we know, not far from the Eagle fountain, and very close to the new excavations that now housed the new Holy Water processing plant.

Virgil had done his research on Di Napolitano. He was a hardened criminal, a mafioso, that's what. He had said, jokingly, to Christian that it would be better for everyone if Di Napolitano were annulled. Christian had replied, it seemed seriously, he would see to it. Christian had insisted on taking Virgil to the Trevi Fountain, then down to the tunnels to show him the amazing waters of Rome. He casually mentioned that it was here that poor Dr. Scalpel had drowned. Virgil wanted to put his arm around his son, and after they had traversed about as far as *Piazza San Pietro,* he finally did it, under the guise of needing help to cross a small underground stream, grabbing him by the shoulder to keep his balance. Christian held him in his strong arm and helped him across. Virgil hoped he would feel the warmth of Christian's body, something to make him feel close to him. But it was cold and dank down there beside the Roman Waters; certainly no warmth between two humans.

Having arrived early, Benitez met them under the Eagle Fountain and led the way to the Gardener's cottage where Di Napolitano awaited them at his center of operations. Benitez eyed Di Napolitano carefully. There were many people buzzing around, shuffling pieces of paper, all of them, without exception, showing the dark swarthy characteristics of Neapolitans. Di Napolitano stood out, though. He was much taller than them all, taller even than Virgil or Christian. Benitez introduced Virgil.

"We are here at your service," said Virgil cheerfully.

Di Napolitano waved at the busy people in the room. "Everything is under control. They have prepared the ballots, just in case we need them, but I am planning on doing what Cardinal Benitez did for Pollagrande, and simply call a voice vote, show of hands."

"Sounds good to me," said Benitez, "now if you don't mind, I need to get back to the rest of the cardinals and pretend that I do not want to be Pope."

"Please do," said Di Napolitano. "My operatives tell me that they have shored up a unanimous vote, with one possible hold-out from Florence." He turned to Christian. "If you would put on your Monsignor attire, I have it here," he gestured to a worker who brought the costume, "then go to the apostolic palace and lead the cardinals across to the Pauline Chapel. I will address them there, before showing them into the Sistine Chapel for the vote."

"So the white ballots. Who burns them to produce the white smoke?" asked Christian.

"That will be your job, but don't worry, I will be there to assist you. I have installed a new contraption," said di Napolitano with satisfaction.

"And me? What is my task?" asked Virgil.

"You have the most difficult task," answered the Di Napolitano. "You must make a speech that says how important it is to elect this new Pope quickly, why we need to do it efficiently, why we need a Pope who is urbane, worldly, has the reach and foresight of the great world empire of the Roman Catholic Church. A new dawn, that sort of thing. Didn't Benitez tell you all this?"

"No he did not. Whenever I asked he said that it was not right for him to tell me what to say, because he was a potential candidate for Pope. But no problem. I am used to giving rousing speeches at my Pentecostal."

Di Napolitano was about to ask what a Pentecostal was, but thought better of it. "If I may say so, the success of this whole venture now depends on your speech in the Pauline Chapel."

"But it's a done deal, isn't it?" asked Virgil, a little annoyed.

"Nothing is done till it's done," said Di Napolitano conveying the wisdom of a consigliere.

*

As the cardinals entered the Pauline chapel, Virgil found himself humming the tune of "When Johnny Comes Marching Home," a song he used often to rouse the crowds at his Pentecostals. An old civil war song, they loved it in the south. He smiled and nodded at each couple as they passed through the low marble-edged doorway, counting them as they went. Di Napolitano had predicted that just forty two would show up. His network of Mafiosi had worked diligently to discourage the rest not to come to Rome. Alphonso had provided all the money to convince them, so with very few exceptions, additional incentives were unnecessary. Cardinal Benitez brought up the rear and as soon as he entered he passed by the corner table behind which sat Di Napolitano arranging the paper ballots, with Christian at his elbow.

Benitez carried what looked like an old leather satchel from the 15th century with large iron buckles and a wide carrying strap. He handed it to Christian, who gave him a knowing look. He nodded to Di Napolitano and moved on to join the group of cardinals, his main supporters, from South Asia.

Virgil counted forty two cardinals just as Di Napolitano had predicted. He climbed up on the makeshift dais, a rough wooden box the size of a large packing crate that would house a Cinquecento, with smaller boxes arranged into steps. He decided that he should look low key, but that his talk should be short but rousing. So, he had dressed in a novice's rough brown cloak, bare feet in Roman sandals. He also wanted to look and feel like a novice of old, to give the air of tradition, the great tradition of the Catholic Church. So he wore a wig with long straggly brown hair that hung down well past his shoulders. And at the last moment, when he saw his clean shaven face in the mirror, contrasted with the unkempt long hair, he went out and bought a false beard and wore that as well. No one could claim that he did not belong in the Pauline Chapel. He fitted in much better than the cardinals who were all to a man, well-scrubbed, well-shaven, with short hair if they had any, well covered by their red caps. He stood high up on the dais, at first with his hands on his hips and sang loudly, "And the animals went in two by two! Hurrah! Hurrah!" waving his arms, the palms up, addressing the throng. The excited buzz of cardinals consulting with each other immediately stopped and the silence of the Pauline Chapel ruled for just a few seconds.

Virgil raised his hands to the Lord and cried, "birds of God that you are! Cardinals of the 21st century! Join us in the arc of the future, Noah's animals did not get a vote, but you, our most precious birds of Heaven, of the air, as said Matthew, are here today to vote for your next holy leader! I implore you! Think deeply! Act wisely! For his future is your future! Stand tall, rise above all opposition, vote with your hearts and souls! The 21st century needs a Pope of great foresight, who reveres tradition that is the foundation of our Great Catholic Church, who is the holiest of the holy! Please take a paper ballot from our pontificate officials, doctors Di Napolitano and Bunion, and hold them to your heart."

A rustle of clothing rubbing on clothing ensued. Virgil continued. "Now, let us proceed into the Sistine Chapel where we will take the first ballot." The crowd murmured and mumbled, shepherded by Di Napolitano and Christian through the open doorway to the chapel, so narrow that the cardinals could enter only one by one.

There was a problem, at least in Virgil's opinion. There was no dais in the Sistine Chapel. He could easily have stood up on the bench that ran right around the base of the chapel walls. But this was not good enough for him. He liked always to be well above the crowd he addressed. So he beckoned to Christian to come to his aid. He then stepped on to the bench and then on to Christian's shoulders and once more addressed his audience.

"Holy Brethren! I see that you are all ready to vote!. May I suggest that we deviate from old protocol, as I am told you did in electing that great Pope, bless his dear soul, Pope Si, and dispense with the paper ballots and simply take a voice vote right now. So I ask you, all those who are in favor of Cardinal Benitez, who I know is your favorite, raise your hands and say 'Aye!' and please do so holding the paper ballot in your hand, so we can preserve an element of tradition in the vote."

All hands shot up and the deafening, almost irreverent sound of 'aye' reverberated throughout the chapel, bouncing off the walls, the incredible ceiling of Michelangelo, the tiled floor, and into the receiving ears of these red birds of prey. Virgil looked on with satisfaction, it was as though they were all poised to come forward and have him lay on his hands, to be born again, just like his Pentecostal. Unfortunately, in his adoration of the crowd and of course himself, he forgot that he was a heavy weight on his son's shoulders, as Christian began to wobble, his knees giving way. Virgil quickly yelled "Cardinal Benitez is pronounced our new Pope!" just as Christian collapsed under his weight, "by unanimous consent," and fell to the tiled floor. He looked for Christian to help him up, but he had departed quickly. His job was to assist Di Napolitano to send up the white smoke from the oven set up in the Pauline Chapel.

Di Napolitano was already collecting the paper ballots on which nothing of course was written. Christian collected those that had dropped to the floor. He ran to the table to retrieve a leather satchel. Carefully opened it, and pulled out a fifteen inch tube. Under Benitez's instructions, he had watched a YouTube video on how to make a smoke bomb. It took kitty litter packed in each end of the pipe, and in the middle a mixture of sugar and potassium nitrate. He had made two, just in case the first one did not work, again, under the instructions of Cardinal Benitez.

Di Napolitano knew nothing of this. Unaware that Christian had already placed the bomb, he stuffed the paper ballots into the oven, and lit them with his cigarette lighter that bore the Papal crest. Christian had, again, on instructions from Benitez, closed the flue of the chimney. At first the papers burned only very slowly, giving off little smoke. But gradually, the flames grew larger searching for a way out of the oven, but finding none, the smoke started to fill the chapel. Di Napolitano realized that the flue must be closed and leaned in to open it, which required his head to get very close to the opening to the chimney. The timing was perfect. There was a loud boom, as the smoke bomb blew up, taking with it half of Di Napolitano's head. His convulsing body dropped in a heap, blood spoiling the lovely tiled floor, much of it spattering the ceiling covered by Michelangelo's second-rate Pauline frescoes.

The cardinals recoiled in horror and stayed back in the Sistine Chapel refusing to come out. It fell to Cardinal Benitez, now the Holy Father, the Pope himself, to bravely enter the Pauline Chapel and survey the scene, to his satisfaction. Christian quickly retrieved the second smoke bomb from the old leather satchel and tied it to a wooden walking stick, the kind without a handle. He lit the fuse that came from its base and shoved it up the chimney, the flue now open. He had turned the bomb into a rocket, and very quickly it took off with a loud whisshh! and zoomed up and out of the chimney leaving a trail of white smoke as it reached for the Heavens. The muffled sounds of the cheering masses in Saint Peter's square seeped through the thick walls of the chapel.

Di Napolitano's body was packed up in the cinquecento crate and was not seen again. It was a fitting violent end to the career of a great consigliere.

18. Mother nature

Maria knocked softly at the Provost's door. She had waited until after the secretaries and other administrative assistants, whose main purpose seemed to be to keep people away from the Provost, rather like Francisco's henchmen back in Mexico, who kept everyone away from herself. Francisco had been so successful that she encouraged him, once her novices had retrieved all the paper dollars from their compound in Mexico city, to move all the cartel operations to Sinaloa. Since the notorious El Chapo was now out of the way, it was easy enough to merge with what was left of that cartel. This made her gentle giant into the next greatly feared Drug Lord, a role that he dutifully fulfilled. Her only function for the cartel now was to have her novices gradually retrieve the paper dollars from her old compound in Mexico City and reconstitute them with their hot irons into spanking like-new dollar bills. The money was then packed into small handbags that the novices took with them on their many trips to America accompanying the caravans of illegal migrants, to be laundered by Alphonso's Holy Water business.

Hearing no answer, she went to knock again when she heard footsteps behind and turned to face none other than the University President, her husband—soon not to be—Alphonso. Taken by surprise, she blurted, "I have asked Pope No to annul our marriage." The former Cardinal Benitez, now Pope, had taken the name of Pope No, in the contorted honor of his former colleague Pope Si.

Alphonso scratched his head. "I know." He leaned forward and opened the door. "After you," he said with a broad smile. He had such nice manners these days, thought Maria. Being university President had taught him something. There was no time for Maria to respond, because her daughter, whom she hardly knew, was at the door.

"Mom!" cried Julia, "and dad too! What a lovely surprise. I was just leaving to go down to the opening of the new LGBTQ gym for a workout. Do we need to sit, or can we talk on the way?"

"Your father and I are getting a divorce," announced Maria.

Julia stepped back. "OK. You'd better both come in then."

She ushered them to the small couch she had in one corner of her office especially for occasions like this. She peeped quickly behind the couch to make sure there were no spies, then drew up a small stool and sat in front of them. "It's about time," she said.

"I don't know what you mean by that," said Maria curtly, "but it's because I fell in love with Sisto, you know him I think, he's that wonderful man with the lovely tenor voice, and he's so smart, runs the Holy Waters project in Rome, without him it couldn't have happened." The words just flowed out of Maria's mouth, her brain struggling to keep up with them.

Julia, now very much the Provost, took it all as though Maria were describing some new course offering. "So you want my blessing?"

"I don't need anything from you, daughter or son or whatever you are." Maria put her hand to her mouth as if she were trying to put the words back in again. "Oh! I'm sorry!"

Alphonso scratched his head and muttered, "don't mind her, she's in love."

Julia looked one to the other and stood up from her stool. "But you can't get divorced. The Catholic Church will not allow it."

Maria dabbed at her cheeks with a lace handkerchief. She looked at Alphonso and squeezed his hand. He scratched his head again.

"Leave that to me," he said, a big smile, bigger than either Julia or Maria had ever seen. "I will make a deal with our new Pope No and he will annul our marriage."

"You're OK with this dad?" asked Julia, nonplussed.

"It's no problem. Though we will have to go to Rome to get it done."

"It's winter break. Can I come?" asked Julia.

Maria turned to Alphonso. "You mean you've set it all up with the Pope already?"

"Yes, my dear. The Pope will issue his annulment and we will sign our divorce papers in front of him."

"What a wonderful ex-husband you will make!" cried Maria and she grabbed his head in both hands and kissed him warmly and fiercely full on his forehead. "This is how Gloria Steinem would do it!" she cried as she hugged Julia. The two women hugged each other, as Alphonso almost pranced around the office. If only they knew the deal he had made! "We will take the Lear Jet tomorrow," he said. "Is Sisto here or is he back in Rome?"

"He went back yesterday. He couldn't stand being away from his rushing waters. They are his life," replied Maria.

*

Pope No was the fourth Pope to claim Cesena as his home. Three Pope Pio's came from there, Popes Pio VI and VII born there, and Pio VIII adopted. Pope No decided that he wanted to adopt Cesena as his native village and he did so the very first day after he was elected Pope No. He wanted to embrace all the Italian cardinals who he was sure resented his papacy. They routinely resented any non-Italian Pope, but this time especially so, given the most unorthodox tactics that rogue Di Napolitano used to get him elected. He could argue, of course, that Di Napolitano's tactics were classically Italian, but that was neither here nor there. One had to be born in Italy to count. The next best thing to that was to be adopted by Italy, and that was what he planned to do on this first day of his papacy. It cost quite a lot of money, but he had a lot left over from Alphonso's generous outpouring of good will to get him elected Pope and the seed money to get the Holy Waters of Rome project off the ground. The people of Cesena were elated to adopt him, convinced that it would be a great boon for their tourist trade. In fact, they insisted on giving him a gift, the gift sent by Saint Francis, who once journeyed through their tiny village as it was then, a *Lagotto Romagnolo* dog, his hair like human hair, beautifully cream colored, a few flecks of red around his eyes and on his back near his happy, uncropped, tail.

The day before he was to annul Alphonso's and Maria's marriage and to preside over Maria and Sisto's wedding, Pope No insisted on visiting the Pollino National Park, and to take his new dog that he had not yet named, to forage among the old Heldreich's pines. The dog breeders of Cesena had told him that the dog was a special breed, one that would forage for mushrooms in the forest.

Pope No's inherited slaves placed his litter on the damp grassy ground. Exhausted from the busy days since his election, he struggled to step down. He felt that, perhaps with all popes, he had aged another twenty years in just a couple of weeks. *"Funghi! Funghi"* he called and sure enough the happy dog busied himself sniffing among the exposed tree roots, darting this way and that, the four slaves following him and collecting the mushrooms as he found them. Pope No ne Benitez smiled with great satisfaction, crossed himself, and said, "thank you Lord" as he sat back on his litter, "I could not do anything without your blessing."

The mushrooms collected, Pope No returned to his Papal apartment in the apostolic palace, indeed he had moved into the official apartment, so recently occupied by Pope Shorty. And as he stepped into his apartment, the dog ran forward, seemingly always excited, and got tangled up in Pope No's feet. The Pope fell forward, putting out his hands to save himself, a heavy baggage, dressed as it was with the countless garments that a Pope has to wear.

We need not go into all the unpleasant details of his visit to the hospital, but the end result was that both his wrists were broken, so both arms had to be placed in a sling. This created no end of difficulty because he was no longer able to make the sign of the cross for himself or others. He had tried to move his arms, against his doctors' wishes, who were adamant that he not move his arms at all. In the end they pinned his arms to his upper torso with a straight jacket. He now had to hire a full time translator for the hearing challenged to include the sign of the cross in their signing when he signaled, and he arranged to convey that with a wink. There were of course, other physical difficulties, which we need not go into, suffice it to say that his slaves took care of everything.

But Pope No, if nothing else, wanted to be looked on as the undaunted one, the perpetual optimist, the Pope who overcame every obstacle in his way, the Pope who would never take 'no' for an answer, making this his motto. And, carrying this idea in his head, gradually getting used to the weight of the papacy, not to mention the weight on his head of the various Papal hats, crowns even, he forged ahead. He had an annulment and a wedding to attend tomorrow. And his last instruction to his slaves before he fell into a fitful sleep was for one of them to take a handful of mushrooms that he selected using his nose to indicate which ones, down to the chef to desiccate them and seal in Holy Water vials.

*

Pope No's trusted attendant Christian insisted that the correct protocol was for the annulment to be implemented in the Vatican, in the Pope's palatial office in the apostolic palace. The marriage afterwards must be conducted outside the Vatican, otherwise America and other countries might not recognize the marriage as an official one. This because the Vatican wasn't really a country, just a little principality. Pope No had vehemently disagreed with this silly argument, pointing out that the Catholic Church's geographic presence reached all over the world, inside every so-called country of the world, its population close to one and a half billion.

Besides, Sisto and Maria had insisted that they must be married in the midst of rushing water, and although Sisto would have been more than happy doing it underground, maybe under or even above the Trevi Fountain, Maria would have none of it. She wanted a very big wedding, one too big for the Trevi fountain with all its tour groups and gelato slurping hordes. She wanted to get married under God's beautiful blue sky, water gushing down a mountain, spurting out of fountains. She wanted to invite Gloria Steinem and many other same sexed celebrities.

The thought of Gloria Steinem excited Sisto and he let out a loud long middle C wail, reaching to an upper C crescendo. "I know the perfect place," he said. "We will take over the *Villa D'Este*. It's not far from Rome, and it has fountains you would not believe, water running down the terraced hillside, gushing water everywhere you look."

Much to the consternation of his Vatican bureaucracy, Pope No agreed, and with much enthusiasm. It was important, he said, for the Pope to get out among the ordinary people of Italy and everywhere else. To preside over a wedding in such a public place was a wonderful idea.

Maria thought she had better find out a little about the place so she googled it. And there she found a location in the *Villa D'Este* for their ceremony, right in front of the Fountain of Mother Diana Ephesus, or "Mother Nature," according to Wikipedia. While it was not the largest fountain in the gardens, it was the most effusive, abundant even, the picture of fertility and a reservoir of love, spurting out to all, the holy water of her breasts, all fourteen of them! And she sat among lush green ferns and moss, encircled by round stones the size and shape of udders, built into a flat arch above her head crowned with a basket of a growing sheath of wheat.

It was impossible to put together a list of persons to invite, so she simply sent out a blanket invitation to everyone and anyone on all the social media she could. "Come to our wedding! The wedding of the century!" she proclaimed.

The main street of the small town of Tivoli was always clogged with traffic, but the wedding created almost a catastrophe. The Vatican had to enlist the help of the Italian army's Grenadiers of Sardinia to patrol the roads and direct the traffic. In the end they surrounded the entire town of Tivoli and cut it off from the rest of the world. Included in those who were not allowed to cross the barriers was Gloria Steinem, even though she waived her printout from her Facebook page showing that she was a special guest.

*

Alphonso had requested a private audience with the Pope just an hour before they took off in the helicopter for Tivoli. Something was wrong and he knew not what. He didn't feel happy any more. The excitement and pride of his recent accomplishments, the Holy Water project in Hopewell, his transformation of New State University into Virgin Hall, saving both from extinction, were no longer enough. And now came the annulment of his marriage to Maria, even though he had promoted her to the position of Drug Lady, to run the largest drug cartel in the world. And she had thrived, became a sister of our Lady of the Waters of Mary, did amazing things for the Catholic Church, her little seminary she turned into an imposing, fabulous structure. And what had she gone and done? Fall in love with an effeminate Roman water engineer! He had done so much good for so many people, and yet there was no recognition, everyone took all his good work for granted.

When Alphonso recounted all these worries to Pope No, ne Benitez, the Pope told him to sit down on the sofa with its extravagantly carved legs and delicately embroidered satin cushioned top. "Your problem is," he said with a very serious look on his face, so serious that it might have been fake, "that you are bored."

Alphonso looked up at Pope No who was climbing on to his litter, the slaves getting ready to carry him to the waiting helicopter next to the Eagle fountain. He had not noticed Christian standing passively in a corner of the large living room. He addressed Pope No. "I'm tired of ordering people around, I have to admit. It's no fun anymore. Most of my people act as though I gave them an order, they do things without my having to tell them."

"Many drug lords and CEOs would envy you for that," observed Pope No. He climbed off his litter, with the help of his slaves since he could still not use his arms very well, though they were no longer strapped to his body. Each wrist was in a plaster cast. He nodded to his slaves who immediately went off down a narrow passage, to the old bedroom where Pope Si used to keep Estelle. "You know, my son, I have seen this coming. And I have the perfect solution, or should I say solutions."

Two slaves returned carrying a large metal chest.

"Is that what I think it is?" asked Alphonso.

The slaves opened the box and there, neatly packed inside was Estelle. "She will need to be polished up a little, and perhaps reprogrammed to suit your particular tastes. But I can assure you, she will do wonders for you, and will easily make up for your impending loss of Maria. And again, I admire and support you for what you have done for feminism in the world, making Maria into the greatest Drug Lady ever, and being man enough to let her forge her own life of success and love. Gloria Steinem I am sure, would approve of you, even if she does not approve of any other men."

"Holy Father!" Alphonso slid off the sofa and on to his knees. "I thank you for your Christian kindness, thank you! Thank you! You have reached into my heart as though you were Jesus himself!"

Christian stepped out of the shadows of his corner. Something about Estelle attracted him. He felt something he had not felt for a long time, as though he and she had something in common, that they were soul mates. But he stayed in his place and just watched, his eyes unable to leave the amazing form of Estelle as it slowly emerged under the agile hands of her makers. The slaves busily retrieved the various parts of Estelle, connecting them together, rather like a Lego model.

"I haven't finished yet," Pope No said with a gleam in his eye. "OK, Bring him out! He called to a slave who had remained in Estelle's bedroom.

Alphonso heard the muffled noise of a barking dog. He looked out the window thinking it had come from outside. Then, scampering on the slippery marble floor, out came Pope No's *Lagaretto Romagna*, yelping and jumping, the picture of happiness. Pope No settled himself on his litter and the slaves raised him ready to go. "You are bored with bossing people around. Now you have a dog who will do everything you ask and more, he will give you unadulterated love and obedience. He will obey you because he loves you, nothing more, nothing less."

Alphonso, on all fours, chased after the dog and the dog immediately took to him. They laughed and rolled around the floor together. He had even for a moment forgotten all about Estelle who was fast emerging from the metal trunk before their very eyes. Finally, she was put back together and pretty soon she stood tall, a smashing beauty as she always was for Pollagrande. A slave switched her on. Her body gave a small shiver as though jolted by an electric current, which she was, then her eyes, those big beautiful eyes, and her voluptuous red Monroe lips moved. "El Padrino! I am so glad you have come at last. I have dreamed of you every night, and this last night seems to have been forever!"

Alphonso, suddenly feeling like Superman, grabbed the dog and stood up effortlessly from his prostrate position on the marble floor. He rose up, feeling like he did that day of his first epiphany in the Mexico City Cathedral. His body rose all on its own, as though he floated up. And soon he had the dog in one arm and Estelle in the other, the dog licking Estelle's cheeks. "I am so happy!" he cried, tears in his eyes, "so happy!"

Pope No leaned down from his litter and handed, or more correctly elbowed some papers to El Padrino. "Before we start. Please sign these papers. They say that you agree to the annulment which I will announce at the wedding."

Alphonso grabbed the papers, fell to the floor and lying on his tummy, his navel feeling the nice cold of the marble, signed all papers with a flourish. He then stood up, again as though his body was so light it floated and handed back the papers. And Pope No called out "Onward! Onward Christian soldiers!" and the slaves carried him out of the apostolic apartment, followed by Estelle who called, "wait for me!" and the dog barked joyfully, snapping mischievously at Alphonso's heels.

"Wait for me," called Christian from his corner of the room.

*

Pope No appeared above the crowds and the gardens, sitting on his litter, his wrists still in a sling, suspended from a helicopter borrowed from the emergency wing of the *Gianicolo* Hospital next to the Vatican. It circled over Tivoli and the *Villa D'este.*

Sisto and Maria were already waiting at the fountain. They had reached it mostly underground, following an ancient aqueduct out of Rome and into the hills of Tivoli. Sisto, of course, his curly beard combed as best he could, but clipped and groomed perfectly by the Pope's barber, was ecstatic, overwhelmed by the rushing water, the beauty of Diana Ephesus and her abundance, eyeing Maria's fulsome breast, licking his lips in anticipation. Alphonso and Christian alighted from the helicopter, Alphonso dressed in his vintage shorts and Roman sandals, a white Italian fitted shirt that did not suit his bulging belly, the buttons stretched tightly, his belly button on full display.

A second helicopter appeared, the insignia of the keys of the Vatican with chains of St. Peter and Paul, painted on its side together with "ASP" in big elegant letters. It did a circle of the gardens and the masses of crowds surrounding Tivoli, then eventually landed on the road at the upper level of the Villa. Out stepped Virgil and Julia, hand in hand. Virgil wearing his all white priest's costume of tapered pants, a satin stripe down the side, a white satin vest, light silk long sleeved shirt with starched collar, all topped off by a Panama hat. Julia, now very much into her Steinem style, wore red tapered slacks, white see-through blouse with wide fluttering long sleeves (to comply with the Pope's new edict that one may not wear short sleeves within six meters of the Pope), and beneath, a bra pulled up and full, of red lace. And her hair done in the style of her mother of yore, tightly bound into a top knot. It was important to retain a little of history, Julia thought. "Do you have all the paperwork?" she asked Virgil. He squeezed her hand as they jogged along the path beside the long array of fountains, swinging their arms as they went, looking like teenagers in love.

*

Weddings aren't what they are cracked up to be. Yet people are offended if they are not invited. Guests can't wait to get to them, but once there, they must bear the tortures of small talk, and can hardly wait to leave. This is why the loving couple spends an enormous amount of time choosing the place for the wedding. If it is an amazing place, somewhere that people can feel it was worth it, then many more guests will be happy. So choosing the *Villa D'Este* was a stroke of genius. Maria and Sisto stood beaming before Diana of Ephesus, her bountiful breasts spurting with the waters of love and plenty. And of course, Sisto was ecstatic. Maria had to pinch him on the bottom continually to stop him from breaking out in one of his tenor's wails.

People, especially women, as Maria well knew, obsess over what the bride wears. She had given it much thought. After all, this wedding was as much an acknowledgement of Gloria Steinem's genius as anything else. So why not glorify her vagina? She chose, therefore a red single piece spandex and satin costume, that clung to every inch of her body from head to toe, arms and all. Except that a striking ovular gap revealed her fountain of privacy, the hair down there having been combed and twiddled to match the curly sinews of Sisto's beard. And her face was revealed just as it was when she wore her habit, a tight oval drawn around her face, made white by makeup, signifying her purity and devotion to the sisters of Mary. But then her hair was threaded through a wide opening at the back of her head so that it flowed voluminously on to her shoulders, surely a sign of fertility!

From a distance, the most that guests could see was a lithesome body moving this way and that, rather like Spiderwoman. And Maria played the part, gently though, pulling Sisto with her, parading before the many guests. After all, no one had been overlooked. All were invited. It was an open wedding. So when the word went out, not to mention that Pope No would preside, half of Italy turned out to see the spectacle.

The Garda di Finanzia made up the honor guard from the helicopter pad to the Fountain of Diana. Used to taking abuse from their tax avoiding clients, they firmly held hands to keep back the swooning crowds, even though some were calling out, "down with the Euro!" Maria and Sisto led the procession, such as it was, followed by Alphonso and Estelle, arm in arm, Christian walking close behind them, looking despondent, head down, then Virgil and Julia, holding hands and swinging them with gusto.

Now the hospital helicopter hovered over Diana of Ephesus and gently lowered the Pope on his litter. The slaves followed sliding down the rope like they were special forces. They stood at each corner of the litter as Pope No stood up on his litter and the slaves raised it up and unlocked its folding legs so that it became a platform. Pope No immediately raised his arms high and surveyed the throngs of wedding guests, and, hampered by the casts on his wrists, made the sign of the cross to all as he turned 360 degrees. "In the name of the Father, the Son and the Holy Ghost, I bless you all!" he cried into the microphone attached to his Papal collar, transmitted by Bluetooth (patented) to the massive loud speakers embedded all over the gardens that were used for sound and light shows.

The loving couple stood before the litter, their chins just high enough to see the Pope. Maria held on to Sisto who was swooning as though he were drunk. He was not, but it was clear that he was having trouble standing on his jelly legs. "Hurry," called Maria, "I can't hold him up much longer!"

The Pope began. "Blessed be our couple before me. I now pronounce you man and wife!"

But the crowd all of a sudden jeered and cried in unison, "the vows, the vows, what about the vows!"

Pope No looked over the crowd with disdain. What had this world come to? Was there no respect for the Catholic Church anymore? "You better do it," muttered Christian standing close to one of the slaves.

The Pope gave a sigh. "Do you, Maria, take this man as your lawful wedded husband, to have and hold etcetera, etcetera?"

Maria cried out, "I do! I do!"

"And Sisto do you take this woman as your lawfully wedded wife and promise to etcetera, etcetera?"

Sisto's crooning off-key tenor voice penetrated the buzz of the excited crowd, "I dooooooo! I dooooo!"

Now came the part that Pope No had tried to avoid. "If there is anyone here who objects to this sacred joining together of this loving couple, speak now or forever hold your peace!"

The crowd shuffled in silence. A loud gruff voice, rose above the noise, "At least one of them is already married!" The crowd swooned again and Christian set off to find the offender. But he had disappeared into the throng.

"Whoever you are," cried the Pope, "that was a very bad joke. And just for the record, Maria here was once married to Alphonso who stands behind her, giving her away. Their marriage was annulled by me this morning."

The Pope sat down on his litter, but then Alphonso pushed forward. "Holy father!" he called. "I do have a request, though."

Pope No stood up and looked down, worried. What was Alphonso doing, trying to spoil everything? "What is it my son?"

"Estelle here, and me, we want to get married too."

The crowd once again sighed as a chorus. The Pope reached down and held each of their hands. "I now pronounce you, Alphonso and Estelle, as you promise to love each other until death do you part, man and wife, by the grace of God!"

Alphonso turned to Estelle and she responded accordingly, placing her voluptuous lips right on his. They hugged each other tightly, Alphonso rubbing his navel into her taut abdomen. Pope No sat down again, relieved that all had ended well. The crowd swayed back and forth, excited by the public display of love of humans and the Holy Spirit. He now realized that it was time to close the wedding ceremony, with the crowd in such good spirits. So he raised his hands high ready to say the benediction and was about to speak when another voice came from below.

"We also wish to be married, Holy Father!" cried Virgil, his Protestant tongue trying to resist saying those words to a Catholic priest, the Pope, for heaven's sake. Pope No looked down and there, standing together, holding hands, raised high, big grins on each of their faces, clearly two young, well Virgil not so young, two people madly in love. Christian felt himself drawn towards them. He struggled to get past the crowd milling around the litter. But finally managed to face them both. "I wish you the very best of happiness for the future," he said flatly, without emotion.

Virgil looked at him. "My son," he said, "that means a lot to me. I know you will understand, you are such a great human being. And I'm sorry we are being married by a Catholic."

"That's OK dad. Anyway, Julia's a Catholic isn't she?"

Julia stepped close to Christian. "I am, but I may convert to Protestantism, I love Virgil so much." Christian turned away and reached out to Alphonso and Estelle. "Congratulations to you both," he said, without a smile. "Perhaps you would like to use the Great Godfather's villa for your honeymoon? Pope No is sending me down there to clean things up a bit. They have lost their two top leaders, Great Godfather and now consigliere Di Napolitano. He has already told them that I will be taking over the operation, filling both positions, Great Godfather and consigliere. Hopefully, he mentioned to you that you could be of some assistance to me as I settle in down there."

"He never mentioned it, but it sounds like a great place for a honeymoon," Alphonso replied. At that moment, the crowd swooned this way and that, and Alphonso's dog appeared among the forest of legs. "Dog here, will also be joining us. That OK?" asked Alphonso.

"Of course," said Christian, "he can help us forage for mushrooms. Pope No says he is amazing."

Alphonso picked up the dog and with his other arm embraced Estelle. "We're going to be one big happy family, aren't we Estelle?"

"Whatever you say, El Padrino."

Pope No leaned down from the litter and took both Virgil's and Julia's hands. "I now proclaim you husband and wife and may you live in holy happiness forever!" The crowd cheered and the Pope sat back on his litter, feeling a job well done. There was just one small matter he had to attend to. He looked down at Christian and handed him a small package wrapped in white shiny paper, imprinted with the Papal crest. "This is a wedding gift for the happy couple. You can give it to them when they join you in Sicily, not before, and of course, only when you have arranged for the necessary accommodations." Estelle reached for the package, but Christian stopped her. "It's bad luck to open wedding presents at the wedding. Better to let me take care of it, right El Padrino?"

The Pope's helicopter circled above, dropping handfuls of Euro notes and coins, these *bomboniera* paid for by the most generous Maria. Sprinkled in among them were small gold trinkets depicting Diana of Ephesus, her voluminous breasts exaggerated in size, and a small button on the base which, when press, spurted holy water from her breasts. These had been carefully made by Maria's sisters of Mary.

Naturally, the crowd went crazy, and the *Garda di Finanza* was overwhelmed. But the Pope's litter was raised by the hovering helicopter, creating a spectacle of its own, with the four slaves hanging on to each corner as it flew towards the Heavenly city..

19. Upgrades and downgrades

Alphonso, the greatest of Godfathers, looked out over the fields of vines dotted here and there with olives. He was now responsible for the many peasants who served the old Great Godfather of yesterday. Their livelihood had depended on him, and they now depended on El Padrino. It was too much of a responsibility for Alphonso, unused to bothering about such things as families, women and children, unless they were his own. As drug lord he was used only to a coterie of male oversexed thugs for protection and running day to day activities of drug manufacturing and dealing, and when necessary putting down any attempts from rival gangs. Managing his own small family was hard enough, though he had to admit that he had not really tried to run it or even manage it. The challenges of the past few years with Julia or Julio, had caused him to withdraw from his family. They were problems that could not be fixed by a gun and bullet. He leaned back in his rocking chair and put his hand down to pat his dog's curly head. The dog barked, then ran off down the crumbling steps of the villa. Alphonso called to him, "*Nieto! Peña Nieto!* Come back here!" Nieto ignored him and set off chasing a sparrow that hopped easily out of reach. "*Enrique!*" Alphonso called again and this time the dog looked back, wagged its tail, maybe even laughed at him.

Alphonso sighed and rocked his chair some more. He had reached such heights of power, could even become governor of New Jersey if he wanted to, that was his own opinion of course. But this dog, surely chosen for him purposely by Pope No to teach him a lesson about what power is all about. The fact was, he had no power over this dog, yet the dog already loved him, licked his hands and face if given the opportunity, and mostly, if he understood the Italian, obeyed him, when he was not too excited or distracted. They went for long walks together around the foothills of mount Etna that made up the expanse of territory left to him by the Great Godfather. The Great Godfather had no children to leave his land to, they had all been killed in various acts of vengeance. So Pope No, ne Benitez, had arranged for the estate to be left to Alphonso on the understanding that Alphonso would continue to be a great friend of the church.

And now there was Christian. Alphonso squinted at him through the early morning mist, down in the fields with the peasants, doing their work, a happy peasant it seemed. Alphonso had never taken the time to study the people who worked under him. He simply barked orders and they obeyed. It was very simple. Nobody ever disobeyed him, none of his workers. Only his family disobeyed him, so he had given up barking at them. And look how it turned out! Maria left him (thank goodness) Julio turned into one of those LGBTQ people, if that's what you could call them. It was Julio's fault for bringing Christian into his family, and when Julio turned into Julia, Christian promptly went and had his neuteronomy and now he was only half human and seemed to answer to nobody or anybody. He made an excellent operative, though, a mechanic you could say. He might as well be a robot. Ah yes! There are robots and there are robots! He called for Estelle.

"Coming my darling Padrino!" she called from somewhere inside the old villa's walls.

"Come, Estelle! Make me happy!"

He had already taught her what made him happy, and she put it into action. "Is this what you did with Pollagrande?" he asked with a silly sneer.

"Who is Pollagrande?" she smiled as she caressed him in ways that no human he knew could or ever would. She lifted him easily onto the old wicker couch and they dropped onto the soft cushions. Alphonso rubbed his navel against hers, then slid his tongue between her luscious lips. But then another tongue, cold, wet and rough, licked his cheek. Nieto was on top of them, wagging his tail, wanting to join in the fun.

"Fuck off!" snarled Alphonso. But he already knew it was useless. "Nieto! Peña!" he cried as he laughed. Who else but this dog could make him do that?

Christian suddenly appeared beside the wicker couch. He looked on their naked bodies without interest, as though they were a natural part of the furniture. He snapped his fingers at Nieto and it immediately came to him and sat at his feet, looking up, as though awaiting its next order. Alphonso felt a

tide of anger rise up from his navel. This person, this asshole
had taken away Julio and now he was taking away his only
trusted friend, Nieto. He instinctively reached for his gun, but
then realized that he had long gotten out of the habit of carrying
one, ever since he became President of Virgin Hall.

Estelle sat up straight in a stiff robotic movement, a rare
occurrence. It was Christian staring at her that did it and she did
not know why. There must have been something in her recent
upgrade that Pope No gave her. He had said something at the
time that she could not serve two masters. Again, she mechanically put out her hand and Christian took it in his, and helped
her off the couch. "Was there a dim fire in those eyes?" she
wondered. An LED glimmer perhaps? She smiled as Christian
ran his usually limp fingers, up the full length of her arm, across
to her Monroe breasts, circled them, and moved gracefully and
lightly down, right to her toes. Nieto sat on his haunches, his
tongue hanging out, panting as though he just came back from
chasing a rabbit.

Alphonso rolled off the other side of the couch and stared,
unable to believe his eyes. This Christian, sent by the devil,
without a doubt, to torture him, never let him enjoy his simple
pleasures. To proffer these pleasures like waving them under his
nose, then taking them away. He thought he had enough of
everything, but now he saw that he did not. He thought he was
boss of everyone, but now he saw that he was not. And that rat
Benitez, now the Pope, made the Pope by him, had pulled a
dirty trick. He could see that he had already lost Estelle because
of her upgrade by that bastard Benitez. He had given him a dog,
knowing that he would lose Estelle.

"You OK boss?" asked Christian as he put his arm around
Estelle who shivered, feigning cold. Alphonso pulled on his
shorts and fitted shirt, left open at the front. Christian continued.
"Tell you what. Let's take Nieto and go look for mushrooms,
and I'll cook up tortellini with mushrooms tonight."

Alphonso looked at Christian and then to Estelle. "You
coming Estelle?" he asked.

"I don't think so. I am not feeling well. I think it's my new
upgrade. I need to lie down and get charged up. This happens
with upgrades. It takes a while for the electro-neural circuits to
adapt."

*

Nieto, what a lovely dog! He rushed around, sniffed and foraged among the tree roots, pushed at mushrooms to indicate those to pick.

And when evening came, Christian, assisted by Estelle, took over the kitchen, giving the staff the night off. Estelle, freshly updated, recalled a recipe for tortellini and mushrooms, with green peas. They set about washing and chopping the mushrooms, Christian keeping his jar of desiccated mushrooms given him by Pope No aside, ready to add at the right moment. It would enhance the flavor no end, according to Pope No, smiling as he said it.

Alphonso stayed out in the warm breeze of the autumn evening, the clear Sicilian sky full of stars. He looked up, holding Nieto in his arms and pointed. Nieto struggled, and licked Alphonso's cheeks. Then dropped down, running around, snapping at the heels of the waiters and attendants, still dressed in their faded gray satin uniforms and dirty white wigs.

Christian opened the jar of dried mushrooms. When Pope No had proffered these mushrooms to him, and explained to him who they were for, Christian, unusual for him these days, asked why Alphonso? Pope No had taken a deep breath and looked away, then back at him. "Surely you know why," he said in a croaky voice, "Alphonso is an evil man obsessed with power. He poisons and demeans everyone he touches."

"Including you?" injected Christian, a touch of sarcasm.

"Including me. I'm ashamed and embarrassed to admit it. He knew I wanted to be Pope, and played on it. I resent it, even though I also know it was he who made it possible. That's the trouble, he has the power—money that is—to make all things possible."

"So for this reason you want me to kill him?" asked Christian flatly.

"I wouldn't put it like that. But surely you have had the same experience with him?"

Christian looked away. "He gave me many opportunities, though he was against me with Julia, so I'm told. I remember nothing of that supposed affair. I know he's not a likable man, but he's done only good for me. And look what he did for my father, he literally pulled him up out of the gutter. And now he is CEO of one of the biggest companies in the world."

"All true," answered Pope No ne Benitez. "But that's what the devil is like. He takes on many forms, plays shrewdly on our

wants and desires, parades as a Samaritan when all the while he
plots and plans our destruction."

Christian added a spoonful of the enhancing mushrooms to a
separate bowl of tortellini and set it apart. He was truly torn. He
did not know what to make of the Pope's tirade. Alphonso had
done nothing bad to him as far as he could see. Gave him tremendous opportunities at Virgin Hall, and now here, in charge of
an enormous estate. He went to add another spoonful, but hesitated. Indecision is one of man's worst enemies, and usually it's
driven by cowardice. And certainly as far as he could remember
that was who he was. A coward. He looked across to Estelle
who busied herself straining the tortellini. It is said that looks
can kill. He would do anything to have her for himself.

He added another spoonful.

*

Alphonso lay on his back on the old wicker settee, his belly
no longer protruding, one arm covering his forehead, the other
hanging listlessly over the side. Estelle sat beside him, singing
old lullabies in one of her many touching voices. The mushroom
tortellini had not agreed with him, and he blamed this on Nieto
for picking the wrong mushrooms. Yet, Alphonso was not able
to bring himself to order Nieto's annulment. Had it been anyone
else who had poisoned him, he would have had no compunction
in doing so. He could not even manage to ask Estelle to do it. In
any case, he suspected that she was programed not to kill. He
hinted at it to Christian who pretended not to hear. Christian
certainly would kill the damned dog, he would kill anyone if
asked, no doubt about it.

Estelle saw that Alphonso was at last beginning to take notice
of his surroundings. He had been very sick. The local doctor had
lamented that he may lose his kidney function, which would
mean that one of the local peasants would have to give up a
kidney to save him. She helped him sit up, pulling him forward
and placing a big pillow behind his back. Now he was at last
able to look out over the misty fields and watch the sun slowly
rise and chase away the mist. What a wonderful garden of
plenty God had provided us, thought Alphonso. He was thankful
for his life, and as he surveyed the fields and watched the
peasants at their work, even Christian who loved to work in the
fields. He gave thanks that he still had life ahead of him.
Though he wanted for little. More life, yes, but one thing he

now pined for was to sleep with Estelle and taste more of her legendary talents.

Christian was at his favorite task, remaking the old stone fences, a skill that a local peasant patiently taught him. He stood and wiped his brow with his arm, and looked back to the old villa. Alphonso was now sitting up and Estelle tended him so sweetly. Pope No had phoned Alphonso last night to wish him well and tell him that he had prayed for him every night and every morning on his knees beside his Papal bed. Estelle then brought the phone to Christian and the Pope admonished him for his failure, the first and only time Christian had failed him. Christian took the abuse without flinching, he was in total agreement. It was a botched job. And all the time he listened to the abuse, all he could do was watch Estelle and wish she were attending him as she was to Alphonso. Things could not go on like this. Something had to be done. He was about to place a large stone on the fence when he heard the phone ring and saw Estelle bring it to Alphonso. Alphonso listened, then suddenly with a huge effort pushed himself up and climbed off the settee, a huge smile on his face, his free hand searching for his belly button, now hiding away inside a roll of loose skin that hung down over his boxers. Christian ran up to see what it was. Alphonso threw the phone up in the air and Estelle ran to catch it. "I have been awarded the Nobel Peace prize!" he said, as he bent down to grab Nieto to kiss and to cuddle him. "They cited my devotion to spreading holiness around the world, and the peace that will surely follow. They even said I have surpassed the Pope!"

Alphonso danced and cuddled with Nieto who licked his face all over. Christian tried to shake his hand to congratulate him, but Nieto was in the way. Instead he went to Estelle and put his arm around her and said, "isn't he wonderful? You must be so proud of your master." He felt Estelle's warmth seep into his body from head to toe. She knew it too, he was sure of it. How could this be? How could he be in love with a robot? And it was a love that brought a yearning with it, a yearning for something from his past, a vague feeling that he had been there before. But he was brought back to earth when Estelle mildly rebuked him. "I do not serve a master. Alphonso is my equal partner in life."

"But you do serve him," quipped Christian," and you will never be his equal."

Alphonso, still dancing with Nieto failed to notice the exchange. "I must go back to Mexico City. Pope No has appointed a new bishop there, and they want to celebrate my prize and rededicate the painting of the Annunciation, where I fell with my first epiphany. It will be a fabulous homecoming. And Maria will be there too. She has already divorced Sisto, I knew she would, she only married him so she could divorce him!"

Christian, his arm around Estelle's waist, tugged her to him and reached out to Alphonso to pull him in. Alphonso dropped Nieto who then barked happily and snapped at their heels. This was the first time that Christian had ever danced. But no one noticed.

After two days of feeding Alphonso pasta to try to fatten him up, a still gaunt Alphonso with Nieto in his arms, boarded the Lear jet for Mexico city. He had insisted that he formally divorce Estelle, so that all things would be clear and unsullied when he made his return into Maria's loving Steinem arms. So the local priest had prepared annulment papers and Christian would accompany Estelle to meet with the Pope and have him sign them. There, Christian hoped, Pope No would approve his marriage to Estelle, and they would live happily ever after at the Sicilian Villa. He as the Great Godfather, and she as simply his Goddess.

*

Alphonso and Nieto stopped over briefly to load the Lear jet with bottles of the Holy Waters of Rome, then continued on to Mexico city where Maria's Francisco would be waiting to whisk him off to the Cathedral. How strange it was to see Francisco standing on the tarmac, no AK47, no *bandi* anywhere in sight. Those were the bad old days, Alphonso said to himself. He adjusted his toupee, which for reasons unknown, he had an urge to resurrect from the bottom of one of his suitcases. And as they sped to the cathedral he wondered what the new bishop would be like. Perhaps another Pollagrande, or maybe a relative of Benitez. He wouldn't be surprised.

A small gaggle of reporters gathered at the grand entrance of the cathedral. From habit, Alphonso looked around quickly to see if there were any opposing drug cartel *bandi*. But there were none. The entire operation had been shifted to Sinaloa, thanks to Maria's excellent diplomatic skills. But waiting at the baptismal font was Maria, looking resplendent in her red habit she had made especially for this occasion. They ran to each other and

Maria grabbed Alphonso in her strong muscly arms and swung him around, kissing him voraciously on his bald head, knocking the toupee to the floor.

"What's it feel like to be the man of peace?" called a reporter.

"Like I'm in Heaven," answered Alphonso, "but in my wife-to-be's arms, I am in Heaven," he proclaimed with a big smile.

Maria put him down, held him by the shoulders and looked into his little eyes.. "Are you sure about his?"

"I have only you and one other in my life."

"One other?" asked Maria, it's not…?"

And Nieto ran up barking and nipping at Alphonso's feet. He leaned down and scooped him up and said, "meet Nieto, my constant companion." He threw Nieto to Maria who caught him and tucked him under her arm.

"He will not come between us?" She handed Nieto back to him.

"Oh, yes, he will. He'll join us like glue."

The happy couple proceeded to the altar. "Have you met the new bishop? I thought he would be here to meet us," said Alphonso.

"Haven't seen him. I hear he's a bit of a recluse. Stays in his private chapel praying most of the time."

"Then let's go find him."

Alphonso led the way to The Assumption of the Virgin, eager to revisit the place of his first, and life changing epiphany. Francisco followed them, carrying a large carton of Holy Water vials. Alphonso stopped in front of the great painting and looked up. Out of the corner of his eye he saw a small, bent figure in a dark brown robe of a novice, walking unsteadily towards him, his hand extended, the other holding a walking stick. Alphonso did not want to take his eyes off the Virgin-to-be-no-longer, thinking that maybe another epiphany would befall him. The staggering figure grabbed him by the arm.

"It is a great honor to welcome our own Nobel Peace Prize winner to our humble cathedral," he smiled, the many creases in his face appearing as stark contours on a map. "I am your new bishop, Francis himself, lover of all creatures, and I see we are the same, this is your little doggie, no?"

"Meet Nieto, the smartest, loveliest dog in the world." Alphonso felt in his pocket, again from habit, looking for the usual roll of money he always brought to the cathedral. But this time, he had brought none. Hadn't even thought of it! A change had come over him! Then Francisco pushed his way forward. "The vials as you asked, El Padrino."

"I am very pleased to offer you, free of charge of course, a box of the Holy Waters of Rome, a gift of holiness to you, Monsignor bishop." Alphonso even bowed before him. And just as he did so, his legs buckled and he fell forward, striking his head on the stone floor. Stars flew before his eyes and he rolled over on his back, looking up at the Virgin-not-to-be. Another epiphany, or was it an accident? He shook his head and tried to stand, and felt Maria's reassuring strong hands under his armpits.

Maria cried, "Water, he needs water!"

The new bishop suddenly came to life and ripped open the carton to retrieve a vial of holy water. He twisted off the tamper-evident top and thrust it into Alphonso's mouth. It was not much, exactly six ounces according to the legally approved label. And in the smallest of print, the label also stated, again at the requirement of New Jersey State Department of Agriculture and the FDA regulations: NOT TO BE TAKEN BY MOUTH, FOR EXTERNAL USE ONLY. But whatever the label, Alphonso recovered immediately. He had no epiphany, there was no new insight or idea or whatever inside his head. Just a little fuzziness. He was a great Nobel Laureate and benefactor of the world. What could a new epiphany do for him that he had not already done?

Unfortunately, Virgil, in a cost cutting decision had decided not to install a pasteurizing plant to kill any bacteria that might be present in the water. Besides, it was Holy Water, from the tombs of the saints, in particular St. Peter, which was by definition pure and clean. The next day, as Alphonso was holding a press conference on the steps of the cathedral, black blotches appeared all over his face, blood started to seep from his ears and nose, and he fell down, gasping for breath, vomiting up the foulest black muck one could imagine. An ambulance came, but it was too late, and the crowd, now frightened, pulled back, and then ran away in all directions. Perhaps the devil had descended upon him, he had after all committed many sins. But the devil's form this time was Ebola, the plague of the centuries. Clearly it had been waiting deep beneath the catacombs of the Vatican, to be released on the world.

Maria threw off her red habit revealing no clothes beneath and ran screaming naked back into the cathedral crying as she went, "you bastard! You bastard!" She shook her fist. "I always knew that the devil was the worst of men!" And she ran out of the cathedral and through the streets of Mexico City, shaking her fists, until she was exhausted and fell down in a dirty street, joining the many others who lay there with nowhere else to go, until Francisco the jolly giant came by in his green truck and scooped her up in his arms, and took her back to her nunnery. And there she remained, never to be heard of again.

In Alphonso's will, it was stated that the Diocese of Mexico City would embalm his body and place it in a glass coffin next to the Assumption of the Virgin. When some members of the church complained of the ugliness, the bishop pointed out that many of the embalmed bodies of the popes in St. Peters didn't look all that good either, many a dark awful green, verging on black.

All of this could have been disastrous for the Waters of Rome project, except that Virgil, in a deft move, had foreseen something like this, and sold the franchise to Pepsi. So if there were any law suits brought against the Waters of Saint Peter, the deep pockets of Pepsi would have to cough up the money. The FDA did, in fact, hold a hearing on the Ebola incident and it resulted in the requirement that the Waters of Saint Peter increase the size of the warning label by point one of a per cent. And in a show of good will, Pope No in an important Bull, issued orders to all pastors and priests who anointed their flock with holy water that they make an oral statement saying," I anoint thee with the Holy Waters of Saint Peter and hereby state that the water is not pasteurized and is recommended for external use only and any other use may result in you going to hell."

*

Though his neuteronomy had apparently made Christian devoid of any emotion to speak of, at least none in respect to other humans to whom he felt no attraction at all, nor any from them, he was driven by some bodily urge that befuddled him. He had often wondered, since that radical surgery, what it was that made it so easy for him to dispose of enemies at will, without the slightest personal regret or feeling. He thought it was the absence of emotion. But it could not be because he did feel for Estelle, he wanted her more than anything else. But when he put down the phone after speaking with Pope No, he recognized that the urge that drove him was ambition. He had watched, even helped, Benitez become Pope. If Benitez could do it, why couldn't he?

Pope No had agreed to meet Christian and Estelle at the Eagle fountain. He had refused to come down to Sicily, he was too busy to travel at present. And he had refused to meet in his apartment because he did not trust Christian, and besides, he wanted to be free of his four slaves who were beginning to get on his nerves. They were very high maintenance. They would need to be sent back to Louisiana where they came from.

Christian appeared at the Eagle fountain, Estelle in tow. Her memory of Pope No and of course Pollagrande had been erased. She still carried a torch for Alphonso, but when Christian explained to her that he was dead, she did not quite understand. "You mean he does not remember me anymore?" she asked. And Christian replied, "something like that."

Estelle squeezed his hand as they stood some distance from the fountain. She kept away from water. It frightened her. Soon, Pope No came, flanked by his incessant entourage, but no litter. He approached Christian and held out his hand to be kissed. Estelle did so. But Christian took it and shook it as man to man.

"My son..." said Pope No.

"I am not your son," said Christian bristling.

The sun, usually bright this time of day, went behind a black cloud. Pope No and Christian looked up in unison. Estelle took no notice. "You want to marry Estelle, are you sure of that?" asked Benitez.

"It is the only thing I am sure of," said Christian, continuing belligerently, "did you ask Alphonso that? I bet not. He just told you to do it and you did. And that's what I'm telling you to do."

Both kept their eyes on the dark cloud above. Pope No muttered, "You are not Alphonso and never will be."

"Thank goodness. You know he was struck down?" countered Christian.

"Of course, It was meant to happen. God's will, after all."

Estelle stepped between them. "I want to get married," she said, the picture of innocence.

"I'm not marrying the two of you," said Pope No sternly, true to his title. "It's not good for you Christian. You are not made for it, if you understand me."

Christian turned to him and grabbed him by the ears. "You will marry us or suffer the consequences. Alphonso has given her to me. I have the signed papers for annulment of his marriage to her."

"Well he's dead. It's unnecessary," responded Pope No with a frown.

"Of course. I forgot. Marry us, do it now!" ordered Christian.

Christian pulled the Pope forward and heard the noise of people running. The Papal entourage was about to descend on him and would no doubt beat him to death, or maybe drown him in the fountain. He pulled Pope No further, still holding him by the ears, and butted him on the forehead. Or at least, so it seemed. At the same time, a huge bolt of lightning flashed down from the a dark cloud above and the whole fountain exploded in a thousand colors, the waters suddenly flowing backwards into the ground, and the Pope as though taken up by a cyclone, flew into the air then dropped with a plop on the soft grass of the garden beside the fountain. He lay there, his eyes transfixed, and his mouth moving, the words not coming forth. Then suddenly, a great scream came from deep within him and the words, clear to all who were staring in fright, that came forth would change the Christian world forever:

"Allahu Akba! Allahu Akbar!"

The Pope had become a Muslim.

*

Upon seeing this Papal conversion, Christian had only one thought. Maybe he could become the next Pope? But at the sight of this tremendous transformation, his ambition quickly subsided. What better life could there be but living quietly on the estate in Sicily, Estelle serving his every need. Toiling in the fields with his simple peasants. That was the kind of power that satisfied. And free of fear or discontent.

Our story could end there, except for a few loose ends. You may be wondering what happened to Julia. She became university president, replacing her father, bless his soul. Unfortunately, the LGBTQ community drummed her out of their LGBTQ community because she got married. And besides, she wasn't a transgender anymore, because she got completely changed into a woman and nothing else. So there was no longer anything LGBTQ about her. This turned into a very nasty fight resulting in the university severing all ties with the LGBTQ emergency care center, all funds cut off, and the closing of the facility. The university continued to blossom, enriched by the enormous profits from Virgil's highly successful Waters of Saint Peter franchise. Julia was asked to run for governor of New Jersey, to be the first transgendered woman governor, but she declined. She had much more power where she was, in an unelected position, not subject to the whims of democracy.

And ah, yes, what of Sisto? So quickly married and divorced? A creative genius that he was, he easily turned misfortune into an amazing venture and success. He convinced RAI Television (helped with a large donation from his share of the Waters of Saint Peter) to produce a pilot of his new TV show, DIVORCE ME! Hosted by Sisto and featuring as its first guest Gloria Steinem who presided over his own divorce from Maria. And the prequel of the second show, assuming the pilot would be enormously successful (and it was) would be the showy divorce of the University President Julia with her LGBTQ history from Virgil, former homeless bum and user of Starbucks toilet, televangelist and now CEO of the richest corporation of the world, Waters of Saint Peter.

What better fodder for binge viewing?

THE END

Other fiction by Colin Heston

Available from all bookstores around the world and digital platforms everywhere.

9/11 Two.

It's politics as usual when criminologist Maciver tries to thwart a terrorist drone tack on New York City Iranian terrorist Shalah Muhammad and his neurotic Russian American apprentice, Sarah Kohmsky, hire a Russian mafia boss, Uncle Sergey, and his evil nuclear scientist, Turgo, to hit Ground Zero on the anniversary of 9/11. Hearing of the plan from the CIA New York Mayor Ruth Newberg enlists Professor Larry Maciver, world renowned criminologist to thwart the attack. While the terrorists quietly orchestrate their attack, the drama unfolds as a battle between MacIver the careful scientist, and the impatient Buck Buick, Newark cop and former Marine bomb squad specialist. Will it be a drone, a missile, or a repeat of the 9/11 bombings? Das, Maciver's geeky assistant, thinks he has the answer. Can they save NYC or must it save itself?

The Tommie Felon Show
and Other Outrageous Stories.

A collection of stories ranging from the absurd to the improbable, with a cynical twist. These stories will keep you guessing, their deeper meaning will haunt you forever. "...engaging, hilarious, unique... a commentary on human desires, shortcomings and the society we live in...vivid and real...some of the stories jump out pf the pages." "Almost as sarcastic and cynical as Kurt Vonnegut, Colin Heston is an author to watch out for, now and in the future. —*Readers' Favorite*).

Miscarriages

Teen Chooka grows up in the weird world of 1950s Aussie pub life. When his alcoholic dad dies, he searches for his identity, and that of his shadowy underage girlfriend, Iris. Captivated by the pub's many crazy customers and their raucous stories, Chooka becomes a boozer just like them. But Iris, after a miscarriage, disappears and Chooka sets out on a search that takes him to foreign places including Melbourne university and Vietnam. The search ends in a Melbourne pub, where they start over, but this time there's a different ending. "...a brilliant, unforgettable book about real people...a sensitive, touching and poignant story." —*Reader's Favorite.*

Ferry to Williamstown

In this raucous Aussie story, corpses pop up in the Yarra river while Lizzie entertains her powerful and kinky clients in her Winnebago, parked on the ferry to Williamstown. Tightly bound Detective Striker, confronted by the mob of Catholics, wharfies and communists who rule Williamstown, struggles to solve the mystery. Lizzie gets engaged to her uncle Bobby, the lame ferry driver, and her mum, Babs, spellbound by the strange Father Zappia, tries to solve her own mystery of St. Robert's toe. She throws a raucous send-off party for Lizzie, and out of the chaos emerge many truths. "...a gritty but comedic family drama ...with many threads to unravel, Ferry To Williamstown will reward those who can untie its hilarious Gordian knot." — *Reader's Favorite.*

MONA and Other Twisted Stories

The opening story of MONA, inspired by the Museum of Old and New Art located in Hobart, Tasmania, sets the stage for this collection of short stories that adds an Australian flavor to Colin Heston's acclaimed *The Tommie Felon Show*. The stories range across many styles, prose poems, jottings that are almost aphorisms, classic stories of human emotion and the contradictions of human existence, dystopian themes and settings, all engaging, never dull. "Many of the stories appear straightforward, but their simplicity brilliantly reveals many truths about modern society—so-called—and the impossibility of human ambitions reflected in the societies they have created... one has to look beyond the words and the events in these stories to really appreciate them." —*Reader's Favorite.*

About the Author

Colin Heston is the pen name of a criminologist of international repute. He has written nonfiction books on the history of punishment, edited a four volume encyclopedia on *Crime and Punishment around the World,* and regularly contributes to a variety of criminology and criminal justice periodicals. His forthcoming nonfiction blockbuster *Civilization and Barbarism* will be released by SUNY press in May 2020, authored under the name of Graeme R. Newman. Heston is now hard at work on his next novel, tentatively titled *The Perfect Liberal.* A two volume pictorial history of punishment is in the planning stages as is a new edition of his classic *The Down Under Cookbook.*

Other books published by Harrow and Heston
All available on Amazon and most other e-book publishing outlets.

A Primer in Private Security by Mahesh Nalla and Graeme Newman.

A Primer in the Psychology of Crime by Mark Seis and Shlomo Shoham.

A Primer in the Sociology of Crime by John P. Hoffmann and Shlomo Shoham.

Close Control: Managing a Maximum Security Prison by Nathan Kantrowitz.

Corporate Crime, Corporate Violence by Michael J. Lynch.

Crime and Social Deviation by Shlomo Shoham.

Delinquency and Identity by Jim Sheu. **New 2nd edition 2020 now in paperback and digital.**

Discovering Criminology: from W. Byron Groves edited by Graeme R. Newman and Michael J. Lynch. **Now in paperback.**

From Gangs to Gangsters by Marylee Reynolds.

God as the Shadow of Man by S. Giora Shoham

Justice with Prejudice by .Michael J. Lynch

Migration, Culture Conflict, and Crime edited by Joshua D. Freilich, Graeme R. Newman, S. Giora Shoham, Moshe Addad.

Personality and Deviance by S. Giora Shoham.

Punishment and Privilege edited by Graeme R. Newman. **New 2nd edition 2019, paperback and digital,**

Race and Criminal Justice edited by Michael J. Lynch and E. Britt Patterson

Representing OJ: Murder, Criminal Justice and Mass Culture by Gregg Barak

Salvation through the Gutters by S. Giora Shoham

Sex as Bait by S.Giora Shoham

The Mark of Cain by S. Giora Shoham

Valhalla, Calvary and Auschwitz by S. Giora Shoham

Vendetta (Italian) by Graeme R. Newman and Pietro Marongiu.

Vengeance: The Fight against Injustice by Pietro Marongiu and Graeme R. Newman. **New 2nd edition 2020 paperback and digital.**

Who Pays? Casino Gambling and Organized Crime by Craig A. Zendzian.

276

HARROW AND HESTON PUBLISHERS

Australia, New York & Philadelphia
www.harrowandheston.com